I0671362

Quest for Truth

Mantle of the Gods

Quest for Truth

Unmasking Truth

Truth Revealed

Anthologies

Discovering Truth

Quest for Truth

Book 1 of Mantle of the Gods

Tricia Sparks

Trinity Gateways LLC

QUEST FOR TRUTH, BOOK 1 of the *MANTLE OF THE GODS*

Cover Design by Doris Ross

A Trinity Gateways LLC Publication
www.TrinityGateways.net

ISBN: 0988195151
ISBN-13: 978-0988195158

Dedications

To my parents, you've been my life's compass, showing me my true north.

To Mrs. Dent, my high school English teacher, who took an interest in my writing and put the wind in my sails to pursue my dreams.

To Doris Ross, the captain of my ship. You've been behind me every step pushing me to go further and never give up.

To Lisa Gastineau, my creative partner and crew. You're the one that works behind the scenes and keeps my voyage smooth.

To Dustin, my life's partner on this grand adventure, you make each day brighter because you're in it.

Thank you all for helping me to reach this stop in my journey and I hope that you'll sail with me into the future as well.

1

Jerusalem, Israel
Thursday
9pm

"I'm taking a few days off."

The words echoed in her mind as Anna burst through the door of her hotel suite. It hit the wall with a bang then slammed behind her. Startled, Anna jumped. She turned, expecting the enemy at her back. Finding no one Anna let out a deep breath, she'd been unaware of holding. She was alone.

"Get a grip Anna. They don't know your intentions…yet. It won't take them long to figure it out though," she muttered to herself. After a momentary pause, she steadied herself. Willing her racing pulse to subside, she sighed again. Surveying her spacious junior suite almost like it was the first time; soft green wallpaper was complemented by sensible dark wood furniture. A queen-sized bed covered in a white with a strip of golden damask fabric running along the foot of the bed. A few of the traditional landscape-style portraits lined the walls. Her desk was piled high with electronic gadgets, her computer, and specialty tools the only sign of her presence in the room. It was neat – tidy. Just the way she liked it.

"Better get moving, girl." She ordered her stiff legs to respond. Knowing she was about to swath a path of destruction through the space – already regretting it.

With determined strides, she threw open the closet door. Reaching inside, she pushed the clothes hanging crisp and pressed on the hangers into two groups. Organized by color and style, she wrapped her tanned arms around the first bundle. Heaving them off the metal rod then throwing them on the bed. She repeated the process with the second bundle and moved onto the shoes. Grabbing them up by pairs and tossing them beside the clothes.

Closet emptied, she spun on her heels; raced for the dresser.

Pulling open; the top drawer then filling her grip with neatly laid out undergarments and a couple of silk nightgowns. She tossed them into the clothing pile. Slammed the top drawer shut, almost catching her fingers. She yelped. Yanked her hand back, glaring at the offending inanimate object.

Then she hauled open the second drawer, seizing her socks and tank tops, before removing her shorts and work pants from the bottom drawer. With her hands full, she turned; strode to the bed, dumping them into the pile then charged into the bathroom.

Pulling open one of the storage drawers in the sterile-looking off-white bathroom, she grabbed her travel bag; unzipped it. She swept all her toiletries and makeup into the case, tugging the zipper closed. She pitched it out the bathroom door onto the bed. Anna contemplated grabbing her personal travel shampoo bottles and soap. She thought better of it. They'd ooze out onto her other stuff since she didn't have time to put them away properly.

She hurried over to the desk, near the flat panel T.V. The dark semi-reflective surface capturing her harried look and disheveled clothes. She groaned turning her focus from the surface. The screen sat perched like a sentinel guarding the room; reminding her of the endless stare of some black-eyed creature. Anna thought of little green men and other oddities that didn't exist. She shook her head with disgust. She'd been contemplating such peculiar things far too often of late.

Snatching her black purse from the back of the chair, she dug for her keys; then threw the bag absently onto the dresser beside the television. She crammed her keys in her pants pocket. Racing back to the closet, she dragged out her suitcases and luggage cart; wrangling both up next to the bed.

Anna cringed. Looking at the pile on the bed made her uneasy. The tops of the hangers twisted and curled at odd angles like tangled claws. Suits and other apparel formed the long curved lines of limbs and a body. The clear plastic makeup bag and black purse resembled a disembodied eye and mouth.

"It looks like some weird monster," she said; disgusted by the tousled mess and the strange beast lurking therein. Her skin crawled. Her thoughts wandering back to her work. The implications of what she'd unearthed made her palms sweat. "No time for that now," she chastised herself. "Slay this beast first."

Even as she attacked the pile, stuffing clothes into the suitcase, she grimaced at the thought of having to undo this destruction whenever she did make it home. Everything would have to be sent off to the dry cleaners again to be pressed…She hadn't even worn half of these clothes. What a waste! Fear lingered in her belly; threatening to turn the small shiver within into a wracking shudder. Dropping her travel case atop the pile, she stomped the items down with her foot. Wrestling the zipper closed on the hunter green suitcase. She lugged the heavy bag upright, bumping the thick leather corners against her shins. She cried out in pain. The suitcase was designed to take a severe beating in transit—her legs were not.

Packing in haste was not something she was accustomed to. Given the mounting situation she didn't want to stick around too much longer. "Find a safe place. Gather your thoughts. Make sense of all this madness," she told herself for the hundredth time.

Anna turned her attention to her workstation and groaned—the last bastion of organization was about to be thwarted. Here haste was more problematic. Items could be too easily damaged, but she had to find a way to make it quick. Reaching for her smaller suitcase, she set it on the dresser next to the desk, flipping back the top. She steadied herself then began packing her workspace with a sigh. If her employers found out what she was up to she'd be going nowhere.

Frustration hit her. She slammed her palm down on the desk. "Damn it! This isn't fair. I shouldn't have to go. It was bad enough they pushed me out of my work at the main site – now this. If it weren't for me, there wouldn't even be a site," Anna grumbled with frustration. She mashed a button; shutting down her laptop. Taking hold of the annoyance and letting it drive her she jerked the cables from wall and machine. Wrapping them up, cinching Velcro ties. She placed small electronic items in their protective cases. Anna slipped her laptop into its padded sleeve in the top of the suitcase. Locking it in place then loaded her camera and the other tools. Each was tucked away in its specific place.

Her gaze fell on her field kit. The soft roll of well-worn camel-colored canvas perched on the far side of the desk. She picked up the kit, feeling the familiar weight of picking and cleaning tools. The soft clang of the tools contained within gave her an odd sense of peace. She placed it gently inside the suitcase. Her hand lingered for a moment on the fabric. How long would it be before she came back? That didn't matter right now. Just focus, she told herself.

Anna turned back to the desk, looking over the scattered paper items and small miscellaneous objects. She grabbed the suitcase, placed it in the seat of the desk chair. Shut her eyes then swept the remaining items into the bag. An assortment of note books, sketch pads, journals, pens, pencils and photos fell into the bag with a clatter. Anna's eyes popped open. She nearly wept at the sight before her.

She loved her work. It pained her to mistreat any of it. Discovering secrets from the past was her obsession. She was a truth-seeker, wherever it led. It was making the fact she was leaving her dig difficult. It can't be helped, she told herself. I've seen things I cannot explain. Why won't they listen to me? There must be a reasonable explanation for what we found. How could they shut me out?

Anna had to get away. Gain some perspective. Ground herself again in truth. She blinked; now wasn't the time to rehash her reasons for going. She needed to finish packing. Get out of there, now.

Anna moved to the bed and dropped to her knees. Pulling the blanket up, she reached under. Her fingers brushed against cool wood. Having located the most important of her possessions, her grip tightened. She pulled the smooth cigar box to her. She shuddered as she moved it afraid to disturb it too much. The contents within were worth more than anything she owned. She'd wrapped the item within to the best of her ability. Still she worried it wouldn't be enough. This wasn't protocol for transporting a priceless antique. However, she couldn't have her little clandestine act discovered. Anything crated would normally be photographed, coded, and properly cataloged. The contents within the box had not. If her employers knew what it contained, she'd be in more trouble than she cared to consider.

Anna piled her suitcases onto the hand cart, stacking the larger one first; topped by the second. She pulled a canvas carrying tote out of a suitcase pocket. Wrapped the cigar box in the tote and added the package to the cart. Tacking everything down with cord to ensure nothing fell off. She shouldered her purse; then grabbed the handle for the dolly. Anna took one final survey of the room to ensure she hadn't missed anything. Satisfied, she opened the door leading into the main hall of the hotel.

2

Anna peered down the passageway in both directions certain someone would be waiting to spring on her. She entered the hall; relieved to find no one else there. Anna walked at a fast clip down the corridor to the elevator. Her heels thudded a faint sound on the patterned carpet. The wheels of her cart squealed behind her drowning out her foot falls. At the end of the hall, facing the antique-white metal elevator doors, Anna pressed the down-arrow. She waited. Her foot tamped in a show of impatience as the elevator groaned, responding to the call. Nothing like foreign hotels, she thought glibly. She contemplated taking the stairs, but then thought better of it. Besides she was carrying precious cargo, how would she get the cart downstairs without a total disaster?

While she stood, she considered her next move. Once she got back to the states, she wouldn't be able to stay at home for long. They would come looking for her. She'd go elsewhere, but where? Family was out of the question. That'd be the first place the company would go looking for her. Anna shoved the matter aside as the elevator dinged announcing it's coming arrival. She'd cross that bridge when she came to it. Besides, she'd have plenty of time to figure it out on the airplane. Not like she would be sleeping anyway.

The doors of the elevator slid open. Anna hurried inside. She pressed the button for the garage then focused on turning the bulky cart around inside the small space. After a few moments of struggle, she managed to get it facing forward, as the elevator descended. An errant sleeve had spilled out between the zippers of her suitcase. She muttered a curse.

"Is it pinched in the zipper? Oh no! I love this blouse," she sighed, exasperated. Anna shoved the sleeve back inside, closed the bag. Then inspected the other bags making sure nothing else was hanging out. Seeing not a thing out of place, she turned to her reflection in the glass, and smoothed out her hair. She rubbed at the small shadow of mascara under her eyes and realized it was dark circles, edged with obvious lines of stress. Anna tried to relax. She had to look normal, put together, ordered. Otherwise the wrong people might take notice of her unusual behavior.

"Breathe Anna," she murmured. The doors opened in the parking garage. Anna looked out at the gloomy grey lot with distrust. It didn't look very inviting or friendly for that matter. She took a step forward and stopped, glancing around ill at ease.

"Perfect, Anna. You just had to watch that stupid psychological horror flick last night with the woman who got attacked in the parking garage. When will you learn? How long after the last one were you afraid to take a shower?" Anna felt her heart race. Her lungs tightened as shadows deepened. Seeming to grow, sprouting to life in the dark corridors of the concrete garage. Panic swept over her like a tidal wave. Her feet wouldn't respond, though she knew she should walk forward. "I can't do this," she breathed.

The open elevator buzzed; a loud and annoying sound of protest at being left ajar too long. Anna cursed. The noise startled her out of her frozen state. If anyone was out there she'd just let them know where she was. The new jolt in her nerves propelled her forward. She set off at a rapid pace towards her car. Looking around to make sure no one would see her hurrying with so much, luggage in tow. The echo of her boot heels clacked on the concrete floor, which only served to amplify the squealing cart racket and garner her sense of urgency.

Car doors opened and closed, engines roared to life in the distance. Patrons came and went about their daily lives, oblivious to her newly discovered truth…something that would change what the world believed in. How can humanity not know? How could her employers hide something this important? A huge scientific discovery and they wanted to muzzle her. They had excommunicated her from her site; tossed her back to do dredge work. It was insulting!

She shook her head clearing her thoughts; allowing the frustration to fuel her. Chasing away her anxieties; seeing the navy blue rental car parked another thirty feet in front of her Anna slowed her pace. Someone's car alarm beeped nearby. She jumped then hurried on. Anna pressed the car remote, popping the trunk. Reaching the rental Anna tried to catch her breath. She loaded up the trunk, taking care not to jostle the items in the smaller bags too much.

Anna slumped into the driver's seat, started the ignition and drove around to the main entrance. She looked about her for suspicious cars or people. Saw only tourists and tired travelers.

She put the car in park but left it idling in front of the main glass doors of the King David Hotel. Stepping out of the car she walked into the lobby; heading straight for the front desk clerk with purpose. Anna was careful steeling her nerves; putting on her normal aura of being in control. The clerk spotted her and smiled.

"Ah, Miss Gallagher, good evening, how may I help you?" Liam's smile was genuine. Anna had always liked him.

"Hi, I…" Anna searched her mind trying to draw back the plan. Why was she there? The room keys in her pocket burned in her mind. The reflex of returning the plastic items to their rightful owners hit her with some demand. "Stick to the plan, Anna," she thought to herself.

"Miss Gallagher?"

"Oh sorry, I wanted to say don't worry about the fresh towels. The ones I have are fine. I don't need them changed."

"Are you certain? I apologize that you have had issues with the maid not changing them out the last couple of days." His accent was thick, but his English was well-spoken. She had appreciated the fact that most Israelis did speak some English while she was learning her Hebrew.

"No, no, its fine – todah."

"Of course, is there anything else we can do for you?" he asked.

"Oh, cancel my wakeup call tomorrow morning. I'm going to sleep in for once."

"I'll see to it Miss." She watched him scribble something down on a notepad then level his gaze on hers once more. She felt the flicker of concern in his eyes more than she saw it. Maybe she looked worse for wear than she thought. Anna had been told she wore her emotions on her sleeve.

"Thank you, Liam." She said before she turned and left. Once outside, the heat struck her. Thoughts of her endeavor weighed in on her once more. She hoped this little tactic would buy her some time…a couple of days at least. Like her, they were over thirteen hours away by flight. She would have at least from the time of her discovered absence until the time it took for the plane to reach D.C. before they could track her down. That was assuming they didn't discover her missing until at least tomorrow sometime. It was a lot to presume. A big gamble, but she didn't have a choice. She'd seen too much to go on ignoring it. The museum back home had to be informed..

3 American Coast line near New York
Thursday
9pm

Anna sat with her head resting on a small rectangular pillow pressed against the shade of the airplane window. She groaned finding yet again that she couldn't get comfortable. Giving up she switched on her light. Sleep it seemed was beyond her reach. Anna stowed the pillow. Took out a stack of newspapers she bought while at the airport in Israel. She unfolded the one on the top of the stack; began flipping through the pages. Looking for anything on the discovery near the Dead Sea.

Seeing nothing she muttered a curse. Setting the paper aside she switched to the next in the stack and moved her way through each.

"The find of the century and no one knows anything about it. How was it possible?" Anna muttered with disgust. Not one paper showed any sign of being aware of the dig. It didn't make sense. They couldn't all be bought off, could they?

"When the director of the Smithsonian sees what I have to show him that'll change." Once Anna got off the plane she'd call him personally and tell him what was going on. There'd be a press conference. They'd have no choice but to let her back in the main site, Anna assured herself.

The fasten seatbelt light came on. The captain announced they were beginning their approach for landing at the JFK Airport in New York. It was a short hop from there to DC then home.

4 Los Angeles, California

"Two minutes Miss Walsh." A young woman with short cropped brown hair called as she moved past Pamela's cramped dressing room.

"Thanks Mina. I'll be right out," Pamela called to her assistant. She clipped a mike to her blouse then turned her attention to her hair. As she fixed it her thoughts wandered.

It wasn't fair. She should have been working as anchor for the national station in DC. She was well on her way when her fool ex-husband wrote the story that lost him his job; crippling her career. Even after she divorced him, nothing changed. She was marked as the woman whose ex was crazy enough to take on the status quo.

The local news station in DC had refused to renew her contract. The results, she was back on the gossip circuit for entertainment. It burned her, she was struggling, even after taking everything from him in the divorce, while he was thriving. He'd inherited some money after the divorce was finalized, moved out to Vegas and opened a gym. He was looking at the prospect of fame on the horizon. It wasn't right. Where was the justice? She asked herself.

Pamela made her way to the set to film her next segment. She sat down behind the desk, waited for her cue as the intro music played. When the director pointed at her and the camera light lit she was ready.

"Tonight we look at former heart throb turned director James Hardagen. His last few movies having been lack luster he's hoping that tomorrow's premiere of Heart of Glass, his directorial debut will shine. We tried to get a word in with James but were unable to make contact. He is closed up in his L.A home reviewing the script for his next project."

"What are you hearing about the new film, Pamela?"

"The buzz is it's hot. James has found his niche in Hollywood once again."

"We'll keep our eye on this story and see how it plays out. Is she or isn't she? When we come back we'll take a look at which Hollywood leading ladies may be pregnant. "

"We're clear."

Pamela Walsh took off her mike. She headed backstage to her dressing room done with the shoot for the day. It really wasn't fair but next week it would all be different.

5 Washington DC, Virginia
Friday
12am

Anna sighed with contentment. Her green eyes locked on the traditional Georgian home so common to the area.

"How long has it been since I last looked at this place?" She considered the matter. Doing the math she was shocked.

"Too long," she murmured then unlocked the front door. She stepped inside. Three years was more of an extended visit than she'd planned. When she left for Israel she'd only planned on being gone a few weeks. She should have known Ian would find a way to keep her from home longer.

Switching on the light she hung her purse on the hook specifically for it. As she made her way to her work room she did her best to ignore the layer of dust on the furniture making a mental note to set it to rights later.

Entering the space she worked out of Anna supposed that most would look at it with surprise. This was no small, simple office space with an oversized desk. Anna had it built special. She'd taken the dining room and den, combined them into one space. A fireplace sat as the main focal point. The hearth was framed by windows and book cases of various sizes. In the back left corner was set up a space for reading. The back right corner was a designated gaming corner. In the center of the room was a large round table. Throughout the wall space between the book cases were various statues, art and historic pieces.

Anna unloaded the cigar box then her work bag. She secured the rest before moving the cart out of the room her clothes like the dusting could wait. She had things to deal with. Her first order of business was to get her work organized; ready for presentation tomorrow. Turning her focus to the bag containing her electronics and journals she opened it up. Attacked, setting to rights the mess she'd made in her haste.

Pens and pencils were gathered first. She slipped them into a small zipper liner separating them from the rest. Next she gathered the photos in a pile and set them on the work table with the small wooden box. Anna sorted through the various pads and journals separating writing from drawing into two organized piles. She moved them to the table as well. The printer and laptop joined her other things on the workspace then Anna closed up the bag. She'd get to the camera and her tool kit later.

Her work gathered, Anna moved on to the next task on her mental checklist. With care she lifted the lid of the wooden box to get out her prize. Digging past the packing she felt the touch of cool metal against her skin. Anna trembled with a strange mix of excitement and fear. She'd felt the same wave when she discovered it too. Anna wrapped her fingers around the relic and drew it out.

The disk was approximately seven inches in diameter; made of a strange melding of a yet unknown metal and granite. The two had been smelted together in a way that didn't currently exist. This melding made the disk appear to be like molten silver. Varying from white to black, it seemed to be divided into five sections. The outer ring was white. Inscribed in it was a form of strange writing.

The second track was like fine silver. Carved within were four intricate symbols she didn't recognize. Lines at odd angles came off the symbols. Small leaves extended from them. The third section was like pewter. It depicted the image of various objects and possessed the only bit of color each image held a small gemstone at its heart.

The inner track was black; contained within it white distinct dotted patterns and lines that made no clear image. The center ring was no bigger than a quarter. It held an image she had yet to decipher; some sort of writing maybe.

Anna shook herself no time to ponder it. She had lots of work to do before she turned in for the night. Anna plugged in the laptop. Connected the printer to it then switched it on.

While she waited for it to power up Anna took her suitcase to her room, and laid it on the bed putting the task out of sight and out of mind. She stopped in the kitchen on her way back to the work room. Grabbed a bottle of water and moved on.

Back in her work space she crossed to a bookcase. Pulled off the shelf a book on Grecian art. Anna then began the process of putting her work into a report for the director to review.

6 Jerusalem, Israel

Gina made her way down the hall to room 410. She groaned. Miss Gallagher was the most demanding of the hotel patrons. She was a major neat freak. If things weren't just the way she liked them she complained. Her major complaint since arriving was the lack of clean towels. She'd changed them out three times already that week. With a sigh Gina tried to look at the bright side. Miss Gallagher's need for cleanliness meant very little work.

Opening the door Gina blinked. She turned, looked at the number on the door again. Seeing it was indeed 410 she stepped into the room filled with disquiet. The closet door gaped open bare. The drawers to the dresser stuck out. The bedding was disheveled. Peering into the bathroom she found the drawers in the same state. Nothing belonging to Miss Gallagher remained. She checked her notes to see if the room was being checked out of. Saw it wasn't. Shrugged, she'd check with her husband once she finished her rounds. For now it was time to get to work. She set the requested bottled water on the table then turned her attention to the bed.

7

"Liam."

Liam looked up from the desk at the sound of his wife's voice. "Ah, my love, done already."

"Yes."

"Did you remember to leave additional water for Miss Gallagher?"

"Yes. Did she say anything about checking out?"

"No, she asked me to cancel her wake up call for tomorrow. Why do you ask?"

"The room was a mess. None of her things were in it."

"You're sure?"

"Positive."

"Let me check in with Mr. Broody. Find out what's going on." Liam picked up the phone. Dialed the number he'd been given for the work site if he had any questions or concerns about their patrons. The phone rang several times before he was greeted by a cool hello.

"Hello Mr. Broody this is Liam at the hotel."

"Of course. How can I help you Mr. Cohen?"

"I was wondering if Miss Gallagher in 410 was checking out today and forgot to mention it."

"As far as I know of she is not. She's taking a few days off to rest. Why do you ask?"

Liam explained what his wife had told him.

"I see."

"Should I keep the room open for her sir or check her out."

"Leave it open for now."

"Very good sir. I hope that Miss Gallagher is okay."

"I'm sure she's fine," Broody assured him.

8

Ian Broody mashed the button on his cell phone severing the call. He tried Anna's phone and got no response. Ian groaned then reminded himself she'd requested time off. Her refusal to respond didn't mean anything. The hotel manager's description of the room bugged him though. If there was one thing he knew about Anna it was she was as neat as a pin. The state the room had been in was not like her.

Turning his attention to the computer on his desk Ian began to dig. His fingers flew over the keys running a search on Miss Gallagher's passport. He cursed finding that she'd passed through customs in the states. Ian pressed a button on the desk and a moment later a man with dark hair and brown eyes entered the office.

"We have a problem."

"Sir?"

"Miss Gallagher has left the country she's back in the states find her."

"Yes sir."

Ian watched as Mr. York's hired gun walked out of the office. He drew a breath then reached for a crystal glass and his decanter of brandy. His hand shook in a display of nerves as he poured himself three fingers.

"Damn it Anna, why did you have to go and run off," he grumbled.

"Understand that if Miss Gallagher gets out of hand I'll deal with her and hold you responsible." Russell York's warning replayed in his mind and Ian felt his palms slicken with sweat. He hoped Mr. Handal found her and got her back before she could cause any real trouble. Russell York was not the sort of man he wanted to cross.

9

Washington DC, Virginia
Friday
9am

Anna woke to the buzz of the alarm with a jolt. The shadows of a dream slipped into the recesses of her mind. She rose from the bed and crossed the room to the closet. Anna picked out a sharp suit, for the meeting she would arrange later that day, with matching heels then headed for the master bath. As she went through her morning routine she reflected on the night before.

She'd stayed up far too late. First completing the report for the director of antiquities at the Smithsonian; then still on Jerusalem time she'd moved into the bedroom. She unpacked her suitcase ironing the whole mess, washing anything that needed it or putting it in a pile to go to the dry cleaners. Once the laundry was handled she'd set to putting the house to rights dusting and cleaning it until everything shined.

With a sigh Anna put the finishing touches on her makeup. She examined her reflection, making sure she'd completed the task at hand to her satisfaction.

Anna wore a white blouse with a black pencil skirt and matching blazer. Her golden blond hair was pulled into an elegant up-dew. She was the picture of professionalism. Anna passed herself for inspection then turned from the room. She made her way to her work space. Picked up the report she printed up the night before and placed it in a black portfolio. Anna set the strange disk from the site on top of it. Picking up the phone she dialed the number for Phillip King the director of antiquities. She waited for him to pick up.

"Come on Phil I know you're there," she grumbled.

"Hello?"

"Hello Phillip, this is Anna."

"Anna, so good to hear from you. How are things in Israel?"

"Well sir I'm back in the states. I took a few days off and wanted to run a few things by you. I was concerned that you may not have been apprised of the full situation over there."

"I see."

"I've put together a full report for you. I'm sure once you read it you'll want to call a press conference."

"A report you say well, why don't you bring it by. I've got an hour before things get busy here."

"Of course I'll see you shortly," Anna said with excitement. She hung up her phone, grabbed her work and the purse off the hook. To keep the artifact hidden she wrapped it in a black scarf. She tucked it away in her purse then left.

10

Phillip King turned his attention back to the new acquisition from the auction. He'd collected it not for the main gallery but the private collector's wing. The horn was made of fine silver. Etched in it were multiple layers of an image he couldn't quite determine. Perhaps they were leaves, feathers or maybe scales. Philip wasn't sure. The rim of the horn was overlaid with gold. Encrusted in it were several small sapphires. Spaced between each in silver was a smaller rendition of the same detail. It was an unusual piece. Few horns were made of precious metal. Carved from ivory or bone that was normal. Seeing one so ornately carved and jeweled was less common. The piece would fetch a fine price he figured. He was just preparing to look closer at the carvings when the phone rang again.

"Blast what now," he grumbled. Setting down his magnifying glass. Phillip answered the phone. "Hello."

"Good Morning Philip."

"Mr. Broody, hello. What can I do for you?"

"Phillip. you haven't by any chance had contact with Anna have you? She asked for a couple days off. No one's seen or heard from her since. We're starting to worry."

Phillip sighed, it seemed his best student Anna had not made peace with Dr. Ian Broody as he'd feared but had called a temporary truce. If she'd failed to tell him where she was going he'd not tip him off. "Not in some time. Is everything all right over there? It's not like her to just run off."

"Phillip, I don't know how to tell you this but Anna's not herself. She's pushing too hard on this one. Her behavior of late has been strange. She's been making outrageous claims and accusations concerning the dig; things that have no basis in reality. I'm concerned she's become delusional."

"Oh dear," Phillip said with alarm.

"Phil, if she contacts you I want you to meet with her. Get whatever documentation from her she may have and have it sent to me. We can't have one over worked woman destroying the entire project."

"Of course sir," Philip said before he hung up. He sighed before putting the horn away in the wall safe. He'd finish his appraisal of it later. He turned his attention to a small stack of packing slips. Working his way through them he considered Anna and what Dr. Broody had said. Yeah he'd send him her stuff in a pig's eye. It seemed Ian was up to his old tricks again. Well he'd play no part in aiding Mr. Broody in stealing the credit for whatever they'd discovered near the Dead Sea.

Phillip King jolted when his secretary buzzed the office to announce Miss Gallagher's arrival.

"Send her in." Phillip steeled himself for what was to come. Relief hit him at the site of her. She looked like the same Anna who left over three years ago just with a tan. There were no outward signs of hurt or betrayal. There were no sighs at all to substantiate Ian's claim of her having lost it. As soon as the thought had finished itself another followed. "Don't judge a book by its cover."

"Good morning Phillip, thank you for agreeing to see me on such short notice."

"It's my pleasure dear," he assured her and waited.

"As I said on the phone I have a report I think you should see. There's a lot about the dig you've been kept unaware of." She sated. Anna opened her portfolio and pulled out a multiple paged document. She set it on his desk then took a seat across from him. She waited.

Phillip flipped through the pages counting them; studying the work. It was neat and well organized. It contained among the text references and photos. The work was complete, rational and fully Anna. He wondered why Ian had elected the insanity card to discredit her until he noted one word; then groaned. A claim like that would seem crazy coming from anyone but Anna. He set the report down.

"Aren't you going to read it?"

"I'll read the rest later. I think you should know Ian called looking for you."

"You didn't tell him I was here did you?" Anna asked alarmed.

"No, my dear, I'll not help him to find you but he was anticipating your contacting me."

"Damn. What did he say?"

"He told me that you're pushing too hard on this one seeing things that aren't there."

"He said I was going crazy?"."

"I'm afraid so." Phillip replied.

11

Anna cringed at the accusation then laughed and sighed. It was ironic because ever since she found the artifact she'd been questioning her own sanity. "Well, as you can see I'm my usual charming self, and our dear friend Mr. Broody is lying to you. In fact he's keeping things from you."

"Do you have proof of that?"

"It's in the report."

"Reports can be falsified." Phillip pointed out playing devil's advocate.

"Phillip, this is me Anna. You know me. I have never tampered with any of my research. That paper comes straight out of it."

"Your research is at the dig site. How can you possibly have taken this paper from records in Ian's office in Jerusalem?"

"I have my own copy."

"Good girl."

"I learned my lesson after Ithaca I know Ian signed a contract giving me rights to the credit for my work at the dig but I don't trust him anymore."

"About the second site you indicate are you sure?" Philip asked.

"Yes. I have proof. Look." Anna pulled the silk scarf from her purse and set it on the desk. She unwrapped it with care, revealing the disk.

Anna watched as her mentor's eyes grew wide with shock. He stared at it mouth agape. It was ornate and made of various intricate parts. A strange and complex machine made of a material she was sure he'd never seen before because neither had she.

"You have gone mad. Taking an artifact from the site."

"I know. It's not something I would normally do but I had little choice the same day I found it Dr. Broody and his team discovered something else. I was sent back to Israel without a word of warning. It all happened so fast I never got to document it at the main dig. I've had it ever since. But have had no time to look at it."

"Anna, if Ian finds out what you've done you could be arrested."

"On what grounds?"

"It's museum property." Phillip answered reaching for the disk. Anna snatched it up shoving it back in her purse before he could touch it.

"I know it is. But it's also the only proof I have of my discovery. If I give this to you now then Ian can deny I was ever at that dig."

"Anna, I can't help you with this."

"I realize that now. I'm sorry I've put you in this position. I should go."

"Jean, call security," Phillip shouted. "Anna, as your friend I'm asking you now to turn over any stolen materials from the site. I don't want to see you get into trouble. I'll have no choice but to phone the authorities and inform Ian." He said as he took her hand in his in a fatherly gesture.

Anna pulled her hand back as if burned. She got to her feet. "I can't."

"Be reasonable Anna, dear," Phillip persuaded. The office door opened. Security moved towards her.

"I will not be reasonable. We're talking about the find of the century here. I won't let Ian cut me out of it."

"Miss Gallagher, lower your voice please," Phillip requested not wanting a public scene. The guard got closer. Anna turned to face him.

"Don't you dare, touch me. I'm in no mood to be civil," she snapped before storming out.

12

Anna felt panic set in as she made her way down the street towards her home.

"What have I done?" She asked herself as she moved through the morning crowd. She felt the weight of the artifact in her purse then groaned. Why had she taken it? It didn't belong to her. She had in point of truth stolen it from the dig just as Phillip had said. No one else had been aware of its existence, but that didn't change the facts she'd taken it off museum property. She'd planned to leave it with Phillip but something within her had insisted she not let him touch it.

"What if I am going crazy?" Anna muttered. She hadn't been acting rationally since she found the damn thing. The chamber she'd discovered it in was undocumented none of her colleagues were aware of its location. It wasn't like her to withhold anything at a dig. That room had put her on edge. She'd felt like some dark secret lurked within it that shouldn't be discovered. Then she'd found the disk. Something inside her had urged her to get it out of that room. Tell no one of it.

After that things at the dig had gotten weird. She'd seen Ian removing artifacts that weren't cataloged; observed him conversing with the security guy and some other man she didn't recognize about them. Then the relic would vanish. She'd been investigating it, trying to figure out the reasoning behind it. When they'd found IT.

Not even a day later she'd been sent back to the original dig to help with the cataloging there. They'd needed to get her out of there she realized now. They were doing things at the site that weren't legal. Anna was sure of it. She had no real proof. Now they were working hard to discredit her.

"Why? What is going on out there?" Anna asked aloud. She crossed the street, stopping in at her favorite coffee shop; needing some kind of breakfast.

13 Jerusalem, Israel

Ian Broody hung up the phone with disgust. The news from Phil was worse than he'd figured. Not only did Miss Gallagher have a copy of her reports she'd also managed to remove an artifact from one of the dig sites. He considered the matter as he pulled up the photos she'd taken. There was nothing like Phillip had described, which meant she'd kept it out of her records. Why? Where had she located it? What else might there be to discover? All these questions weighed heavily upon his mind as he called his hunter.

"Hello?" The voice on the other end questioned.

"Mr. Handal, have you located Miss Gallagher?"

"Yes sir."

"Don't lose her. She has in her possession a copy of her research and an artifact I need both."

"Understood sir."

"Good," Ian stated before he hung up. The issue addressed he turned his attention back to more pressing matters.

14

Washington DC, Virginia
Friday
11am

Anna sat sipping a tall coffee. She picked at a slice of coffee cake no longer hungry. Still reeling from what had happened at the Smithsonian. It was apparent that Ian's employers were taking no chances with the discovery coming out before they were ready. If that was the case and they got word from Phillip of what transpired in his office what did that mean for her? How far would they go to keep it a secret? She wondered. Anna took a gulp of her coffee. It was stone cold but she swallowed anyway. She rose from her table, tossed out the cup. Wrapped the coffee cake in a napkin then set off for home.

As she walked through the press of the crowd she spotted an all too familiar face. Anna groaned. "What's he doing here?" she groused. She'd thought she'd left him in Israel. He'd followed her. Why? She'd told them she was taking a couple days. Why follow her? "To make sure you don't talk to anyone," she muttered. Anna made her way up the steps to her front door. Her tail stopped on the other side of the street; turning down a side street as if he'd just been strolling through. Anna wasn't buying any of it. He was lurking just out of her line of sight. Let him. She was going inside; so what if he knew it.

Once in the house Anna moved into her workspace. She opened the safe concealed behind a shelf of fake books. She stuck the disk and her work in the safe then locked it up. Anna headed for her room; the lack of sleep from the night before was catching up with her. She lay down promising herself it would be a short nap.

town.

15 Los Angeles, California

Pamela Walsh ran her fingers through her bangs getting them out of her eyes. She stood silent waiting for her cue to start her report. Her thoughts turned to tomorrow. Pamela smiled.

"Good evening, the city of angels bid you welcome. Tonight we're coming to you live from the Tokyo theatre. They've rolled out the red carpet here for the premiere of *Heart of Glass*; James Hardagen's directorial debut. Hollywood's finest have come out for this gala event .We'll be bringing you all the tidbits from the fashion do's and don'ts to the hot summer flings. Stay tuned."

When she was clear Pamela paused to grab a cigarette. Damn she needed to get away from this gossip gig. It left a bad taste in her mouth being back; so much so she'd started smoking again. She shrugged; it was steady pay at least until she moved on to something better. That thought had her looking beyond the night.

She'd requested a few days off. It was going to be good to get out of LA for a while. If things went as she anticipated she just might never come back to this god forsaken

16 Washington DC, Virginia Saturday 1am

Anna woke with a moan. Her head was pounding. Her throat felt as dry as a desert. She blinked, noted it was dark. When she'd lain down there had been day light streaming through the window. Glancing to the bedside clock she cursed. Her short nap had been anything but.

"Jet lag," she hissed with disgust before getting to her feet. Anna made her way down stairs to the kitchen wanting to get a bottle of water. As she came to the bottom of the steps a sense of disquiet washed over her. Did I lock the door? Anna wondered. She tried to recall. Finding she didn't know, Anna made her way towards the front of the house.

As she came to the entry of her work area she caught movement out of the corner of her eye. Turning she froze. Her dry throat got tight. A dark clad figure stood in front of her book case. His back was to her. He was busy working at her safe. Anna felt something inside of her stir. Her fingers wrapped around the first thing within reach. She felt the ivory handle for a moment before she let it fly in the intruder's direction. She saw the metallic glint for a moment. Heard the curse as the sword replica letter opener hit its mark.

Anna stood dumbfounded; mouth agape as the reality of what she'd just done caught up with her. The intruder lumbered toward her. Panic set her in motion. She raced for the living room and dove left. Behind her the thief stopped in the entry way; pulled the letter opener out of his shoulder. Anna crept past the couch to the end table. She picked up the vase – hid. When the burglar came into catch her she hit him over the head. Turning she raced back to her workspace; grabbed the phone and locked herself in.

✦ ✦ ✦

The sound of sirens filled the night as the police arrived on the scene in response to her call. Anna heard her name called.

"I'm in here," she shouted. A sense of relief flooded her.

"Where is the intruder?"

"He was in the living room," Anna replied. She heard the sound of footsteps as the officer made his way down the hall. A moment later she was told it was safe. The intruder was gone.

"Can I see the badge before I come out?" Anna questioned.

"Sure." Anna watched as a chain with a shield was pushed under the door. She picked it up.

"Detective Roman, burglary," she read it aloud then unlocked the door. Anna stepped into the hall.

The man on the other side had red hair and ice blue eyes he looked to be in his late thirties. "Annalynn Gallagher?"

"Yes and you'd be detective Roman?"

"That's right. Let's step outside. You can tell me what happened here while the crime scene unit works the place." Anna nodded her agreement. She followed the detective out onto the steps.

17

Once outside Anna drew a deep breath. She began to relax.

"Okay Miss Gallagher, now I need you to tell me everything that happened to the best of your ability."

Anna bit her bottom lip nervously as she searched her mind for the words to convey what had occurred. Her mind was sluggish and she found she felt more tired than she could ever remember being. She blinked and the images flashed behind her eyes as the memory raced in to fill the void. Her lips parted and the words tumbled out woodenly.

"I woke around one am, thirsty. Made my way down stairs and felt the need to verify I'd locked the door earlier. When I passed by my work room I caught movement out of the corner of my eye. I saw the intruder. He was trying to break into my safe."

"You're sure of the time?"

"Yes, I was disoriented when I woke. When I lay down earlier it was daylight. Finding it dark I checked the time. I'd slept a lot longer than I'd planned; jet lagged."

"Jet lagged?"

"Yes, I just got back from a business trip."

"Okay you saw him. What did he look like?"

"I don't know it was dark. He was dressed in black, wearing a ski mask."

"Okay. Height, weight?"

"Um he was a bit short. Maybe a couple inches taller than me. He wasn't heavy; looked athletic."

"So you saw him, then what?"

"I don't know. I reacted."

"How?"

"I picked up a letter opener, threw it at him. It was stupid. I realize that now. He chased me into the living room. I hit him over the head with a vase then ran back to the work room; locked myself in, called you."

"You're right Anna, what you did was very stupid. It was also brave. You're lucky to be alive."

Anna jolted startled by his use of her first name but she did not comment still reeling from the reality settling over her. Her home had been invaded. A stranger had entered her domain, he'd been bold enough to do so with her still in the place. She swallowed thickly. "I'm starting to see that."

"I know this is hard but I want you to think about the past several months. Has anyone threatened you? Do you know of anyone that might want to harm you? Have you received any strange or threatening calls?"

"No, not that I can think of."

"Have you noticed anyone you thought might be following you?"

Anna froze at the last question. Fear seized her. It was like a living thing breathing down the back of her neck; causing the hair to stand on end, with the fright came understanding. The man in her home had not been there at random he'd been there to steal her work. No; that couldn't be right, could it?

Detective Roman watched as dread filled her hazel eyes then understanding. "Miss Gallagher, Anna?"

"Sorry, yes I have. I actually have photos stored in my camera. I can print them for you if you like."

"You do. Why didn't you report this sooner?"

"I didn't view it as a threat. These guys work for my employer."

"I see."

"Detective Roman, hypothetically if you were aware of a case that would change everything you knew about the way the law was defined and no one was talking about it what would you do?"

"What do you mean?"

"It's complicated. Let me get you those pictures. We'll talk about it further someplace less open." Anna said. She then stepped back into the house. The detective followed her. After verifying it was okay she went to the bag where she'd left the camera; unloaded it. Anna hooked it up to the printer. She flipped through the images until she came to the ones of the men tailing her. She printed them.

"Where were these taken?"

"Israel," she said with a shrug.

"What is it you do for a living Anna?"

"I'm an archeologist; detective Roman."

"Call me Lance."

Anna blinked at the request it was far too forward of him they were complete strangers. She brushed the request aside choosing to ignore it. "Can I get you anything Detective?"

"Coffee?"

Anna nodded. She led the way to the kitchen. Measured the coffee grounds, ran some water then started a pot. Anna noted the pile of mail in the basket on the counter; picked it up moving it to the table. She poured the detective a cup of coffee, brought over a tray with cream, sugar and spoon. As he prepared the cup she began the task of sorting through the mail. Bill, junk, work, or other. She labeled each piece in her mind as she divided it into piles.

Lance watched her with interest. Waiting for her to say whatever it was she'd held back outside. Looking around he realized that the simple task before her wasn't just an act of distraction; for her it was a means to restore order to her world, regain a sense of control. Miss Gallagher was a woman driven by structure and order her world had been anything but that.

"I was working a dig in Israel. It led to another site, the location of which I won't disclose. Something we found there was so profound it would change everything that we know and believe in science and history alike."

"What did they find?"

"If I told you, you'd never believe me. Hell, I didn't believe it at first and I saw IT. Anyway, not even two days after the discovery I was sent from the new site back to Israel."

"If you saw it why send you away?"

"I don't know. I saw some things just before then. Artifacts being handled wrong even vanishing. I was beginning to wonder if something illegal was going on around me. Before I could figure it out they sent me away."

"Do you think they were aware you suspected them of unlawful activity?"

"I guess, it was upon returning to the original site that I started to notice those men following me. I also noticed that the reports being sent back to the Smithsonian from Jerusalem were missing information; that made me mad. I was afraid they were trying to cut me out of my discovery."

"Why?"

"The man in charge Dr. Ian Broody has cut me out before. He's a credit hog."

"What did you do?"

"I told Dr. Broody that I was taking a couple days off. I hadn't been away from the dig in almost three years. At first he was reluctant to let me do so, said he needed me. The work he had me doing was shit work. Stuff an intern could do. I told him as much and he agreed. Then I did something dumb."

"What?"

"Rather than hang around there I came back to the states to fill in the head of antiquities on what was happening. I met with Dr. Phillip King this morning."

"How'd he take the news?"

"He was not pleased and a bit skeptical apparently they'd contacted him before I got there and tried to discredit me. Phillip demanded my work. I refused, it's the only proof I have of my discovery. I left in a huff, came back here – locked my work in the safe."

"I see."

"So tell me Detective Roman, if you suspected your boss was looking to prevent something you knew from coming to light what would you do?"

Lance studied her for a moment; considered the story she presented then the question itself. He believed her. She wasn't saying a lot. Lance got the impression that what she was saying was all true.

"There's not much I can do for you except tell you to get an alarm or a dog. You might want to change out the locks. Based on your description I'm figuring this guy had gloves. Other than a bit of blood there won't be much to process. I can look into these guys for you, but I'm guessing I'll hit a dead end. They look like ghosts. Beyond that I'll speak with Phillip to collaborate your story. Since there's no real evidence to tie this evening's break in to the events you've described I can't put you in protective custody."

Anna blew out a breath it was what she'd expected. Turning her focus back to the mail she'd sorted Anna put the bills and work back in the bin then turned her attention back to the 'other' pile. Opening each piece to determine if it was a keep or pitch item.

"I didn't ask what you can and can't do, Detective. I asked what you would do if you were me," Anna said exasperated.

"If I were you Anna, I'd get out of town – fast. To me it sounds like you may be in danger. Do you have someone you can trust to stay with? Maybe a place no one knows about you can hide out for a while?"

Anna considered it for a moment; opening yet another envelope. She couldn't stay with friends or family. They'd be watching for that. She didn't have anywhere she could go that no one else knew about.

So what could she do? Anna pulled the contents out of the envelope. Read it to herself. The glossy flyer depicted an image drawn from a book series.

A pail skinned beauty with golden hair, her hazel eyes wide with fear and desire. Tears tracked down her cheeks. She was garbed in a Grecian toga of white. Her left arm is raised above her embracing the neck of the man behind her. He is as white as chalk with golden hair. His blue eyes gleam with a hidden power. His arms are wrapped around her waist drawing her back against him. His mouth is pressed at her throat his fangs sunk deep in her flesh. Blood runs down her skin to form letters.

Anna's eyes skip over the writing taking in the rest of the image.

A cold stone tower lay directly behind them. A torch lit in the window reveals a pair of eyes the color of steel looking down upon them with hate and longing. Her other arm reaches towards the silhouette of a man in the foreground, who reaches back to her. Behind them to the left another man stands skin ruggedly tan, dark hair long and wild. His amber eyes, inhuman, stare at the woman with hunger. Above it all is a heart of glass it has shattered to look like the moon and stars in the night sky. Anna turned her focus to the writing. She coughed. '

Embrace the night. Enjoy a weekend get way for two at Caesars Palace Hotel in Vegas. Magic awaits you at the Serenity Ball. Congratulations CJ Nichols.'

"Well, it's been a while. Maybe I could use a vacation."

18

Lance read over the flyer she presented him. Laughed then watched as her cheeks flushed.

"Sorry, didn't mean to embarrass you. I just found it funny. You don't strike me as the type of woman to read romance novels," he stated.

"I'm not. My sister, she likes to get me odd things for my birthday, tries to draw me out of my routine. One year it was a subscription to Harlequin's Intrigue series; another it was a wine of the world thing. This year she bought me the Dark Heart Trilogy and submitted the entry for me," Anna admitted. Remembering the card she'd received.

Lance nodded focusing on not laughing again. "I think a vacation could be a good idea. Why don't you give the sweepstakes people a call then get yourself packed? I'm going to give you the name of a friend of mine and the address for his gym in Vegas. You should look him up once you get into town. He may be able to help you. Do you have a number I can reach you at if I learn anything?"

"Sure let me get you my card."

She opened a drawer. Pulled out a business card and handed it to him.

"I'll let you know the second we have anything."

"Thanks. Um Detective, I think I should mention that if you talk with Phillip he may claim I've stolen museum property. I didn't."

"I think I hear a, but in there."

"See, I gave a copy of all my work to the Smithsonian they don't need mine. But um, I kind of took an artifact." Anna paused, took a sip of water. What she said next might land her in jail she realized. That didn't change the fact she needed to be honest with him. Lance waited her out wondering what she'd say next.

"I found it at the main dig; was analyzing it when they sent me back to Israel. I took it with me. I hadn't told anyone about it yet. I had planned to turn it over to the museum when I was done with it. Now I'm not so sure I should." Anna waited, wondering what to expect.

Lance studied the woman before him again; weighed her words. Her fear was palpable. "That's understandable but it is stolen property. However, if you want I can take it as evidence then no one can touch it until the investigation is closed."

Anna considered the offer not sure if she should accept it. She felt an inner struggle. There was something about that disk that wasn't natural something dark. She told herself it was foolishness. She didn't have a superstitious bone in her body but it weighed on her mind in a way that nothing ever had. She worried that giving it to anyone else might endanger them.

"If I give you the artifact can you promise me that no one else will see it or touch it?"

"I can keep it myself. No one else will know about it."

"I appreciate that but understand it shouldn't be handled."

"Why not?"

"I don't know, it's complicated to explain. I feel like there's something evil around the thing."

"Evil," Lance said with disbelief; trying not to laugh.

"I know it sounds crazy. I don't believe in that sort of thing, never have. But something inside me keeps telling me it's not right."

"Okay, I'm sorry I don't mean to make fun of you. I won't handle it."

"I forgive you, now wait here," Anna said. Getting up from the table she stepped out of the kitchen.

Lance sat in silence sipping his coffee deep in thought. He turned at the sound of her footsteps; smiled. She carried with her something wrapped in a black silk scarf.

Anna moved to the table, unwrapped the disk. Lance studied the artifact with curiosity. It wasn't what he had been expecting. He'd pictured some kind of pottery or ceremonial dagger. Something that looked ancient. What lay on the table in front of him was modern in appearance with strange engravings.

"What is it?"

"I don't know. Its unlike anything I've ever come across."

"What are these markings?"

"Some kind of writing I think though it's nothing I've ever encountered."

"You're sure it's a relic it looks like something from today.

Maybe even the future."

"I know. When I found it I thought it was site contamination until I tested it. The analysis dates it before our known history. It's older than mankind. It wasn't made by men either. It's composed of metal and stone fused together in a way that we aren't even capable of today."

Lance felt something in the room shift as he looked upon it – son of a bitch. She was right, the thing felt wrong. "Maybe I shouldn't have made fun of her," he muttered.

"You feel it too don't you," She whispered with relief.

"Yeah, it's set off all my cop instincts." He admitted. "If what you say about this thing is true how can it be here?"

"A good question. One I wish I could answer."

"Where did you find it?"

"I can't tell you that. Whatever this thing is, it can't go back there."

"Why?"

"As bad as this thing feels the chamber I removed it from felt much worse."

Lance reached out to touch it He drew his hand away. "I don't know if I want to take that thing."

"Superstitious?"

"Yeah, maybe a little," he confessed. "I've read enough stories to know this thing might be cursed."

Anna laughed. "Sorry I'm not making fun. I'm just relieved to know it's not just me. I was beginning to wonder if I was going crazy. I mean look at it. It's like a weird paper weight, and I'm afraid of it."

"Yeah, feels pretty stupid when you look at it that way."

"If you don't want to take it I'll understand."

"It's not been reported missing yet right?" Lance asked.

"As far as I know of," Anna said. Wondering why he asked.

"Okay, so I'm not required to confiscate it. So, as long as you skip town before it's reported I can't collect it."

"Are you sure? If anyone found out what you've done couldn't you get in trouble?"

"Possibly, I would rather not have that thing in my charge."

"Okay. I'll lock it up again, make my phone call and be gone before you can speak to Phillip. Um can I get a place to contact you in case things go bad?"

"Here's my card and the contact information for my friend."

Anna extended her hand to Lance in friendship. "Thank you for all of your help, Detective Roman."

Lance took her hand in his. Turning her wrist he brought it to his lips where he brushed it with a light kiss. In a display of old courtly affection that made Anna laugh. "Lance," he corrected with a whisper wanting to hear his name fall from her lips but her eyes widened with alarm at the nudge. He sighed knowing she would not relent and smiled. "It was my pleasure, Anna," he whispered. The care given to her name brought the laughter to an end. He felt her pulse begin to race and let her hand go. As he noted her mounting disquiet at his attempt to coax her out. Having no desire to upset her further he turned his attention back to his coffee.

He'd shaken her with the intensity of his gaze. Somewhere in the midst of their interview his interest in her had shifted from professional to personal. He wasn't sure when it had happened but it was clear to him she was uncomfortable with it. Lance watched as she picked up the disk and covered it once more; without another word she left.

Lance finished his coffee and moved back out to the living room; he conferred with the crime scene unit and then left wishing Miss Gallagher a good night.

19

Lance stepped out of Miss Gallagher's home and pulled out his cell phone. He punched in a number he'd never thought to dial again and waited for it to be picked up on the other end.

"Hello," the reply was cold and gruff. It hinted at the person having just woken. Lance groaned inwardly he'd forgotten the hour.

"Hello Mr. Abrams, its Detective Roman..."

"Damn it Lance, do you know what time it is here?" the other man groused.

"Sorry for the hour."

"This had better be good."

"Oh it is. You're not going to believe who just popped up on the radar."

"Kedar Handal," Mr. Abrams said now wide awake.

"Yeah, I got a call for a burglary attempt at the home of a Miss Annalynn Gallagher. She had photos of a group of three men who were following her lately due to her job. One of the three is your man, figured you'd want to know."

"What line of work?"

"Archeology, I can't sort out the connection for the life of me. I'm sending her your way."

"I'm not in that line of work anymore Lance, you know that."

"Yeah but if it's really Kedar chasing her I figure you're about the best person I can send her to. She's got one heck of a story; maybe you can sort it out, get your life back."

"Not interested. I've moved on."

"Can you at least watch her until I get clearance to come out there myself?"

"Sure, whatever, when should I expect her?"

"Tomorrow."

"Aww hell, figures. Fine. Can't wait," Sam grumbled before he hung up.

Lance smiled at least he knew Anna would be in good hands.

20

JERUSALEM, ISRAEL

Have you got it?" Ian Broody questioned. His voice brimmed with impatience.

"No sir, there's a new wrinkle." Kedar answered.

"What kind of wrinkle?" Ian questioned with irritation.

"The local police are involved."

"What happened?"

"She caught me trying to break into the safe; got the drop on me." Kedar admitted embarrassed. He was a seasoned agent and an assassin; that an inexperienced woman had gotten the better of him left a bad taste in his mouth.

"Damn. Don't lose her Mr. Handal, or I'll have to inform Mr. York of your failure."

"I won't sir. No need to notify him. What do you want me to do about the cop?"

"Go to his superiors, make sure the case vanishes."

"Understood." Kedar said before he hung up. He punched in a number he'd not used in some time. As he waited for the phone to ring he hoped his contact would be able to return that favor he owed him.

21 Los Angeles, California

"Tonight in the city of angels, the stars are shining bright as they celebrate the return of one of their own. James, heart throb, Hardagen has made the transition from teen star to director with Heart of Glass, his directorial debut. For his critics who claimed he was done; James had one thing to say.

"I'm not dead yet." The recorded shout played back. Pamela waited for her next cue.

"Pam, can you tells us what Hardagen and his people have been saying since the film ended."

"Well, moments ago Hardagen and his steady girlfriend Emily got into their limo, rode off into the night. His agent was quoted saying, 'the big premiere was a great success.' After a brief meet with his press agent we learned Hardagen is optimistic. So long as the numbers are good coming off the opening weekend James will be filming Heart of Clay the popular sequel to CJ Nichols Heart of Glass."

"Thanks for the scoop Pamela."

"You're welcome. Good night from the city of angels."

"Cut. You're clear. Nice work Pamela."

"Thanks Mina. Did you take care of the favor I asked?'

"Yes, Miss Walsh, you're all packed the bags in your car. You're on the next flight out to Vegas. Are you sure about this?"

"Positive. I've got some personal business to attend to."

"Good luck then Miss Walsh," Mina said. She turned her focus to packing up the gear.

I don't need luck not with my ex. He may be a maverick but in some things he's as reliable as a ticking clock. Pamela thought to herself. She handed her mike to Mina and headed for the car. It was going to feel good to get out of there.

22

Manhattan, New York

CJ Nichols sat at her desk her laptop was up and running. Pages of notes sat in a pile to her right along with a glass of water. Her fingers flew over the keys, typing up the notes for her newest book concept. It hadn't been easy lately to get anything going, not with all the noise made over Heart of Glass being translated to the big screen. She'd been swamped with fan mail requesting a fourth book for the Dark Heart series. Everyone was asking about Serenity again.

"I should have had Rachel cut off her damn head," CJ muttered with annoyance. She brushed a lock of her red hair out of her face. Serenity, everyone loved her. Why CJ didn't have a clue. She couldn't stand the woman. CJ figured by turning Serenity into a vampire it would have brought an end to her. She'd been wrong the fans still wanted to see Serenity find a happy ending. It was maddening.

CJ sighed. She'd locked herself in her work room this evening though she was sure her publicist would be furious with her for missing the premier. She didn't care. CJ was tired of all the talk about Serenity. She was done with her. CJ had let her publicist talk her into bringing Serenity back for book three. There would be no fourth book.

Besides she'd written much better characters in that series. If Heart of Stone was made into a film, that she would attend – that she was proud of. Rachel and Derek were the happy ending for the Dark Heart trilogy. There would be nothing more. "I've moved on from Dark Heart," she assured herself. CJ finished typing up her notes for the new novel.

Glancing at the clock in the bottom corner of her screen she noted the time, figured the premier was over. Good then there would be no more calls that night. She saved her notes, closed them out. CJ clicked on the second fie open, then turned her focus from notes to scene.

She reread the last couple pages to get the feel for where she'd left off and fell into the scene. It flowed from her fingers like a river. She turned up her music, losing herself in it.

CJ screamed as a hand grabbed her shoulder. She spun in her chair. Looking to see who was behind her. As her gaze fell upon the familiar face of a dark haired man with brown eyes, relief filled her. Knowing she was safe, anger bristled at being pulled out of the scene. Her blue eyes burned with rage. She rose from her chair to face the intruder. "Damn it Bryan. You scared the hell out of me."

"Serves you right, Catharine, I've been calling for over an hour." Bryan said. His eyes cold his jaw tight with anger. "What the hell do you think you're doing skipping the premier?"

CJ groaned at the question. She'd told him yesterday she wasn't going. She had too much to do. "What I'm doing is working. In case you forgot I have a deadline on the current manuscript… Wait, how did you get in here, I locked the place tight before I sat down."

"I told you that your being there was more important than the deadline. You need to be out in the public eye, gaining support for the film and the series. This thing is going to be huge. Book sales for Heart of Glass have tripled since the previews started running."

"Don't change the subject. How is it you managed to get in here and scare me?"

"Remember when you closed on the place; you were busy at the time, in a meeting with your editor?"

"Yes."

"I was asked to finalize things. The realtor gave me a key along with the two for you. I used it to prep everything and move your stuff in."

Catharine's eyes widened with fury. "You still have it? How dare you enter my home without an invitation?"

"I did call and knock. You aren't answering the phone or your door. So I let myself in. We have to talk about Dark Heart."

"I'm not talking about the trilogy until Monday."

"The movie premier was a hit. As long as the numbers hold, Hardagen will be making Heart of Clay for sure. This thing isn't going away CJ, not for a while."

Catharine blew out a breath. She wasn't going to avoid discussing the film now. "Okay, will you get off my back about the premier if I attend the opening night here? Arrange for a book signing?"

"Let's set it up in Vegas."

"Why?"

"You're going to have to take a few days off for a trip out there anyway. I got a call earlier from the contest winner. A Miss Gallagher will be flying in for her personal escape."

"Right, the contest I'd forgotten about it. If I do this thing will you ease up on the Dark Heart thing? I need to get the new book finished."

"As much as I can, but understand the house may not back off it."

"Fine, now go away. I want to get back to what I was doing if I can. I guess I need to pack. Give me my key. I'll see you in Vegas." CJ said her voice was cool as morning frost. She held out her hand, waiting for the key.

Bryan pulled it from his pocket, set it in her palm. She curled her fingers around it then escorted him to the door; locking it she turned, set to work on the task at hand.

23

Las Vegas, Nevada
Saturday
6am

"Time to get moving," Sam muttered, urging himself on. The sun had not come up. The desert air was still cool. It wouldn't be long until that changed. Checking his pedometer he noted his distance then looking to his watch checked the time. He was right on schedule; time to ramp it up into the next gear and push himself. With that thought in mind Sam's light jog became a full run. His sneakers moved from asphalt to dust.

He found his rhythm at the new speed with ease. His arms moving in and out with each stride he took; feet making contact with the dry earth in such a way as to prevent sinking deep in the sand. He closed his eyes as he ran on; allowing his other senses to take over. He knew the terrain well. It was the same path he'd run every morning for the last ten weeks. He'd run it more times than he could remember since moving to Vegas. Each day he pressed a little harder. He ran farther or raced faster. His goal here was to gain more speed or endurance. This morning he pressed for both. Tonight was the night. He would be ready.

His thoughts turned toward his opponent and what he knew of him. Frank "the Avalanche" Clifton was a good fighter, known for his striking and takedown defense. His stamina was questionable. Frank Clifton had never been pushed out of the first round. Sam figured if he could weather the early storm; drag the guy into deeper waters, he'd have the advantage. Sam pushed himself harder than before in preparing for the war to come. When he stepped in the cage tonight he wouldn't lose because he'd run out of gas.

Sam opened his eyes as the ground beneath him changed. He again checked both his distance traveled and the time. Satisfied with the numbers he broke into a full sprint, raced on through the final leg of his journey. His thoughts turned to his plans for the rest of the day.

After the run he'd grab a fast shower, a quick bite before he moved onto the gym for weight lifting. He'd follow that with some strength and conditioning then a light work out on the heavy bag. His next stop would be reviewing film to make sure he had his game plan locked in. Sam hoped to get a brief nap so he'd be well rested and onto the fight. The key for him today was to stay calm – focused. Debut fights had a way of overwhelming the unprepared. He didn't want to fall victim to the infamous jitters.

Sam toweled his hair as he walked into the kitchen. He tossed the wet towel into the laundry room to his left. Opening the fridge he reached in to grab his meal. The sound of the doorbell stopped him. Closing the door of the fridge he made his way to the front of the house to answer it.

"I'm coming, keep your shirt on," he shouted. The bell rang a second time. Opening the door Sam blinked in shock at the face on the other side. She was the last person he was expecting to see this morning.

"Ela," the old endearment fell from his lips before he knew it was there. He couldn't stop it. She hadn't been his Ela since he moved out here. He watched as her brown eyes sparked with delight at the old greeting. Her cherry lips curved into a smug smile.

"Good morning Sam, can I come in?" She said his name in a way he'd once accepted as love. Her voice as sweet as honey poured over him beckoning him to her. Her eyes the color of whiskey tempted him with a sirens song. Calling for control Sam steeled his heart against it; knowing that she was not to be trusted.

"What do you want Pamela?" He asked, his voice icy cold; closing her out.

"Come on Sam, don't be like that. I just want to talk." She said. Brushing her salon made blond locks behind her ear, exposing the bold sapphire tear drops hanging there. He'd bought them for her as a birthday gift their first year together. Sam felt something inside him stir. He stomped it out. Recognizing the move for what it was. The earrings were a tool she was using to soften him, so she could get whatever it was she wanted from him without a fight. Well he wasn't biting on her bait, not today.

"This isn't a good time Pam. I've got a lot on my mind at the moment. Can't it wait until Monday?"

"I know you're busy so I'll keep it brief. Better to get it settled now than later."

"Fine," he said with irritation; knowing she was right. He couldn't afford to let her crowd his thoughts today. Which was why she'd come now. Damn the woman was calculating. Why hadn't he seen it when they were married? Because she was good at manipulating people and he'd been in love. People didn't see the bad things about the people they loved until after they got married. He reminded himself before stepping aside to let her in.

24

Pamela walked past him into the living room, looked about with mild curiosity. She noted that the space had been filled with furniture suited for a man. It was ugly as sin but no doubt comfortable. Pamela noted the leather recliner in the corner. She smiled. Pamela had hated the chair in their home. It hadn't fit so she'd let him keep it when they divorced. After all it was his chair. She crossed the room, took a seat in it, taking his place in a silent display of control. The throne was hers for now.

She watched amused. Annoyance played over his face and went. Sam moved to stand behind the couch across from her and as far from her as possible without being rude. She noted he was just out of her reach and gave him a point. He was getting better at this.

25

"What is it you want, Pam?"

"I need your help."

He laughed a cold humorless laugh. It was his anger here not amusement. "Why the hell should I help you? Haven't you gotten enough from me? I gave you everything you asked for. You still had the nerve to send those damn papers claiming that I somehow jeopardized your career." Sam vision began to haze over with red. He drew a breath, knowing he needed to find his calm.

"You did. Your actions have damaged my reputation as a reporter." Pamela stated with disgust.

"Your reputation; what about mine?" His temper flared. Sam considered the matter again. Before her he'd had a job he loved and was good at. She'd gotten tangled in the middle of it and he'd tossed it all away for her. The fallout had been ugly. "You left when I needed you most – for what?" He said. Admitting for the first time that her walking out had hurt.

"I made no secret of the fact my career came first. If you were too blinded by your emotions to see that it's not my fault."

Sam's eyes left her gaze. He looked at her again with disbelief. "Were you always this cold and conniving and I never saw it or have you gotten worse?" He asked with disgust. It bothered him he misjudged her so far. Maybe his employers had been right to cut him loose, perhaps he had gone soft.

"How dare you?"

"How dare I? That's rich. You have some nerve showing up today of all days, demanding favors."

"Look if you help me I'll drop the suit, never ask you for another dime," Pamela said it in a rush.

He felt his temper ease. "I'm listening."

"I've got a publicist lined up waiting to buy a book but I can't write it without your signing a waiver."

"Okay, I want some time to think on this."

"Fair enough, why don't we meet say Monday, around ten am for brunch? My hotel, I'm staying at the Bellagio. We can discuss it further then."

"Fine." Sam moved to the door, opened it without another word; indicating she was no longer welcome. Pamela rose from his chair with the grace she'd always possessed, crossed the room to where he stood. Perfectly manicured red nails brushed over his arm in an all too familiar caress. He felt the bite of her nails on his scalp a moment too late to react.

The kiss came hard, fast, like a knockout blow. Sam cursed as old feelings and desire swept over him like a tidal wave. Unprepared for the attack he found himself in deep water, sinking fast.

26

"Bye Sam, until Monday," she murmured her voice breathy with the promise of passion and then she was gone.

Sam stood with the door a-jar hands slack at his side lost in the past, caught in a web of desire and need. He was dazed for a moment. Reality crashed in on him, with it came anger. He slammed the front door with disgust, stormed into the bathroom, turned on the water grabbing a rag. He scrubbed at the red stain she'd left on his lips, removing her mark, wishing he could remove it as easily from his memory.

"Pamela Walsh," he spat the name out like a curse. He'd been a fool for letting her in the house.

"I should have gone outside," he muttered to himself. The nerve of her sitting in his chair, acting like she ruled here. This was his house, his life. She had no part in it. Wasn't that why he'd left DC to begin with? It had held too much of her influence. She'd breezed in here, invaded his space all over again. The smell of her perfume still lingered in the air. Damn her, it still managed to drive him crazy.

"How does she do it?" he asked himself. He fought to regain control. Despite the anger she still managed to get to him.

Evaluating the encounter he gave himself credit. He'd done better this time. Hadn't given her what she wanted right? Sam had a nagging suspicion he was wrong. Pamela Walsh had managed to play him like a fiddle yet again. It infuriated him she'd been able to leave him standing in his own front door alone with her ghost. The entryway left open for anyone to walk through. There had been a time when he had been immune to such tactics.

Sam pushed the thought aside. He needed to get his mind back on track. He still had a full day ahead of him.

27 WASHINGTON DC, VIRGINIA

Lance sat reading over his notes from the break in at Miss Gallagher's home the night before.

"Anna," her name came unbidden from his lips like a prayer. Her image filled his mind. He'd advised her to leave town but at the moment he wanted nothing more than to see her again. There was something about Anna; he hadn't been able to get her off his mind.

"Dangerous ground," he muttered to himself. Lance looked over the CSI reports. His suspicions had proved to be correct. They'd turned up next to nothing from the scene. The guy's blood type was pretty common place. His search on the guys in the photos had turned up nothing. Ghosts, just as he'd anticipated.

Lance glanced at the clock, noted the time. It was too early to contact Phillip King at the museum. His shift was winding down. Lance contemplated grabbing a few winks in the crib when a knock sounded.

"Come in." he called. His thoughts having drifted back to Miss Gallagher and the strange artifact she'd shown him. Looking up he watched as his superior poked his head in the room.

"Got a minute, Detective Roman."

"Of course captain." Lance rose from his chair and followed the older man down the hall into his office.

"Shut the door please."

Lance did as requested, taking a seat opposite his boss. His nerves began to hum with anxiety. Something was off.

"You're working the break in called in by Miss Gallagher correct?"

"Yes sir."

"What have you got so far?"

"Nothing much I'm afraid. Very little evidence at the scene. The photos are coming up with nothing. I've got one more stone to turn…"

"I see. Lance, I've been asked to have the case closed on our end. Homeland Security is taking over this thing. If you know where Miss Gallagher is I need you to tell me at once."

"Homeland? Sir what is this about?"

"They aren't saying much. Apparently there are some concerns while she was out of the country that she turned traitor."

"Oh come on! Captain, this stinks."

"I know it Lance. We have to play ball. So, if you know where she went I need you tell me."

"Sir, I spoke with Miss Gallagher last night…"

"I don't want to hear about it not now. Do you know where she went?" The captain asked. His gaze shifted to the phone. Lance tensed with understanding. The office was bugged.

"No sir."

"All right then. Get me those reports so I can hand them over. As of this moment the case is closed."

"Understood."

"Lance, you look dog tired. Why don't you take the rest of the shift off?"

"Thank you, sir." Lance said getting up from the chair. He made his way back to his office for the paperwork. The captain walked with him.

"The Brickskeller, one hour." Lance nodded, handed over the files. He left the police station for the day.

28

Las Vegas, Nevada
Saturday
1pm

Anna sat at a small table sipping her second cup of coffee for the day. Her laptop was open and in front of her. She searched various papers on the net for any news pertaining to the dig site being discovered. She wasn't surprised to find nothing, yet again. She closed out the browser, pulled up the solitaire game. She needed to distract herself for a bit.

Anna flipped through electronic cards, working on sorting them into distinct piles. Her mind ran over the mess she was in. She sat contemplating her next move when her phone pulsed noting a call. She jumped, startled by the sensation, and drew the phone from her pocket, read the screen. She blinked surprised by the number that appeared, pressed the button to accept.

"Hello."

"Anna, this is detective Ro… it's Lance."

"Good afternoon detective. How are things in DC?"

"Not so good I'm afraid. No real evidence to speak of from the scene."

"Sorry to hear it."

"The case was closed this morning."

"Why?"

"Another agency took over. They requested your location. I've told them I didn't know it, but it won't take long for them to track you down out there."

"What do I do?"

"Anna, listen to me. Calm down. Don't make a scene. You should be safe enough. I'm meeting with my boss. With a little luck I'll be headed your way. For now my advice is to go to the hotel manager there request a change of room. If anyone should come asking for you, beyond the person in charge of the contest, have them informed you've checked out. Tell them an ex is after you or something."

"Okay. Then what?"

"Track down my friend's gym, he's expecting you. He'll make sure you stay safe until I get there. You might consider telling him your story, he's a former reporter."

"Right, okay, I'll get started on that then. Thank you, Lance."

"You're welcome. Anna, be careful."

Anna hung up the phone, drew a breath, trying to find her peace once again.

"Man, I could use some chocolate about now," Anna muttered, then tossed out her coffee. She returned to her table, and packed up her laptop. She needed to get started on what Lance had advised.

As she shouldered her bag she noticed a man folding up his paper. Hadn't she seen him before at the hotel? Was it possible they were already on her trail? She'd left false leads in a bid to throw her employers off her scent. She'd figured it would buy her a day at least. Maybe she'd been over optimistic. Anna walked out of the café, made her way back down the strip to her hotel.

29 WASHINGTON DC, VIRGINIA

Lance sat in an enclosed booth in the back of Brickskeller sipping a beer. He heard the jingle of the bell over the door, indicating someone had come in. He looked up to see the captain headed his way.

"Hello, Thomas."

"Lance, I trust you'll tell me what the hell is going on? I can't recall the last time I had another agency breathing down my neck."

"Well sir, it's like this…" Lance set down his beer. Proceeded to explain everything Anna had told him in the early hours between night and day, from the dig in Israel, to her fears that her employers might be doing something illegal.

"You believe her?"

"Yes sir, I did some checking on her as well. I can find nothing that makes me suspicious of her. I was going to meet the head of antiquities a Phillip King but since the case is closed."

"Do you think there's any way she could be a traitor?"

"It's about as likely as you or I turning traitor."

"I see. Okay, I want you to go meet with this Mr. King then I want you to track her down, treat her like a witness, all of this will be off the books. If anyone asks you've decided to take your vacation."

"Understood."

"Good luck Detective," with that said the captain rose from the booth and left. Lance paid for his drink. He left for the Smithsonian, with a little luck he'd be done with the interview and on his way to Vegas before sunset.

30

Lance walked into the Smithsonian. He made his way to the reception desk.

"May I help you?"

"Yes, I'd like to speak with Phillip King."

"Do you have an appointment?"

"No, I only need a few minutes of his time," Lance assured her. He showed her his badge.

"Let me page him see if he's available."

"Thank you."

Lance waited while the secretary picked up the phone. She spoke in a rush. Gave a nod then hung up. "He'll see you detective, right this way," she said politely before leading him through a door labeled staff only. Lance noted the labels on the doors as he made his way down the corridor. Anna's name drew his attention but only a moment. He needed to stay focused.

The hall came to an end at a set of double doors. The placard read Director of Antiquities Dr. Phillip King. The woman opened the door, issued him in. As he stepped in the room a man in his mid-fifties rose from behind his desk. His blue eyes were full of questions but he offered his hand to Lance in greeting.

"Good afternoon detective. What can I do for you?"

"I appreciate your agreeing to meet with me on such short notice. I figure you're a busy man so I'll try not to take up too much of your time. I'm wrapping up details for an investigation of an attempted robbery at one Anna Gallagher's home last night."

"Robbery? Is Anna okay?"

"She's fine a little shaken up. She said that she'd had a meet with you yesterday."

"That's correct Anna came in with news pertaining to her work. She indicated that certain people on her team were keeping things pertaining to that work from the museum. One of her colleagues contacted me before she arrived to indicate she had lost perspective."

"I see. When you met with her did she seem rational?"

"Yes, quite, but then when I requested her research from the dig she refused, walked out of my office with an artifact."

"Has she ever lost perspective on a project before?"

"No."

"Is she the type of woman who would fake a break in?" Lance asked.

"Never, if you're looking at her as making up stories detective then I'd ask you to get out. That girl has never done anything illegal. Despite her outburst yesterday I don' believe she would."

"Is it possible that she was telling you the truth and her colleague is trying to discredit her?"

"It's possible."

"One last question, Miss Gallagher indicated that she was being followed. Have you seen any of these men since yesterday?"

Phillip studied the pictures. He gasped. "Yes the one in the center he was just in this morning asking if we knew where Anna was. He claimed to be her boyfriend."

"Thank you for your time Doctor."

"Tell Anna that I'm glad she's safe."

"Next time I speak with her I will, good day sir." Lance said, before turning and leaving. Phillip King was in the clear for the burglary attempt. He was unaware of his colleague's actions. Satisfied Lance headed for home. He needed to pack then he'd be on his way.

31

Las Vegas, Nevada
Saturday
3pm

Sam walked into the gym, passed the reception desk with a quick greeting for the secretary, making his way back to his office. He tossed his bag and pulled out his gloves. He was still raging from his encounter with Pamela earlier. He had made up his mind to work it off. Gloves on Sam moved out into the sparring room. He was in the cage, trading blows with his sparring partner. He ducked punches and kicks sent his way, countered with blows of his own. He had just finished defending a takedown attempt when his corner man walked in the room; called time.

Sam growled around his mouth guard.

"Don't roar at me. You're supposed to be lifting weights, doing cardio work. I don't know what's got you so fired up. You got to take it down a notch or you won't be able to go in at a hundred percent."

Sam took out his mouth piece. "You're right, sorry the ex, she dropped in, left me mad. I need to work it off."

"Go hit the heavy bag for a while then. You don't need to injure yourself."

"Will do," Sam said. He made his way back to the general workout area

32

Anna parked her rental across from the gym, crossed the street. Opening the door she was greeted by the cool air. She walked over to the receptionist counter, waited for the woman behind it to finish up a call.

"Sir, can you hold on for a second? Someone's just walked in. Thank you." The woman pressed a button on the phone. Set down the receiver. "Sorry about that. How can I help you?"

"I'm looking for Mr. Abrams is he in?"

"He just came in a few minutes ago. I believe he's in the back."

"May I speak to him?"

"To who?" A man questioned. He came in behind them. Anna turned. She was faced with a young man with blond hair and blue eyes.

"She was asking about speaking with Mr. Abrams."

"I'll see if he's in the mood for a visitor Hanna," the young man said, vanishing around the corner.

"If you'll take a seat I'm sure he won't be long," Hanna said with a smile. The phone beeped reminding her that the man on the phone had been holding for at least two minutes. Anna nodded, moved over to a chair taking a seat. The woman, Hanna picked up the phone, continued her conversation. Anna deciding she wasn't going to sit around and wait to be brushed off; rose from her chair, pointed in the direction of the ladies room. Hanna nodded. Anna made her way around the corner the young man had rounded. She slipped into the rest room area, waited a few seconds then moved on down the hall in search of Mr. Abrams herself.

33

"Sam, there you are. I thought you were supposed to be lifting weights," the young man called, seeing his employer.

"It's a long story."

"Sam, there's a pair of hot legs out front asking for Mr. Abrams."

"Right have Hanna escort her to my office. I'm not ready to deal with a skirt yet."

"Will do," Rick turned to head back out front, noticed the blonde speaking with one of the guys. "Looks like she wasn't willing to wait. She's over there talking with Hank."

Sam turned, spotted the blond head facing away from him; cursed. Pamela had some nerve showing up again. "I'm out of here. Rick, keep her busy." Sam crossed the room back to his office. Rick moved to intercept her.

"Miss, you shouldn't be back here members only. Please wait out front." Rick said placing himself between her and Sam.

"I know. I'm sorry. I just really need to talk to Mr. Abrams."

"Mr. Abrams just left. He doesn't want to be disturbed today. Can it wait until Monday?"

"I can understand his not wanting to be interrupted. I'm afraid if I don't speak with him now I may not get a chance to again later."

Anna looked past him. She spotted Mr. Abrams retreating out the back door. "Mr. Abrams, please may I have just a moment of your time? Detective Roman sent me. I know you're a busy man. I wouldn't press but I don't have much choice."

Sam paused. His curiosity pricked; something in the voice there – fear maybe? He cracked his neck as if breaking loose of a leash. Not his business. "Miss Gallagher?" He questioned but before the woman could respond Hanna came around the corner.

"There you are. I'm sorry Mr. Abrams, I was on the phone with a client. She requested to use the restroom."

"It's okay Hanna." Sam said turning to face the receptionist. His gaze landed on the woman.

"Miss, there is a gentleman upfront looking for you. He said he was your boyfriend."

Sam watched as her hazel eyes flickered with alarm. She turned. Glanced back in the direction of the lobby. Sam looked past her to the man in the lobby. As he looked at the middle aged man of Middle Eastern decent he blinked. Doing a double take he knew the face all too well. He'd studied the man for months while living in DC. He'd been working on terrorist connections to government officials and lobbyists. The Man was Kedar Handal a known hit-man for an unknown individual answering to Mr. York, The last time he'd seen Mr. Handal he'd had a gun on him; threatened him and Pamela's life.

Sam looked at the woman. Saw recognition but not relief. "Do you know this gentleman?" Sam asked.

"Not really. He works for my employer. I saw him at the coffee shop earlier today then again at my hotel lobby. Kind of weird he'd turn up here looking for me."

"Right, weird. Hanna, go brush him off. Inform him Miss Gallagher left." Sam instructed.

"Okay."

"Thanks Hanna."

With the goon up front handled Sam grabbed Miss Gallagher by the wrist, dragging her into his office.

Sam closed the door to his office, careful not to make too much noise.

"You wanted to talk to me?"

"Yes. My name is Anna Gallagher," she licked her lips in a show of nerves. Not sure where to begin Sam reasoned. He'd seen it many times over the years someone with a wild tale always worried they'd not be believed. Whatever she had to say it was clear she hadn't thought this through and it left her uneasy.

"Nice to meet you, Sam Abrams," He said offering his hand. She shook it and then seemed to relax.

"Mr. Abrams, I don't know how much Lance told you but that man out there has been following me for at least a month."

Sam switched on the lights, peered through the glass front to the lobby area at the man asking after Miss Gallagher. What did he want with her? He wondered. Sam then turned his attention back to her. He let her go. Realizing he still had her wrist. "Detective Roman didn't say anything about your situation only that you were an archeologist and someone had broken into your home."

"Can he see us?"

"No it's a two way mirror."

"Good."

"Miss Gallagher, that man out front looking for you; I've run into him before."

"You have?"

"Yeah, last time I saw him was in DC. I was working a story. He had terrorist connections then."

"That can't be. He was hired as security for a dig I was working in Israel," Anna said with disbelief. Ian Broody was a lot of things but she found it hard to believe he was connected to terrorists.

"I don't know who pays him now Miss Gallagher, but he's no joke."

"You think I don't know that?"

"I'm not sure you do. If this guy is following you because of this story of yours my advice is to drop it before you get in over your head."

Anna slid down into a chair in front of his desk. "I think it's a bit late for that," she muttered, burying her face in her hands.

"What was that?" Sam asked. He turned. "Oh no, Miss Gallagher, please don't cry. I'm sorry." What had set her off? Sam wondered. He crossed the room to where she sat, watched as she lifted her head, hazel eyes met his.

"I'm not crying Mr. Abrams; just trying to clear my head. If I let it get too cluttered; the past couple days just might overwhelm me."

Sam drew a breath relieved. Her words brought out the reporter in him. What had happened in the past few days that she refused to dwell on? Sam gave himself a mental shake. He didn't care. He wasn't going to get involved any further than he had already agreed to.

"Right, sorry my ex she had a tendency towards tears when she didn't get what she wanted."

"I see."

"Before we go any further let's see about getting you out of here safely. Did you drive over or get a cab."

"I have a rental that should be ditched," Anna said with annoyance.

"Okay, let's get you a cab back to your hotel then."

"Thank you."

"You're welcome." Sam said before he picked up the phone. He called to request a cab. "It'll be here in thirty minutes, just sit tight.

We'll get you out of here without being followed

"Right. Um I'm not quite sure where to begin."

Sam heard panic in her voice. Whatever was going on with her she was scared. He wanted to walk away. Women in his experience were not to be trusted. But he'd promised Lance. "Relax Miss Gallagher, I'm not going to judge you here. I've heard it all over the years." he assured her.

"I doubt you've heard this one Mr. Abrams."

"Sam."

"What?"

"You can call me Sam."

She nodded. "Okay Sam. Please don't take this the wrong way but I don't know anything about you except that you're Lance's friend. I don't really know him either. This guy shows up in Vegas and for all I know Detective Roman led him straight to me so how is it you think I can trust you with what I have to say."

Sam blinked surprised by her words. She was sharper than he'd originally given her credit for. "You're right, you have no reason to do so Miss Gallagher, but if you don't you may not live through whatever it is you're tangled up in."

"That may be so Mr. Abrams, and if it is then it also stands to reason that what I tell you could place you in danger as well."

"I can take care of myself; Anna, you however can't deal with Mr. Handel out there on your own. Face it lady, you need my help."

Anna fell silent and Sam cursed; he pushed her too hard. She wasn't going to say anything more.

The sharp buzz of Sam's intercom broke the silence that had settled over his office. He watched as Anna jumped, startled. Damn she was right on the edge of control. He picked up the phone, listened as Rick spoke. He gave a quick response of agreement then hung up the phone. Anna's hazel eyes met his with question.

"Cab's here."

"Okay, good. The sooner I get moving the better, but what do I do about the rental?"

"Give me the keys. I'll have the rental place pick it up." Anna nodded. Reaching in her pocket she pulled out the key for the rental.

"Come on. Let's get you on your way," Sam said. He led her out the back to where the cab was waiting. She slid in to the back seat. Sam moved to close the door. The sense of being watched pressed heavily on him. He looked around and though he saw no one his instincts told him the guy from earlier was out there, watching. Before he could consider the matter he got in the cab with her.

"Where to?"

"The lady knows the destination. For now just drive," Sam instructed before Anna could react. Sam glanced at his watch then groaned. He didn't have a lot of time to burn. Sam hoped this wouldn't take long. He spotted the black sedan three cars back. Sam sighed, hating that he was right. He didn't have time for this. Seeing the traffic backed up he made a last minute call.

"Here's five, change of plans." Sam opened the door. Grabbing Anna's hand he dragged her from the cab.

Sam ran down the side street dragging Anna behind him. He hung a right headed back for the gym. Looking behind him he was relieved to see they weren't being chased. With a little luck they'd make it back to the gym before Kedar Handal hit the first street. Maybe he wouldn't sort out where they'd gone. As they ran into the back lot Sam pulled out his keys, unlocked the car. "Get in."

Anna did so without question. Sam pulled out of the lot. He was sure to head in the opposite direction the cab had been headed. "Where to?"

"Caesar's Palace," Anna replied through deep breaths. She wasn't used to running that hard. "What just happened?" she questioned. Trying to understand why he'd even gotten in the cab to begin with.

"Your boyfriend was following us. I figured if we lost him that you might get the chance to get clear of his watchful eye for long enough to relocate."

"Thanks."

"You can thank me once I'm sure we're out of this," he snapped irritated. Checking the rearview he was relieved to see that they hadn't been spotted. He scolded himself mentally for getting this involved in her problems.

He'd given up this life style when he left DC. He'd promised himself no more car chases, dodging bullets. He'd given up too many things for that life, a home, family and friends. He believed once that with Pamela he could change that. He'd been a fool. She was never interested in settling down into a normal life.

When Sam moved out to Vegas he'd hoped that down the road he might have a chance at that life he'd given up. This was a step in the wrong direction. He was not going to get tangled up in that life again. This thought in mind he pulled in front of Caesar's Palace.

"Thank you Sam," she murmured.

"You're welcome Miss Gallagher. I hope you'll heed my advice." Sam used her last name to create distance. It annoyed him that he liked the sound of his name on her lips, downright angered him that he felt something stir inside him when he looked at those hazel eyes of hers. He'd been down this road before with Pamela. It was all too familiar territory. He refused to be lead down the same path twice.

"I make no promises Mr. Abrams. Good day," She said. Her words were cold, biting. If he wanted to keep things formal, place her at a distance then so be it. Anna thought with disgust. She opened the door to get out.

Sam blinked he wasn't sure but he would have sworn her eyes had darkened as she spoke. It was a bit spooky. The cold formality of her good bye registered next. It felt like a slap to the face. Her abrupt switch to Mr. Abrams set his temper close to the edge. He couldn't fathom why. He'd wanted distance; she'd given it so why was it rubbing him the wrong way. He grabbed her arm, halting her departure.

She looked at his hand upon her with irritation "Would you please stop man handling me Mr. Abrams?" She requested in the same icy tone.

Sam blinked at the sensation of past and present colliding. In his mind's eye he saw himself draw the car door shut before pulling the woman at his side to him. His kiss had been rough and demanding then. Things had moved too fast with Pamela.

"Not again," he muttered to himself. He let Anna's arm go as if it had burned him. He wasn't going to get tangled up in her problems. Whatever was chasing her he'd walked as far down the road with her as he intended to? "Sorry, please be careful Miss Gallagher." He requested.

"I will," she assured him. Anna got out of the car. "Good luck with the fight this evening Mr. Abrams," She murmured, then smiled.

"Thank you. Here's my number in case you change your mind. Good bye Anna." He said and he handed her his card.

Sam watched as she closed the door, made her way into the hotel. He waited until she was inside, certain there was no sign of the man from the gym. Taking out his phone he called Lance. The detective was not going to be happy.

"Hello."

"Lance."

"Sam, what's up?"

"I just dropped off Miss Gallagher at her hotel. She refused my help."

"What? Why?"

"Our mutual friend showed up here in Vegas. She won't trust me," Sam stated with disappointment.

"Kedar is there already? Shit. Make her change her mind Sam."

"How?"

"I'll give you her number. Call her, talk to her, and convince her you're not her enemy. Damn, I've got to go, good luck," Lance said. He rattled off the phone number where Anna could be reached then hung up.

Sam cursed before pulling away from the curb to head out. He still had lots to do before the fight that night. He'd be lucky if he managed to get it all done in time.

34

Anna crossed through the lobby headed for the elevator. She was looking forward to a few minutes alone. Her mind was far from restful. What had Mr. Abrams meant by not again? Was he as upset for grabbing her as she'd been by his odd behavior? Or was there something else she didn't understand? Anna sighed. Knowing this was one question she couldn't find the answer to on her own. Pushing it aside she contemplated her next move.

"Miss Gallagher, oh thank goodness," a woman's voice called from somewhere behind her. Anna turned, watched as one of the receptionists came her way.

"Oh, hello," she murmured. Wondering why the woman seemed so relieved to see her. "Did you need something?"

"No I just wanted to let you know that we have a couple messages for you, also a gentleman was looking for you. We told him you'd checked out per your request. He questioned my man for details. None were given," the woman explained. She handed over a couple envelopes.

"Thank you," Anna said with appreciation.

"You're welcome. I hope you'll enjoy your stay with us," the woman replied, moving back to the desk.

Anna moved onto the elevators. She pressed the button; she'd look at the messages once she got back to her room. For now, she needed a moment to relax. When the doors opened Anna moved down the hall, the only thought in her mind bed and a bath.

35 SATURDAY 4PM

Sam groaned as he moved from the bathroom into the bedroom. After dropping Miss Gallagher off he'd driven back to the gym, finished out his workout, then driven her rental car back to the airport and turned it in. He'd had to pay a second cab fare to get back to the gym. It still grated on his nerves. He was tired from a busy day. He still had time before he had to be at the hotel. He could grab a short nap and be well prepared.

His gaze moved to the business card sitting by the phone. Lance had sent it earlier 'Make her change her mind.' Lance's voice whispered in the back of his head. How the hell was he supposed to manage that? He asked himself. He lay down on his bed with his back to the phone. 'I make no promises, Mr. Abrams.' The words echoed through his mind. Her hazel eyes appeared through the dark of his imagination.

"Damn," he groused. Sam turned in the bed. His gaze focused once more on the card. "I could call her. Let her know the rentals been dealt with," he reasoned, then cursed again, this was a mistake. He didn't have any reason to call her. If she didn't want him involved; he couldn't force her; besides, he really didn't want to get tangled up in whatever she was. Sam reminded himself even as he sat up. He reached for both the phone and the card; he'd promised Lance. Before he knew what he was doing he dialed the number. He was listening to it ring. Just when he was about to hang up he heard the sound of the line connecting.

"Hello?"

The voice on the other end registered as male. Sam checked that the number from the card matched the number he dialed. "Lance?" he asked.

"Yeah."

"When did you get in?"

"About an hour ago."

"Good."

"What did you need?"

"I wanted to let Miss Gallagher know the rental car was handled."

"Lance, who is it?" Anna questioned.

"Some guy," the man replied. Sam heard the sound of the phone being handed off. He waited.

"Hello?" she questioned.

"Anna?"

"Oh, hi Mr. Abrams, – very funny Lance."

"Anna…" Sam called her name bringing her attention back to him. He tried to ignore the jealousy stirring within him at her use of the detective's first name.

"Yes," she said. Letting him know he had her undivided attention once again.

Sam froze, trying to recall why he'd contacted her. "Anna, I'd hoped we might meet again and…"

"Mr. Abrams, since Lance is here now I don't see why I need your help."

Damn there it was again, that icy, high society disapproval. It grated on his nerves in a way that he couldn't understand. It wasn't her speaking it was someone else. He wasn't sure why he thought it but he was sure of it. "I know more about this guy than detective Roman does."

"That may be so, but I don't believe you're really interested in helping me Mr. Abrams. You know where the hotel is. You strike me as the type who prefers to hear a story first hand; so you can see the truth of it from your source." Anna commented.

"You're right. I called because I wanted to let you know the rental was returned."

"Thanks."

"You're welcome. I'm sorry for the way I acted earlier. I was in a bad mood when you showed up. I was unfair in the way I treated you."

"Apology excepted."

"Did you tell the detective about our little adventure earlier?"

"Yeah."

"What's he doing in Vegas?"

"He said his boss sent him out here to keep an eye on me." Sam heard a door close. He pictured Anna moving into a room where she could speak without Lance hearing her. "Sam, I think he's keeping something from me. Before I left he said he couldn't put me in protective custody. Now he's here on orders. I can't figure out why."

"Do you trust him?" Sam asked.

"Yes, I don't think he's a threat. I just get the feeling that his being here means that things are worse than I originally thought," she confessed.

Sam cursed himself for a fool. "I still have some contacts in DC, do you want me to try and find out what's going on back there for you?"

"I'd appreciate it."

"Okay. I'll do some checking; drop by in about an hour."

"Thank you."

"Don't mention it," he whispered before he hung up. Sam pulled out his laptop, started running a search on Anna Gallagher. If he was going to get involved in this thing any further he wanted to know what he was walking into. While the computer ran his request he picked up the phone, set to work finding out what Detective Roman was hiding.

36

Sam sat in Caesar's Palace café sipping a cup of coffee. He pulled out his phone and sent the signal to Miss Gallagher to meet him. As he waited he reflected on his phone call earlier. His contact had not been happy to hear from him; until he mentioned Kedar, then he'd been more than cooperative.

Sam spotted Anna from the lounge where he sat waiting. She was just stepping off the elevator and headed his way. He also spotted detective Lance Roman shadowing her. Sam cursed. He rose from his seat, leaving money for his drink, meeting her midway.

"Change of plans," he whispered. Sam drew her to him in a hug. He felt her tense, struggling to resist the urge to push him away. Good; she understood they needed to appear close as opposed to a pair of strangers meeting in case anyone was looking on.

"Why?" she murmured in question as he let her go.

"Your cop followed you."

"My; damn, I take it you found something."

"That's right doc, lets roll," Sam stated. He led her out of the hotel to his car. He escorted her around to the passenger side; opening the door for her, then got in himself. Lance stepped outside. Sam pulled away from the curb. He noted the detective still standing on the steps. Good he wasn't following. Now that he was sure they were alone Sam relaxed. "Are you sure you want to hear this?" Sam questioned. He switched lanes and waited to turn.

"Yes, better to know than move in ignorance," she replied.

"Okay, I checked with my contacts in DC. I learned the burglary case for your home was closed this afternoon by Homeland Security. It seems they've marked you as a possible terrorist suspect, Anna."

"What?"

"You asked," he reminded.

"Oh, hell, you're serious!"

"Now it's not public yet. I imagine if our friend from earlier doesn't find you soon, it will be."

"No, I don't think that they will let that happen. There are things I have that I know which my employers don't want becoming public knowledge."

"What sort of things could an archeologist know that has national security running around? Do you work for the government?"

"Been checking up on me Mr. Abrams?" Anna asked. From her tone he figured she wasn't sure if she should be flattered or insulted.

"Yeah a little, old habits."

"Fair enough, far as I know of – no. I wasn't employed by the government."

"You didn't answer my entire question." Sam pointed out. Anna noted there was a bit of annoyance in his voice.

"I gave some thought to what you said earlier at the gym. I'm just not comfortable with sharing my story with you or anyone else for that matter."

Sam blinked, surprised by her refusal. He turned to look at her. She looked troubled and confused. Something had shifted since he dropped her off. The energy she'd been surrounded by had lessened. She'd been diminished somehow.

"Anna, what I said before about not knowing if you'll be alive long enough to tell your story; I meant it. Kedar is on the payroll of a very dangerous man."

"So you say, Mr. Abrams, but as far as I know the only man he's working for is Dr. Ian Broody, I've known him for some time now. Ian maybe a lot of things but he is no terrorist."

"Are you sure you want to stake your life on that?" Sam asked with disgust. Recognizing a connection to the other man, he cursed inside. How close were they, Dr. Broody and his Anna? Sam's mind froze at that. Anna wasn't his. He barely knew her. What was wrong with him? He admonished himself for the possessive claim. Anna spoke.

"Yes Mr. Abrams, Ian is a good man." She stated.

"Your eyes, say you don't believe a word of that."

"Maybe you're right and I don't believe it. Perhaps you're wrong. What I do know is there's something in your gaze that wasn't there earlier."

"Good or bad change?"

"I'm not sure. I can't sort it out." She muttered more to herself than him. He could practically hear the gears in her mind turn as she lost herself in the matter. His gaze moved back to the road, trying to stay on topic and on task.

"Don't go silent on me, Anna, to try and protect me. I can take care of myself. I've been down this road before," he assured her. Sam caught sight of the black sedan from earlier. He cursed with frustration. He'd been so focused on making sure the detective didn't follow them he'd missed the fact Kedar had spotted them. Sam made a quick turn – poured on the speed.

"What's happening?"

"It seems we were spotted coming out of the hotel. Hang on I'm going to try and loose this guy again," Sam said, rounding another corner. He heard breaks squeal. The sedan cut off another car to pursue them. Sam glanced in the rearview. He saw the sedan closing fast. The passenger window was open just enough for a gun. He heard the familiar pop of a silenced bullet. The back window shattered. "Get down doc," he ordered. Sam made another sharp turn. Anna slumped down in the seat. "If we live through this I want some answers Anna. I'm not getting shot at for nothing."

She said nothing. Her head nodded. They rounded a corner. He realized she'd never faced anything like this before. He cursed. He reminded himself she wasn't Pamela. She wasn't versed in this kind of danger. Sam made his way through the city snaking up and down the main roads in a maze of turns. They had no apparent rhyme or reason to them.

"Got to get someplace safe to hold up," Sam muttered. He turned down another side street. There was only one safe place he could think of at that moment though. He noted there was no sign of the sedan. Sam figured they'd lost Kedar in the turns. Satisfied they'd gotten clear; he made another turn. This one pointed him in the direction of home.

Sam made a mental check. Was that where he wanted to take her? Once he crossed that line there was no turning back. He'd be in this thing, whatever it was up to his ears. Glancing over at his passenger, he noted she showed signs of early shock. He had to get her out of the open and make sure she was okay. His mind set, Sam made a final turn into his neighborhood, pulled his car into the garage. He closed the door, concealing their destination then got out. Sam rounded the vehicle to the passenger side and opened it.

37

She didn't move.

"Anna, you okay?" She gave no reply. When he reached in to shake her he felt something warm and sticky. Fear settled in the pit of his stomach, like an icy ball. He felt it writhe and coil, like a snake. Sam didn't know what he'd felt. He couldn't until he saw it. Sam moved back to the driver's side toward the door, switched on the lights. The sudden illumination was blinding. He closed his eyes until they had adapted.

Upon opening them his gaze fell to his hand. He felt himself tremble. The red smear on his skin was unmistakable – blood. Sam rounded the car once more to the passenger side with the lights on. He could now make out at least a half dozen bullet holes. Had she been hit? Why didn't she react or say anything. As he reached her side once more he calculated the last time she'd said anything to him. Sam realized it had been at least ten minutes.

The light pouring through the open door revealed a spreading blood stain on her white blouse. Sam cursed. He'd been so preoccupied, first with his jealousy for Dr. Broody then with the chase. He'd not been aware of her. "Nice going Mr. Abrams," he muttered to himself. Sam decided he could scold himself later. He reached in to verify she was alive. It took a couple of tries but he found her pulse. A steady beat under his fingers. He let out a breath; he'd been unaware of holding. With care he unbuckled her seat belt, lifted her out of the car.

Sam carried Anna into the house, laid her down on his bed. Moving into the bathroom he grabbed the needed supplies to take care of his charge, a bottle of peroxide, rubbing alcohol, cotton swabs, and a towel. Moving back to his bed he placed them on the night table then made his way to the kitchen for a bowl and water.

His tools gathered Sam returned to Anna's side, unbuttoned her blouse. With hand towel and the water he cleaned up her skin, revealing the wound. He noted that the shoulder was pierced on both sides; that meant the bullet was gone. He knew how to treat her but if he did so it would lead to questions he'd rather not answer.

He'd already broken protocol earlier by placing that call to find out about what was happening in DC for her. If he started showing signs now of reverting back to his former life – it would mean trouble. On the other hand Sam didn't want to risk the hospital. Kedar would be watching there no doubt. So what was he going to do? Sam heard the trilling of a phone. Reaching into Anna's pocket he pulled out her cell phone. The name on the screen registered. He pressed the talk button.

"Anna, where are you. Are you okay?"

"Lance."

"Abrams, where's Anna?"

"She's here, in a lot of trouble."

"What happened?"

"I'm not sure. We were tailed when we left the hotel. Detective, she's been shot."

"Where are you?"

Sam rattled off his address. He did his best to slow the bleeding.

"I'm on my way," Lance said before the phone went dead. Sam dropped it on the bed. He cursed his need for secrecy. If he'd not been so hell bent on getting her away from the detective then she might still be all right. Turning his focus from the woman on his bed, Sam moved down the hall to unlock the door so Lance could get in when he arrived.

38

Lance pulled onto the empty drive matching the address Sam Abrams had given him. He ran across the lawn, burst into the unlocked front door. “Abrams?”

“In here.” The answer came fast from the back of the apartment. The voice sounded weary, broken even to Lance. He raced down the hall in the direction it had come from. Lance rounded the door frame. The sight before him stole his breath. Anna lay on the bed her shoulder bound. Blouse beneath her stained with blood.

“How is she?”

“The same, I managed to stop the bleeding but she’s still out.”

Lance’s gaze moved to Sam. The guy looked sick with worry and guilt. “How long?” Lance questioned. He crossed the room to inspect Mr. Abrams work.

“The last thing I remember her say is ‘What’s happening?’ at the time I thought she was asking why I’d taken the corner wide and sped up. Now I wonder if she was aware something was wrong with her. Unaware of what.”

“Unaware of a gunshot?” Lance asked with disbelief.

“It was silenced.”

“Possible then. You’ve done nice work here.”

“Thanks, though if I hadn’t…” Sam began.

“Don’t, as much as I’ve wanted to see you taken down a peg due to recklessness in previous encounters this one isn’t all your doing. I can share in the blame also.”

“It was Kedar.” Sam said.

“Aww hell. This is worse than I thought. I know I asked you to watch her until I got here but I can’t handle this one on my own. Do you think you could get clearance to…” Lance began.

“When my story was discredited it was the company burning me.

I am no longer in that line of work. I broke an agreed silence when I called a contact in DC at her request."

"Is that why you're not treating her yourself?"

"Yeah too many questions I can't afford to have surrounding me right now."

"I got to admit; I had thought to work this one on my own, not get you involved but if he's tied to this that means Mr. York is. I know this thing is over my head."

"I'm in, but I'm rusty," Sam said with disgust.

"Rusty or not glad to have you aboard," Lance admitted.

"Thanks, now what do we do for her?"

"I need a knife or a cigarette, a lighter to cauterize the wound and a needle and thread to close it up."

"Knife and lighter I've got. A needle…"

"Wait, I've got an idea. Where's her purse?"

"Still in the car, I'll get it." Sam rose from the bed, disappeared down the hall. When he returned a few moments later he had the knife lighter and purse.

Lance opened her purse and started rummaging through the various liners and pockets.

"What are you looking for?"

"From what I saw of her place it was neat, organized. I'm playing a hunch she'll have one of those emergency sewing kits."

"Makes sense," Sam commented.

"Why'd you ditch me?"

"She wanted to know about what was going on back in DC. Since you weren't answering her I figured it was a conversation best kept from you. I'd hoped to establish trust with her."

"Works, I suppose."

"Yeah, but I was so focused on losing you I never saw Kedar."

"It happens… Aww, yes; got it, a needle," Lance said. He held up needle and thread for Sam to see. "You know what I can't understand about this?

"No, what?"

"Why did he shoot at her now and not before?"

"Maybe he recognized my picture at the gym and decided he didn't want her talking to me," Sam suggested. Mentioning the gym brought the fight back to focus in his mind. "Oh man, what time is it?"

"Almost Six, why?"

"Oh, nothing much, it's just I'm supposed to be at the MGM Grand in about 20 minutes for the biggest fight of my career to date,"

Sam muttered.

"You're thinking of not going?" Lance questioned in disbelief.

"It hardly seems important now."

"You can't explain your reason for canceling. You'd be throwing away your career."

"It wouldn't be the first, besides I've got the gym."

"Sam, you should go. There's nothing else you can do for her now. I've got her in hand." Lance assured him.

"I don't know…"

"Mr. Abrams, go win your fight," Anna murmured as she came around.

"Anna…"

"I'll be fine,"

"Are you sure?"

"Yes."

"I want to hear about everything when you're up to it."

"Deal," she whispered. She watched as Sam grabbed his things. After a brief good bye; he went on his way.

"Now that you're awake, let's see if Sam has any alcohol," Lance muttered. He left Anna on the bed and went in search of the kitchen.

39

Sam clinched his taped hand into a fist. He struck the hand pad his trainer held out for him, testing the wrapping. Finding it was ready he checked the other.

"How's it feel, Sam?" His coach asked.

"Feels right to me," Sam answered.

"Okay then let's glove up. Get you loose."

Sam nodded then picked up his UFC gloves. He pulled them on waited as the gaming commission rep taped them closed, marking them legal and un-tampered. With the gloves ready Sam turned his attention to his coach and corner man, practicing his moves. Once he was in the octagon he would respond without thought. He would focus on the move several steps ahead. Sam had learned over the past several years that Mixed Martial Arts or MMA as most called it was as much about the mental game as the physical. He was fast and athletic but the thing that had gotten him to this big chance was the head game, his ability to out think his opponents.

Unbidden his mind drifted to the earlier events of the day. His emotions rose to the surface.

"Sam, where you at? Get your head in the game man," his coach scolded as he missed an easy block.

"Sorry, I've had a busy day," Sam muttered.

"Yeah, you've been off all day. First coming in all worked up then the interruption. Whatever it is you got to put it away. It's almost game time."

"Right," Sam said. He closed his eyes to clear his head. He saw the image of Anna Gallagher laying on his bed bleeding. He hoped she was okay. Then he tucked the day's events in a dark corner of his mind, focused his thoughts on the fight. After all; she'd told him to win.

40

Anna woke in a green field. She yawned, stretched stiff limbs lazily. A strange sense of inner peace surrounded her, bidding her not rush. The ground beneath her was flat and even. Yet it seemed to mold around her to comfort and support her. The earth itself was soft, inviting her to lay still – rest.

"Where am I?" she murmured. Her voice moved like a whisper on the wind, fading into the silence around her. She closed her eyes. Tried to remember what had come before but found nothing. A gentle breeze moved through the tall grass, setting it to dancing around her. The smell of spring flowers surrounded her. The grass moist with dew brushed against her skin like waves, rocking her to sleep. The wind sang a sweet lullaby.

She blinked feeling strangely like sleeping beauty waking after a long slumber. Lifting her head she sat up, trying to determine her location. Anna was surrounded by tall grass and wild flowers as far as she could see. The grass was made of the deepest greens she'd ever seen. So brilliant in its coloring that it shown with a radiant inner light like that of a gem. The flowers too were the boldest colors she had ever known. So beautiful they almost hurt to look upon.

"How did I get here?" Anna whispered. She turned her gaze to the sky above. The expanse of the heavens, were a brilliant blue. The sun blazed above like a great ball of fire. Its light so bright it was almost blinding. Anna closed her eyes to shield them. She set her gaze once more to the field. The wind shifted. Its song changed to something warm, wistful.

Anna became aware of the sound of running water in the distance. The sun above warmed her skin. The sound of the water called to her. She became aware of a thirst within her. It was near fevered pitch. Anna felt as if she'd crossed a desert. She had been without water for many days. How long had she slept she wondered. She got to her feet.

The grass danced in the wind, tickling her toes. She looked down at her feet and saw they were bare.

"Where are my shoes?" she questioned. Then recalled she'd not worn them. Looking about she sought some sign of the running water, saw nothing. Whatever it was, it was beyond her sight. The heat of the sun beating on her became greater. Her need of water grew unbearable. She set off through the field following the sound.

She soon came to a flowing river. The water was a crystalline blue. Anna knelt at the water's edge, dipped her hands in. It was cold against her skin. A shock to the system that set her to shivering. The water shown like a mix of aquamarine, and turquoise in her palms, it ran between her hands, splashing back into the river before she could drink. Her gaze fell to the water, landing upon her reflection. She looked upon her own face. The image was wrong; her mind whispered. Anna studied the woman in the jade green Grecian toga.

"MY DEAREST ANNALYNN, AT LAST WE MEET."

She turned; startled by the sudden realization she wasn't alone. Anna looked about her but saw no one.

The voice had been strong, powerful –it seemed to come from nowhere and everywhere all at once. Something about it stole her breath, dropped her to her knees, breaking the peace about her. She closed her eyes trying to make sense of it all. When she opened them the voice had taken shape. A man, with hair darker than the night sky and eyes like sapphires, stood behind her.

"This is a dream," she whispered with understanding.

"THAT'S WHAT I TREASURE MOST ABOUT YOU ANNA, YOUR QUESTING MIND THAT SEEKS AFTER KNOWLEDGE. IT'S THAT THIRST THAT HAS BROUGHT YOU HERE." He said. He reached out lifting her chin to look upon her face. His touch was like ice, cold, unnatural but burned like fire. She moaned in pain. Yet the touch swept through her stirring her with desire and longing. The song of the wind grew louder, more insistent.

"Who are you?" She asked. The mild disquiet she felt at hearing his voice became a living breathing fear coiled deep in the pit of her stomach. She wanted to turn away from his touch but felt she couldn't.

"YOU KNOW ME, ANNA. I'VE BEEN CALLING YOU YOUR WHOLE LIFE. YOU'VE SOUGHT ME AT EVERY TURN. I AM YOUR GOD. HERMES, LORD OF KNOWLEDGE," he said. He let go of her face, offering a hand to her to help her to her feet.

Anna looked away from the hand, afraid of it. Her gaze fell to the ground. She saw before her, his feet. They were clad with golden sandals, ornamented with the design of wings at his heels, depicting the image, the god he claimed to be was known for. The sensation of being a supplicant bowed at his feet washed over her. She lifted her gaze. He was not her god.

At his waist was a golden belt of olive leaves wrapped about pristine white, from it hung a finely made leather pouch, the strap draped from his hip. Her eyes lifted. She met his gaze. The blue glowed with power. She felt the urge to look away but refused to shrink again before him. On his brow was a crown of golden leaves.

"You can't be. He's not real – a myth," she said with disbelief.

"COME ANNA, LIES DO NOT BECOME YOU. WE BOTH KNOW YOU'VE COME TO BELIEVE IN ME." He said with amusement. Taking her hand in his he helped her to stand.

"I have?" she questioned.

"YES, IT'S THE REASON WHY YOU CAN NOW HEAR MY VOICE. I'VE CALLED TO YOU MANY TIMES BEFORE MY LOVELY ONE. UNTIL THIS NIGHT YOU'VE NEVER HEARD ME," he said. Brushing his fingers through her hair, she gasped startled by the touch and shrank back from him.

"Please…" she began. Her full request was drowned out as the song on the wind grew louder.

"WHAT CAN I DO FOR YOU MY LADY?" he asked, taking hold of her wrist.

"Why have you brought me here?"

"YOU HAVE BEEN CHOSEN ANNA."

"Chosen?"

"TO BE MY BRIDE," he said caressing her face.

"Oh God," she breathed the words in panic. The old stories of the gods chasing mortals filled her thoughts.

Now he laughed at her. His eyes gleamed like blue fire. "AFTER A LIFETIME OF DENYING HIS EXISTENCE YOU CALL OUT TO HIM NOW. DO YOU THINK HE HEARS YOU?" He mocked her. He drew her to him. "You are mine Anna."

"No! Please no," she breathed the words breaking free from his grasp. She then turned running from him. "Wake up Anna," she muttered to herself.

The gentle breeze became violent, shoving against her and slowing her flight. A frantic sprint became a jog. She chanced a glance back; found the man had not moved. He stood on the other side of the river with a smile upon his lips. It occurred to her then she was playing his game. Didn't every myth always portray mortal woman and nymph alike fleeing from the gods' advances only to be pursued?

God what was she going to do? "It's a dream Anna, just wake up," she told herself. The song that seemed to be everywhere became unbearable. She covered her ears to drown it out. Still she ran. The song became more like the roar of some beast. It held words in a language long dead. Words that tore at her will – vied for control.

Pain exploded behind her eyes fierce and horrible. Her vision darkened, bringing her to her knees. Anna closed her eyes against the pain. She gasped for air. Aware now her lungs burned from her flight. "Have to keep going," she told herself. When she opened her eyes she found she'd reached the end of the green pasture. Before her loomed a vast chasm. There was nowhere to run but back the way she'd come.

Looking back she saw the river in the distance. Hermes stood at the water's edge. His hand outstretched beckoning for her to return. She closed her eyes, drew a breath searching for calm. Her mind flooded with images of her surrender. She trembled, though why even she wasn't sure. Her emotions were a jumbled mess; she couldn't sort through. Her will was not her own.

Anna opened her eyes, turning away from the images in her mind. She became aware she was moving. Looking back she saw the river loomed closer. Hermes held a gilded chain pulling upon it – pain registered. She became aware of a golden collar around her neck. He was slowly pulling her back.

"No! God, please help me," she cried out in desperation.

The sun above exploded with a blast of light that was blinding. Anna closed her eyes to protect them. When she opened them again she screamed. The world around her had changed.

The lush green grass she'd been kneeling in was now a writhing mass of serpents and flames. The river was molten rock. Looking to the sky; she found it was black, heavy with ash. The only light to be seen was a bright white that blazed in the midst of the darkness. Its descent from above was slow. Anna seized hold of the long chain. She could now see it hanging from the collar. Anna pulled fighting against Hermes control; fearful of the river.

The light landed upon the ground between her and Hermes. It spread – growing, taking shape. When the light faded a man stood before her, his hair shown like the sun and his eyes were a blue bordering on violet. They burned with a fire from within.

"Fear not Annalynn Gallagher, the Father has heard your plea,"

He said, before turning his gaze upon the god. "Peace!" His voice sounded like a thunder clap above all other things around her. At his command the wind fell silent –still. The nightmare images faded back to the lush green field. The pain in her head eased. She felt her strength return.

"BE GONE FROM THIS PLACE. YOU HAVE NO CLAIM HERE," Hermes raged.

"She has called. I was sent."

"HER SOUL IS MINE."

"IT IS NOT FOR YOU TO KNOW THE WILL OF THE FATHER."

"SHE'S GIVEN HER WORSHIP IN MY TEMPLE. HER LUST IS FOR MY POWER," Hermes boasted. To prove his hold upon her he pulled upon the chain, dragging her closer to him.

Her defender reached down where she was, touched her brow. She felt peace wash over her.

"Wake now," he whispered. She felt the image fade.

Anna heard the roar of the god's raged cry. She moved beyond his reach, from the dream realm to waking.

She came to with a scream. Pain registered in her mind. Lance came into her view.

"Easy, slow you shouldn't move just yet. You've been shot."

She blinked. Reality came into focus. The dream faded to shadows.

41

"Two minutes."

Sam froze mid punch. He felt sweat pool in his palms. His stomach clenched. Pulse raced. Fight or flight kicked in. His adrenaline was flowing early. Sam swore in frustration. He'd heard of this happening, even seen it on T.V. It was weird going through it now first-hand the first fight, on the big stage, adrenaline dump.

He took a deep breath, worked to relax. Telling himself it was just another fight. Reminding himself he'd done this a hundred times before. He'd do it again after tonight regardless of the results. The battle was just on a larger stage tonight. There was nothing to be afraid of Sam reasoned. He made his way down the tunnel from the locker room to the arena.

Sam passed through a sea of faces toward the UFC Octagon. Lights flashed overhead in an artful display of chaos. Music blared through the arena. Fans cheered or jeered. It was so loud he could barely hear himself think.

"Our next match-up is a bout between two light-heavy-weight fighters. Frank "the Avalanche" Clifton is fighting Sam 'the Tank' Abrams in his UFC debut."

Sam stepped out of his shoes, removed his hat and shirt, then waited for inspection to enter the octagon. While he waited the announcers returned to their commentary.

"Sam 'the Tank' Abrams is 31 years old. He's a new up and comer to this sport, versed in several martial arts styles. This former news reporter turned fighter is no stranger to the martial arts world. This guy is violent. His record is 10 and 1."

"That's right Mike. Abrams is well versed in Muay Thai kick boxing. He's not afraid to brawl. Sam will stay in the pocket; go toe to toe with anyone. But what makes this guy so dangerous is he's fast and smart. All his wins have been either by knockout or submission. It'll be interesting to see how he does here tonight against a tough opponent in Frank Clifton."

With his brow greased, his mouth piece in place, Sam stepped into the octagon. He began his routine to loosen up. The announcers Mike Goldberg and Joe Rogan went over his opponent's information.

42

Anna lay on Sam's bed watching the T.V. She'd turned the volume down afraid of being caught watching the UFC fights. They were a wicked indulgence her parents would not approve of, one she had yet to own up to. MMA fascinated her. Sam's intro had been a good one. She watched now as Frank Clifton began his walk from the locker room to the cage. It had been a good night so far. The fight coming up promised to be just as good. A pair of brawlers would make for a good show.

"There are a lot of celebrities in the house tonight. We got James Hardagen director of Heart of Glass in theatres now." Michael Goldberg stated as the camera showed a close up of the actor speaking with another man. "Now let's look at this tale of the tape. Frank "the Avalanche" Clifton is fighting out of Los Angeles California. Sam "the Tank" Abrams is a local boy. His gym is here in Las Vegas Nevada. Clifton is 27, four years younger than his opponent Abrams. Sam stands 6'1 and will enjoy a two inch height advantage. They both weighed in at 185 pounds. For this evenings fight Abrams will enjoy a three inch reach advantage.

"Are you ready? The ref asked. Sam nodded in confirmation. He asked Sam's opponent the same question. Frank also nodded in response. "Fight!"

43

At the command Sam watched as his opponent came out of his corner to meet him in the center of the octagon. They gave a quick touch of gloves from one fighter to another in a show of respect. The battle was on.

Sam circled toward his opponent. He threw a left jab testing his reach. The first jab was short. The second was blocked by a gloved hand. Having found his range Sam went on the attack. He threw an inside leg kick to weaken his opponents stance. Sam followed it with a left jab. Frank switched levels grabbing hold of a leg for a takedown. Sam sprawled. Pushing back on the other fighters head he stuffed the attempt, breaking his hold on the leg.

His rival pushed back, driving Sam into the cage, initiating the clinch game. Sam grappled for control, throwing a few knees to the body. His opponent answered with foot stomps and knees of his own – fighting for the take down. Sam frustrated his efforts with dirty boxing. Landing a few punches.

An elbow caught Sam's right eye. Pain exploded in his head. White light hazed his vision. Sam cursed. Aware he was right on the edge of losing the war, he felt his legs weaken. Sam growled calling for the adrenaline he hadn't dumped, to avoid being sucked down to the mat. He struck back with an uppercut. It found its mark. Striking the chin he felt Frank's grasp weaken. Sam pushed him away, creating distance. He threw another jab. Followed by an inside leg kick. Sam blocked a counter strike, answering with two more leg kicks. His eyes looked down at Frank's leg. He watched his opponent react, guarding against another blow there. Sam threw a head kick instead. He watched as Frank Clifton crumbled, his legs having given out. Frank fell in a heap to the canvas. Sam moved to strike. The referee leapt between him and Frank stopping the fight.

"And it is over!" He heard Mike Goldberg call out. His corner man handed him a shirt. Sam paid it little mind. He instead looked to his opponent to verify he was okay.

"Bruce Buffer has the official decision."

"The winner by – knock out; Sam 'the Tank' Abrams!"

"I'm here with the winner Sam Abrams. That was an impressive first battle in the octagon. You got hit early on by a few blows. One in particular in the middle of the round, I thought the fight was going to be over. Were you ever in any trouble?"

"Yeah that elbow. I didn't see it coming. It left my ears ringing. Thought I was done. Frank is a great fighter. The best I've faced so far. It was an honor to go to war with him. I know he's going to come back from this the better for it."

"Congratulations on your victory. We look forward to seeing you again, Sam 'the Tank' Abrams."

Sam pulled the detective's car onto his drive. He cursed, seeing a glimpse of himself in the rearview mirror. Sam turned off the engine. The adrenaline he'd been running on ever since he took the elbow was beginning to fade. He was now keenly aware of a sharp pain behind the right eye. He got out of the car, slamming the door with disgust. Sam felt light headed as he made his way for the door.

Stepping into the house he watched Lance rise from the couch. "I wasn't expecting you so soon."

"I didn't feel much like celebrating." Sam grumbled.

"Did the fight not go well?" Lance questioned surprised. Abrams wasn't the type of guy to get involved in something unless he was sure he could win at it.

"Oh it went well. I won but I won't be making a repeat appearance for a while," Sam said with disgust.

"Why not?" Lance questioned surprised.

"Frank Clifton hit me with an elbow I didn't see coming and broke my orbital bone."

"Bad luck."

"Yeah, tell me about it. I'll be out of the game for at least six weeks."

"Too bad."

"Figure you need to get back to the hotel for whatever things the two of you might need." Sam said, changing the subject.

"I got a few things but yeah I don't think staying there any longer is a good idea. I'll have to get Anna's room key."

"How is she?" Sam questioned. Allowing himself to think on the matter now that he was away from the fight.

"Okay, she slept through the work but not peacefully."

"Nightmare?"

"Yeah, she didn't say what about. I've seen that look enough at the station. I can guess."

"Where is she?"

"Anna's still in the room. She hasn't come out since requesting fresh clothes."

"I'll go get that key from her for you. Grab what I need also, so I won't have to intrude on her again this evening," Sam said.

He moved down the hall to his room. As he approached the room the sound of his T.V. caught his attention.

"Tonight's main event of the evening…" Sam blinked. Was that Mike Goldberg? He wondered puzzled. Opening the door his gaze looked to the T.V. He watched as Jo Rogan and Mike Goldberg went through their normal routine before the main event. Sam groaned. Recalling he'd set the T.V. up to record the fight. Wanting to see it himself later. Now he wasn't all that interested.

Turning his focus to the bed he swallowed. His eyes fell upon Miss Gallagher. Her blond hair was pulled up off her neck and shoulders into a makeshift bun. Several strands had worked their way lose. The ruined blouse was gone. It had been replaced with a silky green tank. Her midsection was partially exposed. Her legs which had been hidden earlier were uncovered and on full display. Black slacks replaced with a pair of cutoffs.

Rick was right she had a great set of legs. Though they weren't her best feature he thought to himself. He took in the whole picture. Sam tried not to stare. Every inch of her was beautifully tanned. Was that her natural skin tone or a result of extra time spent out in the sun while working in the field? Sam studied her for a moment; decided it was the latter. There was a hint of pink in places suggesting a tendency towards burning.

Sam watched as Anna yelled at the ref. He laughed. The woman in front of him was not the prim and proper professional he'd met with earlier. The woman before him was a free spirit. She was the real Anna. He watched as her hazel eyes shifted from the T.V to where he stood. A blush colored her cheeks.

"Sorry didn't mean to startle you," he said aloud. Sam watched as the relaxed free spirit vanished. The stiff doctor returned.

"Mr. Abrams, I didn't hear you come in," Anna said. She switched off the T.V.

"I should have knocked," he admitted, though it was his room. He moved from the doorway to his closet drawing his attention from her. He began the task of getting the things he would need for the evening and the next day.

"No, it's your room I shouldn't have touched anything," she said mortified she'd been caught watching the fight. She shifted in the bed, covering herself.

Sam came out of the closet. He noted Anna looked more reserved than before ashamed even. He crossed the room to her side. Sat down on the edge of the bed then turned the T.V. back on. "You're a guest Anna, not my prisoner. You're welcome to whatever you like. So let your hair down. Relax. I think it will take a while before they find you here."

She smiled. He felt something in him stir. "Thank you." She whispered it. Some of the polished professional vanished. There was in her place now a lost girl. The image shook him. Sam rose from the bed. He had no business there. He didn't know her.

"I'm sorry about what happened before. I wasn't careful. I…"

Anna reached off the bed with her good arm. She grabbed his wrist stopping him from leaving. "Sam, it wasn't your fault. I shouldn't have gotten you involved."

Sam sat back down at her side. "Anna, don't – you promised…"

"Yes, and I will tell you all that I can tomorrow." She murmured. Anna brushed her hand against his cheek. Sam winced at a quick jolt of pain caused by her touch. He turned his cheek into her palm, moving the broken bone away from her. He looked down at her. "Why tomorrow? Why not now?"

Sam felt her hand grow warm. It soothed bruised skin and grew stronger, rushing out to wash over his face. His blue eyes widened with shock and panic. The pain lines that had knitted his brow receded. What the hell was that? He wondered.

Anna drew her hand away from him. Sam stared at it. Half expecting it to be glowing or something like they portrayed in the movies but it was no different than his. Sam's gaze met hers. He noted she was as spooked by what had just happened as he was. Sam was aware that the pain in his head had faded. He took her hand in between his, looking at it.

"What just happened?" He asked.

Sam watched as a storm of emotions passed over her face. Acceptance came first then contentment. Fear washed over her like a tidal wave and was followed close by uncertainty. Anna drew her hand away from him breaking the connection he'd felt. Sam wondered what she had been thinking that had upset her.

"I don't know." She admitted. Sam watched as her demeanor became cool once more. He figured she'd made some sort of decision, though what escaped him.

"As to your earlier questions Mr. Abrams, I'm not ready to look at it again tonight. These matters are best left for daylight."

"Why?"

"I don't know."

Sam ground his teeth together in frustration but he let it go. Whatever it was it would keep until morning, he reasoned. Sam tried to brush off her switching yet again to miss proper. What was with her? He sighed. Deciding that too could wait. She should be resting. "Lance needs your key. He's going to get the bags for both of you."

"It's in my purse." She murmured. "Where's my other bag?"

Other bag, did she have another bag? "I guess it's in the car."

"Can you bring it to me?"

Why was she asking for it now? Couldn't it wait until morning? Sam wondered. His reply was, "Of course."

"Thanks."

Sam rose from the bed, drew her key from the purse. Taking his things with him he moved back into the living room. He set them in a chair then handed the key to Lance. Sam moved onto the garage to look for her other bag. He found it tucked under the seat. It was a small leather carry on. He slung it over his shoulder. Sam made his way back to the room. He was aware of the car outside driving off.

Anna looked up from the bed at him and the bag. Was that relief he saw play across her face? What's in the bag? He wondered. When he removed it from his shoulder to look, Sam watched panic bloom on her face. This time he saw it clearly; those hazel eyes, darkened becoming the color of an emerald.

"No, don't," she gasped.

Sam nodded respecting her wishes. "What's in the bag doc?"

"I don't really know Mr. Abrams. Whatever it is again, it can wait until morning."

Sam crossed the room and set the bag on the bed beside her. He watched as she drew it into her grasp. Whatever it was, it was important, Sam reasoned. "I won't take it from you Miss Gallagher," he assured her.

"I know an I'm sorry, it's just..." Anna began but he interrupted her.

"Good night Anna," he murmured before he turned and headed back out to the living room.

44

Once the door was shut Anna let out a breath she'd been unaware of holding. She'd been frightened by her reaction to Sam's touch. She'd liked it. There was something in it she'd never felt from the men she normally associated with. Despite his cold demeanor she realized she liked him. She felt panic rise within her again. How could she? She didn't know anything about him. He hadn't been particularly nice to her. He'd made no secret of the fact he wanted nothing to do with her. So why was her heart still racing from when she touched him.

What had happened? She felt a jolt of pain stab behind her right eye and then heat pour out of her. What was happening to her?

Finding no answers; Anna groaned then opened the bag. She drew out of it a bound leather book. She shook her head.

"Anna you are going crazy," she muttered to herself; studying the gold engraving on the cover. She'd seen the symbol a million times before and paid it no mind. Despite the words she flipped open the cover and began to read.

"When men began to multiply on the face of the land and daughters were born to them, the sons of God saw that the daughters of men were fair, and they took wives of all they desired and chose. Then the Lord said, My Spirit shall not forever dwell and strive with man, for he also is flesh, but his days shall yet be 120 years. The Nephilim were on the earth in those days—and also afterwards—when the sons of God came into the daughters of men, and they bore children to them. Those were the mighty men of old, men of renown." (Genesis 6: 1-4)

Anna's thoughts wandered back to the dream. The image of Hermes entered her mind. He fit that description. She brushed the thought aside. Flipping over a number of pages and began again.

"Then behold a hand touched me that set me trembling on my hands and knees. He said to me O Daniel, man of high esteem, understand the words that I am about to tell you and stand upright, for I have now been sent to you. And when he had spoken this word to me, I stood up trembling. Then he said to me do not be afraid, Daniel, for from the first day that you set your heart on understanding this and on humbling yourself before your God, your words were heard, and I have come in response to your words. But the prince of the kingdom of Persia was withstanding me for twenty-one days; then behold, Michael one of the chief princes came to help me, for I had been left there with the kings of Persia." (Daniel 10:10-13)

In her mind the dream resurfaced once again. She pictured the image of the one who came to her aid. He could have been an angel.

Anna groaned with disgust as she threw the book away from her. What was she doing? It was a dream, nothing more. One she barely remembered. "Angels, demons, sons of heaven, gods and goddesses, a divine Creator I don't believe in any of this nonsense." She said with disgust.

"Just because you don't believe in something doesn't mean it's not real." A voice answered. It came from nowhere and everywhere. Anna looked up with alarm. Standing at the foot of her bed holding the book was a man with golden hair and deep blue eyes.

Anna tried to scream but before the sound could be freed he was by her side. "Fear not," he whispered then touched her shoulder. She felt warmth spread through the wound. The pain eased.

"I'm dreaming," she whispered with disbelief.

"No, you are wide awake, perhaps for the first time ever."

"What is happening to me?"

"As you were told in the dream you have been chosen but you in turn have a choice. You can serve the one who holds your chains. Who enslaves your mind to his will. You have seen him as he wants you to see him. You know what he desires from you. He'll continue to call to you now that your ears are open to him."

Anna trembled. The dream came back a clear haunting image in her mind. "He's not my god," she murmured.

She watched as the man smiled. "Or you can open your eyes. See the truth. You called out to the Father in your desperate hour. He heard your plea. I was sent to spare you from him. The Father's been watching, waiting, listening for this day when you would awaken. Rather than submit to your jailer you can serve the one who sent me. All you need do is repent and believe. "

"I don't know what I believe anymore." Anna muttered.

"You have time still. Consider with care the matter." He said, setting the Bible at the foot of her bed once more.

"What is this?" she asked holding up her satchel and its contents.

"Now is not the time. Rest."

Anna nodded. She lay back, blinked. When she opened her eyes again he was gone. "I'm losing it," she said with a laugh then closed her eyes. She drifted into a dreamless sleep.

45 Sunday 6am

Sam woke as the first light of the rising sun poured in through the living room window. He lifted his head. Sat up on the couch where he'd slept. The house was still. Sam sighed with relief. He wasn't ready to face his house guests. After rising from the couch, Sam crossed the room to his chair where his clothes for the day had been placed the night before. He moved down the hall to the guest bath. Changed into his running clothes then stepped out of the house to begin his day.

He started out with a fast walk. As he rounded the corner onto the main street he picked his pace up to a jog. His music played in one ear. The sound of his feet on the asphalt kept pace. Sam's mind drifted back to the night before. His head which had been pounding after the adrenaline of the fight, wore off, no longer hurt. It hadn't since that strange moment in his room when Anna had touched his face. He'd felt a strange jolt. The pain had dulled as warmth had spread over his skin under his eye.

It had been odd, unusual, not just for him but for her as well. Anna had looked at her hand after he moved away with eyes full of questions. She studied her palm as if it were some foreign object rather than a part of her. Something had happened in that moment. She'd felt it too. It had happened. It wasn't just a dream despite her look of disbelief.

When he'd taken her hand in his to look at it; she'd spooked. He'd seen that too; when he touched her. In truth so had he. Sam hadn't been prepared for the second shock to the system. There had been nothing foreign about that one though, he mused.

It had been a pure physical response to her, was why he'd let her end the discussion with such ease last night. He hadn't been ready for the sucker punch of desire that touching her had triggered. In the car he'd felt it too but dismissed it as echoes from the past. The intense moment they'd been caught up in. This however had been under ordinary circumstances. It had hit him with more force than the earlier one. Yes he'd needed the space she sought just as much.

He turned his focus from his guest. His feet moved from asphalt to desert sand. He'd come out here to clear his head; not clouded it further with her.

"These matters are best left for daylight," Her comment from before played over in his mind. Sam cursed at his inability to put her from his thoughts. The statement had almost pushed him to stay despite his need to get away from her. What could be so terrible it would not allow for discussion then? What was it she was afraid of? Sam wondered as he poured on more speed, starting the final leg of his morning run. He couldn't think of anything but he was going to find out. He'd get to the bottom of it when she was awake. His mind made up Sam set his course for home.

46

Lance groaned. The sunlight hot and bright streamed in the room. Opening one eye he noted the open curtains. "I thought I closed them when I got into the hotel," he muttered. Lance pulled the pillow out from under him and covered his head. Attempting to go back to sleep. The room grew warm. The sun poured in; making him hot. He kicked the sheets off, turned, trying to get comfortable. Lance cursed. The move had him rolling off the edge of the bed, falling onto a cold hardwood floor.

He blinked. Wait the hotel had been carpeted. Where was he? The detective wondered as he sat up. He noticed his bag sitting at the foot of the bed. Sleep slipped away. He recalled the night before. Calling Anna after she and Mr. Abrams left to find out what was going on, getting Sam instead. His relaying the news she'd been shot. He was in Sam's guest room.

Lance yawned. Seeing the time he grabbed a change of clothes from his bag. He needed to call the captain back in DC. Let him know what was going on before it got too much later. Lance took his clothes down the hall to the guest bathroom. He busied himself with getting ready to face the day.

47

Anna's mind became aware of the sound of water running. Fear seized her as the memory of her dream tried to resurface. Her eyes opened. She spotted the leather book at the foot of the bed. Recalling her visitor Anna stretched. She found that the pain from her wound was gone. Sitting up she noted her bags on the floor. Good she'd have no reason to return to the hotel. She'd just call the contest people. Inform them she was unable to stay due to personal matters. Send Lance with her apologies.

Looking back to the Bible she sighed. It was time she familiarized herself with the myth surrounding her discovery. Anna considered the question; was it myth or more. Picking up the Bible she opened it and flipped over to Genesis chapter 19. She read the story to herself, scribbled a few notes before getting up out of the bed. She changed her clothes to something more comfortable for a crowd then gathered her work before moving into the kitchen to find a light meal.

Anna spotted a note on the fridge from their host. "Stepped out for my morning run, feel free to help yourselves to whatever you want, Sam." She opened the fridge. Peering inside she looked for something to eat. Anna sighed when she came up with nothing. "Man not even bread for toast. What does this guy eat?" Anna muttered. She heard the sound of the front door slam.

"Morning, sorry there's not much too eat. I picked up bagels on the way back," Sam said as he stepped into the kitchen.

Anna smiled with gratitude. She closed the fridge. "That's perfect."

Sam handed her the bag. He moved past her for a glass of water. She opened the offered bag. Pulling out a plain bagel and set to toasting it.

48

Sam studied his guest with interest. She moved about his kitchen preparing her morning meal. The cut offs from the night before were gone; he noted with disappointment. The more professional attire was back. Her long shapely legs were hidden by a pair of light brown slacks. She wore a green blouse that her hazel eyes changed to match. Her hair was pulled back into a high and tight braided ponytail. All business he thought with annoyance. Sam finished his water then set the glass in his sink.

"Would you please quit watching me Mr. Abrams," she said. Her voice conveyed annoyance and he tried not to let it get to him. Sam noted her gaze never rose to meet with his.

"Sorry, I wasn't meaning to…" Sam's apology slid away in his mind. Wait, why is she using her bad arm to reach for a glass? "Don't do that! You'll tear your stitches," he snapped. Moving to her aside, he pulled down a second glass for her. "Go sit. I'll get the rest of your things."

"I'm completely capable…"

"You were shot Anna. You shouldn't aggravate your shoulder."

"I'm fine, Mr. Abrams." She assured him but she sat down. Doing as he asked.

Sam collected her bagel, got out the cream cheese and a knife. He set them and the glass in front of her. The sound of the shower running ended.

"What do you want to drink?"

"Juice," she replied. Lance made his way into the kitchen. Sam pulled the juice from the fridge and set it on the table for her.

"I'll leave the two of you to your breakfast. When I'm done with my shower we can talk."

Anna nodded. She turned her attention to her meal as Lance

busied himself with preparing his own meal. Sam watched as Lance took a cup of coffee and moved to the living room to call his boss. Satisfied his guests were settled; Sam moved down the hall to clean up.

49

Sam made his way back to the kitchen. He watched Lance step through the archway ahead of him. Anna was rinsing her plate when Sam joined them in the kitchen. Lance pulled out a chair on the left side of the table. Sam sat down across from him leaving the head for Anna. They both waited. She turned off the water then joined them at the table. Anna drew a breath. Trying to relax Sam figured.

"You okay?" Lance asked concerned.

"Yes it's just trying to decide where to begin. A lot of this is so far beyond my normal range it's going to come across as madness," Anna muttered.

"Try us," Sam encouraged. He pressed record on a mini-cassette recorder he brought with him.

Anna gave a stiff nod then opened her bag. She pulled out her research. "I got a call three years ago when a construction site in Israel found an artifact. They called in several experts on the area's history. Due partially to my lack of bias I was brought in."

"What did they find?" Lance asked with curiosity.

"Don't interrupt her," Sam said with irritation. He had questions too and understood Lance's rush but he'd worked as a reporter long enough that he could see whatever it was she had to say, she was right on the edge and if pushed would not say it.

Anna pulled out an 8 x 10 photo of what looked like a vase. She set it on the table. "It was a vase. The problem was that until I arrived no one could really decide where it had originated from. The pottery style is consistent with that of the people of the area. The image depicted is mostly seen in Grecian art. Some of my colleagues had been prepared to dismiss it as a hoax. They had unearthed nothing else where the vase was found. All the tests ran though dated it according to the pottery style. It was a legitimate find. They'd all but given up when I stumbled on the site."

"What do you mean stumbled?" Lance asked.

"I moved up onto higher ground hoping to spot something we missed. When I came back down I tripped on a loose stone. At my fingers was a pottery shard. We started to dig there. What we unearthed was the city of Sodom."

"Wait, the biblical city destroyed by the judgment and wrath of God?" Lance asked with disbelief.

"Yes. A lot of cities mentioned in the Bible are real places. Sodom and Gomorrah are no exception."

"What did you find there?" Sam questioned, prompting her to go on. He didn't want her distracted from the story for too long.

"A lot of strange things that made little sense; the strangest was the chamber that contained a map of the kingdom. It depicted the location of Gomorrah. On the wall with it was an inscription. A riddle really." Anna replied. She pulled out a photo of the wall for them to look at.

"Was Gomorrah where it said?" Lance questioned.

"Yes we unearthed Gomorrah at the point indicated."

"Is that where you found it?" Lance asked.

"It?" Sam prompted. He was irritated the detective seemed to know more about what was going on than he did. His temper pushed at the surface at Lance's continued interruptions. Sam needed her to stay on topic. What was more he needed to focus so no detail was missed.

"No I didn't find the disk there…"

"Disk?" Sam questioned now needing an explanation. He had no clue what that meant. The only reference he had was for a computer and he was certain that wasn't what she was referring to.

"I found an artifact at a location disclosed within the map rooms. It's unlike anything I've ever encountered in my work," Anna explained. Her demeanor had shifted, she wasn't comfortable talking about the artifact whatever it was and he cursed Lance for bringing it up. In order to help her; he had to understand what he was dealing with. It would have been better if she'd been allowed to come to it on her own now he had no choice but to push.

"Is that what was in the bag?" Sam questioned. Recalling how protective of it she'd been.

"Yes."

"May I see it?"

Anna nodded her consent. Sam was relieved but it was clear to him she was unsure if it was wise. He watched with growing interest and concern as the detective rose from the table. Lance left before she even opened the bag. Sam looked on with interest as she pulled out something wrapped in a black silk scarf. When she drew the fabric away what he saw lying on his table baffled him.

The disk was approximately seven inches in diameter. It was made of a strange melding of metal and stone. The two had been smelted together which he knew was impossible but there it was. This melding made the disk appear to be like molten silver, varying in color from white to black. It appeared to be divided into five sections. The outer ring was white. Inscribed in it was a form of strange writing. The second track was like fine silver. Carved within were four intricate symbols he didn't recognize. There were lines at odd angles with small leaves coming from them. The third section was like pewter. It depicted the image of various objects and in the center of each was a different gem stone. The inner track was black. Contained within it, in white, were distinct dotted patterns and strange lines. The center ring was no bigger than a quarter. It held an image he couldn't make out.

"Where did you find that?"

"Atlantis," she breathed the word. It took him a moment to register what she'd said. He blinked, stunned by the admission; true or not she feared the word and dared not utter it too loudly. Almost as if it held some dark secret power she dreaded would seek her out.

"You're kidding?" The words escaped before he could stop it.

"I wish I was. I helped discover the lost city. What we found there beyond this disk I'll not speak of. You'll have to see it for yourself."

"What are you afraid of?"

"Things that until recently I didn't think were real."

"Things you've been dreaming about lately?" he asked. Recalling what Lance had said about nightmares.

Anna nodded. "I wrote it up if you want an idea, but I don't want to talk about it. Things that are happening around me right now have me questioning my own sanity. Everything I've ever thought of as truth."

"What did you mean by I'll have to see it?"

"I was always going to go back to the dig in Israel. This trip back to the states was meant as a brief one. Just a quick getaway so I could think things out. Now I've got to go back. Things I believe are worse than I originally feared. I think you need to come with me."

"Why?"

"I don't know. I just have this feeling that you have to be shown first-hand what it is that I've found. That you're a part of it all."

Sam looked at the pile of notes she had beyond the photos. He felt his fingers itch. He wanted to dive into it. To see and understand but he hesitated. His gaze fell upon the disk sitting between them once more. The sense of something not right weighed upon him heavily and he wasn't sure he wanted to delve too deep into anything that would have him exploring that darkness more closely. But he felt it too; a nudge from within. To follow wherever it was she would lead him.

"How soon do you want to leave?" He asked.

"A day or two," she murmured

"Doesn't give me much time to think about this does it?"

"I'm sorry," Anna whispered. She set the pages she typed that morning in front of him then got up from the table taking the disk with her.

Sam watched as she went on her way before turning his attention to the pages she set in front of him.

50

Anna sat on the bed. She turned her focus from thoughts of dreams and travel to the disk in her charge. It was time she took a better look at the thing. Now that Dr. Broody was aware she possessed it she'd need to leave it behind if she was going to avoid it falling into the wrong hands. That meant before she went anywhere she needed to have every detail of the thing recorded for further study. Photos were out. Those were easily recognizable. If she brought those Ian would be able to sort out what she was hiding from him.

A drawing then was what was required. Anna pulled out one of her many sketch books. For the first time since leaving the dig site she busied herself with a closer look at the disk. Anna started with an overall image of it. No real detail just the whole as she saw it. Anna noted her impressions of it. Once that was done she began to focus on the various sections within the whole. It was set in what appeared to be five concentric rings. Each ring was marked with strange images.

Pulling out her magnifying glass Anna began in the center of the image, drawing the smallest circle. Within it were carefully engraved a mess of text. Looking closer, she noted some of the letters were Hebrew. Others were Greek. She paid careful attention to put in all the letters as they appeared in the disk. She started on the next detail image. Working her way through each ring until she reached the outer edge with its strange writing unlike anything she'd ever seen before. Once it too was drawn she turned back to the page with the inner circle. Anna looked at the letters for anything familiar.

51

Sam swore as he set Anna's pages aside. He buried his face in his hands. Angels and gods how did it connect with what she'd told him. What had they found at Sodom? How did it connect one to the other? It didn't matter. This whole thing was absurd. He wasn't going to Israel with her. Sam had things to deal with here. He still had to meet Pamela tomorrow, settle things with her. He had a gym to run. Whatever was in Israel it didn't concern him.

"You never were a good liar Samuel."

Sam looked up from his palms. Fear gripped him as he looked upon the man he'd moments before read about. He blinked thinking perhaps his mind had conjured the image. When his eyes opened once more the man remained.

"The name is Sam," he stated annoyed.

"Yes, but it is never the less the shortened form of Samuel or Samson if you prefer," the angel said with amusement.

"Whatever. Look I'm really not in the mood for whatever this is so…"

The being laughed aloud, a thunderous sound that shook the house. "Ever stubborn. You mortals never cease to amaze me. You cling to your science and history like an infant to its mother's breast. When will you learn that there is more to this world than what you can see and touch?"

"What do you want?"

"I'm here to make sure you go with that girl."

"Why?"

"The first question of all men when faced with the divine. You always have to know the reason behind the act. I'll never understand your kind. You take what's dark and worship it; shunning the light," the angel muttered with irritation. He looked up to the heavens above as if someone had spoken interrupting him.

"Huh?"

"Now's not the time for that, perhaps another discussion," the angel replied. Once more he looked to the human before him. "You ask why. The Father has decided that you will see. Remember you brought this on yourself."

"What are you talking about?" Sam questioned.

"You're being given a glimpse." The angel replied. For the second time in less than twenty four hours Sam felt a flood of heat wash over him as the angel touched him. He jumped, startled by the flood of power. There was a brilliant flash of light. Sam closed his eyes to protect them. When he opened them again his home was gone.

"Where am I?" Sam questioned. The light faded. Darkness surrounded him. Then a light, faint and weak, pierced the darkness. He heard the sound of footsteps. Sam was aware that he was no longer alone. He watched as Anna appeared with a torch. She lit a series of lights in the chamber.

The room he found himself in was cold and dark even though it blazed with fire light. In the center of the earthen chamber was a throne carved of smoky quartz. Behind it the wall was engraved with strange markings he couldn't discern. A presence was here with them. Something dark and foreboding hung in the air waiting.

"Anna, we shouldn't be here," he breathed the words. She gave no response. Sam watched as Anna pulled the disk from her pack. She moved towards the wall as if drawn by some unseen force. Her hands brushed dirt from it, revealing a strange crevice.

Fear gripped Sam as Anna placed the disk inside. There was a click like a key fitting in a lock. Then a strange sound as if a series of pieces moved seeking their place. Something distinctly mechanical sounded. The wall began to open.

"Run!" the command came from him though he didn't understand it. Anna heard nothing. Sam watched helpless as a shadow that looked like a man stepped past the door. His hair was darker than the night sky. It shown like it held the light of the stars. He had eyes like molten fire. His gaze fell upon the woman before him. He smiled. A cool unfeeling smirk that sent shivers down Sam's spine.

"My dearest Anna, at last we are together. I've waited long for you to return for me. Now all will be as it was before," he whispered. Sam recoiled at the sound of his voice. In one ear his words were like that of a hissing snake. In the other they were sweet as honey. Sam watched as the man's hand brushed a lock of Anna's golden hair from tanned skin in a loving caress. He felt disgust wash over him. "Anna, get away from him he's not what he seems," Sam warned; his words fell on deaf ears. He realized in that moment she didn't hear the hissing snake only the seductive voice. He reached out to draw her back from the invader but his hand passed through her. Sam cursed with understanding. He could do nothing but watch.

"My lord, long have I waited for this day. I am at your command," she murmured before kissing the palm of his hand. Sam watched as the man's appearance changed from handsome to a grotesque beast. He felt anger rise within him at the deception before him. His stomach churned at the display. There was nothing romantic about this meeting – nothing natural. Anna's words were those of one enslaved to a master not born of love. Her voice was cool and lifeless as if she had no will of her own.

"Dear God, what is this?" Sam questioned with disgust. He looked on as the thing from beyond the door drew Anna against it, devouring her lips in a savage kiss. Her hazel eyes became black as coal. Fear flooded through her but she was now far too late. The torches blazed bright for a moment then went out. Sound faded from around him. Silence reigned, leaving him once more alone surrounded by darkness. An ear shattering scream pierced the dark. Blinding light surrounded him.

When he opened his eyes again Sam found he was sitting at the table in his kitchen. The angel was gone. Sam muttered a curse as he became aware of a blooming headache. "Okay, I got the message. I'm going," he muttered. Sam rose from the table. He made his way back to his room to let Anna know he'd made his choice.

52

Anna set her sketch pad down with frustration. There was no clear message to read in the letters. She could make out words but there was no sense in them. Anna picked up her brush. She swept the bristles over the lettering. Making sure she hadn't miscopied anything. Her finger brushed over the stone. Anna looked on stunned as the letters vanished. She watched as they rearranged themselves. When they were done she heard a click. The piece came off the disk to reveal a brilliant crystal.

She stared at the center with wonder. The bedroom door opened behind her.

"Anna, I've made up my mind…" Sam's voice trailed off.

Anna looked up and noted his gaze was locked upon the disk in her hands. She blinked as both fear and disgust played over his face at the site of it. Something had shifted since she left him; when she showed it to him he'd exhibited no signs of fear. He'd been puzzled and uncomfortable. She opened her mouth to comment but he found his words before her.

"Don't touch that thing. Put it away," he snapped with irritation.

Oh yeah, something had changed. She wondered what but didn't argue. He was right the disk was not something she should be messing with. Anna covered it with the silk scarf. The small piece she picked up like a coin, shoving it in her pocket.

"You made up your mind?" she asked surprised.

"Yeah, I'm going with you."

"Okay, we've got to make a stop first before we head over to Israel," she muttered to herself.

"When do you want to leave?"

"Once I get things straightened out here."

"We're leaving?" Lance questioned as he walked into the room.

"Yes I have to get back to the dig site. Make my walking away from the project official."

"I can't follow you out there." Lance stated.

"No. I didn't think you could. I want you to take care of this for me. I can't take it back there. They know to look for it." Anna said, handing him her bag.

"Anna, I…"

"Yes, I know but I think it'll be safer now with you. There's something in DC you need to take care of. Not sure what, I know it's there," she whispered.

"All right I'll take it just be careful both of you."

"We will," Sam assured him.

Anna watched as the detective took the disk from the room. "I've got to make a quick call then we can get started, Mr. Abrams."

"Fine, phone's in the kitchen while you do that I'll pack," he said. Anna detected a hint of annoyance in his voice. She wondered at it as the phone rang, but said nothing.

Anna sighed with relief as the phone connected. She'd been afraid there would be no answer. "Hello."

"Miss Gallagher, is that you?" A man's voice asked with relief.

"Yes."

"Thank goodness. We had begun to worry. The hotel called. They said you'd checked out last night. What is going on?"

"That ex is causing a lot more trouble than I originally thought. I had to get out of the hotel. I'm afraid I have to cut my vacation short."

"That's a shame. We could tighten security for you if you want."

"No thank you. I'd rather leave quietly," Anna said in a rush.

"We still need to present you with your main prize this evening. If you don't show at the ball room by seven you'll forfeit your winnings. The prize will be awarded to someone else."

"I see." Anna cursed. She could use that extra money right about now. She'd been counting on it for her trip back to Israel. "Well then I'll be there with a guest."

"Very good, your package for the evening will be waiting at the front desk. I'll have a room reopened for you and your guest."

"Thank you."

"Until this evening Miss Gallagher."

Anna hung up the phone. She sighed. Given his signs of irritation; Anna hoped that Mr. Abrams wouldn't be mad at the delay.

53

"Tell me again, why are we doing this?" Lance questioned as they stepped into the lobby of the hotel.

"It's simple; I don't have enough money to cover Mr. Abrams ticket to Israel at this time. So, unless he wants to use part of his winnings from last night's battle I need to make an appearance at the Serenity Ball. So I can collect my prize money."

Lance blew out a breath. "Right."

"Since I don't have the money to cover that right now we're back here. Though, it's probably a mistake. Do me a favor detective?" Sam requested.

"What do you need, Sam?"

"Hang around. Keep your eyes open. If they try for her again this will be their opening."

"I don't appreciate your treating me as if I'm incapable of looking out for myself Mr. Abrams."

"I'm sorry if my going around you offends you doc, but the fact of the matter is that if Lance doesn't stay I'm not going through with this."

Lance nodded. The trio approached the front desk. Lance hung back a bit and kept watch.

As Anna approached the desk the receptionist waved. "Miss Gallagher, welcome back."

Lance winced so much for keeping a low profile.

"Please, not so loud," Anna admonished. She looked over the lobby, eyes uneasy.

"Right, sorry. Here is the key for your suite, head up to the penthouse. Your package will be there."

"Thanks."

"Once you're ready your host will be in the ballroom."

Anna nodded. Sam led her to the elevator; Lance followed after the pair a few steps behind. When the trio reached the penthouse suite they stepped into the room to find a staff employee waiting.

"Three? I was only expecting two of you," the woman said with surprise.

"Only two of us will be attending the event. Detective Roman is just keeping a look out for my ex."

"I see. Well, he can't be hanging around like that. You're fortunate it appears that the detective and your guest are about the same size. I think I can accommodate both of them."

"Accommodate us, how so?" Lance asked.

"Gentlemen, in the room behind me there are a couple garment bags. Please change clothes then come back here and have a seat. I'll get Miss Gallagher out to you as soon as possible." With that said she took Anna by the hand, leading her in the opposite direction. Lance sighed he wasn't fond of suits they reminded him of funerals.

54

Sam loosened his tie for the third time. He muttered a curse. Rolled up his sleeve and checked his watch. It was almost seven. What the hell was taking so long?

"You like her don't you?" Lance questioned. Sam noted a hint of amusement in his voice.

"What?" Sam asked distracted.

"Don't play dumb, Abrams, it's not believable. You heard me. Anna, you like her don't you?"

"Maybe a little, when she's not calling me Mr. Abrams," Sam muttered.

"You didn't mind it when Miss Walsh called you that," Lance commented.

"From her it was natural with Anna it isn't."

"Why do you say that?"

"Instincts; It seems like a trained response."

Lance considered the matter and nodded. "She's…"

The sentence dropped off as the door from the other room opened and Anna emerged.

"Lance, you okay?" Sam asked. Lance muttered a curse. When Sam looked up to see what had caught the detective's attention he understood. Anna stood in the doorway she shifted from foot to foot uncomfortable in her heeled sandals. She brushed a stray lock of her golden hair behind her ear unaware she'd been noticed.

Damn, the woman was full of surprises. Experience told Sam it made her dangerous. He was usually able to sort out who a person was within ten minutes of meeting them. The lovely Dr. Anna Gallagher continued to throw him curve balls.

She was dressed in a lilac silk gown styled like a long Grecian toga. Her hair make-up and jewelry were done up to match the style.

The single piece that was not the same gold was a small coin of black with strange symbols. It hung about her neck from a copper chain.

Sam turned his focus from her as she became aware she was being watched.

"You guys, look sharp," she said. Her voice held approval. Sam reasoned she was turning the focus away from herself.

"Thanks, you're looking pretty good yourself, Anna," Lance murmured.

"Shall we go?" Sam prompted. He was uneasy with how good she looked.

"Of course, let's get this over with, Mr. Abrams," she said, her voice cool and distant. Lance chuckled. Sam felt annoyed but did his best to let it slide. At the moment he felt like hitting Lance for making fun.

The trio made their way from the room to the elevator in companionable silence. Sam stayed close to Anna as they made their way to the ballroom. His attention was beyond her. His mind was on full alert for any danger. He wasn't going to let her get hurt again on his watch.

55

He stood at the edge of the crowd in the ballroom. His eyes moved through the guests looking for something. Catharine sat listening to Bryan go on about the Dark Heart trilogy. He referred to Heart of Glass's bright future as a film and his hope that the fans would appreciate the work that she'd done on it. Catharine mentally groaned. Not for the first time she cursed the book and herself for ever writing it. She turned her attention once more to the man off on his own. She saw that his attention was now on the guest of honor.

The woman, Annalynn Gallagher, she'd been called earlier that day by homeland security. They'd all but ordered her to keep Anna at the ball that night. Who was she? Why did they need her there? Whoever she was she looked stunning in the Grecian gown. Anna could easily have been Serenity. Catharine felt the urge to draw her guest but there was no paper at hand to do so. Her publicist had forbidden her from bringing any kind of work with her tonight. She had to focus on the Dark Heart series.

Catharine watched as the stranger's eyes filled with longing. She felt a pang of envy as he stared at the blonde. What was it like to have a man like him desire you? She wondered. Catharine watched as another emotion played across his face. What was it disappointment? Maybe an acceptance of something he didn't like.

She felt a familiar itch as something about the scene she found herself sitting in, captured her imagination. Maybe it was the lighting or the mood; she wasn't sure. Despite her publicists wishes she rose from her seat at the table. Catharine made her way across the ballroom floor towards the mystery man standing alone.

56

"Can I buy you a drink?" The voice was distinctly female, warm, smoky and inviting. Lance blinked startled by the question. He'd gotten lost in his own thoughts. A dangerous place given the fact he was supposed to be keeping a look out for danger. His gaze moved from Anna and Sam to the source. He found the woman that the voice belonged to was just as appealing.

"Can I get a rain check?" he asked the ivory skinned red head.

"Not drinking?" She asked disappointed.

"No, I'm not a guest. Just added security," he explained.

"Really?" Surprise flashed in her eyes. They were the deepest blue he'd ever seen. Something flickered over her face that he couldn't quite place.

"Yeah, Miss Gallagher is having problems with an ex."

"Playing body guard then," she said amused.

"Yeah."

"Do you do this often?" She questioned.

"No, body guard is not my normal role. Why do you ask?"

"No reason," she said. Her voice was distant though she stood before him her mind was miles away. Lance saw the lie immediately.

"I'm not buying what your selling this evening Miss."

"Okay, I was curious" She licked her lips in a show of nervousness. She tried to relax. "I spotted you standing here alone. Wondered who you were? Why you weren't enjoying the festivities?"

Lance grinned amused. She was telling the truth but holding something back. He studied her and tried to figure it out. "Well, I'm not enjoying the festivities because as I said I'm not a guest. As for whom I am, the names Lance," he said.

She giggled at that. The sound was like the jingling of bells. "Lance, that's wonderful a modern day Sir Lancelot," she murmured.

Lance blinked, surprised by the comparison. He was a little disconcerted as she studied his face more closely.

"I suppose," he answered with a shrug.

"Oh dear, I'm sorry, I've offended you." She said alarmed. "I can't believe I said that out loud. Will you forgive me?" She asked. Her gaze eased.

"Sure, no harm done. I don't know that anyone has ever compared me to a knight before."

"No, I don't imagine they would." She said. "Writer's habit," she muttered it under her breath more to herself.

"You're a writer?" Lance asked. He considered the matter; shook his head. Of course she was. That explained the close study, the curiosity. She was looking at him not as a person but a character.

"Yes, oh I didn't introduce myself. I'm Catharine," she said then offered him her hand.

"A pleasure to meet you."

"So, what is it you do Lance, when you're not playing body guard for Miss Gallagher?"

"I'm a cop in DC."

"A cop," she said it with such enthusiasm and delight he laughed. "What department?"

"Burglary."

"How do you... no never mind not now."

"What not now?" he asked. His own curiosity piqued.

"It'll wait. Are you going to be in Vegas for a while?"

"Not sure," he said with a shrug.

"Can you grab that drink after this thing is over?"

"Maybe."

"Then perhaps I'll see you in the bar around ten," she said amused.

"Okay."

"Can I get a business card in case you aren't able to make it?"

"What for?"

"In case I'm ever in DC I can look you up. If not tonight, I will be having dinner with you Lance," she said with a laugh.

Lance blinked at the certainty in her words. He didn't understand why but he gave her the card. She thanked him. Brushed a kiss on his cheek then whispered, "Thanks. I suppose I should let you get back to work."

"Yeah, but it was nice meeting you."

"Indeed," Catharine said with a smile. Lance watched as she melted back into the crowd.

57

Catharine tucked Lance's card away. She made her way back to the main table. Bryan looked at her with irritation as she took her seat.

"Now without further delay I give you CJ Nichols."

Catharine rose from her seat, taking a bow before moving to take her place behind the mike. As her publicist past her, he muttered a warning about reprisal later for the holdup.

"Good Evening ladies, and gentlemen, it's an honor to be here this evening. I'm sure you're all aware a number of years ago I wrote a trilogy titled Dark Heart. I'm delighted that Heart of Glass has been made into a film. I hope it's just the beginning of a trend that will see other of my works hit the big screen." Catharine paused. She struggled to maintain her cool. She hated that of all her work, the trilogy was what they'd bought.

"CJ, we've heard rumors that you're rewriting part of the novel for the movie is that true?"

"Yes."

"Will those changes include a happy ending for Serenity?"

"I don't know. It'll depend on where the scene goes when I get to it."

"When we last saw her Serenity was enslaved to the vampire lord. Is there any chance we'll see a fourth book as a result of the films."

"There wouldn't be anywhere to take it. Serenity is a vampire. In the world I've created they are evil. All I could do is make her the villain."

"What about an anti-hero?"

"I am working on a novel separate from the series at the moment. I haven't thought about Dark Heart any further. Tonight isn't about me, it's about our guest Miss Gallagher."

58

Anna sat silent listening as her host gave a speech of presentation and waited for her cue. She felt a sense of being watched. Her gaze roamed over the crowd, searching for the source. She felt Sam's hand clasp her own under the table. He gave it a gentle squeeze. Her gaze met his. Anna was scared. She wished that the ceremony was done. Sitting there she was too exposed.

"I won't let anything happen to you again," Sam whispered as he leaned closer to her.

"Thank you. That's very kind of you Mr. Abrams," she murmured as her host wrapped up her speech. As CJ came to the end of her intro Anna rose to her feet despite her nerves to reply.

"Thank you very much for that warm introduction. It's an honor to be here, a real treat."

"Congratulations Miss Gallagher. I trust you'll enjoy your stay in Vegas." CJ said. She drew Anna into a hug then presented her with her prize. Anna tucked her award in her purse. "Now, will you allow me a small indulgence before you go on your way?"

"Perhaps."

"Will you speak with me for a few minutes?" Anna prepared to refuse but in that instant she spotted the man who had been following her. She nodded her consent. Anna gave Sam's hand a squeeze then walked away from the table, staying close to her host.

Anna moved across the dance floor in the direction of a quiet balcony. She was aware that Sam had followed after them. He watched and waited.

"He's here isn't he?"

Anna blinked, surprised by the question; concerned her host had so easily picked up on what was happening. Anna nodded as CJ stepped out onto the terrace.

"He's not an ex is he?"

"No." Anna whispered. She tried to relax recalling all too well the feeling of waking to find she'd been shot.

"What's going on? I was told to keep you here. Homeland Security claims you're a threat."

"It's better for you and everyone around you if I don't answer that. I can assure you that I am no threat to you or the American people."

"He's headed our way," Catharine whispered as Anna's unwanted guest approached them. CJ let Anna go on her way. Anna melted back into the crowd her eyes searching for Sam. Where had he gone? She jumped, startled as she was grabbed by the wrist. Turning she found herself face to face with him.

"Time to go doc," Sam whispered. He drew her closer to him giving her tail no clear shot at her.

"Right, let's lose this guy Mr. Abrams."

"Sam," he muttered as he reached the doorway leading back to the lobby.

"What?" She questioned as they made their way to the elevator.

"My name is Sam." He stated as he pushed her onto the elevator. He pressed the button to close the doors but kept her close to him in case they were ambushed on the penthouse floor.

"I know that Mr. Abrams," she said baffled. What was wrong with him? Did he think she'd forgotten?

Sam turned her so that she faced him. Anna felt her checks flush with heat as his close proximity; awoke within her – desire. She turned away from his gaze afraid he'd see all too clear what she was feeling. Her hazel eyes were prone to changing color with her emotions. She glanced at her reflection checking that nothing was wrong.

Staring back at her were a pair of lilac eyes rather than hazel and she sighed. He lifted her chin so that they looked eye to eye. Anna watched as his blue eyes widened with surprise. A new rush of blood through her face deepened her blush, apparently he'd noticed.

Something lit in Sam's eyes as he looked on her. Anna felt her palms begin to sweat. She felt her lungs tighten making it harder to breath. The smell of her perfume crowded in on her. Anna hoped it wasn't as strong as it seemed. Her nerves were getting the better of her. She didn't remember being this uncomfortable around Ian. So why was she panicking now?

They were too close; her mind warned. She felt fear wash over her and the urge to retreat but there was nowhere she could go that would be far enough from him to calm the storm building inside of her. The man had managed to get past her defenses it was unsettling and thrilling all at once. She turned from his gaze, afraid he'd see in her eyes too easily what she was feeling.

Lilac eyes swirled with color growing darker then fading and changing becoming more of a stormy grey as her emotions warred within her.

He laughed. "Call me Sam," he requested. The tone had some heat to it coming across more like a command.

Anna stiffened in his arms as her temper flared. "Don't laugh at me Mr. Abrams," she said coolly. "I don't appreciate being bossed around either."

"It's Sam," he growled in frustration. The elevator came to a stop and a ping sounded indicating they'd reached their floor. Sam shoved Anna into the safety of a corner as the doors opened. He looked for any signs of danger. Seeing none he grabbed her by the arm, dragging her from the car down the hall to their suite. Anna sputtered protests at his behavior but he ignored them. His focus was no longer on her. He was thinking of one thing getting her safely back to the room and inside.

As he stuck the key card in the door Sam drew Anna in front of him keeping her hidden from anyone moving in the area. He opened the door, pushed her inside, stepping in behind her. She heard the door click shut behind him. For a moment the room was dark until he switched on the lights.

"For heaven sake I don't understand why you feel the need to man handle me. I am perfectly capable of walking on my own. You don't need to shove me around and drag me about. If you think for one minute I'll tolerate this kind of treatment you are sadly mistaken, Mr. Abrams." She snapped in anger.

Sam swore and she started again.

"I absolutely won't stand for being cursed at Mr. Abrams."

Anna watched as frustration and arousal washed over his face. He took a step towards her and in reflex she took two steps back retreating from him. She hated herself for the fear running wild through her as he'd shown her nothing but kindness. He didn't deserve her distrust.

Her demeanor changed to alarm. "Relax doc. I wasn't laughing at you. It wasn't my intent to order you around and I wasn't swearing at you either. I won't apologize for man handling you as it was called for under the circumstances. I won't be doing so again this evening."

Anna nodded her acceptance and felt the fear inside her abate.

"I'm sorry…" she began.

"I wasn't finished doc, so you may want to save your apology."

"Why?"

"I'm going to tell you flat out. I like you Anna, despite the prim and proper act. I want to kiss you but I won't, not tonight." He said. With that he walked past her to his room to change, giving her no chance to respond.

Anna crossed the main room of the suite to where she'd left her things. She stepped inside and looked back across the room to where Mr. Abrams had moved to change. His words echoed round in her head. They set her nerves on edge. "I like you Anna, despite the prim and proper act." What did he mean by that? She wondered. Anna shut the door. She crossed the room to the bed where she'd left her own clothes.

Anna slipped off the heeled sandals. Set them back in the box. Crossing to the mirror she removed the Grecian jewelry and the clip from her hair. She put the various pieces back in their boxes, closed them up. Anna noticed a small envelope with the CJ Nichols insignia on it and carried it back to the bed with her.

"I want to kiss you Anna, but I won't, not tonight." Anna drew a breath trying to relax. What kind of man told you he wanted to kiss you then refused to do so? And what had he meant by that not tonight thing. Was he saying that he wouldn't ever or just not right then?

"Why do I even care?" she muttered to herself annoyed. He wasn't anyone she could be with. She was the intellectual. He was a thug that's how her father would view it. Her mother would look at him as the wrong sort of man, someone who might hurt her. They would view him as beneath her, she was supposed to, but damn it she liked him. Being near him she desired him and it scared her.

Anna unzipped the gown, pulling it off over her head. She set it on the bed careful not to let it touch the floor. Anna put on her own blouse and slacks. Stepping into her shoes, she put the dress back on its hanger, closing it in the garment bag. She'd enjoyed wearing it; Anna admitted to herself. She had liked stepping beyond her usual business attire into the fanciful. Just for one night to play the role of the princess in the faerie tale and dance at the ball.

She'd really liked dancing with him. It had been magical, thrilling and dangerous. Having him so close had stirred feeling in her she'd never experienced with Ian or the men she'd dated before him. Anna froze. "We aren't dating," she told herself sternly. It was an impossibility, they'd never approve. The truth of it stung more than she'd expected. Anna realized she'd wanted him to kiss her. Tears unbidden threatened to fall and she brushed the entire matter from her mind. Turning she set her focus on the envelope.

Opening it she found a card similar to the kind that came with flowers. "Miss Gallagher, as a souvenir of this night's festivities please take with you the wardrobe provided. Best wishes, CJ Nichols." Surprised and touched the tears fell after all. Anna mentally thanked her sister for entering her in the contest before drying her eyes.

Anna had always done what was expected of her. She'd nearly married Ian because her parents approved of him. They'd been disappointed in her when she called it off. Only her sister had supported the choice. She sent romances novels because at the time it had been what Anna needed. Even put her name in the contest. On her own, Anna would have never entered – never even read the Dark Heart trilogy.

Anna behaved prim and proper because it was what had been required growing up. It bothered her that Sam had seen the truth she worked so hard to keep hidden. That it was just an act. Underneath all the polish she was someone else, someone that her parents would find to be a disappointment. Anna turned her thoughts from this track. She didn't want to dwell on it. Instead she gathered up her things, moved into the main room to wait. As soon as Lance got back they'd get out of there.

59

Lance watched as hotel security returned to their stations. When Anna's tail had been spotted they'd moved in to assure the crowds safety. Kedar had slipped through the net. How? Lance didn't have a clue. He only knew that for now Anna and Sam were both safe that was enough. Glancing at his watch he noted it was almost ten. He considered his next move. Lance wanted to head back to the room but at this point Kedar would recognize him. He didn't need to lead the guy back to her.

Instead he made his way back to the ballroom. As he stepped through the threshold he found it was empty, only Catharine and the host remained.

"Damn it CJ, I told you tonight was about Dark Heart. You needed to stay focused. You left your fans twice."

"Bryan, I'm sorry I just…"

"I don't want to hear it Catharine. I need you to stop dodging these people's questions about Serenity. The house is making noises about it."

"I will sit down this week and resolve the matter, now please back off."

"Fine," Bryan turned. Spotting Lance he glared, his brown eyes fierce with hostility. He muttered an oath before going on his way. Catharine sat down at a table and buried her face in her hands. Lance crossed the room to where she sat.

"You okay?" he questioned as he took a seat across from her.

Catharine lifted her head, smiled. "Yes, Bryan is just a little frustrated detective. It's nothing serious."

"He looked pretty mad. I hope we didn't get you in any trouble."

"No, it wasn't you or Anna just me. I skipped the big premier for Heart of Glass. He's still steamed about it."

"Did you still want to get that drink or would rather pass?"

"No a drink sounds great." Catharine replied. She rose from the table. Crossed the room to her seat during the dinner and reached over to grab her purse. CJ he noted was wearing a similar style gown to that of Anna's. The toga was a traditional white. Her adornments of gold looked vaguely familiar. His mind clicked back to the flyer Anna had shown him. She looked like the woman depicted except for her red hair.

She was smaller than Anna was, more feminine somehow. He mused as he watched her. Stronger though and bolder. Anna was cold and distant by nature –like ice. Catharine was her opposite. As she turned he studied her face. There was something almost ethereal about her. She reminded him of a faerie. He laughed at himself. Lance hadn't thought in terms like those since he was a boy. Fantasy was a realm he'd left upon reaching adult hood. He watched as her blue eyes lit with questions. He wondered what she'd ask him.

The pair made their way from the ballroom to the bar. They took a seat in a quiet corner.

"I didn't think you'd show," Catharine confessed.

"Neither did I but I can't head back to the room. Beyond that I was curious."

"Oh really, curious, how so?"

"I wondered what kind of host misses their own party to talk with a body guard."

"Fair enough, I don't know why I did. There was something in the room. The lighting, the way you looked at her with such longing but refused to interfere. My mind was intrigued. It set you as the unrequited love. I wanted to know more."

"Miss Gallagher and I are just casual acquaintances. Whatever you thought you saw."

"Is none of my business I know, but after the scene where he swept her away in the crowd from unknown danger, I'm curious to know who she is also."

"That kind of curiosity could land you in a lot of trouble Catharine."

"So I've been told, but I can't help it. How did you two meet?"

Lance opened his mouth to speak as the waitress appeared.

"Good evening, what can I get you?"

"I'll have a Bud Lite," Lance replied.

"And for you miss… Oh wow you're her. CJ Nichols. You wrote Dark Heart."

Catharine sighed not again it seemed she was destined to endure the endless subject of Serenity. "Yes. I'll have same."

"Can I just say I loved the trilogy and can't wait to see the movie? I love Serenity she's just so romantic."

"Thank you," Catharine said graciously.

"Could I get you to sign my copy of the book?"

"Sure."

"Hey CJ, did you want anything with your beer?" Lance asked, steering the conversation back to their order.

"Not really."

"Oh, I'm sorry I'll get those drinks for you," the waitress said. She withdrew.

"Thanks," Catharine said with relief.

"No problem. You don't like the Dark Heart trilogy much do you?'

She blinked surprised by the question then laughed recalling he was a cop. "It's not the series I don't like it's her."

"Her who, Serenity?" he asked. Recalling the name mentioned repeatedly that evening.

"Yeah, her."

"Why not?"

"Have you read the series detective?"

"I could lie to try and flatter you but I'm not going to. Until tonight I'd never heard of CJ Nichols," he admitted.

Catharine smiled pleased to hear it. "How did you meet Anna?"

"You don't waste any time do you?" he said amused.

"No. Not really."

"I met her on a call. Someone had broken into her home."

"Really? What were they after?"

"Something she found at a dig."

"A dig? What does she do for a living?"

"I don't think it's my place to answer your questions about her."

"Fair enough, let's drop the subject of Miss Gallagher for now."

"Okay, what do you want to discuss?"

"You, tell me a bit about yourself. Where are you from? Do you have family? Have you always wanted to be a cop?"

Lance laughed "Full of questions. Okay I'm from DC, yes I have family. No one close. Yes I have wanted to be a cop for as long as I can remember. My father was a cop." Lance said.

"Sorry to disturb you but here are those beers," the waitress said. She set Lance's in front of him and Catharine's across from it. She set a well worn paperback book down in front of the author along with a pen.

“Who do I make it out too” Lance heard the question but the response escaped him.

The image on the cover was the same blonde from the flyer. She stood under the shattered heart moon. A wood lay behind her in the distance rather than the tower. The dark haired man with amber eyes stood behind her one arm wrapped about her waist, much as the vampire’s had been. The fingers of the hand dug into her thigh eliciting a desperate cry from her. His other hand held her left breast, his nails tearing the gown. Her eyes were wide with the same fear and need. Her hands outstretched to the silhouette of a man in the distance. Across the image in blood red was written “Heart of Glass”. Lance watched as Catharine opened the book and signed it for the waitress.

“Have you read it?” the waitress asked him.

“No, can’t say that I have,” he replied. Embarrassed to have been caught drooling over the cover image.

“Here have a look,” she said. Putting the book in his hands the back facing him before Catharine could protest. He noted that there was no author’s photo, Lance wondered at it, only a simple golden bird. He read the back cover to himself and curious flipped it over. Thumbing open the cover he read the teaser.

“Serenity trembled in his grasp, her body tensed. His amber eyes lit with hunger. She felt fear seize her, recognizing all too well his rising desire. He pressed his need against the curve of her rear. She gasped. Felt her flesh stir with passion, then moaned. What was happening to her? Why did she want him after what he’d done to her? How could she feel anything for him but hate? He drew in a breath scenting her and growled. His hands began to caress her hidden curves. “That’s right my love don’t fight me. Not this time. It’ll be better for you if you want me.” His words were both a demand and a tool of seduction. His warm breath brushed over her ear as he whispered them. Fingers sought bare skin tempting her further. Serenity felt her body awaken at his touch and cursed him for it. He turned her to look at him. His golden eyes burned with desire. His lips curved into a wicked smirk aware he had her where he wanted her. “I hate you, my heart is Davrik's” Serenity whispered it, willing it to be true. He laughed at her. “That may be so, but he’ll never make you feel anything like I do,” he countered. His lips met hers plundering, concurring her, bending her to his will. His hands played over her porcelain skin stirring her with need, readying her to accept him – her mate."

Lance blinked. The image faded. He swallowed a swig of his beer and tried to cool his blood.

"It's hot isn't it?" the waitress asked. Lance gave no reply, just a simple nod. He'd forgotten about her and the author of the book, sitting across from him. Lance handed the book back to the waitress. He looked up at Catharine. Lance cursed. The woman was good, just the short glimpse had him wondering what else she'd written. How steamy it got.

Once the waitress was gone Catharine spoke again. "So, what did you think?"

"It was hot definitely – but dark. Something there suggested the encounter was not planned. She's weak your Serenity. That's why you don't like her," Lance stated, keeping his assessment of the text analytical.

Catharine smiled. She took a sip of her beer. "Yes." She replied then Catharine leaned across the table. She put her hands on his face and kissed him. It was a quick peck. Nothing like what he'd just read and yet it hit him just as hard with desire.

"What was that for?" he asked.

"For getting it," she said. Catharine rose from her chair.

"Where are you going?" Lance questioned. He didn't want her to go not yet. There were questions he wanted answered now. Things about her he needed to know.

"I'm tired Lance. You've got a long day ahead of you tomorrow, I imagine, so I'm going to bid you good night," she replied.

"Good night?" He asked confused. Lance rose from his own seat. He wanted to stop her from going but short of forcing her to stay didn't know how to.

"Yes, but I'll be in touch," she assured him. With that she turned and walked out of the bar.

60 Monday 8am

Anna walked up to the ATM out front of the Bank of America. She glanced over her shoulder. Sam and Lance sat in the car, engine running, and waiting. She stuck her card into the machine. Typed in her pin and waited. As she put in the request for her money, a man walked past her, brushing against her shoulder. He made a quick apology before walking into the bank. Anna took her cash and informed the machine she didn't want another transaction. Her mind went back to the man. "I've seen him before," she muttered as she made her way back to the car.

"All set?" Lance questioned.

"Yes," Anna replied distracted. She tried to recall where she'd seen the man.

"Something wrong?" Sam asked as she opened the door, slipping into the back seat.

"No, it's just that guy who walked into the bank I've seen him before."

"You think we've been spotted?" Lance questioned.

"No, he's not one of the guys from before. He's just got a face I know."

"Like he's famous or something," Sam commented, having the same reaction.

"Yeah. I know. I saw him on the TV yesterday. He was at your fight."

"Hardagen," Sam said putting a name with the face.

"Yes, wonder what he's doing here?"

"It's not important come on we need to get to the airport before we miss our flight," Lance reminded. They pulled out of the bank's lot and drove away.

61

Lance pulled up to the curb in front of the airport, put the car in park. He knew the plan but he still didn't like it. "I think we're making a mistake. It would be better if I were going with you to DC."

"We've been over this detective. It's better for you if you go alone. I really think you have something you'll need to do once you get back. If you're counted as among our number you won't be able to do it."

"Right."

"Lance, I really appreciate all of your help." Sam said. He offered the man his hand in friendship.

"Don't mention it just take care of her," Lance said. He watched as the pair got out of the car. Bags in tow they made their way into the airport. He pulled away from the curb, then drove his car back to the rental place, grabbing his own bag. He shouldered it and turned over the key. Lance made his way inside, heading for the airport lounge. He had a few hours before his own flight would be boarding.

Lance listened as the departure of Sam and Anna's flight was announced. He hoped they would arrive in DC safe. Lance sipped a beer as he passed the time. His thoughts moved from the pair leaving to the night before. He'd dreamed that night for the first time in as long as he could remember of something other than the dead.

In it he'd rode out upon a black stallion into an enchanted forest on a moon lit night in search of Serenity. His mount had spooked. The woods had barred his path at every turn. He'd seen a glimpse of her in the distance blonde and beautiful staring up at the moon light. She'd looked like a goddess that had deemed to wander the earth.

He'd called her name but she'd not heard him. She instead turned into the embrace of a shadow. The trees had hidden them from his gaze. He'd thought that the shadow was using the woods to stop him from reaching Serenity. He'd been wrong, it had been her. In his dream she'd taken the form of the faerie he'd pictured her as. In the dream she'd teased mercilessly, until he forgot his Serenity; then she'd been his.

After waking he'd gone out, bought her book. He claimed it was a gift for a friend. It mortified him he wanted to read it. It was a romance novel after all. He blamed Catharine for it. Between the book and her calling him Lancelot she'd woken his imagination. He had to know the rest or his mind would try to fill it in for him. Dangerous to let his mind wander in the realm of fantasy too far.

"Is this seat taken?" the voice was warm and inviting. Looking up he was faced with the woman in question.

"No, what are you doing here?"

"I figured I'd find you here. Look I want to go with you to DC."

"What?"

"You heard me?"

"Why?"

"I want to know more about you and Miss Gallagher. See I've got this itch to write about what happened in the ballroom and…"

"Are you crazy?! You saw that guy; he's a former mafia hit-man. If you're seen with us you're risking your life."

"No. You split off. My guess would be to try and keep you out of the line of fire. Now we both know that they have to get out of DC relatively quickly. I can help with that."

"How do you figure?"

"I have a private plane. They can take it to wherever and avoid leaving a trail."

"Okay."

"In exchange for this favor Lance, I get to go with you to DC. Spend a few days in your life. I'll exact a price from her as well later."

"Really? Do you do this often?"

"What hop on a plane out of the state with men I barely know, or ask to invade upon their private lives?" Catharine asked amused.

"Never mind, forget I asked," Lance muttered. Realizing he didn't want to know the answer.

"Relax, the answer is neither. This is definitely a first for me."

"Fine, you can come, but I'll warn you my life isn't all that exciting," he relented.

"I doubt that Lance."

"You mentioned Anna; didn't you want to talk to Sam?"

"Is that his name? No."

"Why not?"

"He's not important," she said. "What were you thinking about when I walked up? You seemed far away."

"A dream."

"Cool. Have you ever imagined yourself as an animal?"

Lance laughed. "No, can't say that I have," he replied. "Have you?"

62

Washington DC, Virginia
Monday
12pm

Sam looked at the traditional Georgian house intimidated and disappointed. This fit the prim and proper Dr. Anna Gallagher. It wasn't Anna. He followed her up the steps, his eyes moving about the streets searching for danger. Once they were inside he drew a breath.

"We shouldn't be here doc. They're watching the house."

"I know, but I need to get a couple additional books. I have an idea about a couple of the images on the disk and…"

"You don't have that anymore."

"No, I don't. That doesn't mean it's beyond me to interpret it. I drew the thing. I still need to sort out what it is so that I can better understand what I'm protecting and from who." Anna stated. She moved into her office toward the back right corner.

Sam followed her past the entry way. He watched as she switched on the lights. He was grateful to find the drapes pulled tight so no one would spot the light within. It was better for the place to appear empty.

She moved deeper into the room her eyes skimming over the shelves in search of the right book. As he followed her he noticed that the books were all science, history or something of a scholarly nature. There was no fiction to speak of. It struck him as wrong.

"Anna, I don't think you should be messing with that thing. It could be dangerous," Sam warned.

"That's why I need to finish deciphering it. To learn if it is."

"Did you ever consider it might be connected to him? To Hermes..."

"Of course I have. Do you think me a complete fool Mr. Abrams? I've looked at it repeatedly I see nothing to connect him to it." Anna muttered. She pulled a book from the shelf, moved on.

"What if you're wrong? There's a tie you just don't understand it yet? What if you solve the thing and it binds you to his will forever?" Sam questioned. Recalling all too well the glimpse he'd seen.

"What's going on? Why are you pushing so hard to stop me from doing my job Mr. Abrams?" Anna questioned. She pulled the second book.

"I..." Sam began but he fell silent at the sound of glass breaking. He lifted his finger to his lips. Indicating she should be quiet. Sam cursed as he heard glass crunch, followed by footsteps. Anna's eyes widened with alarm. Rather than head for the entryway she moved into the corner with the chess game set up. She flipped a switch there pitching the room into darkness. Sam swore as he followed her. The dark wouldn't protect them for long.

63

Anna moved from the switch to the statue of the thinker. She felt along the base. Her fingers latched hold of a concealed trigger, pressing the button to access a hidden passage. She listened as the lock sprung and pulled.

"What are you doing?"

"Help me," she muttered. Sam grabbed hold of the corner. The statue moved to reveal an opening. Anna slipped through it. She watched as Sam did the same then grabbed the bookcase on the other side. Anna pulled it towards them closing the gap sealing the door.

"What is this place?" Sam whispered from somewhere close by.

"My private library," she replied. Anna felt along the wall until she brushed the controls for the gas fireplace. Pressing the button she lit it. Providing them with enough light to see but nothing the intruders would notice.

"A secret room?"

"Yeah I hide my personal collection of books and art here. I never thought I'd be hiding myself," she whispered. Anna took a seat in one of the chairs. She watched as Sam looked over the shelves and tried not to be embarrassed. He pulled one from a shelf and took a seat close to her. The time to talk ended. The intruders had entered her office.

64

Lance stepped off Catharine's private plane. He made his way from the hanger to the parking garage where he'd left his car a few days earlier. He heard the sound of heels and cursed. He'd almost managed to forget he had a traveling companion. He still wasn't sure how Catharine had managed that. Her being there with him put her in danger. He knew it. Glancing back he waited for her to catch up.

She wore a simple purple sundress with matching heels. Around her neck was the same gold chain he'd seen the night before. Whatever was on it was hidden under the neck line of her dress. He wondered what it was. Her blue eyes were hidden behind a pair of dark shades. Her red hair pulled back into a simple pony tail. Bringing her was a mistake. She was a distraction

Lance groaned seeing she was struggling with her bags. He took the main case from her and started in the direction of the car again. He unlocked the unmarked cruiser. Letting Catharine in, then moved to the trunk loading it up. Once all the bags were settled he slipped in behind the wheel, started up the car.

"So, is this one of those cars where you can't get out of the back from the inside?"

"Yeah."

"Cool. How does it work? No, never mind. Save that for later. What's our next move?"

Lance studied her for a moment fascinated by the way her mind worked. He was not sure how he felt about the way she'd included herself in his arrangements. "My first stop is home to unload my stuff. I'm not sure where you wanted to settle in at."

"You got a guest room or a free couch?" She asked.

"You want to crash at my place?" he asked with disbelief.

"Yep I want to immerse myself in your world," she replied.

"Catharine…"

"Think of it as a business arrangement, I'll pay you room and board for the time I spend there."

"Fine, I have a spare room it's being used for storage at the moment. I can clear it out for you."

"You don't need to go through all that trouble. I can sleep on a couch."

"That's not going to happen," Lance grumbled insulted.

"Okay, suit yourself then. Um after we get situated then what?"

"Next move is to give Miss Gallagher a call. Find out where she and Sam are. Then arrange a meet. See to it they get on their way."

"Sounds easy enough; why not contact them first then get settled? If the people chasing her have narrowed you down as a point of contact they could be watching your place, follows us to her."

Lance blinked he hadn't thought of that – sloppy to miss it. "And you still want to stay at my place?"

"Of course, it's not you they're after it's her. The sooner she's out of DC the safer your place will be."

Lance muttered a clever retort. He pulled out his cell phone and punched in Anna's number. The phone went straight to voice mail and he cursed. "She must have forgotten to turn it back on after landing. I'll try Sam's." Lance broke the call. Punched in Sam's number and waited.

65

Sam jumped, startled as his phone vibrated indicating an incoming call. Pulling it from his pocket he noted it was detective Roman and sighed relieved. He pressed the talk button, whispered a greeting.

"Sam, where are you and Anna at?"

"Her place."

"What the hell are you doing there? It's probably being watched."

"A point I made to the good doctor but she wouldn't listen. I was right. We're hiding in a secure corner of the house. Last I heard they were still tearing the place up trying to find us. Hurry."

"On my way. Sit tight Sam, and stay quiet."

"Will do," Sam answered before hanging up. He put his phone back, glanced over at Anna. She'd drifted off into sleep not long after sitting down. She was still resting quietly. Sam closed his book. He returned it to the shelf, listening for signs of the invaders presence. All was still and silent. Were they gone? Sam didn't know not for sure. Until Lance got there he had no intention of trying to find out.

66

Anna sat at her work station studying her drawing of the disk trying to decipher the other images. Her hair was pulled into a neat up-dew, keeping it off the drawing and out of her eyes. The single piece hung from her neck. She had music playing in the background though she didn't recognize it. The dots and lines – she was getting closer "planet alignment maybe?" she muttered it to herself, exhaled when it proved not to be.

"MY LOVELY ANNA; SO BUSY. CAN'T YOU SET IT ASIDE FOR JUST A MOMENT? IF YOU LIKE I CAN TELL YOU MUCH ABOUT YOUR TRINKET," the voice was gentle. It swept over her like a caress, coming from everywhere and yet nowhere. Anna looked up from the sketch. Hands like ice took hold of her shoulders from behind. She trembled at his touch. Knowing instantly who was with her.

"I want nothing from you," she whispered. Getting up from her chair Anna withdrew from him. She watched as the candles lit themselves. The fireplace burst with flame.

"OH BUT YOU DO ANNA. YOU SOUGHT ME AT EVERY TURN OF YOUR LIFE, STILL DO. WOULD YOU DENY YOUR LOVE OF KNOWLEDGE?"

"Not knowledge. Truth," Anna whispered.

"TRUTH IS RELATIVE, MY DEAR," he stated, materializing before her, taking her hand in his and kissing it tenderly.

"You're not welcome here Hermes," she snapped in irritation. Her flesh awoke called by its master.

He drew her against him, brought his lips to her ear. "YOUR MIND CAN'T KEEP YOU FROM ME FOR LONG ANNA. IT HEARS MY SONG. WEAKENS EACH TIME, WE MEET, TO MY WILL." To prove it he drew the lobe between his teeth. He watched with delight as her eyes widened with arousal. A pleasured gasp escaped her lips.

"Don't," She said her voice weak with need. Anna pressed her hand against his chest, shoving him away, creating space between them. "This is a dream. You're not real." She said with confidence.

"I'M AS REAL AS YOU ARE HERE. WHAT YOU FEEL HERE IS MORE REAL THAN ANYTHING IN WAKING. WITH EVERY MOMENT THAT PASSES HERE, WHEN WE ARE ALONE, YOU BECOME MORE MY WILLING BRIDE." He whispered. Hermes pulled her too him once more. His lips met with hers in a fierce and demanding kiss.

Anna pushed him away. She wiped her lips with the back of her hand. "No Hermes. Do you hear me? No."

He laughed "YOUR WORDS ARE POINTLESS. DO YOU THINK YOURSELF THE FIRST TO BE CHOSEN? I'VE TAKEN MANY A BRIDE OVER THE CENTURIES. OTHERS HAVE TRIED TO DENY ME. MOST SOON CAME OF THEIR OWN FREE WILL. YOU'LL BE NO DIFFERENT."

I will never come to you willingly. I swear to God in heaven I won't.

"SO BE IT, IF THAT'S HOW YOU WILL IT. KNOW THIS I WILL HAVE YOU WILLING OR NO," he hissed. Anna watched with horror as he transformed before her eyes. The man replaced by a monster.

67

Sam watched as Anna's peaceful rest became fitful in the blink of an eye. She began to thrash around in her sleep, fighting off some unseen threat. Sam cursed having a fair idea of whom. Rising from his chair he moved to her side. He shook her gently. "Anna, wake up it's just a dream," he murmured. But she gave no sign of being aware of him. He watched with disbelief as cuts manifested on her cheeks. Blood began to flow.

"God what's happening to her?" he questioned in horror.

"She did something stupid."

The voice was distinct and familiar. It came from everywhere and yet nowhere. "What?" Sam asked. Looking up he found himself faced with the angelic being.

"She challenged his authority over her. He in turn has revealed his true face to her. He's tormenting her."

"Help her."

"I can't interfere unless she asks for help. You people think all battles can be fought with your own will or the flesh. You teach it in film. You don't understand that there are things that your bodies cannot war with."

"Is this because of what I said earlier?"

"No, it's happening due to the fact he senses his hold on her diminishing. He knows his time is short. So he moves to break her will."

"What can we do for her?" Sam asked. Additional injuries began to appear.

"We can tend to her injuries. You can pray."

"Why are the injuries appearing? It's a dream right?"

"Yes, the injuries are a result of how much of her he's drawn into the dream. Her mind is making it real."

"What is he doing to her?"

"I don't know for sure; whatever he wants. He has a claim to her."

"What happens if she doesn't wake and he breaks her?"

"It depends. She'll either end up as you saw in your glimpse or he'll kill her."

68 Monday 1pm

Anna's eyes shot open. She woke with a scream. Fear surrounded her, a living thing. Her eyes ran over the room expecting to see her tormenter. The first thing she saw was the angel. She gasped with relief before she began to cry. Anna felt herself drawn from the chair against a warm body. Turning she found herself looking at Sam. He brushed his fingers through her hair, rubbed her back.

"Shh, it's okay now Anna. He's gone it's all over. You're safe," he assured her. Anna buried her face in his shoulder, clung to him. He was real she knew that. In the dream he hadn't been there. She hadn't even been able to think of him. It was as if he didn't exist.

"It was so real," she murmured. Shaken though now upon waking she didn't remember what he'd done to her. Only that he'd hurt her.

"It was real. You were cut and bleeding here," Sam breathed.

"Oh God, I don't want this. I don't want to serve him."

"Then don't," the angel said. He placed his hand on her brow easing her mind and spirit. "You still have a choice here. The time draws near."

Anna nodded, said nothing. She drew back from Sam. He didn't let her go. She noted he was shaken and rather than push him away as she knew she should Anna allowed him to hold her until he was steady enough to let go.

69 Las Vegas, Nevada

Pamela sat at the Bellagio's bar her red nails drummed on the counter. She sipped at her martini. Glancing down at her watch she noted it was almost noon. Where the hell was Sam? It wasn't like him to be late. She'd been waiting over an hour now. He hadn't shown. Not even a peep. Crushing out her second cigarette she laid down money for her drink, made her way out of the hotel. She wasn't waiting any longer she'd just go find him herself.

She made the short drive from the hotel to his house each passing minute had her temper building. The nerve of him, making her wait. He'd pay for it she swore. Pulling up in front of his house Pamela mentally crushed him under her high heel like a bug.

She made the short walk up the drive; her heels clicking out her growing impatience. A manicured nail mashed the bell. She took off her sunglasses as she waited. Pamela fixed her hair, making sure it was perfect, touched up her lipstick, evening out the blood red stain. No one answered. The house was still, the place dark. Pamela pressed the bell again. She banged on the door. Again she waited. Adjusting her breasts in the push up bra; reapplying her perfume, dabbing it on her throat and wrists. She spritzed it in her hair, applying a hint of it in her cleavage. It would overwhelm Sam, always had. Lead him where she wanted him.

She'd use it to weave her spell. Draw him to her. When she was done with him he'd sign the consent form. He'd give her anything else she wanted too. Pamela thought with satisfaction. But still there was no response from within. She wouldn't let that deter her. Pamela reached above the door to where Sam had always hidden his spare key. She pulled it down, laughed. He might as well have invited her in.

Unlocking the door she stepped into the house. Something was off. She felt it as soon as she saw the living room. It looked as if someone had slept on the couch. Who? Pamela wondered. She crossed the room to the kitchen. Found three sets of dishes in the drying wrack. He'd had company. Perhaps he'd celebrated his victory too long into the night, Pamela reasoned. She moved on from the kitchen to the guest room. The sheets looked as if they'd been slept in. Who had been there? Where were they now?

Crossing the hall she stepped into his bedroom thinking to catch him sleeping. The room was empty and dark. "What the hell? Where is he?" Pamela muttered, anger beginning to bloom again. Flipping on the light she found the bed sheets stained with blood. Her instincts began to hum; something here – something big. Moving to his closet she found most of his clothes gone along with his suitcase. "Gone but where? Why the rush? No word."

Spotting the laptop she smiled. That would hold her answers. She assured herself. Pamela powered it up. While she waited for it to load she drew a shirt from his closet. She held it against her, drew in his scent. She was looking forward to finding him again. Sam had thought by moving away he'd be free of her. He was mistaken. She wasn't done with him not by a long shot. She may have ended their marriage but that didn't mean they were over.

70 Washington DC, Virginia

Lance pulled up outside Anna's home. Fear grabbed him seeing the front door flung wide. He glanced over at his passenger, cursed. He'd forgotten her in his haste to get there.

"Catharine, stay in the car. I've got to go in, get Sam and Anna. I'm not sure they're alone. I can't have you with me in there. If something went wrong your life would be in danger."

"But…"

"No buts on this one. If you argue with me our deal's off."

"Fine," Catharine muttered.

Lance got out of the car and made his way up the steps. He walked into the house, turned on the lights. A path of destruction lay before him. Pictures frames were busted glass shattered, decorations smashed, furniture broken. Who ever had been here was pretty angry at losing them. Lance moved down the hall in the direction of the living room. Behind him he heard the sound of glass cracking. He turned gun raised. Found himself faced with Catharine.

"Damn it Catharine, you almost got yourself shot. Deal's off…"

"You can't. You didn't say anything about not following you. Just no arguing," Catharine snapped. Lance blinked then growled. She was right. He wanted to tell her to go back out to the car but seeing the intensity of her gaze knew he'd have no luck. Her mind was already hard at work.

"Do you know how to use a gun?"

"Yes, I took one of those firearms courses, practiced at a shooting range. It was research for…"

"Okay, take this. Go upstairs and look around. I doubt they'll be up there."

Catharine smiled her eyes lit like a kid at Christmas. She took the offered weapon, gave his a quick peck on the lips. "Thanks and good luck." she murmured, then started up the steps.

Lance blinked then shook himself out of his shocked state. The woman was crazy. He grinned despite his annoyance. Admitted to himself he kind of liked her spontaneity and impulsiveness. So long as she wasn't driving him mad.

As he walked past Anna's work room he noted it was in a similar state to that of the entry way. Books thrown off the shelves, pictures smashed. Fragile items destroyed. Anna would be devastated. Her world was in chaos; the place in shambles. Seeing no sign of her or Sam; he moved onto the living room.

Lance surveyed the damage here as well. Muttered a quick prayer that his friends were okay before calling out to them, "Sam, Anna you can come out."

71

Sam lifted his head from Anna's. She looked up at him in question.

"I think I heard Lance," he whispered. He wasn't surprised to find the angel had vanished once again. Sam cursed. He had questions he'd wanted to ask. In his fear he'd forgotten them. Sam let Anna go, rose to his feet. He took her hand in his and helped her up.

"Oh, then it's safe to go out now," Anna said with relief.

"Guess so," Sam whispered. He followed her over to the picture on the wall opposite the fire place. She pressed on it. The frame moved opening to reveal the living room. Anna turned from the sight of her destroyed belongings. She buried her face in Sam's shoulder. Sam wrapped an arm around her protectively. He looked on the devastation. "Someone was mad," he muttered as he led her into the room toward Lance. The detective turned at the sound of Sam's voice.

"What in the hell is the matter with you, coming back here? You might as well have called this Broody guy, told him you were coming."

Anna stepped away from Sam and faced Lance. "I needed a book for my research."

"Couldn't you have bought a new one?"

"Not easily, no. They could be watching for me to make purchases of that nature," Anna snapped.

"Um sorry to interrupt you, but don't you think we should have this discussion elsewhere. I mean whoever trashed the place could come back," A woman's voice called from the entryway. Sam's gaze shifted to see a petite red head with blue eyes.

"Who…wait aren't you CJ Nichols? What is she doing here?" Sam asked.

CJ crossed the room to where the others stood. "The name's Catharine. I'm here because I offered to let you use my private plane to get out of DC in exchange for the chance to invade Lance's life for a short time."

"Thanks I guess," Anna said. Sam chuckled at her price for her services and wondered just what Catharine meant by invading Lance's life. He wondered why Lance had agreed to the terms from what he recalled of the detective Lance was not one to let others into his private life.

"In exchange for the help I want to know about what happened at the ball last night."

"Now wait a second…" Lance began in protest.

"No, she's right she helped get us out of there. She is going to help get me back to Israel she has a right to know what she's getting involved in." Anna stated cutting him off.

"Thank you," Catharine said with delight.

"Can it wait until after we get out of here?" Sam questioned annoyed.

"Of course," Catharine answered. The four made their way from the house headed for Lance's car. Sam helped Anna into the car and watched with irritation as Catharine took the seat next to her. Cracking his neck, he took shot gun and listened as Anna recounted the events at the dance. Answering the novelist's questions as Lance drove them back to his place.

72 Las Vegas, Nevada

Pamela smiled as she made it past Sam's password prompt. She clicked on the folder housing his work. Seeing nothing new there she shrugged; too much to hope that he'd already written it. Pamela clicked on the internet browser, pulled up the machines history. Looking through yesterday's files she found a search run on the name Anna Gallagher. Pamela clicked on the link. She was sent to the bio of a Dr. Annalynn Gallagher, an archeologist working for the Smithsonian.

"What are you up to Sam?" Pamela muttered then closed out the laptop. She made her way out of his house and locked it up. Put back the key. Pulling out her phone she booked a flight for DC. If Sam was looking at this Anna there was a reason. She was damn well going to find out what.

73 Washington DC, Virginia

"It's all set," Catharine announced as she joined the others in Lance Roman's living room.

"When do we leave?" Sam questioned.

"As soon as you're ready the plane will be waiting for you in hanger twenty-three."

"Thank you for your help," Anna murmured grateful.

"Don't mention it. Thank you for answering all my questions earlier. I know it must seem odd…"

"Not at all. I hope it's enough to get your imagination running. I'm sorry it has to all be so vague."

"I understand why it is. Perhaps some other time we can discuss it further privately, no work."

"Maybe," Anna said.

"Here take these," Lance said, handing a set of keys to Sam. "Cars in the garage take it. Just try to bring it back without bullet holes."

"I'll see what I can do."

"Thanks now get going. Good luck to you both," Lance said. He gave Anna a quick hug, took Sam's hand in his to shake it. "You take care of her Abrams. If I hear she's gotten hurt or that you've hurt her I will not be pleased," Lance whispered before letting Sam's hand go.

"I'll take good care of her," Sam promised. Catharine watched as the pair left. She hoped that their journey would be an uneventful one.

"They'll be fine," Catharine assured Lance once they were alone.

"I hope so."

"You care for her a great deal don't you?"

"Yeah, but she's not interested at least not like she is in Sam," Lance muttered.

"I'm sorry."

"Don't be, it's not her fault or his, it just is. It's my problem. I'll get over it," he assured her then chuckled. "Come on Catharine I'll give you the nickel tour of the place since you'll be staying here," He said. Lance offered her his hand. She took it, allowing him to show her his home.

Rising from the couch he started off to the left down a short hall. Opening the first door on the right she found herself looking into a good sized room. It was littered with boxes and bags. Dust covered the few pieces of furniture. It looked like it hadn't been set foot in for a while.

"This is the guest room. Once I get it straightened up you'll be staying in here."

It was a nice space; it would provide her with enough room to set up her work station. "Once we do." Catharine corrected.

"You don't have to help," he assured her.

"It'll be fun, interesting too. You'd be surprised what you can learn about a person by going through all these things. What they hold on to can be telling," Catharine commented.

"If you say so," he said. Lance led her out closing the door. Opening the next door she found it as neat as the other was not; boxes here, but ordered and labeled for easy access. "This is my office here at home. If the door is closed and the light is on please don't disturb me."

"Right I can respect that. Will you allow me to observe you here at work one time?"

"So long as you stay out of my way," he replied then closed the room off. The door next to it is the guest bath. Across is my space stay out of it."

Catharine nodded. Let the matter go. She'd stay out so long as she wasn't invited. Heading back towards the front he indicated the kitchen and dining area.

"When do you want to get started on the guest room?" She asked.

"In about an hour I need to report in."

"Do you mind if I start on it alone?"

"No go ahead," Lance said, waving her away. She watched as he vanished into the kitchen. Catharine sighed. Turning she made her way to the guest room. Getting to understand the detective was going to be a challenge.

74

Pamela Walsh looked up at the two story traditional Georgian home with curiosity. She wasn't sure what she had been expecting but this wasn't it. Moving up the steps she knocked. The door creaked open. She slipped inside. The house was dark – silent as a tomb. Pamela closed the door behind her. Flicked on a penlight she kept with her for just such occasions. She shined the light about. The small beam illuminated a pile of broken glass.

Pamela cursed, recognizing the early signs of a break in. She'd need to be sure and wipe down the door when she left. Slipping on a pair of gloves she turned on the light, looked upon the destruction. "More than a break in here," she muttered.

The place had clearly been tossed. Whoever broke in was looking for something, but what? Also more important where was Dr. Anna Gallagher? What was she working on? Pamela sighed. Crossing into the workspace she saw no signs of anything remaining. Whatever it was she'd either taken it with her or the people who tossed the place had it.

75

Catharine flipped open the lid on a box. She stared at what lie within it. On the top was a 5x7 frame face down. Beneath it was an article of clothing. She picked up the frame, turning it over. The image was of a woman with short cropped brown hair, soft wide brown eyes like that of a doe. She had skin as white as her own. The woman was long lean and athletic, her body possessing subtle curves. She wore a simple blue sundress that showed off long legs.

"Who is she?" Catharine muttered, brushing a strand of her own red hair from her face. She heard the door close behind her – turned. Lance's gaze moved to the picture. Before she could speak he'd snatched it away from her. Shoved it back in the box faced down.

"If you want to stay here don't ask me any of the questions in that head of yours right now," he snapped; closing up the box. Catharine nodded her understanding, swallowed back the words that wanted to break free. His eyes were haunted. There was pain there, sorrow and even anger – great loss. She felt her heart ache within her at the sight of it. "You know what, I don't want you going through this stuff after all. I can handle it. You go on back into the living room. Watch a movie or something. I'll join you when I'm done here," He said.

Catharine did as he asked, respecting his need for privacy. There were secrets here, in him, wounds too, that still bled. Things he wasn't ready to share.

"I'm sorry," she whispered before she turned and walked out of the room.

76

Lance heard the door click shut behind him, drew a breath. He'd forgotten that box was in here and had managed to lock it and her away in the dark recesses of his mind. Only in dreams could she reach him. Seeing the photo brought it all back. He cursed. Opening the lid he drew the blue fabric out, stared at the sundress. He drew a breath and took in the smell that surrounded it – her smell.

"I miss you," he whispered to the empty room. Lance set the dress back in the container and closed it up once more. He carried the package across the hall to his own closet. He didn't want Catharine poking through it again later. With the box tucked away he moved back to the spare room, began the task of straightening it up for his guest.

Lance was grateful she hadn't protested his demands. He wasn't ready to tell Catharine about her. He didn't want to. Dana was a subject he tended to avoid as much as possible. What had happened to her still hung like a dark cloud over his mind. He wondered; if he'd not made the changes in his life that he had, if his fate would have been the same or worse.

77

Catharine looked up from the TV at the sound of footsteps. She watched as Lance crossed the room to sit on the couch.

"It's all set for you," he said.

"Thank you. You have a nice house. It means a lot to me that you've opened it up to a stranger."

"No problem, I'm just grateful for what you did to help Anna."

"I was happy to do it. Normally my fame is troublesome. I'm glad it was useful for a change. Besides she's no terrorist."

"You know about that?"

"Yeah, Homeland contacted me before the ball, requested I keep Anna there as long as possible."

"You could get in a lot of trouble if they find out what you've done," Lance warned with disbelief.

"How will they? It's not like Anna's going to go advertising how she got back to Israel. Besides, we both know that whoever is after her doesn't want this thing public."

Lance blinked. "You should still be careful they may not take too kindly to your helping her."

"No, I don't think they would, but I don't care. I like Anna. If I can help her get free of whatever is hunting her I'm happy to…" Catharine cursed as her phone rang. Seeing the number she groaned. She connected the call despite her dislike of who waited on the other end. She'd have to face the music sooner or later.

"Hello."

"Catharine, where the hell are you? You were supposed to have a book signing this morning. When you didn't show I stopped by the hotel. They said you checked out!"

"Bryan, calm down I had a personal matter come up. I'm out in DC for a few days…"

"DC. Why the hell are you in DC? You're not there with Tom are you?"

"No, of course not..."

"Who was that guy you were seen with at the bar last night?"

"I don't see how that's any of your business."

"Oh it is my business princess, every detail of your life is. I'm your publicist. It only takes one bad choice to end up in the spotlight for the wrong reasons. It's my job to protect your image and the interest of the house. You're failure of late to keep your contracted engagements has the house questioning your commitment to the book and them."

"That's not fair I've been working..."

"They don't see it that way Catharine. Dark Heart is hot right now. They want it ridden for all its worth, as the author, you have a responsibility to uphold. You know that, yet you can't be bothered to meet with your fans!"

"I..."

"No more apologies CJ, they want action. When you finish up whatever or whoever it is your working on out there you're expected in New York. Unless you hear otherwise they want to meet."

"How dare you imply for a second..." Catharine began in a rage. The phone on the other end went dead signaling he'd hung up. She cursed, throwing the phone.

"You okay?" Lance questioned. She jumped, startled having forgotten where she was and him.

"Fine, just a little steamed with Bryan."

"Who's Bryan?"

"Nosy, overbearing publicist who thinks he has the right to poke around in my personal life," she said with irritation.

"Tell me how you really feel about him," Lance said amused.

"He's a royal pain in my ass."

"What did he want?"

"I missed a book signing today and didn't attend the premiere of Heart of Glass. He's still roaring about it."

"I see. What was it he implied that had you so mad?" Lance questioned. He picked up her phone and handed it back to her.

"That I was out here shacking up with the guy from the bar last night for a hot tryst," she muttered.

"Nice, but isn't that what this could look like to the press if they figure out where you are?"

"I don't care what it looks like Lance. I know what it is and isn't. That's enough for me."

"Aren't you worried about your reputation?"

"No, why would I be? It's all just noise. The part of the life I hate. Let them think what they want. I could care less." She said with disinterest. Catharine turned her focus back to the movie. Lance said nothing more; he rose from the couch and retreated back to his room. Catharine sighed relieved he'd respected her wish to end the discussion but certain he'd had plenty of questions of his own.

78

Tel Aviv, Israel
Tuesday
3am

Sam and Anna stepped off the private plane of CJ Nichols. Bags in tow they made their way from the hanger in the direction of the parking garage. Anna had left her rental there a few days earlier. Spotting the car Anna popped the trunk and moved to unlock the doors. Sam began loading the trunk with their things. She felt the car sag under the extra weight and studied it making sure nothing had been disturbed.

The sound of a door slamming echoed through the lot and Anna looked about uneasy. She heard the sound of footsteps and turned. Anna opened her mouth to nudge Sam to hurry. The words died on her lips as she found herself faced with her pursuers. Sam lay on the concrete motionless.

"What did you do to him?" She asked, afraid to round the car and find him in a pool of blood.

"Relax Miss Gallagher. Your associate is fine, just unconscious. You shouldn't have left Israel doctor. They were willing to let you work the site so long as you didn't cause trouble."

"I had no intention of causing trouble. I just needed a couple days away from everything to clear my head."

"Afraid that's not good enough doc, certain people have questions and concerns in regard to you. Those have to be addressed. Give me the keys and get in, unless you want your sleeping friend here to suffer a far worse fate."

Anna did as he requested. Handing over the keys she watched as two other men came out of the shadows. They loaded Sam into the back seat, sitting one on either side of him. Anna slid into the passenger seat. She watched as the man pulled out a cell phone. He punched in a number as he got into the car. She heard him say, "We got them," he listened to a voice on the other end.

"At the airport in Tele Aviv. We're on our way."

79 Washington DC, Virginia

Lance set Catharine's novel aside. He tried to close out the mental image of Serenity fleeing before the rogue werewolf Kovrin like a frightened rabbit. Her heart hammering with terror even as her body stirred with desire and want for his… "Damn it," Lance groused, unable to shut off his imagination. He never should have started reading it.

Why had he?

Okay he'd been curious after the teaser page. He'd wondered about the back story for the scene presented. Picking up on something darker implied. What he'd found had been darker than even he'd figured on. He could understand why Catharine hated Serenity. There wasn't much there to like. She was fixated on the man who had hurt her, nothing romantic about it.

Unbidden the image of another woman's face surfaced from the depths of his memory. She sat at a scarred wooden desk her back to him. A stack of folders lay piled in front of her the top one open. "Put it away Dana," he heard himself urge. She turned those doe brown eyes, lit with a fire of determination, her mind so focused she didn't see him.

Lance turned away from the image slamming the door of his mind on it and her. He wasn't going there not tonight. He wasn't going to compare her with Serenity either. The circumstances were completely different. Dana was never weak. Not that way, he told himself. Needing the distraction he picked up the novel to read further.

80

Somewhere in Israel
Tuesday
5am

Anna woke to find herself tied to a chair. Where was she, how had she gotten there? She wondered. She lifted her head and looked about. She spotted Sam he lay in a heap on the concrete floor in the corner.

"Ah good you're awake. We've got some questions you need to answer," A voice said from the opposite side of the room. Turning her focus she found herself faced with the man Sam called Kedar.

"What do you want?"

"Who have you been talking too?"

"I tried to speak with Phillip King. He wouldn't listen to me."

"Anyone else?"

"No."

"How did you get back into Israel? We've been watching your passport. It hasn't popped."

"We took a private plane."

"Who's helping you?"

"No one. Look I said I was taking a couple days and I did…"

"Don't lie to us Anna. Someone has been helping you. We have ways of making you talk."

"Don't touch her Kedar," Sam snarled in warning as he swept the legs out from under the man closest to him.

"Mr. Abrams, good of you to join us."

"She's telling you the truth she hasn't talked to anyone about the dig site. She came back to think. She was convinced she was missing something at the site. She couldn't sort it out, needed to get away to clear her head. She decided that she needed help. After doing some checking she contacted me as a research assistant."

"Why you, after all, you were a reporter?"

"What you're trying to keep under wraps will break sooner or later. I figured if we let a reporter in on it he'd keep things the way we want them perceived. Besides, he's not exactly credible among his peers, even if he tries to break it early no one will believe him," Anna added. Picking up the thread of the lie hoping they'd accept it as fact.

"One problem with that doc; since you were gone and avoided being found we figured you weren't coming back. We brought another expert in to manage the dig. So if you'll just turn over the artifact we'll send you home again."

"Another expert, who?"

"Dr. Lynch. I believe you know each other."

"Damn, Zaharrah Lynch, yes, I know her."

"She came highly recommended. They said her skills in the ancient languages and cultures of the area are even better than yours."

"Oh yes, I'm sure they are, hard not to be when you're native to the area…"

"See we don't need you, Miss Gallagher."

"You're wrong about that. As I said before I know Zaharrah. I know for a fact if she's working this thing she's not working for you."

"She's signed a contract…"

Anna laughed cutting him off. Sam looked at her with question. "Zaharrah only works for one person – herself. If she's here she has an angle."

"We've taken precautions…"

"Whatever she finds you won't get it."

"You're sure of that?"

"Positive. Now, you can either let me back on the site to sort this thing out for you or you can leave it in the tomb raider's hands and watch your prize vanish into the night. The choice is yours gentlemen."

The phone on the desk rang. Kedar answered it. He listened to a few words then hung up. Cut Anna loose from the chair. "Welcome back doc. Understand she's still on the team."

"Whatever. Is she at the site now?"

"No, she's elsewhere."

"Fine, just keep her out of my way," Anna snapped as she stood up.

"No promises, come on we'll get you settled in then you can get your assistant up to speed."

Anna nodded. The pair was helped into a car.

"Who is Zaharrah Lynch?" Sam asked with curiosity once they

were in the car.

"I'll tell you about her later once we're alone. Let's just say for now we have a less than friendly history." Sam nodded. The pair fell silent as they were driven out of Tel Aviv.

81 Washington DC, Virginia

Pamela Walsh made her way up the steps of the Smithsonian, stepped inside. Her trip to Dr. Gallagher's home had turned up little to explain Sam's interest. It only managed to raise more questions. Who had gone through her home, why? What was it that Anna was working on? How did Sam know anything about it? Pamela set the questions aside. She made her way to the information desk. She hoped that someone here would be able to shed some light on the matter.

"Can I help you?"

"Yes I need to speak with Dr. Gallagher."

"Miss Gallagher is not available…"

"Can you help me find one of her colleagues? I'm a friend of Anna's. I'm concerned something may have happened to her," Pamela said. She leaned against the counter pressing her breasts up against the surface, lifting them to reveal more cleavage to the young man.

"Um she reports directly to Dr. King. I believe he is in. Let me see if he can speak with you," the young man said distractedly; his focus drawn to her supple chest. She'd worried the money for the boob job had been a mistake. Pamela grinned pleased to know it hadn't. She wondered if Sam had noticed the difference when they met. She dismissed the thought. It didn't matter. She watched as the young man picked up the phone. He spoke quickly to someone on the other end.

"He'll see you Miss; follow me," he said with a shy grin. Pamela gave him a grateful smile. She walked through a door labeled "staff only"; just behind him she noted the various offices. At the end was a set of double doors. The sign above it read Dr. Phillip King Director of Antiquities.

"Here you are. Dr. King is waiting for you."

"Thank you," Pamela purred. She brushed a kiss on his cheek leaving her cheery red lips on his skin. She watched as his face flushed, ruffled his hair. After she finished with the good doctor she'd see about bribing the young man into letting her have a peak in Anna's office. He'd be an easy sell, Pamela reasoned. She opened the door and stepped into the office. An older gentleman in his late fifties sat behind an oak desk, eyes studied her with question and mistrust.

"Good day Miss."

"Hello, Dr. King, I'm sure you're busy so I'll keep this brief. I swung by Anna's place earlier for a visit. I was shocked to find the door a jar the place was a wreck. There was no sign of her…"

"A wreck you say?"

"Yes, it looked like it had been tossed."

"Oh my, that's terrible have you contacted the police?"

"No, I just wanted to make sure Anna was safe. I was hoping she would be here but…"

"No, I'm afraid I haven't seen Anna since she stopped by Friday to report on the dig in Israel."

"Israel?"

"Yes. I'd heard she'd met with a bit of trouble. A detective came in asking questions."

"A detective, why?"

"There was a break in Friday night. I should probably call him."

"What was his name, this detective?"

"Um, I've got his card here somewhere," Phillip said. He began looking through an assortment of papers. "Ah here it is Lance Roman."

"I guess I should talk to him next then," Pamela said with worry. "Would you mind if I took a look around in Anna's office. See if she left anything that might tell me where she is. What is happening to her?"

"I don't…"

"Please Phillip, it would mean so much to me," she murmured. Pamela batted her eyelashes at him working up tears.

"I suppose it can't hurt anything," he said taking her hand in his to comfort her.

"Thank you," she whispered. Turning she left the office. Pamela found the young man waiting. "Dr. King asked you to show me into Anna's office."

"Right this way," he said, leading her back down the hall to Miss Gallagher's door. He unlocked it, followed her in. Pamela gave a mental curse but made no outward sign of annoyance at his being there. She flipped through a stack of papers. Made a mental note of anything she thought might be important. Anna had been working on researching an earthen cup. In the margins of the notes she'd scribbled; discovery in Dead Sea – a vase of unknown origin.

"Find anything?" the young man asked.

"Nothing much I don't suppose you could give me a minute alone."

"I'm afraid not. Anything in here is museum property."

"I understand I just need a moment to settle my nerves. I'd be ever so grateful," Pamela murmured as she stared deeply into his puppy dog brown eyes with her whiskey colored ones. She watched as he swallowed uneasy. Pamela brushed her manicured crimson nails through his dark hair.

"Okay," he breathed before stepping out of the office, closing the door behind him.

Pamela turned and flicked on Anna's computer. Connecting to the net she typed in the site for Sam's creditor. As she waited for the site to load she hoped this risk paid off.

82

Jerusalem, Israel
Tuesday
6am

Sam swore as he and Anna made their way into the hotel. His head was pounding from the sucker punch. Since his luggage was nowhere to be found he had nothing to quiet it. As they made their way across the lobby he spotted the small shop.

"Hang on Anna," he murmured. She stood and waited as he stepped inside, made a quick purchase. He swallowed down two ibuprofens then crossed to her side.

"Ah Miss Gallagher, so glad to see you're well," the concierge said in greeting as they approached the desk.

"Thank you Liam, I wanted to…"

"We've held your suite and opened the one next to it for your friend per Dr. Broody's instructions. I hope you had a safe trip in."

"We did thanks," Anna said. She took the new key and the spare to her own room.

Together she and Sam crossed the lobby to the elevator. They waited in silence for the car; neither voicing yet the question on both their minds. When had the hotel been contacted?

83 Washington DC, Virginia

Pamela smiled with delight as she made it past the password prompt. She found a list of Sam's recent transactions. There was one listed only a few hours old for a hotel in Jerusalem. "What the hell are you doing in Israel Sam? What is Anna working on out there?" she whispered before shutting down the computer.

"Miss, are you okay in there?"

"Yes, I'll be out in a second," Pamela assured the young man, then wiped her eyes with a tissue smearing her makeup so it would appear she'd been crying. She checked her reflection. Verifying she looked the part of the worried friend then stepped out into the hall rejoining her escort. He led her back down the hall, out of the staff only area to the main lobby of the museum.

"I really appreciate all of your help."

"It's no problem miss."

"Could you do one more thing for me?" Pamela asked. She let her eyes plead for her, silently giving him the illusion of a lady in distress.

"Of course."

"Call me if you hear anything about Anna," Pamela requested. She handed him her card.

"I will," he assured her."

Pamela smiled. To ensure he did, she thanked him again and gave him a quick kiss before turning and walking away. Israel, damn that put it beyond her scope she was supposed to be back in LA later that night. If she didn't show and this turned out to be a wild goose chase it would get her fired. On the other hand she still needed Sam to sign off on the book. Taking out her cell phone she punched in Mina's number. She hoped she'd be able to clear a few extra days off. "

84

JERUSALEM, ISRAEL
TUESDAY
6AM

Sam slid his key card in the door, opening it. He flipped on the light.

"Ah hell," Sam muttered at the sight before him. In the middle of the room near the foot of the bed were his bags. Whoever had grabbed them at the airport had already been here. It didn't bode well. For all he knew the place might be bugged.

Anna blew out a breath, the hotel had been informed they were coming and had prepared for their arrival. It made her uneasy. She crossed to the door joining the two rooms. Opening it she cursed as well. The room was left in the same state as when she departed. The drawers hanging open, bed unmade; laying on it her suitcase.

"Great now I get to put it all back together again. They couldn't have fixed it; no I'm just sure Ian told them to leave it for me. When I…"

Sam cleared his throat ending her private tirade. "I think you had better explain this if you can," Sam stated keeping his tone cool and even. Showing his temper now would do him little good.

"Right. Um where to begin?"

"How about with who it is you and the Smithsonian are working for," Sam suggested.

"Well, as I said I was called to the site because that pottery was found. It was unearthed by a construction crew. They were beginning to build an embassy building for the UN."

"Great so they do have government connections."

"As far as I know of no. But given all that's been happening I'm willing to assume that they do."

"How did they take the news their site was a historical one?"

"Not so well at first until we located the city. When we found the chamber with the map they were excited. They moved their embassy building site back a few hundred yards."

"Did you at any point see anything to indicate that there was anyone working their own project?"

"No, I…wait the day they found IT the environment at the Atlantis site shifted. Anyone not working hand in hand with Broody was shipped out."

"What is this IT you keep mentioning?"

"Fossils that predate man. Things that until then we never dreamed really existed," Anna answered. She licked her lips nervously still not comfortable with talking about it.

"Such as?" Sam prompted.

"Monsters," she murmured more to herself than answering him. "Look, what's there you'll see in due time for now get changed I'm taking you straight to the site. What you said before about missing something it's true. There's something in my documentation that's been bothering me for weeks; inconsistencies I don't understand. Maybe a fresh set of eyes can interpret them."

"Okay, give me a few. We'll be on our way."

"Take your time, I need to change as well. Can't go out in the field in a suit," she stated before moving into her own room, closing the door.

Monsters the vague answer echoed in his mind. Sam opened his suitcase, pulled out a change of clothes. He shook his head. "There were plenty of monsters in the world today you just had to know how to spot them," Sam muttered to himself. He pulled a gun out of his bag.

Strange to hold it again after years of ignoring it, odder still that he wasn't really chasing a story. He was intrigued by it yes. But it wasn't the reason he was there. No, despite his hesitation earlier he was there for a reason beyond Anna's story. Whoever was chasing her; he wanted to make sure they didn't catch her. More so he wanted to catch them. He wanted the man in charge of the operation be it man or god.

Sam shook himself; it was weird to be thinking of Greek deities as real and threatening to their safety. Angels and gods how did it connect with what she was working on in Sodom and Gomorrah. They predated the Greek pantheon? He set the matter aside. Set the gun on his night table. Sam busied himself with changing, once dressed he pulled on the harness for his gun, slid it in the holster. He covered it with a leather jacket. He wasn't going to be caught off guard again.

85 Washington DC, Virginia

Pamela pulled an old business card from her purse, dialed detective Roman's number. She got his machine. She groaned. Where was he? If memory served her right he should have still been on duty. Flipping over the card she thanked whatever god was out there looking down on her seeing the hand written number for his cell, punched it in. As it rang she made a mental script so she could get the information she needed from the detective without tipping her hand.

"Hello," his voice was deeper, hinted at annoyance. She wondered why the change.

"Detective Roman?"

"Speaking," the temper had eased. He sounded more focused.

"I don't know if you'd remember me or not it's Pamela Walsh."

"Miss Walsh, of course I remember you; hard to forget such a lovely woman. What can I do for you?"

"Do you remember Mr. Abrams?"

"Yes."

"He was supposed to meet me for brunch at my hotel in Vegas. He didn't show. I swung by his house. The place was empty his suitcase missing. I saw some notes on an Anna Gallagher. I flew out here to see if he was here."

"Were you able to locate him?"

"No, and when I got to Miss Gallagher's place the door opened when I knocked. Inside it was a wreck. There was no trace of Miss Gallagher or Sam."

"How long has he been missing?"

"Last I saw him was Saturday. I know he made his fight; so early Sunday I guess."

"I'd tell you to file a missing persons report but they won't let it be filed unless he's been missing 48 hours."

"Yes. I know. So, I swung by the museum. After speaking with her employer I was told you'd worked a previous break in. I was concerned Sam might be in some kind of trouble so I called you."

"He could just be vacationing I heard through the press that he broke his orbital bone. He won't be fighting again anytime soon. He may have wanted to get away from Vegas for a while." Lance offered.

"No, it's not like Sam to miss an appointment and not call. I'm worried can we meet somewhere. Talk. Maybe you know something more about Miss Gallagher from your investigation that would explain how Sam knows her."

"Sure. Meet me at the Brickskeller in thirty minutes."

"Thank you, detective." Pamela murmured. The line clicked ending the call. She turned the car in the direction of the Brickskeller. She hoped that Lance Roman would be able to shed some light on what Sam was up to.

86

Lance swore as he punched in Sam's number. He listened to it ring twice before he was greeted by a distracted hello.

"Sam, got a problem here?"

"What's up?"

"Your ex just called…"

"Ah hell. I forgot about my meet with her at the hotel." Sam said with annoyance.

"Yeah she's here in DC asking questions about how you know Anna. Said you left notes lying out."

"I did no such thing. The house was locked. Damn, left the spare in same place as the old house. She must have found it and let herself in."

"If you don't want her dogging you I suggest you give her a call. I'm meeting with her shortly, what do you want me to tell her?"

"If you can manage it – nothing. She's not worried about me she smells a story." Sam muttered.

"I'll do my best to keep her in the dark," Lance assured Sam.

"Thanks got to go. Anna says we're close to the dig site. Good luck."

"Same to you." Lance hung up the phone then grabbed his jacket. He headed for the door.

"Where are we going?" Catharine questioned as she grabbed her purse.

Lance glanced back at her. He considered correcting her that they weren't going anywhere; he was going and she was staying. He realized there was no point in it. She'd either argue and waist time, follow him or question him about his excursion upon returning. She'd respected his requests for privacy earlier he could yield here. Let her in.

"Damage control seems Sam's ex-wife is looking for him. Says she's worried, he says she's looking for a story. We're supposed to put her off his scent."

"Oh, okay then let's get moving."

87 Dead Sea
Tuesday
7am

Sam stepped out of the car. He looked across the desert terrain and noted an abandoned construction site in the distance. It looked scorched – neglected.

"What happened there?"

"Oh, that was the original site for the embassy. Apparently the way the pot was discovered was a protester tried to bomb the site. He was identified. The bomb went off before he reached it; they still felt its effects."

"Where did they find the pot?"

"See that charred patch of earth about 50 yards from us."

"Yeah."

"That's where the blast went off. They found the pot not far from there. Apparently it caused an earthquake. They thought the city would be there but found nothing else. I climbed the cliff behind us for a bird's eye view. It was there I found the next pottery shards. Come on it's just up there." Anna said. Shouldering her pack she started up the steep hill. Sam followed after her.

As they reached the top of the mount Sam looked about. He felt a chill he couldn't explain. It was quiet here now – still as a tomb. He could see the signs of the workers that had yet to arrive. A tent was pitched in the midst of the crumbling walls. The jagged stones looked like teeth. He wondered if this was a place where the earth would just swallow a man whole so that he vanished without a trace.

"It's a bit intimidating the first time you see it I know, but we can't linger out here. The others will be along shortly. There's much for you to see."

Anna's voice shattered the unearthly silence. It seemed to break the lands spell, the foreboding image fading to the recesses of his mind. The ruined city came into view. The pair stepped through the gate way into the main square.

"So, the city dwellings are divided in quarters. From what we've gathered the ones to the left are suited more for the wealthy and religious figures."

"Why do you say that?"

"Larger wells for one, we've also found finer stone used on them. The dwellings on the right are for your common folk, servants and slaves."

"What are the central structures dividing the city sections?"

"The first one straight ahead of us is the temple. We'll start there. Beyond that is the entertainment district. In the back is the king's palace. We'll go there next." Anna stated. She started across the ruined square to the temple's remains. Sam followed after her. All the while wondering what it had looked like before its destruction.

They walked up crumbling steps past broken columns, into the main chamber of the temple. Sam noted to his left was an empty basin that had once been a fountain. Another lay to the right. Day light spilled in through a broken roof. Illuminating a face cast in stone. Drawing nearer he noted it was not alone.

In a perfect arch at the back they stood. Ten perfectly sculpted images so like that of the Grecian and Roman statues that they predated. It struck him dumb. He had no words at first. Sam saw the altar in their midst; long and ominous a great stone table. Elevated so that whatever took place there was looked on by the gods and goddesses. He noted the space behind the gods was enough for a single person to pass behind. There were sconces to illuminate the images as well.

"I thought there were twelve Olympians," Sam muttered, staring at the images.

"There were but there were more than just the twelve in mythology. This dcpicts the ten that the people of Sodom worshiped." Anna explained.

"Which ones?"

"From left to right you see Hades first, god of the underworld, he holds in his right hand the scales of life and death his left hand clasped tight. Ares, god of war, he is dressed for battle, his sword held high. Next is Hera queen of the gods. She is embraced by her husband Zeus, the king of the gods. His crown is set upon his brow. The next took some research to sort out; she is Hecate, goddess of night. She is held fast by Chaos the god of the void; in his right hand he holds the scroll of destiny. Next to them are Psyche and Eros. He holds his bow, arrow poised ready to strike. Dionysus comes next; he holds his cup of wine. Last of them is Aphrodite goddess of love and beauty, her eyes gaze upon Ares."

"What of Hephaestus and Persephone? Why do they not appear among the statues here?" Sam questioned.

"I'm not sure. We haven't found anything to explain it." Anna admitted.

"Did you find anything behind the statues?"

"Behind them?"

"Yeah I figure there's a space large enough for a man to pass back there," Sam replied.

"It didn't occur to me there might be a passage," Anna said intrigued. She studied the recessed area behind the images. Taking a flashlight from her pack she flipped it on. They walked behind the image of Hades. Sam a few steps behind. As she came to the center she muttered an oath. Behind the carving of Chaos and Hecate was a door. Shining her light in the dark Anna noted a stair case leading down. Sam took the flashlight from her, started down the tunnel before she could protest. If anyone was wandering into the unknown first it was going to be him.

The stairs were steep and narrow, just enough space for one person to pass at a time. They came to an abrupt end in a small chamber beneath the temple. The floor here was split open and charred. Sam let the light run over the room. Not staying long upon any image. Until he found a small black chest marked with the image of a palm. He crossed the floor to it. Lifted the lid, inside were earthen tablets with strange markings.

"Cuneiform, hidden writings, perhaps your answers are here," Anna whispered and she knelt beside the chest to look.

"Not now Anna. Show me the rest. We'll come back to this," Sam said feeling this was something they shouldn't disturb. It was dark. The room was full of it. It held secrets. Knowledge of old that shouldn't be unearthed without care.

Anna blinked he was right the tablets would wait. There was more to show him at the palace, things there that raised more questions about the city – the others as well. Anna rose to her feet, watched as Sam closed the box.

"Right lets go back up stairs and out into the city I'll show you the palace."

88

Sam followed Anna past the ruined columns into the central courtyard of the king's palace. He strolled over a broken bridge into the king's temple. The graven images were here as well. They appeared in a long wall fresco. Rather than ten images this depicted many others. He started in the center and moved right.

In the image, Zeus stood the central figure he embraced Hera. Demeter clung to his back with one arm while the other clung desperately to Persephone's wrist pulling her away from Hades embrace. A woman he didn't recognize stood between him and Poseidon who embraced another. Next came Hephaestus, he held a chain pulling his wife Aphrodite away from Ares embrace. The war god's gaze was fixed upon Hestia.

"Who is between Hades and Poseidon?" Sam questioned.

"She took me a while to identify also. That is Eos goddess of the Dawn. Poseidon embraces his little known queen Amphitrite." Anna explained.

Sam nodded. Then set his gaze to the other half of the image starting from the left and moving back to the center. Eros embraced Psyche; Hermes reached for Iris who stared with longing upon Helios who embraced another. Dionysus stood by watching as Hecate and Chaos embraced. Another figure he did not recognize clung to Hera in a similar fashion as that of Demeter who clung to Zeus.

"The one embracing Hera I've never read any myth suggesting she was unfaithful. Who is he?" Sam questioned.

"It puzzled me also. He is Erebus, god of darkness and shadow. The woman in Helios's embrace is Cybele, goddess of nature."

"Why does the king's temple depict so many others beyond the ten in the people's temple?"

"I wondered the same thing until I saw Gomorrah."

"Where's the map you mentioned?"

"If you look to the right you'll see the map of the empire."

"There are four cities here Gomorrah, Admah, Zeboim and Zoah. You only mentioned finding Gomorrah."

'We've made no effort to locate Admah or Zeboim because the riddles here, and at Gomorrah were solved. Atlantis was discovered. The others were forgotten."

"What about Zoah?"

"Zoah's location is known according to the biblical account; it was spared from God's wrath at Lot's request."

"Did you find Lot's home?"

"No one's looked for it; everyone has been too busy with the temples. I don't think anyone was interested in proving the Bible to be fact." Anna admitted.

"Okay, I assume you have photos of all of this. The findings at the Gomorrah site as well. Is that right?"

"Yes."

"Good, we'll take a look around here for things missed then head back to the hotel. You can show me photos of the rest. I don't think I need to visit Gomorrah it'll be the same or close."

"It is."

"Fine, let's go have a look around in the common man's quarters. See if we can find Lot's house."

"Why?"

"To give you the truth."

Anna nodded. The two of them left the king's temple behind, making their way back toward the city gate.

89 Washington DC, Virginia

Pamela watched as detective Lance Roman stepped into the Brickskeller, a woman with red hair followed a few steps behind. Who was she; a new partner maybe? The pair made their way back to where she was sitting; filled in the seats across from her.

"Hello detective. Thank you for meeting with me on such short notice."

"No problem. Pamela this is Catharine…"

Pamela blinked. "CJ Nichols. What are you doing here? Last I heard you were in Vegas for your contest winner's award presentation."

"That's right I was in Vegas. I came out here to interview the detective for my next book."

"How do you know Lance?" Pamela asked her curiosity piqued; if CJ had been in Vegas then it was possible Lance had been as well. If he was there when he was working a case pertaining to Miss Gallagher then she must have been there too. Maybe she hunted up Sam?

Catharine looked at Lance. Unsure and he nodded. "We met at the Serenity Ball he was there keeping an eye on the contest winner. Miss Gallagher."

Pamela smiled with delight. "Anna Gallagher?"

"I believe so."

"Did she have a guest?"

"I don't see how that's relevant?" Catharine stated.

"Look I'm trying to determine if she knows my ex-husband Sam Abrams."

"Why?"

"He's missing. I'm concerned he maybe in some kind of trouble," Pamela replied.

"No, you're seeing dollar signs – a possible story. I know that look all too well Miss Walsh, I've seen it far too often of late and at this point I have nothing more to say to you." Catharine rose from her seat without another word and walked away from the table.

"Lance…"

"Its detective. Miss Nichols is right whatever your ex is up to doesn't concern you. I imagine he'll be in touch." Lance said then he got up and left as well.

Pamela cursed; she was running out of options; out of time. She had a good idea where Sam was; what she didn't know was why. The trouble was unless she got something more than a hunch she couldn't pursue the lead. She was due back in LA before ten pm tomorrow for the big bash to celebrate Heart of Glass's success. It had been announced by Hardagen earlier that evening. She was expected to be there. As she stewed her phone rang indicating an incoming call and she smiled; it was him.

"Hello Sam," she purred it, hoping to catch him off guard.

"Pamela, I'm sorry about our meet, I completely forgot. Won the fight but didn't feel much like talking. I broke my orbital bone. Can we reschedule or maybe you can drop that form by the gym. Hanna can fax it to me. I'll sign it and have it sent back."

"Where are you? I was worried when you didn't show up. I stopped by the house, you weren't there. Are you okay?"

"I'm fine just decided to get out of Vegas for a while."

"I'll drop the papers with Hanna. Have her send them to you. You're sure you're okay?"

"Yes, I'm sorry I scared you, hope the book is a hit, talk to you later," Sam said then he hung up.

Pamela sighed; he'd been warned she was snooping. What did that mean? It meant whatever was going on Sam was in it up to his ears. She was going to find out how it had happened and why? Rising from the table she paid for her drink then headed back to the airport. It seemed she was headed back to Vegas.

90

Catharine swore as she got in Lance's car. "I'm sorry I wasn't counting on her recognizing me, I'm afraid I probably added fuel to her fire."

"You did fine. I should have told you who she was."

"Well she'll no doubt head back to Vegas. When she finds out what happened there – that Sam was Anna's guest. It won't take her long to sort out how Anna tracked him down and why. I hope the people he works with are loyal enough not to talk to her."

"I'm sure he'll warn them about her."

"Yeah he seems thorough. I doubt he'll be able to shake her for long. She's hungry."

"Meaning?" Lance questioned curious as they started off down the road.

"I've met her type before. She smells a story. Miss Walsh is looking for something big to get her off the entertainment beat, Miss, she's out of her prime, only has a few years left to make a big splash before the axe falls on her career. She's basically washed up and desperate."

"You saw all that in a brief meet?"

"Yeah, had another one like her write up some nonsense about Bryan and I. It took months to kill the rumors."

Lance looked over at her. He wanted to ask the nature of her relationship with Bryan. He'd caught them arguing on two separate occasions. But he held his questions, none of his business. If he went there she'd want to know about the photo. He wasn't ready to talk about Dana just yet with her. "Gotcha."

Catharine laughed. "Wow have you got the look of a character in conflict with himself. You want to know but are afraid to ask."

Lance stammered in protest. She put a finger to his lips silencing him.

"The implication was that we were involved. Bryan is my publicist nothing more. I am not currently attached to anyone. If I were I wouldn't be here with you. I'm not the kind of girl that just randomly shacks up with strange men despite how it may appear."

"I didn't think you were, though I got to admit it is weird having just met you that you're staying at my place."

"I'd rather observe your daily habits, but if it makes you uncomfortable I can get a hotel room."

"No, that's not necessary you can stay with me," Lance assured her.

"Good, I like you Lance. You seem like a nice guy. It's obvious you've got some baggage but who doesn't. I won't pry into who the woman in the photo is, you have my word."

91

DEAD SEA
TUESDAY
10AM

Anna groaned as her knees began to ache. She'd been digging through the rubble of the common quarters of the ruined city with Sam for more than two hours. Other members of the team had begun to arrive. They'd moved on to the king's temple to catalog the findings there. As more people began arriving, she worried someone else might discover the chamber in the main temple. Rising to her feet Anna reached above her stretching out. She rolled her neck popping it and loosening stiff muscles. Anna was about to comment on wasting time but Sam left the small house moving into the next.

Anna blew out a breath. She followed after him. As soon as she stepped inside the dwelling she knew they'd found what they were looking for. The place felt different to her somehow, though why she didn't know. It was like the place was warm where the others held an unnatural chill. The sun streamed into the rubble near where Sam stood he looked as tired as her.

"Do you feel it?"

"What?"

"That this is his house."

"No, seems like all the rest," Sam admitted. He stepped out of the sun light. Anna spotted it in the dust behind where he'd stood – a pottery shard. Kneeling down she lifted the pieces from the earth, turned them in her hand to look upon the design. It was different from the others no imagery of the stone gods or goddesses just the simple markings of the people of Abraham's blood line.

"Look," she murmured; handing him the piece before turning to search for more proof.

Sam studied the piece with curiosity and wonder. He'd seen so many shards among the rubble during the hunt, he'd lost count but everyone had possessed the mark of tribute to the gods of the city. Here was the different they'd been hunting for. Strange she'd known it would be here before finding it. "How did you know?"

"I don't know. I could just feel it. The place feels different than the others. Warm and at peace, no ghosts linger here I guess." Anna replied. She brushed dust from the door near the entryway. There inscribed in the earth were the Hebrew letters declaring the house to belong to the God of Abraham.

"What you feel is the spirit of God."

Anna turned. Found they were not alone in the dwelling. The angel was there now with them. "The house is blessed?" Anna questioned.

"Yes, though it was never meant to be disturbed. It and the city have been lost since the day Lot and his family fled this place. We've worked long and hard to keep it hidden. The enemy at last has managed to reveal it."

"I wasn't supposed to unearth this place?"

"No, you were allowed to when the vase was unearthed. Its discovery started a storm that was building in the shadows. You've seen what lingers of the old world. It waits for a door to open so that it can return this world to the way it was in the days of Noah. But their time has not come. They must not be allowed to enter."

"What is it we need to do?" Sam asked. Anna watched as the heavenly being smiled.

"Sam, we've always enjoyed your willingness to step up to the task at hand. However you have not seen the whole picture yet and you must."

"Why?"

"To complete the task ahead you must see all that has been discovered with your own eyes for within the findings will lay the key to completing your task."

"How do we get back to Atlantis? I was sent away." Anna asked confused.

"Anna, you know what you must do for now. Once you reach the oldest city in the king's realm we'll talk further." The angel said then he was gone. Anna sighed.

"I hate it when he does that," she muttered before stepping out of the house into the city square. She watched as the workers began to make their way to the temple. She felt an inner struggle. Part of her wanted to stop them, desired to keep them from the discovery that morning. She longed to read it for herself. Add it to her discoveries in the area but it was not hers. Sam had found it. Instead she followed her gut instinct, joined them searching for the man in charge.

"Dr. Broody, wait I need to tell you something."

Anna watched as the older man with dark hair and a touch of gray turned to look at her. She blinked; when had the gray begun to appear. Had he looked that old when they started working the dig together three years earlier? Anna drew upon memory and realized he had not. He hadn't looked like that earlier in the week when she told him she was taking a few days off – strange. What had happened between then and now to have him age so?

"What is it Dr. Gallagher?"

"My assistant Mr. Abrams he made an amazing discovery this morning in the temple. The team should start working on it right away."

"He did?" Ian asked with shock and disbelief.

"Yes Ian. It was right in front of us the whole time but we never saw it. Turns out a fresh set of eyes, was just the thing." Anna said. Sam stepped out of the ruined house.

"Really, well then come let him show us this new find," Ian said pleased. The trio moved into the temple Sam leading the way.

92 Washington DC, Virginia

Lance stepped out of the car, made his way to the front door. Catharine was a few steps behind him. He stuck the key in the lock and cursed when it didn't turn. The dead bolt had issues. He'd been meaning to replace it but had yet to do so.

"Hey what's that?" Catharine asked her voice bright with curiosity.

"What's what?" Lance questioned as he struggled with the deadbolt.

"There's a package of some sort sitting by the door. Your right foot's almost touching it." Catharine replied.

Lance looked down on the step and sure enough a small manila envelope lay on his door mat. "Don't know I'm not expecting a package," he said. Bending down he picked up the envelope tucked it under an arm. He turned his focus back to the entrance and sighed with relief as the key turned. "After you," Lance said as he held the door open for her. Catharine laughed and walked past him into his home. Lance closed the door locking it, following his guest into the living room.

He felt much better. Watching Catharine handle Miss Walsh had been entertaining and he'd managed to forget Dana for a while. He'd also done some soul searching and realized that his attraction to Anna had been because of how much she reminded him of being around Dana. The two women though different in appearance were similar in personality. It wasn't Anna he'd understood it was Dana.

"Hey where are you at?"

"Sorry just thinking. So, shall we open this thing and find out what it is?" Lance asked her.

"Sure."

"Here you do the honors," Lance said. He handed her the

envelope and took a seat next to her on the couch.

Catharine tore open the seal and reached inside pulling out a stack of photos of assorted sizes. "Looks like someone sent you photos," Catharine murmured.

Lance felt his stomach churn and his head reel as he stared at the images. "Put it down Catharine and get out," he snapped unable to believe the nightmare before him.

She blinked, startled; the photos slipping out of her fingers which had gone numb at his sudden anger. Lance watched powerless as the horrific images fell like confetti. They hit the floor in disarray. Some face up others hidden. He watched as her blue eyes widened with fear.

Catharine screamed at the sight of a young woman much like herself laid out on green earth. Her brown eyes were wide with pain and terror, blood ran down her face where it had been cut open. She was dressed in a red Grecian style toga. A golden snake about her body, its fangs sunk into her left breast.

Lance drew Catharine's face against his chest hiding the images from her. He swore. "I'm sorry you shouldn't have seen that," he whispered. With one hand he soothed her. With the other he gathered the pictures shoved them back in the envelope.

"She looks…"

"Don't say it. That wasn't left for you Catharine; it was left for me. It's okay, I promise you nothing is going to hurt you," he murmured and he kissed her hair. "I need you to go back to your room for now I've got to look at them and I might have to go out. I'm sorry."

Catharine drew away from him and nodded.

"Try to relax. I'll be back a soon as I can," he whispered and he brushed a kiss on her brow.

Catharine gave him a brave smile and then vanished into the back of the house. Lance sighed. He spilled the photos out on the coffee table and set to work.

93

Lance tucked the photos back in the envelope and sighed. He put it away in his desk then made his way back to the living room. He'd faxed them over to the station and promised to come in first thing tomorrow. Lance didn't want to leave Catharine alone after what she'd seen. He'd told her nothing would happen to her and he meant it. While the snap shots weren't left for her the one who left them was an opportunist. Dana had lost her best friend because he'd seen her. He wasn't going to give this guy the same chance with Catharine.

Lance sat down on the couch to relax. He felt weary in a way he hadn't in years. He closed his eyes blocking out the haunting images from the crime scene photos. So, the Fury Killer was still out there. The thought of it turned his stomach. Dana would be disappointed to hear it. He whispered an apology then contemplated calling the chief back. He thought better of it. He wasn't going down that road again.

Lance laid his head back against the leather sofa. He wanted to rest but his mind wouldn't allow it. He considered calling Sam. After all Mr. Abrams had been hunting for the guy at one point. Lance dismissed the idea. Sam had enough on his plate right now. Besides he had no clue where the Fury Killer was.

Lance heard the sound of the bedroom door creak open and padded footsteps on the carpet. He sighed. It seemed Catharine had decided the coast was clear. He didn't open his eyes but he was aware he was no longer alone. He felt her presence as soon as she stepped in the room. He was aware of her standing in the door way watching him. "It's okay to sit down Catharine."

"Are you sure? I don't want to intrude."

"I'm sure. You must have lots of questions," Lance said. He opened his eyes and looked at her.

"No, just one. What did Anna give you before she left?"

Lance blinked surprised by the question then laughed. She was good. He'd anticipated an avalanche of questions about the strange package. Instead she'd left it alone, changing the subject on him all together. Silently giving him the reprieve he needed, asking him for something in return.

"What makes you think she gave me anything?" Lance asked more curious than evasive.

"Well, clearly she had something the people chasing her wanted. If she'd taken it with her they'd have it now. She wouldn't risk that from what I gather so she gave it to you for safe keeping."

Lance smiled Catharine Nichols didn't miss a trick. She'd have made a decent cop he mused. "Okay, come on I'll show you on one condition."

"What's that?"

"You can't touch it."

"Why not?"

"I think you'll understand once you see it," Lance assured her. He got to his feet. Taking her hand he led her back to his room. "Wait here," he instructed. On impulse he brushed a kiss on her cheek before opening the door. He slipped inside. Lance left the door open. He smiled as he retrieved the silk bundle Anna had entrusted him with.

Lance imagined Catharine out in the hall peering in through the cracked door. He knew from the door way she could see his king size bed on the far wall. Make out the shape of his large oak dresser. She'd be able to note plush carpet the color would elude her though since he left the light off. He wondered if she'd feel the itch to push open the door, others before her had. Could she resist the temptation?

He wasted a few more moments giving her plenty of time to make up her mind; testing her.

"He doesn't play fair," Lance heard her mutter to herself. He blinked. She was a sharp one alright, aware of his test and not taking the bait.

"What was that?" Lance asked as he reemerged, closing the door behind him.

Lance watched as she bit her lip nervously. Her cheeks flushed with mortification he'd heard her. "Nothing."

"No, I don't play fair. Never have. You did well. Other people I've had over haven't been so restrained." Lance teased, recalling that Dana had followed after him. He'd wanted her to Lance was able to admit now. It was a comfort to him that Catharine had not done so. It told him she respected his privacy. While she may be there to observe his day to day life; she wasn't looking to intrude where unwanted.

"You told me to stay out. I will unless you invite me in," Catharine stated. She followed him back out to the dining room. Lance unwrapped the object hidden beneath the black silk. The strange disk was about the size of a small dinner plate. In the center was a white crystalline circle. The top was divided into four unique sections.

As they looked upon the detail of it Lance felt a chill, he watched as goose bumps rose on Catharine's arms. Good, she understood what he meant earlier.

It felt as if some dark secret lay sleeping within its markings, something that if they touched it might awaken.

"It feels cursed," she whispered. Lance watched as her eyes ran over the section nearest the center. He saw a spark of recognition. "Hey, it's out of line," she muttered with surprise.

"What do you mean?" Lance questioned. Wondering what she was looking at.

"The ring near the center, it looks like it should be depicting star constellations but they don't line up right."

"Really?"

"Yeah, here I'll show you. This first grouping at the top is similar to that of Orion the hunter but the stars that create the belt aren't lined up right. Under it is Cassiopeia only the 'w' is broken. Then at the bottom you got the big dipper. Polaris the North Star is in the wrong place."

Her finger brushed the star in question. They watched with disbelief as the images faded and reappeared, the constellations lining up as she explained. Polaris taking its proper, place at the top. They heard a sound similar to that of tumblers lining up in a lock, a moment before the band separated from the disk falling within to reveal more of the crystal beneath. Catharine unable to resist reached in, pulled the loose piece out. It looked now like a strange bracelet.

"I told you not to touch that thing. Anna doesn't even know what it is."

"I'm sorry I didn't mean to. Not originally any way. It feels different now that it's separate from the rest."

"How so?"

"It's safe, like defusing a trap maybe."

"Weird."

"Here take it," Catharine said. She placed the ring in his hand. He held it, noted the weight of it was less than he'd figured. The ring felt clean now for lack of a better word. He studied the series of dots. It now depicted them exactly as she'd described them.

"How did you know what it was?"

"I did some research for Heart of Stone because Serenity as the vampire used the stars to prophecy for the vampire lord. It stuck with me I guess."

Lance nodded before giving her back the ring. He covered the rest of the disk with the silk. "I think I better put this thing up."

"Shouldn't you take this with it?"

"No, it should be kept separate from the rest."

"Why?"

"If it's safe now, then it should stay that way."

"Okay."

"I'll put this up so that it's out of harm's way then we'll decide what to do with the rest." Lance stated and he rose from the table.

Catharine nodded. Lance made his way to the back of the house once again this time alone.

When Lance reemerged he was in better spirits. Talking with Catharine had helped him to distance his thoughts from the past. He studied his house guest from the doorway noted she was studying him. He wondered what she saw when she looked at him. Was he as easy to read as Miss Walsh had been? Had she seen the defeat he'd felt earlier, the sense of guilt and failure? Would she sort it out in that questioning mind of hers? Connect it to the photo she'd seen earlier.

Lance crossed the room to stand behind her chair. He looked down at her. Worry lines creased her brow. "What are you thinking about?"

Catharine opened her mouth to answer but her phone rang interrupting her. She pulled the offending object from her pocket, muttered an oath. "I'm sorry, I have to take this," she murmured before pressing the button to answer the call.

"Hello again, Bryan." Lance stiffened behind her at the mention of the name. He was really starting to dislike the guy.

"I didn't think I'd hear from you for a few days." she said her voice hinted at genuine surprise.

Lance made a mental note of it. Apparently she and Bryan argued often enough to have a set pattern of behavior. He was breaking pattern. Why?

"What's up?"

Was that anxiety in her voice? Lance cursed and wished he could hear what the publicist was saying.

"Why?" Catharine asked. Her voice conveyed heat and annoyance. Her back stiffened a sign of growing temper. Wanting her to relax Lance took her shoulders in his hands and gave a supportive squeeze. "Bryan…" Protest there. She didn't like what was being said.

"All right, fine. I'm on the first flight out." Catharine said her voice resigned. Lance cursed that didn't sound good at all.

"Right, we'll talk about it tomorrow when I get in. Bye." She mashed the button to disconnect the call and blew out a breath. "I have to get back to LA."

Lance let his hands drop away from her. "Why?"

"Apparently the film hit big. James Hardagen is throwing a party in its honor. I have to be there or the publishing house will bury my new book. I can't have that. I need to step away from Serenity. That book is my chance."

Lance nodded. He felt the room around him grow cold. Memories he'd managed to bury creeping in around him.

"I'm sorry. It looks like my visit will have to be cut short."

"Too bad, I was just getting used to having you around." He gave a half hearted laugh.

Catharine rose from her chair, turned in the direction of the guest room. Lance blinked startled to find himself face to face with her. He wanted to look away afraid of what she might see. He watched as blue eyes widened with alarm. For a moment she looked like a deer caught in the headlights of an oncoming car. Afraid of him Lance realized. Damn he hadn't wanted that from her, not fear. Lance reached out to touch her but Catharine looked away from him. He wondered what she had seen there.

"Here you should take this. I have to go pack."

Lance cursed noting she had changed the subject. Was breaking contact with him, looking for an easy escape. He struggled to maintain calm as the past closed in around him; threatening to devour him. A voice in his head he'd not heard in months whispered that she was leaving and she wouldn't be back. He'd never see her again just like Dana. Lance seeking to silence the voice closed her fingers around it. "Why don't you keep it? You can return it to me when you come back."

Catharine smiled. "It may be a while. Filming for Heart of Clay will begin later this week. I'm consulting."

"Oh." Lance's good mood began to fall as he calculated how long that would take. At least a year from what he knew of the movie making process. He didn't like it. The voice whispered; I told you so. He ignored it. Lance realized it was more than being alone with his past he didn't care for. It was the whole thing.

Something was wrong.

His instincts were humming with warning. They had been since the phone rang. He'd been too distracted to recognize it. If she went something bad lay ahead of her. He felt it as clearly as he'd ever felt anything.

"Catharine don't go. I. something..." He stammered looking for the words but could find none.

"I have too," she stated simply. Catharine gave him a light brush of her lips in goodbye. As her lips met his Lance felt fear grip him. He didn't want her to go. He dreaded to be left alone with the ghosts of his past the photos had managed to awaken, more than that he worried for her safety.

Lance took her face in his hands his fingers sliding into her red tresses and kissed her. The meeting was slow and deep drawing her in, demanding nothing, but inviting her to take more.

94

Catharine felt desire spark, yet brushed it aside. She couldn't linger as much as she'd like to; it was a bad idea. This was not the time to be bold and brash; caution was needed. Something had shifted since their meet with Miss Walsh. The photos had changed him somehow from cool and in control to emotional and unstable.

A storm was building in him; one she wasn't willing to face. She could feel it within him threatening to break. If she let him he would use her to drive it back. She'd walked this road before in her youth and she wouldn't walk it again. She needed to go slow here she told herself ending the kiss.

"Too soon?" he questioned before his lips touched her forehead.

"Maybe a little."

"I'm…"

"No need for apologies, Lance it's just bad timing," she assured him. Her thoughts turned to the scene in the ball room. She wasn't comfortable with playing rebound to Miss Gallagher.

"Right."

"Look, I know we just met, but I'd like to know where this thing between us is going. So, if you get a chance why don't you come out to LA to visit me?"

"Catharine…"

She put a finger to his lips interrupting him. "No promises need be made. I'd just like to see you again before the film is done."

He nodded and she moved on to get her things.

95 Las Vegas, Nevada

Pamela smiled as she stared at the front page of the entertainment section. The image depicted CJ Nichols presenting the prize for the Heart's Escape to Miss Anna Gallagher. Sitting next to Anna's empty chair as her guest was Pamela's ex-husband Sam Abrams. "Where did you two meet and how?" Pamela murmured as she set the page aside. She studied the good doctor's image with scrutiny; Anna was blonde and leggy with a golden tan. The doctor was pretty in the girl next door sort of way. She wondered what Sam thought of her and dismissed the question. It didn't matter she reasoned. Even if he'd gotten mixed up with the skirt he wouldn't be for long.

While she was at the airport Pamela did some checking. Sam's name hadn't been on any flight out of DC that would take him to Israel. He'd not been on a plane out of DC period. Yet she had credit records that said he was in Jerusalem. It could only mean one thing a private plane.

Sam couldn't afford that. Neither could Miss Gallagher, but she was willing to bet CJ Nichols could, which meant whatever was going on the author who missed her premier and then book signing in Vegas was in it up to her neck. She'd swing by Sam's Gym in the morning; turn over the paperwork for the book deal. Ask about Miss Gallagher there. She had enough now to take the story to her boss.

Punching in his number Pamela sat and waited for him to pick up, her thoughts running wild as it rang. If things went well she'd be on the next flight out of the US to Israel, hot on the trail of her ex-husband and the elusive Dr. Anna Gallagher. With a little luck she'd soon learn what it was that Sam was chasing. Scoop him on it. She'd be able to get out of the dead end job being with him had landed her in.

"Hello."

"Mr. Blake its Pamela."

"Ah, Miss Walsh, so good of you to call. I trust you're on your way back to cover the gala at Mr. Hardagen's tomorrow?"

"Actually sir I'm still in Vegas. I've got the makings of a story here."

"I'm listening. It had better be good."

Pamela walked him through it step by step connecting it from one person to the next involved. When she finished the phone was silent.

"It's got potential; you can look into it further after the party."

"Thank you, sir." Pamela said. She gave him assurances that he'd not be disappointed before ending the call. She grabbed her bag, leaving for the airport. Just a quick hop back to LA then she was free to chase down the story.

96 Dead Sea Tuesday 11am

Sam made his way to where the statues loomed over the raised table. "As I studied the images earlier with Dr. Gallagher I noted the space behind them was wide enough for a single person to walk through. I asked her about it. We explored the space. If you'll follow me I'll show you what we found." Switching on a flashlight he led both Anna and Dr. Ian Broody behind the statues to the center where Chaos and Hecate embraced. His light illuminated a small door.

"Amazing," Ian exclaimed with delight. Sam stepped through the door, his light revealed stairs leading down. Ian switched on a second light. In single file the trio started down the steps.

They were steep and narrow and came to an abrupt end in a small chamber beneath the temple. The floor here was split open and charred, showing evidence of the city's fall long before. Sam let the light run over the room showing Dr. Broody the dimensions of the chamber first then allowed his light to settle on the small black chest marked with the image of a palm.

Ian crossed the floor to it and lifted the lid. He shone his light inside. He gasped at the sight of the earthen tablets it held.

"Cuneiform, hidden writings – oh this is great." He breathed and looked over at Anna. She gave a nod with a subtle smile. Ian grinned; it seemed Anna's temper had cooled since last they spoke. Maybe there was still a chance the lovely and brilliant lady would forgive him? Deciding that time would tell Ian turned his attention back to the tablets. "Perhaps here are the answers to the inconsistencies of the temples. Maybe even more," Ian whispered.

He knelt beside the chest to look. Yes it was here he could feel it now the voice in his mind whispered it. He had to be the one to study it. Ian looked up from the stones at the pair in the room. He couldn't let Anna see this knowledge. She'd hidden something already. He wouldn't allow her to keep these secrets from him as well. He had to think of a means to keep her away from the tablets. His mind turning with possibilities Ian turned his focus back to his prize.

97

Anna trembled at the sight of Ian kneeling there. She'd seen the look that had passed over his face when he glanced back at them. He was like a covetous miser his fist clinching tight around a prized treasure to protect it from any who would try to come near it. Anger and distrust – when had he become so cold.

Ian had always desired knowledge it was one of the few things they'd had in common. Why, they'd even hit it off once upon a time. His desire for fame had far outweighed his love and loyalty, a fact that still cut into her heart deep and left anger bubbling beneath the surface of her cool exterior.

He'd cut her out of the academic picture once to feed his desire for fame and glory. Destroying her notes and obliterating over a year's worth of research and devotion. The look in his eyes told her he'd do it again and more. Something had shifted in him. The smile she'd given him in understanding at his excitement over the discovery faded.

This man was not the one she'd come to care for. Something dark stirred with in him. A beast that had only grown stronger Anna drew her focus from the man to the room itself and her stomach churned at the site of him kneeling before the open chest, only hours earlier she'd done the same. It struck her now how much like an altar the chest looked. His posture and wonder appeared as worship. Maybe she did give her devotion to the god of knowledge, perhaps she shouldn't.

"Anna, my dear, you've more than proven your point. A pair of fresh eyes was exactly what we needed on the site. You and Mr. Abrams head back to the hotel and rest up."

"Why?" Sam questioned.

Anna glanced at her watch and noted it wasn't even noon.

"Tomorrow I'm putting you on the first flight I can get you to the main dig site. There is still much to learn there. Perhaps you will be able to unlock its secrets where the rest of us have failed."

"We'll do our best," Anna assured him. The pair then made their way back out of the chamber into the daylight.

"I know you will," Ian said to the empty room. Anna turned having heard him she looked back. Ian was once more looking at the chest. He'd lifted the first of the tablets from the box reading it. Anna sighed, turning her attention from the scene toward the light of Sam's flashlight. She was grateful when they stepped out into the daylight once more.

98

Sam stood by the window of his hotel suite staring out at the gardens below. He saw none of it. His mind was far from the stunning display of color and green in the midst of the busy city. He was still in the dark chamber under the earth near the Dead Sea, he'd discovered earlier that morning. He'd seen something there other than the tablets that bothered him. Something had passed between Dr. Ian Broody and Anna in that room he didn't understand. The good doctor had looked at her with excitement, one she'd shared. She'd given him a nod and then a ghost of a smile. They'd spoken without words – understood each other, been close for that moment. Sam didn't like it.

"Rather than take you to Gomorrah I thought I'd show you my research notes like you asked. We can rest up as Dr. Broody suggested." Anna stated as she entered the room through the adjoining door.

Sam turned from the city to look at her. The shorts and tank from the dig site had been replaced by a simple green cotton sundress. Her blonde hair hung free still damp from her shower. She looked better now. Something had happened at the dig though; what he didn't know. Moving his focus from Anna herself he noted she stood next to a pile of journals and photos stacked neatly upon the small table set in the room for either work or dining.

"You knew if we showed him the chamber he'd send us to Atlantis. How?"

"I don't know. I saw something in him that I know in me. He needs to keep whatever is in those tablets to himself."

"What makes you say that?"

"I felt the same desire to conceal them when we found them."

"Why the need to keep it?"

"I don't know, I've never been one to keep knowledge from

others but ever since Atlantis I feel this compulsion to keep things to myself."

"When did it start?"

"It started with the disk but that wasn't the same; something in me said it was dangerous, needed to remain hidden. This is something else."

"What do you mean?"

"It's like a hunger that gnaws in the back of my mind. It wants to devour all knowledge and keep it for me alone. I feel the need to wield it like some sort of weapon."

"When did you first feel it?"

"I don't know. I guess… wait after I found the statues at Atlantis. It was then I started to keep my observations to myself. That was also when I started to notice odd things going on at the dig. It was like my eyes became open. I could see things that had been hidden from me."

"Perhaps it's not you pushing to hide things; seeing more. Perhaps it's your unwanted dream visitor." Sam suggested.

Anna blinked uneasy with the thought then she went cold. "I don't believe in that sort of thing Mr. Abrams."

Sam repressed a curse. Anna was gone. Dr. Gallagher was back. Why did she always revert back to this icy prim and proper professional? Where did it come from? "Yes, you do Anna, you're seeing it the same as I am. Why is it so hard for you to admit it?"

Anna ignored the question, instead she changed the subject steering it back to the original discussion. "I figured the easiest way for Ian to keep the information of the tablets hidden is to send anyone with a claim to them away. He won't want us at Gomorrah looking to see if there is a similar chamber there. He had no choice but to send us to Atlantis."

Sam felt his temper flare. She'd called him Ian. Oh yeah, there was definitely something there between them. Miss prim and proper had used his first name implying a closeness to him they didn't share; Sam repressed a curse. "Makes sense but you didn't answer my question and now I've got another who is Ian Broody to you."

Anna blinked; her hazel eyes darkened with a flash of temper all her own. "Your question Mr. Abrams has nothing to do with why you are here."

"If you think I'm here for a story Anna you're mistaken." Sam crossed the floor to the table where she stood. He eyed the stack of her notes, lifted them from the table. "This is not why I came." Sam stated. He set the stack in her hands. Turned her around and gave her a push back towards her room.

99

Anna stood rooted to the floor, her head spinning. What was he saying? What had he just done? Why? What was happening here? She heard him curse and a moment later felt his hand at her back.

He was throwing her out. Anna dropped her notes and her hands grabbed hold of the door frame. "If you're not here for the story then why the hell did you come?"

Sam laughed behind her. Anna's back straightened as anger began to sweep over her. She hated being laughed at. Her mother always laughed at her when Anna made a suggestion that she found absurd.

She'd laughed when Anna told her she'd landed the lead role in the school play, she laughed when Anna said she wanted to be an archeologist, she even laughed when Anna told her she'd called off the engagement to Ian because he'd cheated her out of her career. Anna was sick of being laughed at.

She turned to face him her hazel eyes lit with anger. Blue widened with alarm and shock.

"Easy doc, I'm not laughing at you."

Anna felt her anger die out in an instant. She really needed to stop over reacting around him. His gaze played over her face seeking the cause of her reaction. Anna turned from his stare, afraid he'd see right through her. She looked down to the mess on the floor.

"Oh shit," she grumbled then knelt down to collect her work. Anna heard the rustle of loose sheets of paper. Aware Sam was helping to gather the scattered pages. He took her pile from her arms without a word. Set the work on the table. Then took her by the hand and drew her to her feet. He brushed a few strands of her blonde hair away from her eyes.

"I came to make sure you stayed safe." He whispered.

100

Sam felt Anna's skin grow warm under his touch. He drew a breath and repressed an oath. Damn he still had questions he wanted answers to. Now was not the time to get distracted. Her eyelashes lowered, hiding hazel eyes, which had gone to a pale green, from him. Cheeks flushed with color as she turned away from his touch.

"Sam…"

He didn't know what she was about to say nor did he care. There were still things to be said between them but it could wait. She'd said his name. Not Mr. Abrams but Sam. Something had shifted inside her allowing him past the icy walls; he wasn't about to waste the moment with words.

Sam's lips met with hers. He kissed her. Slow and gentle with great care, knowing if he pushed her too hard or went to fast she would run from him spooked. Sam felt her initial jolt of alarm and then she melted into him, giving up control before she kissed him.

Sam fought to rein in his desire as Anna kissed him back. There was more here than he'd thought. The icy exterior was gone – underneath it was fire. He felt her heart race and his own answer. Her body yielded to his touch as her lips demanded he give her more. Sam groaned with understanding and disbelief. She wanted him.

He'd been here before with Pamela, let the fire consume them both and to hell with the consequences, it had led to hurt and betrayal. He would not rush here – not with Anna.

Sam ended the kiss abruptly. He took a seat at the table his legs shaky. He fought to steady his breathing, quiet the storm they'd awoken. He watched as Anna opened her eyes. The jade green had become a deep blue. She drew a couple deep breaths. Questions etched her brow and worry. Sam cursed already regretting his choice.

"Why don't you go lie down and rest for a bit. I'll look over this.

If I have any questions I'll ask you when you wake."

Anna nodded then turned to go. "It's hard for me because that's not how I was raised. I was brought up to seek for knowledge and facts. If I can't see it, touch it, prove it then it's not real and unworthy of my time." She said before closing the door.

Sam drew a breath and sighed. It explained a lot. She hadn't answered the other question but Sam didn't push. After all there were things he wasn't telling her either. Sam gave her a silent thank you then turned his attention to her notes.

101

LAS ANGELES, CALIFORNIA

"Good evening America. Greetings to you from the city of Angels. Tonight former heart throb James Hardagen has opened the doors of his LA mansion to his friends and peers. They are celebrating the success of Heart of Glass's opening weekend. He's given us an exclusive peek of the night's festivities. We'll be checking in with you throughout the night with the highlights."

"We're clear. Nice take Pamela. Let's head inside and see what we can get."

Pamela nodded. Together she and Mina made their way past the gates into the luxurious home of their host.

Once inside Pamela surveyed the scene. The guest turnout was larger than she'd anticipated; it seemed that James Hardagen's success with the new picture had managed to ingratiate him with his peers.

Where was there host? Pamela's eyes gleamed as she spotted him and Emily on the 2nd floor landing. She called out the shot to her assistant and laughed as they caught an image of James brushing a kiss on Emily's throat. He nipped playfully, eliciting a gasp. Pamela chuckled, oh yeah, pay dirt – Mr. Blake would be thrilled. Images of the couple together were few and far between.

Pamela heard various voices begin to murmur about the arrival of their host. The spotlight from the camera crew moved to him. James smiled. The room fell slowly from idle chatter to a hushed silence.

"Good evening ladies, gentleman, and distinguished guests. Emily and I are thrilled you could make it for our celebration this evening. We trust you will make yourselves at home. Enjoy the festivities."

"Mr. Hardagen is there any news regarding the rest of the Dark Heart Trilogy. Will we be seeing Heart of Clay on the big screen in the foreseeable future?" Pamela questioned.

"Yes, you will be. I will be playing the role of the Vampire Lord. I believe the author C. J. Nichols has graced us with her presence this evening. She will be consulting on the film which is set to begin production at the end of the week."

"Really? That fast?"

"Yes."

"One last question you and Emily have been practically inseparable since the announcement of Heart of Glass being made. Are things getting serious between you?"

"Now Pamela, be nice. Tonight isn't about me it's about the film. Give me a call. We'll arrange a more private interview at another time."

"Thank you for your time James, and congratulations," Pamela said ending the interview. She laughed with delight as James kissed Emily on camera again.

102

Catharine moved through the vast crowd in the direction of the pool. She needed a couple minutes to gather her thoughts before she took her turn in front of the camera. Bryan hadn't mentioned anything about James playing the Vampire Lord. She shrugged, it didn't matter he had the general look. Catharine had no doubt he'd do just fine in the role. Still she didn't care for surprises.

Bryan had been waiting at the hotel when she arrived just as he'd said. They'd spent a good three hours going over publicity for tonight. She'd managed to talk him out of having to wear the dress from the Serenity Ball. It was a good thing too. Her version paled in comparison to Emily's. She'd come instead dressed like the lead heroine for Heart of Clay, the surrogate mother of Serenity's daughter.

"There she is C. J. Nichols."

Catharine turned, smiled even as she repressed a curse. Pamela Walsh. Didn't she just get around?

"Good evening Pamela."

"Out by the pool we've caught up with the author of the Dark Heart Trilogy the lovely C. J. Nichols. Miss Nichols, and I recently met; it was a brief encounter in Washington DC where she was doing research for a new book. She is dressed in an ankle length elegant blue upper class Grecian toga. Her red hair swept up in an up-dew like a fan. Dressed like the heroine from Heart of Clay I believe."

"That's correct."

"So, C.J., are you excited at the news that Heart of Clay will begin filming at the end of the week?"

"Yes, I'm looking forward to helping Mr. Hardagen bring the book to life on the big screen. The publishing house is thrilled as well. As you know I Just held the Serenity Ball in Los Vegas at

Caesar's Palace in honor of our contest winner. Upon learning the news we've decided to bring out another contest for Heart of Clay. We're discussing it at the moment; it's in the works for a castle escape."

"Oh wow that sounds fabulous."

"I imagine it will be. We'll keep you posted on it."

"C.J., is it true that some of the content in the series is being changed for the films?"

"Yes."

"Why?"

"Translating a book to film you lose things so we've made additions, removed things to make it more suitable for the big screen."

"Readers I understand have been begging for a fourth book to the Dark Heart series is there any chance we may see another book."

"No, based on the world I created there's nowhere else to go."

"I see. Well, congratulations on the series and its newfound success."

"Thank you," Catharine said.

"You're clear Pamela. Nice job."

"Thanks Mina. Can you give us a minute?" Pamela asked.

"Sure, see you back inside." Mina answered before she moved on.

Once her associate was gone Pamela spoke. "Off the record?"

"Yes?" Catharine questioned.

"Did you loan your private jet to Dr. Anna Gallagher and my ex-husband Sam Abrams?"

Catharine cursed realizing Miss Walsh would only be asking off the record if she already knew it to be true. "Yes."

"Why?"

"Anna was my contest winner. She was in trouble, needed to disappear. The best way was to take a flight that couldn't be tracked."

"What is your relationship with Lance Roman?"

"Is this also off the record?"

"Of course."

"He's an acquaintance. I met him in Vegas. I asked to observe his life. I do that every once in awhile to get inside a characters mind."

"Do you know why Anna went back to Israel?"

"I don't know where Anna and your ex were headed or why. Whatever they are up to I am no longer involved in it. I'll be busy here with the film for some time."

"I see. Thank you again for your time."

"You're welcome, Good evening Miss Walsh." Catharine said.

She made her way back into the house; it was time she met her host.

As she stepped into the main hall she found herself faced with him and Emily. They appeared to be looking to get away from the crowd. “Mr. Hardagen. Do you have a moment?

“Of course.” He replied. His blue eyes focused on her and she saw recognition. “Miss Nichols?”

“Yes. I’m sorry to intrude Mr. Hardagen. I won’t take up to much of your time. I thought it was time we met. First I want to apologize for missing the big premier.”

“Please, call me James. No need for apologies we artists are always busy. I imagine you’ve been working hard on both the changes for the script and your new book.”

“I have, thank you for understanding. The publishing house hasn’t been so forgiving.”

“I can believe it. As bad as an over eager agent is; I’d think all they see are the dollar signs. They can’t respect the work involved in the craft,” James said his voice held sympathy.

“Yes,” Catharine said pleased someone understood. Her gaze moved to the woman at his side. Her brown eyes flickered with a hint of jealousy. “I take it you would be Emily. You look lovely, Serenity would be jealous.”

“Oh thank you. Wow. I can’t believe it’s you. I read the series – absolutely loved it. I actually suggested James pick up the script.”

“Really?”

“Yes, Serenity and Rachel are both amazing. I hope the changes you’re working add to them.”

“They will,” Catharine assured her. Worried she was about to get caught up in yet another question session by a crazed fan who wanted Serenity to find her happy ending.

“Can you tell me…”

“Nope I’m not discussing the changes or how they affect Serenity.” Catharine said interrupting her.

“Okay.”

“Sorry I didn’t mean to be rude. I just get asked about Serenity all the time. I was hoping to enjoy myself this evening.” Catharine said realizing she might have just insulted the boss’s girl. Not a good career move.

“It’s okay I think I can understand. It’s like the fan that talks to you like you’re their favorite character,” Emily said with a laugh.

“You could say that,” Catharine agreed.

“I like her James. We’ll have to have her over for drinks or something.”

“A delightful idea. What do you say C. J.?” James whispered.

“Sure. Drinks sound nice. Maybe we can discuss the film.” Catharine answered.

“Sounds good,” James said with a smile. He couldn’t wait to speak with her again without the crowds.

“Oh. If you were looking to get away from prying eyes you may want to wait a few. Pamela Walsh was out there a moment ago.”

“Thanks for the warning enjoy the party,” James said. He led Emily outside anyway.

103

Pamela made her way back through the crowd to Mina who was getting a couple quick shots of the crowd.

"I think we've got what we need," Pamela commented.

"Yeah, I think you're right. It'll make for a good show, Mr. Blake should be happy."

"I don't know if he told you but I'll be off on assignment." Pamela said as they made their way toward the exit.

"Yeah he's got me working with Chuck. Eww. Are you sure you can't use an assistant?"

"I'd take you with me Mina, but I don't think Mr. Blake will foot the expense for two tickets to Israel."

"Israel. What's in Israel?"

"I'm not sure yet. The moment I know enough to warrant help I'll send for you," Pamela promised.

"Thanks. Good luck."

"You too Mina, don't let Chuck push you around." Pamela said before they got in their own vehicles, driving off into the night. One headed for the studio the other for the airport and what she hoped was her ticket out of LA permanently.

104

ATLANTIS, SOMEWHERE IN THE BERMUDA TRIANGLE
WEDNESDAY
8AM

I can't believe we're in the Bermuda Triangle this is crazy." Sam muttered.

Anna laughed. Yes, it was crazy. For more reasons than he could possibly understand. As she led him through security she hoped she wasn't tempting fate by coming back. Anna sighed, pressed her fingers against her temples. She didn't believe in fate. Damn it what was happening to her. She could normally keep her head out of the clouds. Why was she struggling with it now? It was because deep down she knew that the ground she stood on was evil.

"You okay?" Sam asked as they made their way toward the crumbling walls in the distance.

"Yeah, just a little edgy, this place…"

"Feels wrong," he breathed it. She nodded. Sam took her hand and gave it a reassuring squeeze.

"Yes, I'm glad to know it's not just me that thinks it."

"Sodom felt strange but less pronounced." As he drew near the walls it grew stronger. "This whole place says go away," Sam whispered. They came to what had once been the gateway. He noted it was twice as wide as the one at Sodom and twice as high.

"It's weird a lot of the men on the dig have said that. For me it's different."

"What do you mean?"

"Well, the place fascinates me I'm drawn to something here. Yet I'm afraid of it. I feel like I'm walking into a cage. Any minute someone is going to close the door."

"Maybe men weren't allowed here," Sam suggested.

"Interesting, thought, but why?" Anna asked.

"Don't know perhaps we'll find the answers out there," Sam stated. He pointed at the ruins of the city.

Anna nodded. They crossed the threshold into the dig site. She began to explain what she knew. “This place is different. I’m not even sure you can call it a city. Since it doesn’t feature mass housing or even the kind of basic things you would expect to find in a city. Like a market or stables. It holds five large dwellings in the main part and a temple. Well start there.”

Sam nodded, following her into the center of the city. The temple sat in the heart of the ruins. A small stone path lead over a bridge, up crumbling steps into the broken structure. Pillars had fallen. They were overgrown by seaweed and barnacles. Giving testament to the fact the city had once been beneath the sea. The sunlight illuminated the chamber to reveal a glimpse of the past. It did not open into a great chamber as the temple in Sodom; instead it was a small chamber. On either wall facing east or west there were large stone tables over-looking them were the images of Poseidon, Helios, Zeus and Chaos.

“What did you find in here with the tables?” Sam questioned.

“A pair of scales for measuring, broken vases. We think the chamber was a place to pay tribute to the gods, for the provision of things like water and grain.” Anna replied.

Sam nodded, following her through the doorway into a vast chamber with a great table. Within, ten statues of the gods stood overlooking the table. Their hands were open to accept some unknown gift. Unlike the other statues, these depicted each one represented with wings. “It looks like a banquet hall,” Sam muttered. The images in the room felt foreign and strange here.

“I believe it was. This was the heart of this temple. The ones who came here were encouraged to eat drink and make merry, perhaps to comfort them after paying tribute or to prepare them for it.” Anna speculated.

“Why do you say that?” Sam asked curious.

“Well, the chamber directly behind us looks similar to that of the one in Sodom. The raised stone table being looked upon by the gods. Only it’s not all of them Eros, Dionysus, Zeus and Chaos are the ones watching.”

“Doesn’t sound so horrible. What about the other two?”

“The one to my left is a library; Hermes, Chaos and Erebus are looking down on it. The chamber to the right is grim. There is a huge fire pit. We found branding irons, jewelry pieces, and human bones. I believe it was a chamber of pain and murder. The images looking in on the act there are Ares, Hades, Hephaestus, Chaos and Erebus.”

“Lovely.”

“Yes.”

"This room feels weird to me."

"How so?"

"I don't know. It's just that in the other rooms the images of the gods match with the ones at Sodom; they're carved in the walls to look at the scene. These aren't. Why? It's almost like they don't belong here."

Anna blinked the thought had never occurred to her. But he was right. They were out of place. She recalled the dating in the chamber. The statues were older than the rest. She felt a tremor of fear as understanding dawned. "They don't."

"I could be wrong," Sam admitted.

"Wrong about what?" A female voice questioned from behind them. Anna cursed. Both she and Sam turned to face the newcomer.

The woman behind them had long raven black hair which she pulled up into a high tight pony tail. Her brown eyes studied Sam with question. "Really Annalynn, Darcy, Gallagher, such language I'm surprised."

"Sam, this is Zaharrah Lynch our competition."

"I see you're still not big on sharing a dig Anna. I guess you'd be disappointed to learn of my find then."

"What find?" Anna asked worried that Zaharrah had found the throne room.

"A candle, it was in a chest in the northern palace in the main wall. I hear you found a chamber and a disk of some sort. Odd that it was not mentioned in your notes. It's not like you Anna to hide things."

"I wasn't concealing it. They ran me out of the dig before I could report the discovery." Anna explained. It wasn't entirely true but it was close enough.

"I see."

"How are you handling all the security here? I know it's tighter than your previous digs. Not so easy to walk off with something as you're used to."

Zaharrah laughed "Still upset about Ithaca, Anna? Security here hasn't bothered me."

"You haven't noticed anything weird going on around the site have you?" Anna asked casually. Zaharrah might be irritating but she was observant, might have seen something while she was gone.

"If I have I've learned how not to draw attention to what I see."

"Right, look out for your own interest rather than the museums. You were always good at that." Anna said disgusted.

"I see that I've worn out my welcome so I'll move on. Good day,

Sam was it?"

"Yeah," Sam said. Anna watched as the other woman moved into the library.

"Perfect," Anna muttered annoyed.

"Easy doc. Why the hostility? I get she's competition but that doesn't explain the anger your radiating?" Sam teased.

"She's a troublesome tomb raider. Who seems to enjoy upstaging me. We met on my last dig in Ithaca. I put in a year there with Dr. Broody. While we were there an artifact was stolen among other things. I was working on sorting out by whom when in walks Miss Lynch with the artifact. She'd recovered it and, from a guy not on my short list, made me look like a complete idiot in front of my peers." Anna said with a sigh.

"Hence the animosity. What else was stolen?"

"My career," Anna muttered bitterly.

"What's that mean?"

"Nothing, forget it," Anna said with disgust. She wasn't ready to talk to him about Ian just yet she was still embarrassed – she'd been so blind.

"Did you know you look beautiful when you're angry?" Sam asked.

Anna glared at him and then laughed. "No, I didn't, I've never seen myself mad. Come on Romeo let's get moving before she comes back," Anna muttered. She led him to the opposite corner of the chamber, shifted a floor tile with care, revealing a hole and led him into the dark below.

105

When Anna came to a halt it was in a room Sam knew all too well. The black crystalline throne sat at the top of the three steps at the center of the room. Behind it was the wall he knew held the lock for the disk shaped key Anna had left in Lance's care. What lay beyond the door he didn't know nor did he care to find out. Before the steps was a square slab of stone. To either side made of the same crystal was the same graven image of a winged individual, he looked like none of the others above. One looked down at the altar the other gazed upon the steps before the throne. The room was cool and uninviting –evil.

Anna approached the steps sitting down in the center of the first. "I found the disk here, imbedded in the step it just came out as I was brushing it clean."

Sam noted the impression in the step. "It looked like a seal or signet I'd imagine."

"Yes. I think the statues came from this room. They stood on these steps. That's what the image is looking at. The first keeps any visitors in line. The second makes sure the underlings mind their place."

"If your right then why aren't we looking at Zeus? I thought he was the king of the gods." Sam stated.

"He was, but here they are not gods they're the fallen," Anna whispered. As the words left her lips she felt the heat of fire coming from the altar. The present faded into nothing.

Anna coughed. The smell of smoke filled her nostrils. She blinked. Found the room had changed. She sat on the step leading to the throne. The room behind her was empty. A fire blazed in the stone altar. Torches were lit. The ten winged images sat upon the stairs. On the step beneath the throne on the left stood the image of Chaos. Ares was at his side. Beneath them stood Eros and Dionysus. Next came the image of Hermes. On the Right Zeus stood beside Hades. Below them were Poseidon and Helios. Opposite Hermes stood Hephaestus.

Each held out his hand waiting as if to receive a gift. "What is it they wait for?" Anna wondered. She rose to her feet. Looking back at the black crystal image she tried to place him.

"WE WAIT FOR SEVERAL THINGS MY LOVELY ANNA." A voice answered. His voice came from everywhere and nowhere. She turned and watched as the image of Hermes became flesh. His blue eyes gleamed with delight. "I'M SO HAPPY YOU MADE IT BACK MY DARLING LADY. I KNEW YOU WOULD. YOU'RE UNENDING QUEST FOR KNOWLEDGE AND FACTS, HAS BROUGHT YOU TO ME LIKE A MOTH TO THE FLAME. COME TAKE MY HAND. I'LL SHOW YOU THE CITY OF THE GODS," he murmured. She did as he bid her.

His touch was like ice. She shivered at it but still she allowed him to lead her from that dark chamber into the temple. They came into the hall of feasting. A banquet lay upon the table before her. Anna's stomach growled reminding her it had been hours since she ate. Hermes laughed.

"ANNA, MY LOVE, YOU MUST NOT NEGLECT YOUR NEEDS. EAT, DRINK AND REFRESH YOURSELF AT THE TABLE. THEN I WILL SHOW YOU MORE."

"Not so fast, do you think me a fool. I remember full well the consequences of doing as you bid. I'll not be tricked into the same fate as Persephone." Anna stated.

Hermes laughed again. "THERE IS MY CLEVER LADY. COME ANNA, I'LL SHOW YOU MY HOME," he whispered. Hermes led her out of the chamber of feasting into the northern chamber of the temple. What she saw within made her checks flush. Anna moved her gaze to the floor.

Hermes lifted her chin with his other hand, raising her gaze to see all within the chamber. "NO, MY SWEET. DON'T LOOK AWAY. YOU DESIRED TO KNOW THE PURPOSE OF THIS ALTAR NOW YOU SEE."

"I don't understand," Anna whispered as she looked upon the table. In the center of it a man and woman lay lost in the heat of their lust filled passions.

"THIS IS THE WORSHIP WE GODS COVET MOST – YOUR CARNAL DESIRES. NOTHING PLEASES US MORE." Hermes murmured. He skimmed a finger down the side of her neck.

Anna trembled at the icy touch. She gasped as the woman moaned with pleasure. She felt something in her stir. "We should leave," she whispered feeling wrong for watching, this was a private act.

"YOU KNOW HOW THEY FEEL MY PRECIOUS ONE. AFTER ALL YOU'VE FELT IT TOO. THAT THRILLING SHOCK TO THE SYSTEM AS YOUR FLESH WAKES WITH A DESIRE AND NEED YOU AREN'T EXPECTING; A STIRRING IN THE BLOOD THAT SETS YOUR HEART RACING, HEIGHTENS THE SENSES. I CAN GIVE YOU THAT AGAIN," Hermes whispered in her ear. His fingers slid across her collar bone, towards her heart.

Anna saw the image of herself locked in a kiss, recalled all too well what he spoke of, that sudden jolt of hunger, the sensation of wanting more – all – him. But it was wrong. Something about it played false in her mind. As the woman cried out in ecstasy Anna looked away from the couple, drew his hand away from her chest.

"NO NEED TO BE SHY ANNA. THEY CANNOT SEE US OR HEAR US. ONLY IF I DESIRE TO MAKE MYSELF KNOWN WOULD THEY NOTICE ME. EVEN THEN THEY WOULD BID ME WELCOME," Hermes whispered. He then took the hand that had brushed his aside and pressed it against his bare chest.

"I've seen enough of this places secrets. You said you would show me the city of the gods this is not it," Anna said drawing away from him.

Hermes nodded, led her out of the chamber into the daylight. They crossed the bridge side by side. Hermes wrapped his arm around her waist. Led her through the gardens and turned left. Anna's eyes widened with understanding; seeing each structure as it had once been in its time before it was destroyed.

"They are Palaces!"

"YES, ONE FOR EACH OF THE GODS. A HOME FOR US AND OUR BRIDES THIS IS OUR DWELLING PLACE AMONG HUMAN KIND. THE ONE AHEAD OF US IS MINE," he murmured as they rounded the corner to face the south.

"Yours?" Anna questioned surprised. She wasn't sure why maybe because of the position he held in myth. She'd figured he was not gifted with a palace of his own.

"YES. YOU FIND THAT DIFFICULT TO BELIEVE. DID YOU SEE THE LIBRARY IN THE TEMPLE?"

"Yes."

"THAT TOO IS MINE. ALL KNOWLEDGE THAT IS HIDDEN I HAVE. THE PRICE TO KNOW IT IS A HIGH ONE. THE TRIBUTE I ASK IS THE LIFE OF AN OFFSPRING DEDICATED TO MY SERVICE OR THE LIFE OF A DAUGHTER AS A BRIDE."

"But I thought…"

"MAKE NO MISTAKE ANNA I AM NOT THE SIMPLE MESSENGER THAT GREEK MYTH DEPICTS ME AS." Hermes stated. He led her through the threshold of his home.

"I never believed those myths anyway."

"I KNOW IT. BUT YOU DO BELIEVE IN ME. I WILL GIVE YOU THE KNOWLEDGE YOU SEEK WITH NO PRICE ATTACHED IF YOU WOULD CONSENT TO BE MY BRIDE," Hermes whispered. He led her into his chambers.

"I will not willingly give myself to you fallen one – you arrogant beast. Do you think that by showing me this face I simply forget the real one? That after what you did to me last time you brought me into this God forsaken dreamscape that I'm naive enough to let you lead me about like a prized mare. If you did then you're more foolish than many mortals I know." Anna said disgusted.

Hermes eyes glowed with fury. "YOU DARE CHALLENGE ME AGAIN PERHAPS YOU'RE THE FOOL." He spat before he drew her lips to his and took greedily.

Anna broke the kiss, pushing him away. "God help me I want no more to do with this dream or this fallen one." She shouted it. The sound echoed off the roof. It cracked and dust filled the air.

106

Sam held Anna close to him. He ran his finger through her hair. Whispered her name. His heart pounded. She stared back at him with vacant eyes. Cold and empty like the holes in a mask. She'd given no sign of being with him for some time. What had happened to her? One minute she'd been sitting on the step talking with him. The next she'd been gone. She trembled in his arms and her skin was like ice. Fear gripped him as he waited. The look on her face so similar to that of the one she'd had in the glimpse.

"Come on Anna snap out of it," he pleaded before brushing a kiss on her forehead.

"Sam," she gasped the name. Hazel eyes lit with recognition, meeting his worry filled blue ones.

"Thank God," he breathed as he hugged her tight. "What happened are you alright? What did he do?"

"I'm fine. Not sure really what happened. One minute I was here the next I was in the past alone. The statue of Hermes came to life. He showed me around the city as it once was. Offered me all knowledge if I consented to be his bride I refused him."

"Did he hurt you?" Sam asked. He drew back to look at her for any signs of torment, recalling the last time.

"No. I didn't defy him again. I learned my lesson last time just asked for help then I was back here," she assured him. "Are you okay?"

"I'm fine now. We should get you out of here," Sam said and he let her go. Getting to his feet he extended a hand to her, pulled her up off the step.

107

"Thanks," Anna whispered. She looked down at their hands still linked. It felt natural and right. She knew her parents would never approve of him but she didn't care.

What did they know of matters of the heart anyway? They'd been married well over thirty years and were miserable. What did they know of truth for that matter? They believed in a world, that if you could see and touch it then it was real. A world in which angels and gods were no more than myth and nonsense. Where the idea of a loving creator was fantasy and all existed by random chance. A dark thought she admitted. Especially when you knew that those gods no, fallen existed in the world.

She trembled at the thought of a world where the fallen roamed free. Taking what they pleased, demanding of mankind what they desired. A world with them on it but without God in existence to stop them as her parents believed. Her mind whispered a quick thank you to the Creator echoing Sam's.

"Are you sure you're okay?" Sam asked.

"I'm fine. Can you give me a minute?" Anna whispered.

Sam nodded and let go of her hand. He turned to go but seemed reluctant to leave her in that place alone. Fear etched his face a fear she didn't understand. Anna watched as he made his way back to the temple above. Once alone she looked up to the ceiling above her.

"God, I know that I've treated you with little respect over the years; that I've done wrong. Please forgive me. Your messenger said I had a choice: I could serve the god of Knowledge or I could serve you the Creator. I've made my choice. I will serve you. I believe that you are real and that what your word says is truth. I believe you sent your son Jesus to earth, to die for a lost and dying world – for me. I ask for him to come into my life. Teach me your truth."

Anna felt the cool of the chamber withdraw; the overwhelming, sense of, fear ease. Though the place was evil she need not fear it. Peace washed over her. "Thank you," she breathed. Flashlight in hand she made her way back to the main chamber of the temple above.

108

Sam leaned against the edge of the table his gaze fixed on the opening in the floor waiting for Anna to emerge. He worried he'd made a bad choice by letting her be alone in the chamber below. Every minute that passed he contemplated going back for her. When he'd made up his mind to do so he saw her. His blue eyes met hers. Searching them for any signs of distress and found none. He'd feared that when she came forth it would be with the same lifeless eyes from the vision. He was relieved to see they were not.

"Are you okay?" Sam asked noting something was different about her though what he wasn't sure.

Anna slid the tile back in place, rose to her feet. "Yeah, I'm fine, but you aren't. You haven't been since I woke up. What's wrong Sam? Will you tell me?" Anna asked. She crossed the floor to stand beside him.

"Yeah. Um, I'm not sure where to start," he said trying to gather his thoughts.

"Start at the beginning," Anna suggested.

Sam laughed and nodded. "When you said I should come I told you I needed to think. Well, while I was doing so our angelic friend dropped in on me; helped me to make my choice."

"How so?"

"He showed me a glimpse of the future if I let you come back here alone. What I saw scared me enough to get me on the plane over here. When you were dreaming you had these vacant lifeless eyes like in the vision. I got spooked. I was afraid that what I'd seen was happening."

"What did you see?"

"You with the disk, your mind not your own, you're following Hermes lead – open a door. He steps through and embraces you as his bride. While he holds you he releases your mind. It's too late you can do nothing to stop him. You're now his."

"Sam that won't happen. I was given a choice remember? I could serve Hermes or I can serve God…"

Sam looked away from her as fear gripped him tighter. "I know that but…"

"Look at me." Anna coaxed. She waited until he did so. "I've made my choice. My life will not be wasted serving some puffed up arrogant false god. Whatever power that room once held over me it's broken now. That possible future is gone." Anna assured him. She brushed his bangs out of his eyes. Sam took her hand in his then kissed it, before replacing it at her side. He felt his fears subside and kissed her brow.

Sam drew a breath to level out his system. "So, you mentioned Broody had found something. They sent you away. But you've never said what. Care to explain?" he asked getting back to business.

Anna laughed at the abrupt change of discussion. "Well, Mr. Abrams, I haven't said because as difficult as it is to accept the idea of gods roaming about what he found is far more unbelievable. Come I'll take you to where they found IT," she said. Anna headed in the direction of the northern chamber. It was the fastest route to the northern palace.

109

Sam stepped out into the daylight, crossed the narrow bridge. He followed Anna around the ruins of the northern palace inside the main wall.

"You called this place a city I thought you didn't know what it was."

"It is a city. This is the place on the earth the fallen called home – the city of the gods. The reason there are no signs of the goddesses here is because there are no goddesses. They were human women taken by the fallen as brides and were brought here. Each dwelling is a palace of one of the ten gods. A home for their so called brides and the unnatural children they spawned." Anna explained. The pair passed through the gate into the courtyard of the northern most palace.

Ahead a tent had been erected it buzzed with activity. Numerous people moved about, some with sketchpads, others with cameras and equipment. Anna brought Sam to the edge of the crowd. They looked down where the people worked with care to unearth the fossils.

Sam stared at the ancient bones with silent disbelief. He now understood why Anna referred to them as an IT. There in the ground lay the proof of the existence of monsters. He stared down at a massive reptilian head with its jaws agape. It lead into a long neck that could have been a dinosaur but the wing bones coming from the shoulder bones made it clear it was not. There was no mistaking the hauntingly draconic like features.

The beast's talon bones were wrapped around the front leg of what at first glance looked to be a lion until you noted the scorched wing bones, marking it as a griffon. The dragon's rear claws tore into the hind quarters of its combatant. The tail barbs sank into the hip bone of its rival. The dragon had not escaped unscathed; it bore claws where its underbody had once been and the massive jaws of the lion's mouth were agape around the serpentine neck bones. The two had battled here in the air. Neither had won. In the end it had concluded in a stalemate.

Sam marveled at the sight before him. No wonder Anna had felt the world needed to know about what she'd helped to discover. The implications were astounding. He watched as the paleontologists worked to unearth the remains. He noted a second group of scientists working at the bones already unearthed.

"What are they doing?" Sam questioned pointing at the second team.

"I don't know. I haven't seen them here before," Anna admitted. "It looks like they're taking some kind of samples."

"Dr. Gallagher, you and your assistant are not authorized to be here," Kedar Handal stated as he stepped in front of them barring their view.

"I should have clearance to see them," Anna said with disbelief.

"I'm sorry but you're not on my list you'll need to go now."

Sam nodded knowing it was unwise to rock the boat. They'd just gotten here and were for the moment free from the watchful eye of her employer – he wanted to keep it that way. "Come on Anna, it'll keep for now," he whispered. Sam took her by the shoulders and turned her from the site. He noted one of the scientists. A woman with long brown hair had turned from what she was doing to look at Anna.

"But…" Anna began in protest turning her head to look back.

"I'm sure it's just a misunderstanding, you can talk to Dr. Broody about it and clear it up." Sam assured her.

"You do that," Kedar muttered; his brown eyes gleamed with warning. He adjusted his jacket exposing the grip of his gun. Sam cursed. They were on dangerous ground here. Whatever Mr. York was after, it was among these remains. "Come on doc lets go," he murmured again giving her a gentle nudge in the direction of the gateway back into the heart of the city.

"Okay, we'll leave but when Ian gets back I'll be taking the matter up with him." Anna stated. Sam ignored the wave of jealousy that swept through him at Anna's use of Dr. Broody's first name. He'd deal with that later, for now he needed to put distance between them and the remains. Sam heard footsteps from behind and sighed. He didn't want to deal with Kedar just yet. He'd prefer to keep that little matter from occurring with Anna around. Deciding he wasn't going to be caught off guard again Sam stopped walking inside the gateway.

"A little protective of that find aren't they?" Sam muttered. He leaned against the stone his focus appeared to be on Anna but his senses looked beyond her back the way they came for their tail. Sam listened to the steps and dismissed the possibility of it being Mr. Handal; the sound of the footfalls were too light for a man of his size; someone else then, but who?

"Yes, it's been all secrets since they unearthed them. I don't get it. If you'd found proof that two of the beasts of myth were real wouldn't you be telling the world about it. I mean you're talking about the find of the century."

Sam blinked as the brunette scientist from the dig site approached them. Good, not a threat. He recalled the quick glance in Anna's direction. Perhaps she was an ally?

"It sure is but if you were doing something scientifically unethical you might be less eager to discuss it," the woman stated.

Anna turned to face the woman. "What do you mean?"

"I'm saying that they've got us gathering samples from the bones and a second source doing genetic tests."

"What?" Anna asked with disbelief. "You can't get DNA from fossilized bones."

The woman drew out a pack of cigarettes from her pocket, pulled one out and a lighter. She then put them away. "Look I told them I was grabbing a cigarette so I haven't got a lot of time." She stated before lighting the smoke, lifting it to her lips. She took a long draw then exhaled. "You're right DNA cannot be obtained from fossils. We found something else. From it we have been able to obtain samples from the dragon. They're still looking for the other."

"For what purpose?" Sam asked curious.

She took another long puff off the cigarette then dropped it on the ground, crushing it under her foot. "I can't talk about that here. We'll discuss it further later when I can get away. For now just watch your step."

"Can't you at least…" Anna began in protest.

"If they find out I've said anything to you my life is forfeit."

"Why risk speaking to us at all?" Sam asked.

"Dr. Gallagher discovered this place. She has a right to know what's going on here."

"Thank you doctor," Anna stated looking for a name.

"Dr. Silvers, you're welcome. I'll be in touch," she stated, her brown eyes sober before she turned; walking back through the northern gate.

Anna sighed “I hate being right.”

“Yeah, right now I wish you’d been wrong about something not legal going on here.”

“So do I Sam,” Anna muttered. “Come on let’s get back to the temple maybe some of the answers we’re looking for are there.” Sam nodded. The pair moved on.

110

Spotting Zaharrah in the back corner, Anna sighed as they stepped into the library. She had forgotten the tomb raider was in here working.

"On second thought let's just head back to the boat. We can go back to the room to review my notes and try to sort out our next step." Anna suggested not wanting another confrontation.

"Running away?" Zaharrah asked surprised.

"No, just tired," Anna stated feeling it.

"Not surprised from what I understand you've been bouncing around from place to place for about a week."

Anna blinked surprised by the note of sympathy in Zaharrah's voice. She opened her mouth to comment.

"Anna! Anna, where are you? I must tell you about the tablets," Ian Broody's voice carried through the temple interrupting her.

"I'm in the library," Anna answered. Wondering what had him back here so fast; in such a good mood. She watched as Zaharrah turned back to her text and sighed. She wasn't sure what she'd been planning to say to the other woman. It had slipped away. The moment had come to an end.

Anna watched as Dr. Broody stepped into the room with distrust. There was something in his eyes she didn't like.

"Here you are. I'm surprised to find you and Dr. Lynch in the same chamber."

"I figured that we could cover more ground if three of us worked at it." Anna said.

"True. I've been going over those tablets that Mr. Abrams discovered. They're very enlightening. It seems the reason the king's temple depicts all the gods but the city temples only ten is because the citizens viewed certain gods as light or dark. The people of

Sodom followed the dark side of the Pantheon while the people of Gomorrah served the light side."

"Makes sense," Anna whispered picturing it in her head.

"Anna, dear, where is the disk you found? Phillip told me about it. May I see it?"

Anna felt her skin grow cold; there was something in his voice that felt wrong. The look in his eye grew stronger. The beast within him seeking knowledge was still feeding. It was after something specific. "I don't have it with me Dr. Broody. I didn't want to risk it getting stolen. I left it in the states someplace safe." Anna admitted. She watched as temper flared in his gray eyes then cooled.

"I see. Good thinking. We'll make sure it gets here safely then as soon as possible. Where did you find it exactly?" Ian asked with interest.

"When I was working in the central chamber I found a piece of the floor tiling that was loose. I slid it aside, found a passage underneath that lead into a lower chamber. Mr. Abrams earlier today noted that the statues in the central chamber don't seem to fit the room. I now believe they came from this lower chamber."

"Really can you show me this room?"

"Sure. Mr. Abrams why don't you walk back to the boat? Head for the hotel and get some rest. No need to go through the chamber again."

"I don't mind walking through the room again. Besides if I leave now you'll be stuck here waiting for the boat," Sam stated. Anna nodded and the trio moved out of the library into the central chamber.

"What have you learned about the disk since discovering it?" Ian asked.

"Not much I'm afraid. It's about seven inches in diameter and divided into five concentric circles. In each band are different symbols." Anna stated as Sam moved the tile aside to open the passage.

"What sort of symbols?"

"Difficult to say there are several different ones with no rhyme or reason to them." Anna answered.

"Fascinating."

"Why so interested?" Anna asked not caring for all the questions about the disk. Ian knew something he wasn't letting on about.

"From the description Phillip gave it sounds like a truly unique piece," Broody answered.

"What else was in the tablets?" Sam asked.

"I haven't finished researching them, what I read was about the religious practices of the people."

"I see," Anna said certain now that the good doctor was hiding things. The trio fell silent; making their way into the underground passages of the temple in Atlantis.

111 TELE AVIV, ISRAEL

Pamela made her way past customs, in the direction of the passenger loading zone. She flagged down a cab and requested to be taken to the King David Hotel in Jerusalem. As the cab raced over the 29 mile stretch of road into the holy city Pamela contemplated her next move. How was she going to find Sam and Dr. Gallagher? When she did how would she find out what Miss Gallagher was working on without tipping Sam off that she was in the area? Then how did she convince Anna to give her the story instead?

A lot of questions, Pamela mused. The cab pulled to a halt in front of an elegant six story hotel. She shouldered her carry on, making her way into the lobby. As she stepped inside she spotted the shop where Sam's credit report indicated he'd made his purchase. She'd stop in there once she got settled. Pamela hoped she'd be able to answer her questions rather quick. The sooner she got the story the faster she could get home.

112

**Somewhere in the Bermuda Triangle, Atlantis
Wednesday
11am**

Sam and Anna stood in the throne room waiting while Dr. Ian Broody made arrangements to have the statues from the feasting chamber returned to their rightful location on the steps in the chamber.

"You said in the vision that I opened a door."

"Yes."

"Where?"

"It was the wall behind the throne."

"Show me?" Anna asked.

Sam nodded. He led her up the steps past the throne to the wall. He brushed the gathering dust away from where the lock had been in his dream. Found the same indentations. Anna studied them with both interest and understanding.

"The disk it's a key," she whispered.

"Yes. Whatever is on the other side of this door should never be found," Sam said with certainty.

"That is correct," an all too familiar voice said from behind them. Sam and Anna turned to see their angelic visitor standing before the altar of stone. He looked upon the graven images with disgust and shook his head at the throne.

"What is this place?" Anna asked.

"This place is the most cursed location on the face of the earth. Long before man existed the angel Lucifer rebelled against God. He aspired to be higher than the Creator; leading a war against him in heaven. In time he was cast out to dwell upon the earth. While he was here he established a kingdom of his own. One from which he raged a bloody war until the Lord forged Hell and flooded the earth. His army was destroyed or imprisoned but Lucifer escaped. He dwelled in hiding and bided his time."

"For what?"

"His revenge. He took it when he led Adam and Eve to sin. He established his kingdom in the land near the garden. Over time he led both man and angel alike into sin."

"Tell us of the gods. Explain why here they are but men but elsewhere they are men and women.

"The so called gods of this world were once angels that the devil tricked into taking upon themselves flesh. He then set their eye upon the beauty of woman; making them to burn with desire. They took for themselves from the daughters of men, brides with whom they lay polluting the blood lines. These fallen, for the right to take for themselves whatever woman they desired revealed to the leaders of men the secrets of forbidden arts. For their knowledge they were named gods and worshiped. In time the mortal women they took were elevated to goddesses as truth became lost –passing to myth."

"What is it you need us to do?" Sam asked deciding they'd heard enough of the history it wasn't important now.

"The Fallen later forged mantles of power that they gave to the rulers of men who served them. They were made to help men in their quest to concur the world. When the city of the fallen was discovered those mantles woke. They will now seek out a wielder to lead back to this place. You must ensure that those mantles do not fall into the hands of any human."

"Why? What are these mantles? How will we find them?" Sam asked.

"The mantles have turned up many times over the years. They will often appear in tales of myth, legend and folklore. Often where people would least expect them to. As for what they are the photos taken of the images of the gods in the three cities will reveal them. The reason why is because they enslave the minds of the men who find them to the will of the fallen who forged it."

"Is there any way to avoid these mantles from being rediscovered?" Anna asked.

"No, when this city was discovered a clock began ticking. The city itself calls out to the mantles. If any should be found by someone other than you; you must not allow it to reach this city."

"What about the key?"

"It must remain hidden. Do not allow it or the mantles to reach this lock." The angel said then he vanished.

Anna sighed as the room dimmed. "Great, now what are we supposed to do?"

"Anna, we have to get out of here before anyone else figures out what we know. The government is already poking about. Your Dr. Broody knows more than he's letting on. If they come to realize about the mantles they'll go looking for them. They'd make a unique weapon to use against their enemies."

"Okay, but what do we do? I can't just leave my work unfinished. Ian will get suspicious."

"Why? What is there between you two?"

"Sam…"

"Don't deny it Anna, I know there's something, you call him Ian even as the prim and proper Dr. Annalynn, Darcy, Gallagher."

Anna blinked surprised by his temper. He was jealous had been for a while she realized. Understanding now what she'd seen in his eyes the night she was shot. "Okay, you're right there was something between us. You have no reason to be jealous of him Sam. It ended." She assured him.

"Not for him it hasn't."

"Why do you say that?"

"The way he looks at you. A man knows that look. What was he to you? Why is it over?"

"Ian was my fiancé a little over three years ago."

"You were engaged to him?" Sam said his voice going hard and cold.

"I broke the engagement when he cheated me out of my academic credit to a dig in Greece. The only reason I came here was he signed a contract stating I'd get my credit for the work I did. He'll be suspicious if I just walk away."

Anna watched as something passed over Sam's face; she wasn't sure what but he took a deep breath and seemed to relax.

"Damn, you're right. You have to leave it in someone's hands, but not his. Leave it for Dr. Lynch."

"Zaharrah, are you mad?"

"You said if she's here it's not working for him right?"

"Right."

"Then she's not going to reveal to him or his employer anything she finds that doesn't pertain to their research."

"Okay. Maybe, but she's not exactly trust worthy. If she puts it together we'll be racing against her to find the mantles. That's not a safe move."

"Better than Broody," Sam stated.

Anna sighed. "All right, you have a point. Let's go arrange a meet. We can't have this conversation on site." Anna muttered. Together the pair made their way out of the throne room – back to the library.

113 Wednesday 12pm

Sam and Anna stepped into the library chamber. Zaharrah looked up from the scroll she was studying.

"Back so soon, I figured you'd be busy showing Dr. Broody your little secret chamber." Zaharrah said amused.

"We've finished." Anna stated with irritation.

"I see, so you thought you'd just poke around in my work for your missing answers."

"No… Sam, I can't do this…" Anna said struggling with her temper.

"We need to talk but not here," Sam stated.

Zaharrah blinked surprised by the request. Anna watched interest spark in her brown eyes. She figured Zaharrah was intrigued by all the secrets? It wasn't like Anna to hide things.

"Okay when?"

"Tonight around ten pm back at the hotel. We'll sort out the where then." Sam answered. Anna nodded an okay. Sam led her out of the temple into the noonday sun headed in the direction of the boat. What they needed now was back in the room.

114 JERUSALEM, ISRAEL

Pamela walked about the small shop on the hotel lobby floor. She picked up a few things she thought she might need while she was in Israel. The first was a map of the region. The second was a pair of language books: English to Hebrew and English to Arabic in case she had to speak with any locals; along with a bottle of sunscreen. She set the four items on the small counter.

"Hello Miss, will this be all for you?"

"Yes. I was wondering though if you might have seen my husband. He's staying in the hotel. I thought I'd drop in. Surprise him," Pamela said with a smile. She produced her and Sam's wedding photo.

"Oh yes, he came in the shops two days ago. I believe he's staying in one of our junior suites on the fourth floor."

"Thank you so much," Pamela murmured. She signed for her things. She made her way to the elevator. Pressed the button indicated. When the doors opened she stepped inside and pressed a button. A moment later they opened again on the fourth floor.

Pamela made her way down the hall to the room the shop clerk had indicated. Noted the maid was just coming out.

"Hello, can I help you?" The maid asked.

"Maybe. You don't by any chance know where the resident of the room is? Do you?"

"Mr. Abrams checked out yesterday."

"He did? Do you know when?"

"Depends on whose asking and why?"

"His wife. I wanted to stop in and surprise him. I guess I just missed him." Pamela said. She showed the maid their wedding photo.

"I believe it was after they got back from the dig site."

"They?"

"Your husband and Dr. Gallagher."

"I see. What site is that?" Pamela asked.

"Um the one all the archeologists have been working on over near the Dead Sea."

"Any idea where they went?" Pamela asked.

"I'm afraid not."

"I'll ask at the dig site. Thanks for your help," Pamela said. She then turned and headed back to the elevator. Pamela wondered how far away the site at the Dead Sea was from the hotel. She considered how far behind Sam she was.

115

MIAMI, FLORIDA
WEDNESDAY
8PM

Sam and Anna sat at the small table in their joint suite studying the photos she had taken of the statues, the ones taken at the locations in the Dead Sea and the images of Atlantis. The pair had gotten in only a short while ago. They'd shared a quick meal. Now they worked at determining what the mantles were so that they could begin looking for them.

"There's one thing that stands out to me in these images," Anna stated. She repressed a yawn.

"What's that?"

"The statues in Sodom and Gomorrah depicted each god with a unique item. For example Eros holds his bow. Ares his sword. In the images here they have nothing."

"Yeah, but what about Erebus why isn't he among the statues of the Fallen."

"I don't think he was on the same level as the others. In the images here he's kneeling beside Chaos like a servant not an equal."

"So the ten are of equal status. The item they hold in their hands in the images from Sodom and Gomorrah are the mantles. They wait to receive them here."

"Yes, that's what I think," Anna answered. Having said it aloud she felt certain it was true.

"Okay so let's make a note of what we're looking for. Tomorrow we'll start researching where they were last noted," Sam suggested.

"Why tomorrow?" Anna asked.

"Because we have a meeting with Zaharrah in two hours and we're both tired."

"We can…" Anna began to protest.

"In my line of work Anna, you have to know when to rest. It's time. We'll be of no use tonight if we keep pushing. We may even end up missing something important."

Anna nodded. "Okay let's go over the list then we'll take a short rest before meeting with Zaharrah," she relented. The pair worked at putting the list together.

Chaos held a sealed scroll. Zeus had a crown of the king upon his brow, his brother Poseidon held a trident, and Hades held a pair of scales. Ares held a sword dressed for battle. Hephaestus wore a pair of gauntlets for forging. Eros held his bow, arrow at the ready. Helios a whip for controlling the horses that pulled his golden chariot. Hermes had a horn hung from his belt and Dionysus held a cup of wine.

"Didn't Zaharrah say something about a candle?" Sam asked.

"Yes, she said she found it in a chamber in the North Eastern palace in the main wall, Hades' palace. Why?"

"In some minds a candle is the ultimate measure of scale," Sam stated.

"It seems when we talk later I'll have to get it from her. As for the cup I know exactly where it is."

"You do?"

"Yes, I've held it. It was the piece I was in the process of preparing for the secondary museum site when I got the call for the dig at the Dead Sea."

"That's great you can just talk with your boss there and…"

"It's a sort of auction house. I hope the cup is still there." Anna said worried. She'd been gone for three years. There was a good chance that someone else had finished the research on it and sent it to auction.

"Okay, then we'll deal with it tomorrow. For now we'll put this stuff aside. Grab a quick nap. When we wake we'll meet up with Dr. Lynch. Then we'll make preparations to get out of here without raising suspicions."

"Sounds good, by this time tomorrow with a little luck we'll have two mantles accounted for," Anna said with a confidence she didn't feel.

116 Dead Sea

Pamela climbed out of her cab. She pulled a pair of binoculars out of her bag. Scanning the surrounding area she soon spotted a hill in the distance where a group of people were moving in and out of strange ruins. Pamela noted the security check point. She cursed. Faking her way in there was not going to be easy.

"Did you want to see the lost city?" A young woman's voice questioned.

Pamela jumped, startled. Turning she found she was no longer alone. A woman with golden hair and the deepest blue eyes she'd ever seen stood a few feet behind her. She wore a white, filmy, flowing gown that covered her six foot frame from shoulder to toe. The woman looked to be in her mid to late twenties. Her arms and neck were a perfect tan, flawless in color, without line she seemed to glow in the light of the morning sun.

"Yes. Do you know what city that is?"

"I do. I know much about it. If you'd like I'll show it to you. We must wait until dark."

"I'd like that so long as it won't cost too much?" Pamela said eyeing the young woman with suspicion.

"It will cost you nothing up front, all I ask is that you return the favor later." The woman stated with an easy smile.

"It won't be illegal will it?" Pamela asked.

"No. What I'll ask will be a simple task – completely legal." The woman assured her.

"Very well."

"Come we should move out of the open. I'll show you my dwelling. When night falls we will go," the woman said. Turning she lead Pamela away from the cab in the direction of a tent south of the dig site.

117 Miami, Florida Wednesday 10pm

Sam and Anna stepped off the elevator into the hotel lobby. Looking about they spotted Zaharrah sitting at the hotel bar sipping a drink. The pair crossed the lobby. Entering the bar they settled into a booth in the back. A waitress took their drink request. They sat in a companionable silence as they waited for their drinks.

Sam watched as Zaharrah slid down from her barstool; making her way over to their table.

"Good evening, Mr. Abrams, was it?" She asked.

"Yes."

"You know you're wasting your time with that one. Dr. Annalynn Darcy Gallagher is too professional to get drunk or involved with a colleague again for that matter," Zaharrah said before sliding into the booth next to him. Sam had to give her points; if anyone was watching them their meet would look like a spontaneous one rather than planned.

"Oh really as opposed to a woman who when you wake up you may find your wallet gone or something more important," Anna retorted her temper flaring per normal. Sam gave her hand a squeeze. Reminding her they needed to play nice. "I'm sorry that was uncalled for," Anna mumbled.

"It's nothing. Why did you want to meet?"

'We'll be leaving the dig as soon as Anna clears the air with Dr. Broody. We want to leave Anna's work in your hands."

"Why me?" Zaharrah asked surprised.

"Because you don't work for Broody. I'll pay you triple whatever he's promised you if you'll work for me instead," Anna stated in a hushed voice. The waitress returned with her and Sam's drink. Zaharrah requested another beer before she moved on.

"At least I'm a sure thing. A few missing items is a small price for a night of passion," Zaharrah snapped. Picking up the argument for anyone else to hear.

"Slut," Anna hissed with feigned anger.

"Prude," Zaharrah replied. Loud enough to be heard. "Doing what?" she whispered picking up the real conversation.

"What I need is four fold. First the candle you discovered; I need to see it. I may need to take it with me when I leave. Second anything you find not pertaining to Broody's research you have to keep to yourself. Third I need you to keep your eyes peeled and your ears open for anything odd going on. Send it my way. Finally I know you have some less than reputable connections in the field. I need you to have something stolen for me."

"Why?" Zaharrah asked surprised.

"There are some secrets in this world that are never meant to be discovered." Anna replied her answer cryptic.

"Does this have to do with that room you showed Broody today and the disk?" Zaharrah asked.

"Miss Lynch, I think you have the wrong idea we're just going over the day's notes," Sam stated, picking up the quarrel.

"Oh, well, then in that case, may I join you?"

"Yes." He stated in answer to both the real question and the fake one. The waitress reappeared, gave Zaharrah her second beer before moving on.

"Where are you going?" Zaharrah asked.

"It's better for all involved if you not know," Sam stated.

"Fair enough."

"What brought you here Zaharrah? You tend to steer clear of Broody's projects since Ithaca," Anna whispered.

"It's better if you not know," Zaharrah replied echoing Sam's response.

'Will you take the job?" Anna asked.

"Yes."

"Good, the item to be stolen is at the following address. Tell your contact it's important that they not handle the disk directly. If they do it should be as little as possible. Once you have it, keep it clear of the dig site at all costs."

Zaharrah took the slip of paper which Anna passed over the table stuck it in her pocket. Sam imagined she'd look at it later. "Anything else?"

"Yeah, thank you and I'm sorry."

"No need. Here is my account once I see the funds I will have my man make a move. Anna, whatever this is about good luck to you."

Anna nodded. Sam watched as Zaharrah rose from the booth. "Sorry Mr. Abrams, but this is too dull a conversation for my taste. If you decide you've had enough of it and Miss Gallagher's company I'll be over at the bar," She stated. Zaharrah gave him a quick peck on the lips before moving back to her stool.

Sam chuckled. Seeing temper in Anna's hazel eyes he lifted her hand from the table, kissing her knuckles. "She's good at this," Sam whispered.

"Yes, I know things will be in good hands – provided she doesn't get a better offer." Anna muttered. The pair fell silent. Finished their drinks and then headed for the elevator.

They waited for the elevator to reach the lobby. When the doors parted the pair stepped inside. Sam reached for the button to select their floor. A woman with brown hair dressed in kakis and a white t-shirt stepped into the elevator. The doors closed. The woman pressed the button for the floor above Sam and Anna's. As the car began to move she spoke.

"Dr. Gallagher."

"Dr. Silvers."

"You can call me Brooke. You asked earlier what purpose they have in trying to decipher the DNA of the beasts. They want to make a genetic clone. Can you imagine the implications if a few governments had the ability to produce and control dragons."

"No wonder they're keeping it all so secret," Sam said with disgust. His mind reeled he wondered if the US military knew about it.

"How close are they?" Anna questioned.

"They've got a way to go yet. They're missing several key pieces. Until they find those parts they will be unable to complete the project."

"That's good news. Thank you. You should know I and Mr. Abrams will be leaving the dig site once I clear things with Broody. But if anything new develops on your end let Dr. Zaharrah Lynch know. She's taking over on my behalf." Anna whispered. The elevator dinged indicating they were approaching their destination.

118 Dead Sea

As the sun sank behind the mountains of the Jordan; the sky grew dark. Pamela finished up the light meal of nuts and fruit that her unnamed assistant had offered in the cover of her tent.

"It's time, the team will have left by now." her host whispered. She tied her blond hair up and back making it appear jaw length. The white flowing gown of the morning had been replaced by a loose black tunic and black pants that made her appear like a man at first glance.

"What makes you so sure?" Pamela asked.

"No one will come out here after dark."

"Why is it dangerous?" Pamela questioned.

"No. Most digging teams are local hires. They will not disturb the dead after dark."

"Oh. Okay."

"Put these on, it will make you harder to spot. Then we will go." The woman commanded. Pamela did so without protest. Once changed, the pair left the small tent, starting the short trek to the ruins of the city.

Pamela followed her guide through the broken gateway of the ancient city. Crossing the empty courtyard as they came near the city temple the woman drew from her sleeve a small candle. "Let's risk a little light now." She whispered. When the candle wick was lit the moon began to rise behind them, illuminating the ruins. Pamela blinked working to adjust her vision. The woman led on. They passed by what looked like a temple, making their way to the back wall of the city.

"Where are we going?" Pamela whispered.

"The king's palace, we're almost there," her host assured her. Pamela followed on; crossing the palace courtyard they walked over the small bridge to the king's private temple.

"What is this place? Where are we? Those look like Greek art."

The woman laughed with delight. "Ah how wonderful your mind is, I can see why he's picked you. We are in the king's temple in Sodom. Yes the statues look Greek but they are not. I can assure you of that." The woman murmured.

"I don't understand. What do you mean he picked me? Who? For what?"

"You'll find out when the time is right. The gods of Greece walked the earth long before its people ever made up tales of them. The people of Sodom, Gomorrah and the other cities of the plains worshiped them as well. The king's empire which you can see clearly here all worshiped them." The woman stated before revealing the map of the king's territory.

"Who are you?" Pamela asked frightened. The woman before her seemed to change. Her eyes like a bottomless blue sea looked as though they'd seen far more years than her appearance suggested.

"I have many names, Pamela but you may call me Cynthia."

"You said you know much about this place and many other things. Do you know where Sam and Anna have gone?" Pamela asked. She trembled with fear though she didn't know why.

"Yes. The map will show us the way. Watch. I will reveal a great secret that time has forgotten," the woman who called herself Cynthia whispered. She approached the map "Here to the side is part of a riddle. The other half lies in Gomorrah. If one touches the seal of Gomorrah behold the riddle is completed. The location of the city of the gods revealed. That is where your ex has gone."

"You're sure Cynthia?"

"Yes, if you wish it I will take you there."

"Thank you."

"No need just remember when I ask it, you must return the favor," Cynthia stated.

"I remember," Pamela assured her. Together the pair left the temple returning to Cynthia's tent.

119 Atlantis, somewhere in the Bermuda Triangle Thursday 10am

Sam and Anna stepped off the boat, passing through security at the city gate.

"Do you know where Dr. Broody is this morning?" Anna asked.

"I believe he's working in the temple." The man answered.

"Thank you," Anna stated. Together with Sam they made their way through the city of the Fallen to the central temple. They crossed the stone path in the overgrown garden beds. Over the bridge, as the sun above began to rise higher in the morning sky, the pair hiked up the steps, strolled through the chamber of dedication, into the hall of feasting.

Anna sighed with relief finding Ian there. She hadn't been looking forward to the idea of going back into the throne room. After reaching her room last night Anna had busied herself with preparing for departure today. She'd printed up a complete copy of her notes for Zaharrah then gathered her copy, all but the duplicate photos for Ian. She'd then transferred the money from the contest into the account Zaharrah indicated. She'd packed everything but her clothes for the morning away. Once they got back to Miami they'd be out of there.

"Ah, good morning Anna." Ian said with enthusiasm. His grey eyes shone with a strange light.

"Good morning Dr. Broody. I have something for you."

"You do?" he asked with delight.

"Yes. Here is my research to date on the project. You don't need me here any longer. My short trip home made me realize I miss it and my family. I'm going to leave this in your more than capable hands." Anna said. She set a black portfolio on the stone table in front of him.

Ian snatched it up like a greedy child reaching for an offered treat. "Are you sure?"

"Yes, three years is an awful long time to be away. I think I'll take a short vacation. Pay my family a visit then head home."

"Well you have earned a break from all this. Good luck to you. I trust that Mr. Abrams will be going as well."

"Yeah, what you've got here is so unbelievable I could never print it before you're ready to reveal it." Sam assured him.

"If that's what you want?" Ian began.

"It is." Anna assured him.

"All right then, be sure to turn in your security pass when you leave today." Ian stated.

"We will. Thank you for understanding," Anna whispered. She turned, headed in the direction of the library. She spotted Zaharrah working in the same corner. "Well, Lynch, you got what you wanted I'm out of here," Anna muttered. She pulled out of the bag on her shoulder a manila envelope.

"Sorry to see you leave Annalynn, Darcy, Gallagher it's so much fun to ruffle your feathers." Zaharrah stated. She took the envelope; tucked it in her bag. "You never got to see the candle I found come I'll show you," Zaharrah said. She stepped out of the temple into the daylight. Anna and Sam followed her down the street to the northern palace within the main wall.

She led the pair into the court yard where the completed artifact cataloging sat waiting to be shipped. She opened a small crate, pulling out of the protective wrapping a large pewter candle holder inlayed with emeralds.

"May I?" Anna asked extending her hands to take it.

"Why not?" Zaharrah said with a laugh. She set the candle in Anna's hands. The second the metal touched her skin she felt a jolt of power. Zaharrah's brow rose in question.

"Is it?" Sam asked.

"Yes, encrusted with real emeralds. It would be a shame if it were lost," Anna stated. She handed it back to Zaharrah.

"Indeed, I'll be sure to double check the label before it is sent out. Good journey to you Mr. Abrams."

"Thank you." Sam stated. He brushed a kiss on her cheek. He and Anna then turned, headed for the boat.

"Anna!"

"Yes Ian."

"Be sure to send back the disk."

"I will," she assured him with a bright smile. The pair stepped on the boat for the long ride back to Miami.

120

Washington DC, Virginia
Friday
8AM

"Phillip, thank you for seeing me on such short notice after our last visit." Anna said. She extended her hand to the older man.

"Not a problem Anna. It's a relief to see you safe. Last I heard your place had been broken into a second time. A friend of yours was looking for you?"

"Who?" Anna asked puzzled.

"Miss Walsh. She said she flew in for a visit. When she stopped by the house it was open the place was trashed."

"Pamela, I'm sorry to have worried her. I went back to the site to straighten things out with Ian."

"That's good. What brings you in today?"

"I was wondering if we still had the cup I was working on cleaning up before I left."

"As a matter of fact we do. It is still on display."

"May I see it?" Anna questioned.

"Of course, follow me." Phillip said. He led her from his office at the auction site onto the show room floor. The cup sat in a display case in the center of the room.

Anna studied it with relief, asked to hold it. Phillip deactivated the alarm. Anna lifted it from its pedestal. The second she held it she knew something was off. It felt too light. "Sam, call detective Roman."

"Why?"

"This cup isn't the real one," Anna stated; a sinking feeling in the pit of her stomach.

"What are you saying? Are you sure Anna?" Phillip questioned with disbelief.

"I'm positive. The real cup is surprisingly heavy." Anna stated, setting the forgery down. Sam pulled out his cell phone. Dialed Lance's number. He hoped the detective wouldn't be too busy.

"Anna, dear, what is this all about?" Phillip asked, looking a bit green. Anna saw fear in his eyes and understood the reason. As far as he knew the cup held no real value. Why someone would steal it he couldn't imagine? The fact that she was worried about it suggested it might be worth more than they originally believed.

"The cup may have a connection to the dig site."

"Oh dear."

"Yes. It's not alone. There are other items you should be on the lookout for. A sealed scroll, a trident, a scale, a sword, a pair of gauntlets, a bow, a whip, and a horn."

"Did you say a horn?"

"Yes."

"What sort of horn?"

"I'm not sure really. It would be ornate I suppose."

"I have a silver horn in my keeping it's engraved with an image could be feathers or scales not sure which it's got small sapphires set in it."

"May we see it?" Anna questioned.

"Of course but Anna, what is this all about?"

"Phillip, it's better for you if you not know, just trust me when I say it's important."

Phillip nodded.

"Lance is on his way." Sam stated after hanging up his phone.

"Good I've got a line on the horn when he gets here and he's been brought up to speed we'll go take a look at it." Anna stated.

"Sounds good," Sam said with approval.

"Let's just hope that whoever took the cup will be easy to track." Anna stated. Phillip reestablished the alarm. The trio moved back into his office to await detective Lance Roman's arrival.

121

Atlantis, somewhere in the Bermuda Triangle

Pamela stepped off the deck of the small sailing vessel of her hostess Cynthia. Upon waking the next day, after returning from the lost city, she found the tent gone. Cynthia once again dressed in white. Her golden hair fell down her back free from the confines of the night before, a small pack on her back. Just over the dusty hill a car had been waiting to take them back to Tel Aviv. They'd taken a private plane to Miami. After a short drive to the marina they'd boarded the boat.

As the pair moved ashore Pamela again wondered just who Cynthia was. What had she meant by she had many names? Whoever she was, she was well connected. Pulling out her binoculars Pamela looked ahead. Seeing the security checkpoint she cursed. Whomever Anna was working for they were serious about keeping unwanted visitors out.

"Relax; there is a way in to the city of the gods they know nothing of. Come. I will show you," Cynthia murmured. She set off west of the city gate. Running near to the wall she came to the outside of the first palace. Pressing her palm against the stone it slid forward revealing a hidden entrance. It led to the bed chambers. Moving to the center of the chamber she pressed a tile depicting gilded wings. The floor opened. Drawing out the candle from her sleeve she lit it, proceeding down into the dark passage below the palace. Pamela was only a few steps behind her.

122

WASHINGTON DC, VIRGINIA
FRIDAY
9AM

Lance pulled up in front of the address Sam had given him. He cursed. Whatever was going on now it was connected to the museum? He wondered if Dr. Phillip King had finally decided to take action against Anna. As he stepped into the auction house he questioned what in the hell they were doing back in DC.

"Hello."

"Detective, so good to see you again though I wish it was under different circumstances," Phillip King stated. He came out of his office.

"What is the problem doctor?"

"It seems that one of our pieces is not real."

"What?" Lance questioned surprised.

"The cup there in the center is a forgery," Phillip stated.

"You're sure?" Lance questioned.

"Positive," Anna replied. She and Sam joined them.

"I see."

"Phillip, can you give Detective Roman and myself a moment alone?" Anna asked.

"Of course, my dear, take your time." Phillip said. He moved back into the office.

"What are you doing here it won't take long for…"

"Dr. Broody knows I'm back. I turned over my notes – left the project."

"Then, why the interest in the cup?"

"It's a long story. I'll fill you in another time for now let's just say Sam and I were given a task. It has to do with completing that."

"What kind of task, by whom?" Lance asked.

"An important one. If we told you who you'd never believe us," Sam muttered.

"Okay. I'll see what I can find out about the cup."

"Thanks," Sam said.

"You're welcome. Now, do me a favor. Both of you stay out of trouble." Lance grumbled.

"As best we can," Anna promised.

"Good now get out of here so I can get to work," Lance stated. The pair nodded. Phillip reemerged from his office. Lance watched as the trio left. He put a call into the crime scene work team. Hoping they'd find something.

123 Atlantis, somewhere in the Bermuda Triangle

The narrow passage came to an end abruptly at a wall with the same golden wings depicted on it. Cynthia placed her hand upon the image. The ceiling opened up a gilded ladder lowered. Pamela followed her guide up the ladder. She found herself in a vast chamber. Two large black crystalline images towered over her. Before her were a set of stairs leading up to a massive black crystal throne. The steps were lined by the graven images of ten of the gods of Sodom each one winged.

When she stepped forward to take a closer look the opening in the floor closed. A large square altar slid into place where it had been. Cynthia using her candle lit the various torches about the chamber to give her guest a better look, as well as lighting the fire of the altar.

"What is this place?" Pamela whispered.

"This is the oldest chamber on the face of the earth, it is the throne room of the prince of the sky," Cynthia murmured.

"The gods they reach back to the beginning of time?"

"Yes."

"Who are you Cynthia? Tell me the truth," Pamela requested. Her mind swam with wonder. She felt a surge of power she didn't understand.

"I am Artemis daughter of mighty Zeus, goddess of the moon and the hunt, bound to the service of the one who has chosen you, the god of Knowledge." She stated. Her blue eyes glowed with an unearthly power. Pamela fell to her knees. Brought low under the force of it. Her gaze fell to the floor; unable to look upon that beauty or the power within it.

"Please lady, forgive me I meant no disrespect," Pamela whispered. She closed her eyes shaking with fear.

"Pamela, I have hidden myself from you until the appointed time, now sister you will learn much," Artemis whispered. She moved closer to the trembling woman. Lifted Pamela's head and watched as her eyes opened. The brown pools were glassy – lifeless, indicating that lord Hermes had drawn her into the dream realm.

Pamela woke from a pleasant slumber to foreign surroundings. She looked up at a rounded ceiling of gold. The dome was supported by ornately crafted Corinthian columns. Beyond the columns was a sea of green and vivid color. A garden she realized. Sitting up she found she lay upon a golden swing. Pamela yawned. Stretched like a cat. Trying to recall how she'd gotten there. All she could recall was that she had been looking for something.

Getting up she gasped at the feel of the cold marble beneath her bare feet. She wondered for a moment what she had done with her shoes. The thought slipped away at the smell of roses nearby. She made her way down the stone path through the garden, coming to a pool of fresh clear water. It was surrounded by roses of every hue. She gasped in delight.

Pamela knelt at the water's edge to smell a bold red blossom. It was as large as her hand. She wondered whose garden it was. The smell of the flower was sweet and exotic. She closed her eyes, allowing the scent to wash over her.

"Hello my dearest. It's good to finally meet you," A voice whispered. A warm arm wrapped about her waist from behind. She gasped startled. Realizing she was not alone. Pamela was alarmed at her reaction to his touch her body yielded to him. She felt her pulse quicken. Looked up to see who held her.

His face was perfectly tanned. His dark hair was more like that of a lion's mane, long and untamed curls. His blue eyes shone with pleasure as he looked upon her face.

"Who are you?" she whispered. He reached past her with one hand to pluck the rose from the bush.

"I am the owner of the garden, master of this house. I'm so pleased and honored to have you here at last my lovely one," he murmured. He kissed her brow before tucking the rose in her bleach blond hair.

"What do you mean at last?" Pamela asked. She turned to face him.

"I've sent for you many time's my dear. Until this day you have not answered. Today you are with me, my chosen one." He murmured as he touched her face, caressing her cheek and neck. Running his fingertips down her bare shoulders, down the length of her arm to clasp her fingers.

"What do you mean your chosen one? Chosen for what? Who are you?"

"I am Hermes god of Knowledge the lord who you serve. You my darling, have been chosen to be my consort," he whispered as he drew her fingers to his lips, kissing them.

Pamela fell to her knees before him, humbled by his power. She averted her eyes from him, kissed his feet. "Forgive me my lord, had I known you I would not have looked upon you. Who am I that you would desire me?" Pamela breathed.

Hermes touched her head lifting her gaze to meet his. His touch stirred desire within her. Her mind whispering of the power he could give her. The secrets he would reveal to her. He drew her to her feet. "You need not fear me my lady. I mean you no harm. To you I would give all that you desire and more for you are a loyal priestess to my temple. You are fair to look upon." He explained then he kissed her.

Pamela moaned with delight. His kiss assaulted her senses driving her body wild with hunger. She kissed him back taking as he took – seeking more. She groaned in protest when his lips left hers.

"What do you say Pamela, will you be mine? Will you give yourself to me as my lady?" He asked her. His fingers played over her clothed body teasing, enticing with the promises of pleasure.

"Yes my lord, I am yours," she whispered. "I will be yours."

Hermes smiled with delight. "You have given me great joy this day. I will give you all you desire," he vowed then kissed her again.

Pamela gasped as her mind returned from the dream. She blinked. Wept to find herself once again in the throne room, kneeling at the feet of Artemis; her lover gone.

"Shh, do not weep. You will meet him again in time. There is much for you to do here yet my sister." Artemis murmured. She knelt beside Pamela, kissed her brow.

"Was any of it real?" Pamela asked confused.

"Yes, all was real. You have been touched by a god. Your body is now his temple, be careful not to misuse it."

"What is it I must do so I can be with him again?" Pamela asked.

"Seek out the man whom once you called husband. You will find him in DC. He holds in his possession the mantle of your husband's power. Get it from him. Bring it back to Dr. Ian Broody, his champion. You will be rewarded with all you desire." Artemis stated

"It shall be done," Pamela assured her.

"Come, we must leave this place before we are discovered," Artemis said. She put out the fire in the altar. Artemis touched the gilded wings upon it, opening the passage way once again. Pamela nodded. She kissed the feet of the image of her lord then left.

124

WASHINGTON DC, VIRGINIA
FRIDAY
9AM

Phillip King led Sam and Anna into his office at the Smithsonian. He bid the pair have a seat. Moving behind his desk he took down the picture of dogs at poker to reveal a safe. He worked the combination and upon opening it removed a velvet bag. Anna watched from the brown leather armchair in front of his desk as he closed the safe. Phillip took a seat at the desk, opened the pouch.

He pulled from within it a long silver horn. Etched in it were multiple layers of an image. She noted that Phillip had been correct; you couldn't quite determine what the image was. Perhaps they were leaves, feathers or maybe scales. The rim of the horn was overlaid with gold. Encrusted in it were several small sapphires. Spaced between each in silver was a smaller rendition of the same detail.

When she saw it Anna was certain, this was the horn of Hermes god of Knowledge.

"Phillip have you dated it?" Anna asked.

"Not yet, I've just been working on cleaning up the detail. It's truly unique."

"It is that. Unfortunately it can't be sold." Sam muttered.

"Why not?" Phillip asked.

"It's dangerous Phillip. It has to remain undiscovered." Anna stated.

"Why? What is it that you found over in the Dead Sea that has you spooked my dear? How is it connected to this horn and the missing cup?" Phillip asked.

"I'm going to walk you through what I know. Promise me you'll listen with an open mind," Anna murmured.

"I promise," Phillip answered. He sat in silence as Anna related all she knew from the finding of Sodom and Gomorrah to the riddles and the discovery of Atlantis. She told him about the gods of old and about the mantles. As she came to the end of it she prayed that he not think her mad.

Sam took Anna's hand in his, gave it a reassuring squeeze. "I know how it sounds Dr. King, but I've seen it all firsthand. It's true."

"I see. So you're saying this horn is the horn of a god?"

"Yes. It is a danger to anyone that handles it." Anna murmured.

"That explains the strange urges I've had to keep it hidden, to not work on it of late. I thought I was getting lazy but it was a warning. All right, you can take it, though I don't know where you can put it that will keep it safe. Perhaps somewhere in the legends there is a clue how to destroy it."

"Thank you."

"You're welcome. You can rest assured I'll keep my eyes open for any of the others. The second I have a hint of something I'll let you know."

"Thank you so much Phillip. Please don't say anything to Broody I don't know if he can be trusted with this."

"He is ambitious it could get the best of him. I shall say nothing of it. I think you best get on your way. Good luck in your adventure." Phillip said.

Anna thanked him again. Returning the horn to the pouch she handed it to Sam. Figuring if anyone came after them he could protect it. Sam tied it to his belt so he'd be aware of it at all times. The pair then turned and left.

125

Washington DC, Virginia
Friday
4pm

Lance sighed with relief as he looked upon his home. He'd had the busiest morning he could recall in a long time. It burned him that it was during his first vacation in years.

The crime scene team had found nothing of note at the auction house. Not surprising when you considered the fact they'd been unaware until this morning that the cup had been swapped.

As Lance made his way back towards his office to type up his notes the hairs on the back of his neck rose, his senses went on full alert. Something was off here. Lance pulled out a pair of gloves from his pocket, slipping them on before opening the door.

"How the hell is it possible to have my private life invaded upon twice in a 48 hour period? I need a damn dog," he muttered. The room had been tossed papers and photos littered the floor. Lance began the careful task of sorting through the mess to see what if anything was missing. Dread washed over him. He realized this incident had nothing to do with the photos. The only thing missing was Anna's disk.

Lance made his way out of the office, punched in her number. He wasn't looking forward to her reaction when he told her.

"Hello."

"Anna, its Lance."

"Oh, hello detective."

"We've got a problem here Anna. Someone broke into the place. They took it."

"Really?"

"Afraid so."

"Wow that was fast." Anna muttered.

"What do you mean?" Lance asked his temper flaring.

"I hired someone to steal it so I could avoid sending it back to

Broody."

"You did what? You might have warned me."

"No, it looks better for you if you're unaware."

"True," he relented. "So are you going to tell me what this is all about?"

"Soon..."

Lance's jaw tightened at the reply he was sick of that word. If he was going to help them even on a peripheral level he needed to know what was happening. He cut her off. "No. Not soon. You're going to tell me now or I'm out. You know what, put Sam on the phone, I need to talk to him anyway." Lance snapped.

"Lance…"

"Do it Anna."

"Sam, detective Roman wants to talk to you," He heard her say then he heard the sound of the phone being handed off.

"Hello?" Sam questioned.

"Abrams, I've got news pertaining to old matters but first you're going to tell me what in the hell is going on."

"Fair enough," Sam answered. Lance heard the sound of a door closing and figured Sam had moved beyond Anna's ear shot. "Anna and I have been charged with the task of locating and protecting ten mantles of the old gods. The cup is one of them."

"Oh hell – old gods? You've got to be kidding!"

"I wish I were," Sam said with a sigh.

"You know how that sounds right?"

"Yeah, it sounds even more insane when you say that the one who gave you the task is an angel of God."

"Shit. You are serious. Okay, let's pretend for a moment I believe you. Anything I should be aware of if I find this cup?"

"Yeah don't touch it. Also if you start having dreams about gods be afraid."

"Sorry I asked." Lance sighed, ran a hand through his red hair. "I've got more good news for you then; our old friend who likes to create furies is back."

"Damn. When?"

"Sent me a package the night I met with your ex; Catharine saw it."

"Perfect. It's bad enough having Kedar out there – now him! Looks like I'll be putting in another call to my DC contacts. Trouble is I don't have room to work this right now." Sam groused.

"Yeah got that, you have to gather the mantles of the gods!" Lance said with a chuckle.

"Laugh it up cop. Did they find anything at the auction house?"

"Afraid not."

"Figures, keep me posted on all fronts and Lance, be careful."

"Will do." Lance assured him before hanging up. He then put in a call to report the break in.

126

Sam hung up Anna's phone and handed it back to her.

"How did he take it?" She questioned.

"About as well as can be expected, he doesn't believe it. Can't blame him but he knows we do. He'll help us as best he can." Sam answered.

"Did they find anything?"

"Afraid not."

"Figured as much. What else did he want?"

"Update on an old story." Sam said dismissively.

"Oh." Anna drew a couple deep cleansing breaths before punching in Ian's number. She prayed for calm as she waited for him to pick up.

"Ian Broody."

"Ian, it's Anna."

"Oh Anna, did you make it back to the states all right?"

"Yes. I went straight home. I wanted to get that disk on its way to you before I started my vacation."

"Splendid. When should I expect it?"

"I'm afraid I've hit a snag. The person I left it with just called; it seems someone broke into his home. The disk was taken."

"What?"

"I'm sorry Ian. I left it with a cop I thought it would be safe." Anna stated.

"Damn it Anna, I needed that disk. It's… important. You better pray you find it or I'll see you pay for its loss." Ian snapped.

"I'll do my best, good day Dr. Broody," Anna assured him then she hung up.

"How'd he take the news?" Sam asked, joining her in the living room of her home.

"Not well. I think you're right. He knows more than he's letting on. It must have been in those tablets." Anna shivered ill at ease.

"You okay?" Sam asked.

"I think so. There was just something about the last thing he said. It gave me the chills. He's getting worse," Anna murmured. Sam drew her into his arms, rubbed her shoulders to chase away the cold. He brushed her brow with a kiss.

"We'll be long gone from here before he can do anything." He whispered to assure her. "Why don't you go on up to your room, lie down and relax. I'll be up in a few with a cup of hot tea and a bite to eat. Once we're done eating we can get out of here."

"That sounds wonderful. Don't take too long," Anna requested. She brushed his lips with her own in a quick peck. Turning she headed up the stairs.

127

Sam stepped into the kitchen. He whistled with appreciation. The room was neat and spacious. It was split into three distinct sections: the main portion of the room was for food preparation, the smallest space looked to be a breakfast nook tucked in a small corner in the back. Next to it was a dining area. He noted a lack of a fridge; wondered at it. Seeing all the cabinet space he groaned. Maybe I should have asked Anna where to find things.

Considering what he knew of her Sam headed in the direction of the breakfast nook. The counter space near it held a small sink, a microwave and anything else she might require for preparing a quick breakfast. He found coffee mugs hanging in a line next to the microwave. Opening the cabinet he found tea bags and other non perishables associated with breakfast. He took down a mug filled it with water and put it in the microwave. He then selected a tea to sooth her before moving on to look for something to eat.

As he walked about he noticed no sign of a pantry either. Recalling the hidden room in the office, he wondered if perhaps the door to the pantry was disguised as well. It wasn't long before he located it at the end of the counter on the far wall. Stepping inside he laughed there was the fridge. All manner of food stuffs were here as well. A large chest freezer was tucked against the far wall.

Sam pulled out the fixing for a couple sandwiches. He grabbed some chips and moved back into the kitchen. Sam closed the pantry door behind him. The microwave beeped marking the water ready. He crossed the room, took it out, putting the tea bag in the mug. He let it steep and turned his focus to fixing lunch. He was slicing cheese when he became aware he wasn't alone.

"I'm almost done…" He began. The rest of his words died off as he found himself faced not with Anna but Pamela. She wore a clingy red dress with matching heels. Her crimson lips curved in a smile at the sight of him preparing a meal. “Ela, what are you doing here?” He asked. The old endearment fell from his lips before he was aware of it.

She crossed the room to him in three quick strides. Threw her arms around him “Sam, I’m glad to see you’re safe. I’ve been so worried since I found this place torn apart. I was afraid you’d gotten in over your head again. That something bad might happen to you.” She whispered. Pamela moved her left arm around his neck. He felt the bite of her manicured nails on his scalp and blinked.

Get a grip she’s not your Ela any more, hasn’t been for a long time he reminded himself. The smell of her perfume overwhelmed him. He’d missed her, though he’d never admit it. Why couldn’t he get her out of his system? She didn’t care not really. He reminded himself. “I’m fine Pam, what do you want?” he asked his voice was frigid, hinting at annoyance.

She drew back so they were face to face. Her whisky eyes held hurt. She ran her fingers down his cheek and neck to his chest. “Nothing, I just wanted to make sure you were all right. It’s not like you vanishing without a word. Oh, thank you for signing that paper for me. The book means a lot to me.”

“You’re welcome. I trust this means were square.”

“Of course I sent a message to my lawyer to call off the suit. I’m sorry about that, it wasn’t my idea. My agent said that I should do it. I was mad at the time so I did. It wasn’t right or fair,” Pamela whispered.

“I should have known,” Sam said with disgust. He’d never been a fan of her agent the guy was shady.

“Can you forgive me?” she asked. Pamela batted her long lashes at him in the way she always had to get what she wanted.

“Yeah, I can,” he breathed.

“Thank you, that means a lot. I made a lot of bad choices of late. The truth is I still want you Sam,” She murmured then she kissed him.

128

Pamela felt Sam slide into her kiss. She repressed a triumphant laugh. He was so easy. He always had been. It was one of the reasons she'd agreed to marry him in the first place. Her mother had taught her well, it was a shame she'd had to end it. If she'd just waited a little longer maybe things would have been different. It didn't matter now she was moving on to bigger and better things. She would be damned if she was going to let Sam walk off into the sunset with, the good doctor, Anna Gallagher. Sam was hers. He always would be. No other woman was allowed to take her place.

Pamela opened her whiskey eyes at the sound of footsteps. She looked past Sam to see the lovely blonde. Her hazel eyes met with Pamela's and turned gray, pain shown on her tanned face. Pamela smiled before closing her eyes, dragging Sam deeper under her spell. Her fingers tore at his shirt fighting for the feel of skin. Sam groaned his arms wrapping about her tight so there was no space between them. He lifted her from the floor. Pamela wrapped her legs around his waist pressing the center of her against the source of his growing desire.

She pulled off his shirt, throwing it in the direction of the doorway. She heard a sharp intake of breath – retreating steps. Bulls-eye, that's right move on he's taken, Pamela's thoughts murmured. Her lips parted his. She nipped and sucked her way down his throat; leaving smears of her crimson lipstick in her wake. Seeing the possessive markings she laughed with delight before sliding down from his waist. She took a step back. Pausing a moment to catch her breath. She'd done what she came to. It was time to put the brakes on, back away. The idea of having him there in Anna's kitchen was appealing but Pamela remembered Artemis's warning. She didn't want to find out what kind of consequences she might face for sleeping with her ex.

"You still taste good Sam. I don't think we should be doing this here though. I suppose this will have to tide you over until next time," She whispered. Pamela kissed him again. A light brushing of her lips against his. She gave his lower lip a playful nip then stepped away. "I'll be in touch," she murmured. Turing she walked off, leaving him half naked – aroused and confused.

129

Sam stood by the counter in silence. The only sounds in the room were the tick of the clock, and the pounding of his own heart. She was gone. How could she do that? Get him all wound up then throw on the breaks. His body ached with thwarted need. Sam swore with disgust. He realized she'd done it again.

Reality crashed in on him. He became aware of his surroundings. He was in Anna's kitchen for crying out loud. He needed to get a grip. The chill of the air hit his skin and he groaned. Where was his shirt? When had he lost it? How long had he been lost in her? Sam sighed. Spotting the shirt in the doorway he crossed the floor, picked it up.

Sam pulled on his shirt. It was then he noticed that the satchel with the horn which he'd had hanging from his belt was gone.

"Damn you Pamela," he shouted with disgust understanding now why she'd played with him.

"What's wrong?" Anna asked. She came into the living room from the direction of her office. She blinked at the sight of the red smudges on his skin.

"She took the horn," Sam said. He laughed.

Anna's dove, grey eyes darkened to the color of steel as her temper flared. "You think this is funny?"

"No, of course not," Sam stammered surprised by the anger.

"Then why the hell are you laughing?" Anna snapped with disgust. Her eyes didn't meet his blue ones instead her gaze kept drifting away from him. "Because somehow despite how much I can't stand that woman she always manages to get what she wants from me," Sam muttered with annoyance. He looked down at himself to where Anna's gaze kept drifting. He was mortified to see Pamela's lipstick all over him. "Ah hell," he cursed. Moved back to the sink grabbing a rag he turned on the tap. Sam worked at cleaning himself up.

"What do you mean?" Anna asked curious.

"I don't know. I just know that when I'm around her it's like I can't think. She crowds me. I can't push her away."

"I see. So, I've got a question for you. How the hell did she know to take it?"

"I haven't a clue." Sam stated. He rung out the rag, turned off the tap. "Look I know what that looked like but…"

'It doesn't matter I've got to get that horn back."

Not caring for the way she brushed the matter of the lipstick aside he considered her temper, wondered if she'd walked in on that. He felt his stomach twist with disgust. She must have. "Don't you mean we?" Sam asked. He reached for her hand, looking to reestablish their connection. Anna pulled away from his touch. Her hazel eyes he noted were the color of steel in her fury. Sam swore. He'd hoped to keep things civil but she'd seen more than he feared.

"Don't touch me. How could you - in my house? Was she worth it? Never mind. I don't even want to know. It doesn't matter… Look I'll get the horn alone. You said it yourself you can't be trusted around her." Anna said. She turned and walked out of the kitchen.

Sam cursed knowing she was right. He shoved everything he'd gathered off the counter and shouted in a display of his temper. The mug hit the floor, shattering. Cool water splashed out. He sighed. He'd managed to make a real mess of things. What was the matter with him? Why couldn't he resist Pamela's charms? Sam found no answer. He growled in his frustration. It was maddening. He needed to get out of there before he broke something else. Mind made up Sam turned, made his way to the front door.

Stepping outside he locked the door with the spare key Anna had given him. Starting down the street at a slow jog; he hoped a run would clear his head.

130

WASHINGTON DC, VIRGINIA
FRIDAY
7PM

Lance stepped through the green, oak double doors of the Brickskeller. He made his way towards the hostess station. His thoughts drifted to Catharine. It was a shame she had to leave before he could tell her about the place. She'd have loved it. He had no doubt that she'd have asked a million questions about it. He'd have been entertained as he answered them. Another time, he told himself, though he doubted there would be one. It had been a while since he brought anyone here off shift. He normally met here with his boss or fellow officers on the clock when business couldn't be discussed in house. The last person he'd had in was Dana.

Lance sighed. He didn't want to dwell on her or the case that had ended her life. No, he'd come here to get away from all that. At the house her ghost had been crowding him. It had been a long tiring day. Right now all he wanted was a few minutes away from it all to clear his head. He was just wondering if his preferred booth would be open when he spotted a familiar face at the bar. Lance crossed the room to take a seat next to him.

"Sam, what are you doing here? Where's Anna?"

Sam took one look at him and cursed. "She's gone."

"Gone where? Why?"

"She's off chasing down Pamela. She dropped in earlier. Took the horn."

"What horn? Stopped in where? Why would you let Anna go off alone? It isn't safe," Lance snapped.

"Damn it, can you ask one question at a time please, my heads starting to hurt." Sam muttered before taking a pull from his beer. "Anna and I have to find the lost mantles of the gods and make sure no one else gets their hands on them. Weird powers or something like that, Pamela took the one we managed to recover today."

"Yeah, got that, you told me earlier. The missing cup is one of these mantles as well," Lance said. He looked at the former reporter turned fighter and he wondered how many he'd had.

"That's right. As to the where, I was in Anna's kitchen at the time. She just let herself in the house. Put on her show. Fool that I am I fell for it again."

"What's that mean?"

"It means my ex-wife is a horrible tease. She knows how to cloud a man's head. Poor Anna must have walked in on us. Not sure when. It couldn't have been good by the time Pam let me up for air I was standing in the kitchen and my shirt was gone," Sam said with disgust.

"Son of…"

"Yeah I know it. Anna said I couldn't be trusted around my ex. She left."

"You let her?" Lance asked with disbelief.

"Yeah, because the worst of it is she's right. I can't think straight when I get around Pamela." Sam said with disgust. Lance shook his head. His temper flared. Without a thought he hit Sam.

"You're an idiot. So you messed up, it happens. I'm sure it does in the ring too but you get up. Try again right. You're not a news reporter any more. You're an MMA Fighter. From what I've heard a good one. If what you say is true about these mantles then you were chosen to help Anna. I sent her to you for a reason. It's not because you were a reporter. Whatever it is she has to do she's going to need a warrior to stand with her, that's you."

Sam blinked, considered the matter. "Yeah maybe but that doesn't change the fact that I can't be trusted around my ex. She's involved in this mess somehow." Sam muttered.

"So what if she is, that shouldn't matter. Whatever your history you can get past it. You care about Anna right?"

"Yeah and she saw me…"

"What she saw doesn't matter. From what Catharine said about Pamela's type I'm sure that if Anna saw anything Pamela wanted her to see it."

Sam cursed.

"Now, the way I see it you can let her continue to control your life. Ruin what you had going with Anna or you can fight back. The choice is up to you. Personally I wouldn't let your ex-wife win." Lance stated before he slid down from the stool. He moved back to the hostess station. He'd said all he was going to on the matter.

131

Sam took another sip of his beer; found he'd lost his taste for it. He mulled over what Lance had said, rubbed his jaw where Lance had punched him then laughed. He'd been hit more than once today, he mused. Sam wasn't sure he was ready for another round.

"He's right you know." A familiar voice stated. Sam looked over at the seat Lance had vacated. He glared at his angelic visitor. Why wouldn't they leave him alone to wallow in his guilt?

Sam sighed. "I know it. But I'm afraid. What if this happens again? Why can't I think around her? I have no control when it comes to Pamela. I don't know why! We're divorced – most of the time I can't stand her."

"You humans, you think that you sign a piece of paper and that fixes your problems. You don't understand marriage. When you spoke your vows you became one being; your souls tied one to the other. That doesn't just end when you sign on the dotted line. You're still bound to her in the spirit. Until that tie is severed she will torment you."

"What must I do to be done with her?" Sam asked.

"You know Samuel, Abrams. You've known since I told Anna she had to make her choice. You believed first, but you've set down roots; refused to step forward. In waiting you've given the enemy time to move."

"What do you mean?" Sam asked puzzled.

"Do you think it a coincidence Pamela is now in the hunt? The enemy is cunning he will use your weaknesses to distract you from your goal – to break you."

"He hit the mark well. Not only did she get the horn she managed to hurt Anna in the process," Sam said with disgust.

"Yes he did and more."

"Meaning?"

"Pamela does not know it but she is in grave danger. When Anna made her choice the fallen one who pursued her chose another. Her."

"Shit."

"You waste time drowning your guilt here, take it to the Creator. Be done with it. Anna needs you," the angel stated.

Sam set down his beer and the money for it. He nodded and slid down from the bar stool. Turning he headed out the double doors. As he stepped into the evening air he prayed.

Sam stepped through the front door of Anna's Georgian home. It felt wrong to him to be there when she wasn't. It couldn't be helped. He'd left his things before including his phone. He had to get a hold of her. Sam knew where Pamela was headed. He couldn't let Anna go back there alone. Picking up his phone he punched in her number, prayed that she would answer as he paced the floor waiting. He recalled the mess he'd made earlier and headed for the kitchen.

"Come on Anna pick up," he whispered. Willing her to answer but the phone went to her voice mail. "Anna I know you don't want to talk but please call me. I know how Pamela knew about the horn and where she's headed next." He considered leaving an apology. Realized it wouldn't be welcome at the moment.

Sam hung up the phone, turned his attention to cleaning up his mess. He made a mental note to buy her a coffee mug to replace the broken one.

132

Anna groaned as her phone rang for the third time in an hour. She noted Sam's number and sighed. The man was persistent. She was beat. Anna had been to every fancy hotel in the DC area asking to see if Miss Walsh was there. She had come up with nothing. At her wits end she pressed the button to check her messages. Anna cursed. She should have answered the damn phone then maybe she wouldn't have blisters on her feet from all the walking. She'd wasted an hour because of a bruised ego. It was disgraceful her parents would be disgusted. Anna shoved these thoughts aside, pushing the button to return his call.

"Anna, thank God I've been trying to reach you for a little over an hour." Sam said he sounded almost frantic.

She blinked surprised by the intensity in his voice and the clear display of relief. She wasn't used to such open expression of emotions. "Yes, I got your message."

"Where are you?" Sam asked.

"The Mayflower, I've been trying hotels looking for her. I came up with nothing." She stated frustrated.

"Sorry to hear it." Sam said.

"So how is it you think she knew about the horn?"

"Hermes, Pamela has a questing mind, an unending love of searching out a story – facts and knowledge, she would have been a prime candidate for him as a second choice," Sam stated.

"Ah hell, why didn't that occur to me?"

"Don't feel bad I didn't have it either until after our mutual friend dropped in on me, pointed it out." Sam admitted.

"So where is she headed?" Anna asked trying to play catch up.

"The way I figure it there's only one place she can be going."

"Atlantis, but how does she know?"

"He led her there. I've been thinking while I waited. The way I figure it the reason Broody is spooking you is he's been influenced by Hermes as well."

"Why?"

"Well, I'm not sure on the particulars. Our friend said the horn and statue can't be brought together right?"

"Yes."

"Well, in the vision the key opened a door and Hermes came forth. I'm thinking, what if the same is true of the horn; but he needs a sacrifice in order to return to claim his bride."

"Makes sense. We've got to stop her."

"We?" he asked with relief.

"Yeah I may not be able to trust you around her but I can't take on Broody's thugs alone." Anna stated.

"Right. Anna about earlier I'm sorry. I…"

"Save it for later Sam. Where are you?"

"At your house."

"I'm on my way." Anna stated before she hung up.

133

Pamela stepped out of her cab, heading for Artemis's private plane. She had to move. It wouldn't take Sam long to figure out she had the horn or where she would be going. That was the thing she'd loved about him his sharp mind. It thrilled her to no end that she could dull it. He was putty in her hands.

Artemis stepped off the plane, greeting Pamela with a kiss on each cheek. "Welcome Sister. You've done well. Lord Hermes will be pleased. Call to him once we are underway. He will answer. "

Pamela trembled with anticipation. "They'll be close behind," she stated.

"Yes, well I know it. Do not fret I have it in hand," Artemis assured her as they boarded the plane. It taxied down the runway. After a quick check with the tower they took to the skies. Once they were in the air Artemis rose to her feet. "I call upon the powers passed down to me by my father Zeus, king of the gods. Let the sky rage war behind us to hinder our foes pursuit." Her voice came from everywhere and nowhere. Her blue eyes lit from within as she wielded her power. Outside the clouds gathered behind them. Lightening split the sky.

Confident that Sam would be delayed Pamela closed her eyes. "Hermes," the name fell from her lips like a prayer. In an instant he responded, drawing her into the dream world.

134

Sam cursed as rain fell in sheets across the windshield as they approached the plane hangar. Lightning flashed. Thunder rumbled above while the winds howled. The storm that raged had come swift – sudden. The evening sky filled with black clouds that changed a pleasant evening to an ugly night. Weather reports warned of possible tornados. They pulled into the cover of the hanger the rain behind them coming down looked like a waterfall.

Stepping out of the car he heard the roaring of the wind. The pilot came out of the plane.

"All flights have been grounded due to this mess."

"I figured, any idea how long." Sam asked.

"No clue. They don't even know where it came from," the pilot shouted over the crashing thunder.

"Well, we can't go back out in the rain to wait. We barely made it here. Had to pull over and switch drivers." Sam stated. He watched as Anna got out of the car. She was still scared, he could see it, but not like when she was driving.

"Come aboard you can wait it out in the cabin. When it breaks we'll head out," the pilot said. Sam nodded. The trio entered the plane.

Once inside Anna sank into one of the leather seats away from the windows Sam sat down beside her. "You okay?" he whispered.

"Yeah, I just hate driving in the rain. I got caught in weather like this once on a dig in Brazil. I lost control of the car and crashed. I was out in the jungle alone for two days before someone from the team found me."

"That must have been horrible."

Anna said nothing she simply closed her eyes to try and relax.

"Anna about earlier I…"

"No need to explain. She was your wife it's only natural for you to still want her."

"I don't want her Anna."

"How can you say that? I saw you with her. You were in my kitchen. Her legs wrapped around your waist mouth all over you. She threw your damn shirt at me. From where I was standing it looked like you were going to have her for lunch instead, and on my counter." Anna said with disgust.

"I'm sorry you saw that. I can't imagine how you must have felt. But try to understand I didn't want her. Pamela has a presence about her that drags you under. She attacks the senses, overwhelms you before you know what's happening, your mind drowns. All you can do is what she wants."

Anna's eyes opened. She wanted to be disgusted but she understood what he was saying. Hermes had done the same to her in one of her dreams. "I'm sorry, has it always been that way with her?" Anna questioned.

"No, at least I don't think, maybe it was I just wasn't aware of it until we split."

"Why then?"

"After I moved to Vegas I met a girl. She was nice. We hit it off. I was getting ready to have her in for a meal when Pamela turned up. The girl walked in took one look at us hit me and left." Sam said with regret.

"She set you up," Anna whispered; seeing it clearly in her mind then and earlier that day in her home. "Damn. I played right into her hand," she whispered with disgust then laughed. "Oh, she's good. I'll give her that. She left you?" Anna questioned.

"Yeah, when my career went south."

"Cold blooded. She leaves but won't let you move on. You're hers until she says otherwise," Anna murmured. Her temper flaring as she looked at Pamela's nature. Sam was a good man. He deserved better.

Sam swore. She realized he'd never thought of it that way, but was beginning to now. The image Anna described made sense. "So it would seem," Sam muttered.

Anna took his face in her hands she pressed her cheek against his forehead. She kissed it. "Not anymore," Anna murmured before her lips met his. She gave him a short peck then drew back. "I'm still here." She assured him before letting him go. Sam grabbed her hand stopping her retreat, kissed her knuckles.

"Thank you," he breathed as he let her hand go.

Anna was aware of him watching her as she sank back into the chair. She said nothing of it. She was sure he didn't understand why she was so quick to forgive him, but she figured he was grateful.

"You're a good man Sam," she assured him as she closed her eyes. She heard him let out a breath he'd been holding as the tension between them eased.

135

Lance groaned as he stepped into his front door. He was soaked to the skin. That was the last time he was going to walk to the Brickskeller. Where the hell had the rain come from? He'd been on his way home when it started. There wasn't a cab in sight. Lance stepped out of his shoes. He left the soaked shirt as well; hoping not to drip all over the place.

He made his way back towards his room the sound of the answering machine beeping from the kitchen caught his attention. "I'll get to you in a minute," he muttered. Lance opened the guest bath. He switched on the light, grabbed a towel. Then moved on to his room where he stripped off his wet clothes. Toweled off and pulled on dry ones. Having chased away the chill he tossed his wet things in the hamper near the master bath.

His thoughts drifted to the past when the door had been marked over by yellow crime scene tape. His heart constricted. Lance turned away from the door having no desire to remember again tonight. He had no doubt his dreams would run back to it, no point tormenting himself while awake as well. Turning Lance moved out of the room back to the kitchen where the answering machine chirped.

He pressed the button to play it back. Lance listened as the machine informed him he had a message. It ran through the information of the call.

"Hey, it's Catharine sorry I had to run out the other night. You looked upset about something. I hope this finds you doing well. Started filming today it's a little overwhelming. Well, I should probably go; breaks almost up. I'll try later, bye."

Lance sighed she sounded distracted, a bit down. He pressed the button to delete the message. He wasn't in the mood to talk at the moment. Moving into the living room he picked up her book. Set to reading. He needed to get away from the world for a while. He hoped the storm wouldn't interfere with his escape.

136 Miami, Florida

Pamela stepped off the plane focused and reenergized by her visit with Hermes. She'd been afraid at first. Unsure as her thoughts drifted back to what she'd done to get the horn from Sam. As Hermes touched her she'd felt unworthy of him. She'd worried he'd be angry. Had pushed him away and wept, telling him of her moment with Sam.

Hermes rather than rage had kissed her until she was breathless – her body burning with desire. When his lips had parted hers he'd laughed with delight. His words from before, echoed in her mind.

"My dear one, do you think me as weak as a mere man? I know your devotion lies with me. I was there with you as you used your power upon him, watching – reveling in the act. Only the devoted will give their mind body and soul to please their god. I am overjoyed that you are mine."

Pamela smiled as her thoughts ran on to their time together. It wouldn't be long now until they met in this world. She was looking forward to it. She'd soon have everything she ever wanted. He'd promised her.

"I'll send a messenger ahead and prepare you a room at the hotel," Artemis stated interrupting Pamela's train of thought.

"No, need I'm not tired we'll head straight for the harbor. The sooner we reach the city of the gods and meet with this man Broody the better." Pamela stated.

Artemis smiled. "As you like my sister," she murmured and the pair moved on together in silence.

137 Atlantis, Somewhere in the Bermuda Triangle

Pamela stepped off the boat on the lost isle. She looked upon the city as the morning sun began to rise.

"From here you go on alone. You know the way. Broody will be waiting for you," Artemis murmured from the boat deck.

Pamela nodded. "Thank you sister," she whispered then started in the direction of the secret passage

Pamela made her way up the ladder and into the throne room as she came forth a man stared down at her.

"Amazing," he breathed the word as if in a trance.

"Dr. Broody," she questioned. Pamela studied the older man with dark hair and steel grey eyes with question. She'd been expecting someone younger; this guy was no match for Sam.

"Yes, and you would be Miss Walsh?' he said it with a certainty that made little sense as they had never met.

Pamela stepped aside from the passage as the altar slid back into place. She pulled from her bag the satchel she'd taken from her ex. "I am. I was asked to give you this," she stated. Opening the velvet bag she pulled out the horn from within, placing it in his hands.

His eyes gleamed with a strange light as his hands closed around the silver horn. Pamela felt something rush through them. Awareness stirred within her. This was it, what she wasn't sure, but it held the key. Broody's gaze met with hers.

Pamela gasped as she looked in his eyes. They were no longer grey but blue. Hermes voice whispered in her mind urging her to kiss him. She felt his presence coming from the man before her. Saw that he desired her. Recalling Hermes words from earlier she drew Ian Broody into her arms. Pamela kissed him. He answered her with a fierce intensity that stole her breath, thrilling her. Hermes was there just below the surface, waiting for her to release him. She gave herself over to him willingly, mind, body and soul.

Pamela laid upon the cool stone of the altar her body stiff, Broody crushing her. He stirred and kissed her brow.

"I'm sorry my lovely one," he whispered before rising.

"I don't understand I thought I'd be with you Hermes not Broody," she whispered confused.

"Soon my sweet, I'll tell you the story of the ages very soon. It will be me not this vessel. My return draws near then you will know me. All you desire you will have." He assured her as he dressed

Pamela fixed her clothes, kissing him briefly before he bent and picked up the horn. When it was in his hands his eyes returned to steel gray.

"Where did you get this?" He questioned; once again the man.

"I got it from Dr. Gallagher." Pamela murmured. Relieved to see no sign the man was aware of what had happened earlier. It was as if no time had passed for him since she gave him the horn.

"Go back. Learn all you can about it. I must know what it is," Broody said with excitement.

"Consider it done," Pamela murmured. She turned and left heading back the way she came

138

Broody held the horn in his grasp; he stared at it with wonder. What was it? Something within him stirred urging him to set it in the hands of the statues. Why he wondered. Looking up at the statues he studied them. They held out their hands waiting for something. They want the disk he reasoned, but questioned if that was right. It didn't matter Miss Walsh would find out.

Ian felt his blood hum with desire at the woman's name. He'd had the strangest reaction when he saw her. He'd felt for a moment that she'd held all the answers to his question about the horn. That all he'd need to do was take them. He asked himself how; and again in his mind's eye he pictured kissing her. Watching as her whisky eyes went dark with passion; lifting her from the floor taking her upon the stone altar.

The image passed again, Ian swallowed his throat having gone dry. He blinked. The image shifted in her place was Anna. Ian groaned with hunger as the two women traded places in his fantasy. A voice within him whispered they were the same either would serve to unlock what he sought.

"I don't understand," he whispered to the dark room.

"You will," the voice within him assured him. "You'll learn all you seek to in time and more. Protect the horn do not lose it. Keep for yourself the treasures you find they are more precious than you can yet understand."

Ian studied the statues for a moment. They were the only one of their kind in the world. He had to add them to his collection but how. Everyone there at the dig knew of their existence. I'll have replicas made of both them and the tablets. I alone will possess a copy of them. Satisfied Ian smiled. He'd get part of his team started on it immediately.

139

Miami, Florida
Saturday
11am

Anna stepped off the plane. She made her way towards the car. They needed to move. They were over twelve hours behind Pamela.

"We should head straight for the harbor," Sam stated.

"I agree only problem is the boat doesn't run to the island on Saturdays," Anna said with a sigh.

"You're kidding."

"Afraid not, might as well head for the hotel we won't be able to reach the isle until Monday."

"Damn."

"Yes that storm gave Pamela plenty of time to reach the isle. She'll have met with Broody by now. I just hope whatever it is that has to happen, takes a few days or we may already be too late." Anna said with disgust. She cursed herself for wasting time the other night. If she'd taken Sam's call then they might have been able to catch Pamela before she gave the horn to Broody.

"Don't beat yourself. This isn't your fault. Forget about asking what if. Let's just get moving," Sam said "If you let them, the questions will drive you crazy."

Anna nodded. The pair got in the car. Sam drove out of the airport headed for the hotel. She prayed they'd be able to reach Atlantis in time.

140

SATURDAY
8PM

Pamela walked into the Aqualina Resort and Spa. She headed for the front desk to get a room. As she walked, she spotted Sam and Anna sitting in the restaurant. She fumed; she'd have thought the good doctor would have left for good after finding Sam in the kitchen with her. Perhaps she'd underestimated just how low the woman's self-esteem was. Pamela wondered what Sam had said and done to keep Miss Gallagher around but dismissed the matter.

She smiled, on the plus side of things she'd not have to travel after all to get the information she needed. Besides it had been fun playing with Sam. Now that she knew how Hermes felt about it she'd be sure to enjoy it. She was looking forward to seeing that broken look in Anna's eyes again. As she reached the desk she considered her next move.

"May I help you Miss?"

"Yes I'd like a room for the night."

"Very good was there anything else?"

"Yes do you see the couple in the restaurant? She's my sister. I came in to surprise her for her birthday could you tell me which room their staying in?" Pamela said her voice sweet as honey. She batted her eye lashes at him.

"Of course Miss Gallagher is staying in suite 510."

"Thank you; please don't say anything to her. I want to keep this a surprise." Pamela murmured. She slid him an extra fifty.

"My lips are sealed," he assured her, handing over her room key. Pamela palmed the key. Thanked him again before moving on. She hoped they hadn't spotted her.

141

Sam sat with Anna on the sofa of their joint suit. He watched as the credits began to roll. After checking in they had agreed to not worry about Pamela or the horn. They would enjoy the weekend. Treat it like a mini-vacation. They'd shared a nice dinner in the restaurant then come back to the room, sat down to a movie.

Anna yawned. "What time is it?" she murmured.

"After eleven I think."

"I'm going to call it a night Sam. Thank you this was nice." Anna brushed a kiss on his cheek. Getting up she moved on to her room. Sam whispered a good night then turned off the TV and headed for his own room.

Sam was beat from a long couple of days but not quite ready to turn in. He stepped out of his shoes in the dark not bothering with the lights. He crossed the room to the bathroom, feeling the need of a shower. He felt grimier than he had in a while. He wondered if it was all the travel or just the after effects of yesterday's actions: first with Pamela then in turn the visit to the bar. Sam hadn't set foot in a bar since he moved to Vegas. It bugged him he'd wound up in one yesterday. It was just another way he'd let Pamela take control. He sighed, no point dwelling on the matter it was over.

Sam flipped on the light in the hotel washroom, walked inside closing the door behind him. He got out of his clothes, switched on the shower, stepped inside.

Sam stepped out of the bathroom a few minutes later, towel drying his hair. Light spilled into the bedroom from the bath casting shadows, illuminating the dark. Through the dim light he spotted someone else in the room with him. Sam froze.

"Hello Sam," her voice was sweet like honey and all too familiar. A voice he'd come to so many times. Drawn to like that of a sirens song. Tonight it had no effect upon him.

Sam switched on the lights unwilling to face her alone, in the dark. He blinked as his eyes adjusted. She stood at the edge of his bed blonde hair spilling out of her loose bun. In a way that had always driven him crazy showing off the curve of her swan like neck, inviting him to taste it. She brushed a lose strand of her bottle blonde hair out of her whiskey brown eyes, tucking it behind an ear. Drawing attention to the sapphires he'd given her.

She wore a blue silk blouse with plunging neck line. He'd always loved it when they were together. It was snug across the chest making her breast look bigger, revealing plenty of cleavage. She'd paired it with a black low waist mini skirt that showed off her flat belly, emphasizing her long shapely legs. He knew the look well; it was one that on more than one occasion she'd seduced him with when they were still together.

Sam had no doubt in his mind that was her intent. As he looked at her now he couldn't understand why it had held such appeal. She was trying too hard - came off looking trashy. "What are you doing here Pamela?" he said his voice neutral.

She licked her crimson lips in a false show of nervousness, drawing his attention to her mouth. Getting him thinking about their last kiss. Sam saw right through her act for the first time since they met. Realizing that every step she took was calculated – meant to control him. His temper flared with disgust. He wondered what he'd ever seen in her.

"Sam, I'm sorry about yesterday. I had no choice." Pamela whispered. She closed the distance between them boxing him in as she had so many times before. The smell of her perfume filled his nostrils and he struggled to breath. What did she do bath in it? He wondered. The smell became so thick he could taste it.

"I followed you out to the dig in Israel. I was worried. I thought I smelled a story. I ended up here at the Atlantis dig. Dr. Broody caught me at the site. He threatened my life unless I brought him that horn." Pamela murmured. She reached out her blood red nails brushed through his wet hair.

Sam said nothing. He waited. Aware that she was lying. Broody had known nothing of the horn when they left and nothing of her connection to Sam. She'd not been threatened by Broody or anyone for that matter. She'd been told about it by her god Hermes. She had done as he asked willingly.

"I was so scared I did as he asked. I tracked you down at Anna's - took it. I'm so sorry Sam, can you ever forgive me," she asked. Pamela threw herself into his arms, buried her face in his chest and cried.

Sam pushed her away. He wanted to knock her down but was gentle. She was being used here, though she didn't know it. He needed to try and make her see that. Sam decided that if she was there to seduce him as he suspected he needed to get her away from her goal, his bed.

"Let's talk about this in the living room," he whispered. Sam led her out of the room. She clung to his side. Not giving him any space to breathe; still trying to work her will upon him. Sam sat her down on the couch, stepped back. She snatched his hand holding it tight. Not allowing him to put too much distance between them.

"I can forgive you Pamela, but I need you to tell me why you are really here? Broody didn't know anything about the horn." Sam stated.

Pamela stood up. She brushed his dark hair away from his blue eyes, her brown ones pleading with him to listen to her. "I'm here because I missed you. I felt bad about before. I still care for you Sam. I don't want you to think that what happened yesterday was just to get the horn. I wanted you, I still do. I know we've made our mistakes. I made a lot of them. I should have stood by you," She whispered. Pamela wrapped her arms around his neck, kissed him.

Sam pushed her away. Reaching up he tried to pull her loose. "I don't believe you Ela." He said his voice cool as a winter's day. "I want to know right now what are you doing here?" He demanded.

"Broody does know about the horn. He found out about it in one of his documents at the dig. He caught me just like I said. He had his goons rough me up until I told him what I was doing there. Then he threatened my life unless I got that horn from you. I gave it to him. He sent me back for everything you know about it. If I come back empty handed he'll kill me." Pamela wept. She held him tight refusing to let go.

"You're lying Pamela; Broody didn't know we had the horn. We'd just obtained it that day. You're here because Hermes sent you here. He told you he chose you for his bride. Did he mention he chose Anna first? She refused him. Listen Ela, don't get into this thing any deeper than you already have. You're dealing with a force far greater than anything you can imagine – a power that will destroy you. Get out now while you still can."

Sam watched as temper flashed for a moment in her whiskey colored eyes. It disappeared. Something else flickered there and then her lips crushed his with a bruising force. Teeth nipped at his lower lip parting them so she could take more. Her hands were everywhere nails biting. She straddled his leg, road it using her thigh to press against his groin. Teasing him and demanding he finish what they started yesterday.

Sam shoved her away disgusted. She fell to the floor. "Get out," he snapped. She gasped and stared at him with disbelief.

"What?"

"I said get out. You're not welcome here Pamela. You have no right to touch me."

"What do you mean I have no right? You're mine damn it. I want you. I will have you," she snapped outraged.

"No you won't. I am not your plaything any more we're over. Get out before I call security. Don't bother coming back. You'll get nothing more from me," he stated. His blue eyes met with Anna's hazel ones from across the room pleading with her not to leave.

142

Pamela sputtered and hissed like a spurned cat. She got to her feet. Rage filled her. She measured both of them for a coffin. As she contemplated her next move the door burst open. Six of Broody's men rushed in.

"Anna, run!" Sam shouted as he moved to intercept the intruders.

Pamela's gaze fell upon the troublesome scientist. She attacked. If it wasn't for her Sam would still be wrapped around her finger. Somehow the bitch had broken her hold on him. Broody needed to know what Anna did, so be it. She'd take the troublemaker to him. Let him deal with her. She broke a lamp over Anna's head knocking her out cold.

Sam fought off Broody's goons. She watched with a thrill. He was holding his own. Given time, would win. She had no doubt in her mind. Grabbing Anna by the hair Pamela dragged her away, slipping out of the room in the confusion.

143

Sam threw a Super Man punch knocking out one of his attackers. He dodged a right hook from another, answered with a head kick. The guy went down like a felled tree, leaving four others. He'd lost sight of Anna. He prayed that she'd gotten out of there safely. Sam wrapped an arm around one guy's throat, choking him out. Another came at him like a linebacker tackling him to the floor. Sam saw stars with the impact but shook it off. He blocked the guy's first punch with his feet, caught the second before dragging him down into his guard. The guy struggled to break loose. Sam threw his legs up catching the guy in a triangle. He held him until the guy went limp.

"Damn who is this guy," one of the two remaining men muttered. He watched them run away. Sam drew a breath, getting to his feet. The metallic taste of his own blood was in his mouth from a couple punches he'd taken early on. No real damage just a couple bruises he figured. Sam looked around there was no sign of Pamela or Anna. He spotted the broken lamp with a few strands of blond hair. A few drops of blood on it. He cursed with annoyance. He pictured Pamela hitting Anna with the lamp, dragging her out in the confusion. He kicked the glass and pulled out his cell phone.

"It's me. That package I failed to deliver I've got it wrapped up, ready for you in suite 510 at the Aqualina. I'll fill you in with what I know at another time." Sam stated before hanging up. His own business handled, he dialed another number. He hoped Catharine could help him reach the island before Monday. He didn't want to think about what might happen to Anna if he didn't.

144 Washington DC, Virginia

Lance cursed as his phone rang, drawing him out of Catharine's book. He was almost done with it too. He contemplated ignoring it then saw the number, pressed the button to answer the call.

"Hey Sam, what's up?"

"Sorry to call this late. I need to talk to Catharine."

"What? Why?"

"We got hit, they got Anna. The boats out here don't run over to the island until Monday. Pamela must have her own otherwise she couldn't have been here. I was hoping Catharine could pull some strings and…"

"She's not here."

"What?"

"She got a phone call, went back to LA. Filming for the second movie started."

"Damn."

"She left me her number out there. I'll give her a call, see what she can do then I'll call you back," Lance said.

"Thanks."

"Right you owe me big," Lance muttered as he hung up. Moving to his home phone he pulled up the caller id list looked for the call from Catharine earlier. He dialed her number then waited.

"Hello, detective," she murmured her voice was warm and inviting but distracted.

"Catharine, you okay?" he asked concerned.

"Fine, just worn out. It was a long day. What's up?"

"Sam called from Miami they got attacked. He lost Anna, needs a ship so he can reach an island."

"Oh dear, yeah I can set something up for him."

"Thanks."

"No problem. Though I must admit I had hoped this was a social call," she said with disappointment.

"Sorry I've been busy," he stated simply.

"Don't suppose you'll tell me what with?" She said with a sigh.

"Work."

"That's what I thought. I'll let you get back …"

"I'm in no rush. I'm done with it for the night," he assured her. Not ready to let her go just yet.

"That may be so. You should get back to Sam. I'm beat. I'll talk to you later detective," she murmured then hung up.

Lance sighed he'd made a mess of that. He'd call her later and explain. But not tonight. She was right he needed to get back to Sam.

145

**Atlantis, Somewhere in the Bermuda Triangle
Sunday
5am**

Anna woke. She was first aware of cool stone beneath her. The sense of, a dark presence close by; hit her next. Opening her eyes she blinked. Faint torch light played over the darkness giving the space around her an eerie glow. Her eyes began to focus. Marble images stood like sentinels before her. The evil she had picked up on radiated from them.

Anna screamed aware of where she was. The throne room, it looked just as it had in her dream. The statues of the fallen were flanking the throne. She lifted her head. It pounded with pain. Reaching up, she felt the lump on her scalp from where Pamela had hit her.

Anna sat up realizing she was laid on the altar. She rose from it, stumbling in her haste. Anna fell to her knees on the floor. She felt the eyes of the statues upon her. Aware they watched. Waited, though for what she didn't know.

"I see your awake good. Now, perhaps you can explain what these images tell you that I can't see. What is the significance of the horn?" Ian Broody shouted. He tossed her notes on the floor in front of her as he came out of the shadows.

Anna gasped. She looked upon him with terror. His eyes were not his own. They glowed, blue, lit with madness, birthed by an unnatural power.

"She knows the answers," Pamela murmured from where she stood beside the graven image of Hermes. She caressed the stone cheek then kissed it "My husband has confirmed it."

"Tell us about the horn Anna or you will suffer," Ian stated. He drew a gun from his jacket. Then approached her where she knelt on the floor to press the barrel against her temple.

A woman with golden hair and eyes so blue they hurt to look upon came into the room. She knelt at Anna's side then touched her brow. Anna groaned at the contact in protest.

It was like ice. "You waste time with this mortal. She'll tell you nothing. All you need do is set the horn in the hands of the god of knowledge. He will tell you what you want to know," Artemis murmured.

"No Ian! Don't do that, you don't understand what's happening here. You're in great danger."

"Danger?"

"That's right, Ian, you're being deceived." Anna sputtered in protest.

"Deceived?"

"Yes if you do as she asks something terrible will happen to you."

"She lies, only seeks to keep the knowledge it holds for herself." The woman countered.

"That's not true, Ian, please, listen to me. If you ever loved me don't do this."

"I did love you Anna, I still do but you left me. You've been hiding things from me…"

"I know Ian, and I'm sorry but it was for your own safety. Give me the horn please it's dangerous."

"No Anna, I don't believe you. I think you'd say anything to keep its secrets for yourself, you've become mad with power," He hissed. Anna watched as Ian did as the woman bid – unable to stop him. When the horn touched the image of the fallen, the earth trembled beneath her. Anna felt a dark power spill in around her. It poured out of the graven image into Ian. Something left him. Anna looked on with horror while Ian's appearance changed. The grey in his hair darkened. Lines of age melted away. Features altered, his face becoming more pleasing to the eye. His body grew stronger. Steel grey eyes became blue as the god from the dream realm was flesh once more.

Hermes lifted the horn from the statue. He laughed with delight. "I'M FREE, AT LAST – AFTER CENTURIES OF WAITING. ONCE MORE I SHALL MOVE UPON THE EARTH." He declared. Then turned from the image where the mortal Ian Broody now laid trapped within.

146

Hermes gaze fell upon Pamela with both hunger and gratitude. After all she had been the instrument of his release. He was pleased to see that her eyes gleamed with excitement at seeing him. Hermes reached out for her. His hand brushed her cheek in a tender caress. She moaned at his touch, overwhelmed by the reality of him. He smiled aware of her desire for him. "THANK YOU MY DEAREST, FOR ALL YOUR HELP, YOU WILL BE REWARDED FOR YOUR ROLE IN MY RELEASE." He murmured then he kissed her brow.

Anna rose to her feet while the fallen one spoke with his bride. She would not fear him nor would she kneel. She knew what he was. Anna dusted the earth from her skin. Hermes turned. His gaze fell upon her, his blue eyes lit with anger.

"MY DEAR, ANNA, YOU DISAPPOINTED ME. YOU WHO SOUGHT KNOWLEDGE WITH SUCH HUNGER REFUSED ME. I'D HAVE GIVEN YOU ALL YOU EVER WANTED IF YOU'D HAVE ACCEPTED ME." He moved closer, took her chin in his hands so that her eyes met with his. "I STILL WILL IF YOU WOULD ONLY REPENT," he murmured.

Anna felt his power move over her. Seeking a means to enter her mind then obtain control over her. She asked the Creator for strength. Steeled her resolve then spoke. "I will not surrender my will to you again fallen one. Nor will I serve a false god." Anna snatched the horn away from him.

Hermes roared in rage at her refusal. His hand flew striking her in the cheek. The blow was strong. Her ears rang and her vision blurred. The horn fell from powerless fingers. It clattered to the floor. She felt the bite of cold hard stone. She blinked aware his strike had knocked her back onto the altar. She lay upon it in a heap.

"IF YOU'LL NOT SUBMIT TO A GOD THEN I'LL TAKE WHAT I NEED OF YOU BY FORCE," Hermes raged. Anna struggled to get up. She groaned her head pounding from the blow. She fell off the back of the stone slab. Hands and knees protested at the jarring pain of catching her. Her arms gave out and stars exploded before her eyes as her chin hit the earthen floor. Her hand brushed against cold metal resting near the horn. Anna wrapped her fingers around it. The altar slid away behind her. A pair of strong arms reached out from below, grabbed her ankles and dragged her out of the chamber – into the dark corridor below.

147

Sam pressed the button closing the tunnel entrance once Anna was clear. The earth shook. He heard the god above rage at losing his victim. Sam made his way down the ladder into the hallway the angel had shown him. With Anna cradled in his arms, he fled back the way he'd come. Anna stirred in his grasp. He was relieved she was okay.

"Sam?" Anna struggled with sorting through the fog in her mind.

"That's right. You okay?" He asked; aware of footsteps behind them. Someone was on the ladder coming down after them.

"Yes, head hurts, visions still cloudy, but it's clearing," she murmured.

"Do you think you can run if I set you down?"

"Don't know," she admitted.

"Then hang on we don't have time to waste," he stated. Sam reached the end of the corridor. He pressed the tile which gave them passage through the palace. Sam was relieved when he heard the floor seal shut behind them. He crossed the chamber to the wall. Opening the secret way he began the final leg of their journey.

"How?"

"A little help from CJ and our angelic friend," Sam stated. They came out of the dark corridor near the wall of the city and into the light of the rising sun.

"Set me down. I think I can manage now," Anna stated.

Sam slowed his pace then stopped setting her down on her feet. He waited until she was steady before taking her hand in his. Turning he ran again. A woman with golden hair and fierce blue eyes emerged from the passage. She cursed as Sam and Anna reached their waiting vessel.

"I don't know how you've eluded me mortal but you will not escape," She shouted her voice filled with rage. "Lord Hermes needs the woman. He will have her and I will have my revenge!"

Sam looked back as his ship taxied away from the dock. The woman lifted her gaze to the heavens.

"Who is she?" Sam asked.

"Artemis." Anna stated; recalling the name from while she was on the ship.

"I thought there were no goddesses," Sam said confused.

"She's the child of a god half mortal half god. What is she doing?"

"I don't know but it can't be good."

"I Artemis, daughter of mighty Zeus, king of the gods, call upon my birthright. Hear my command oh sky. Do my bidding. Rage now upon the sea slow their escape."

"Oh shit. You have got to be kidding me," Sam said with disbelief. He watched as the sky darkened. The winds around them began to howl.

148

Hermes swore. He became aware that both the intruder and Anna had escaped the isle. Artemis pursued them but her efforts were being slowed by the interference of a servant of the Creator. It was no matter, in due time he would have all he wanted. After all he was free.

Of his brethren he alone had managed to escape the prison created for them. He'd be the only one. The first thing he'd do was replace the real statues with the replicas he'd had Broody make. Any other mantle found would find no place to go. He would be the new king of the gods. There was nothing any of them could do to stop him.

Pleased with himself the god turned his gaze once more to Pamela. He smiled at her then moved to her side. She still stood beside his image lost in her desire for him – waiting. "COME MY LOVELY. I WILL RAISE YOU ABOVE ALL YOUR KIND," he whispered. Hermes held out his hand. She took it without hesitation. He drew her against him. His lips met with hers in a fierce bruising kiss that demanded she surrender all.

She melted into him willing and eager beneath the gaze of the other graven images. Hermes laughed as the spirits within them hissed. They writhed with hatred of their brethren who was free. Hermes taunted them with his enjoyment of mortal flesh. He laid Pamela upon the stone altar bare before them allowing them to look upon what they had been denied for so long.

They roared in their rage as thunder crashed above and the earth trembled. Hermes eyes gleamed with triumph. His fingers played over her eliciting cries of pleasure from the mortal, protests as well, for the delay.

"LOOK NOW UPON YOUR KING AND HIS QUEEN," he

whispered. The spirits trapped within cursed the declaration but looked on unable to turn away helpless to interfere. Hermes turned her so that she faced the throne and the others. He drew the part of her he sought to claim as his own back against the part of him she now begged for. There before the throne of the dark prince and the other fallen he claimed her.

The time of the Fallens' reign had begun anew.

149

Sam stood on the deck of the speed boat racing away from the island. The sail boat closing in fast behind them. Above a storm raged wild and out of control. The seas churned beneath it threatening to flood the boat. The storm didn't touch the other ship. He cursed in his frustration; they were getting nowhere fast.

"We can't take much more of this storm," he muttered noting the boat was beginning to fill with water.

"I know. What I can't figure out is why she's serving Hermes? She should be working for her father Zeus." Anna stated.

"Whatever her reasons she gaining on us. This storm is working in her favor. If we don't get out of it we're done for."

"She created it with her father's blessing. That's where the storm came from that slowed our chase of Pamela."

"Well, unless we can lose her this whole effort will be in vain."

Anna nodded "I know it. I'm not sure what else we can do," she murmured then laughed at herself. "We can pray," she stated. Recalling how doing so in the dream realm had freed her from Hermes reach. Perhaps it would help here as well. Anna looked up at the raging sky. She whispered a prayer for aid. Sam muttered one of his own under his breath.

Light cut through the dark sky parting the clouds. The seas around them grew still as a lake. The boat shot across the smooth water like a bullet. Anna looked back at the sailboat. She watched the waters behind them swell once more. The clouds became fog. A scream carried on the wind.

"Sounds like we lost her," Sam said amused.

Anna heard Artemis rage. "We did, it doesn't matter much though. We've already failed." Anna said with disgust.

"What do you mean?"

“Ian put the horn in the statue’s hands. When he did the spirit trapped within was released. It took him over. Hermes is back, unless he was too angry, with you for getting me out of there. He’d be bedding his new bride about now.”

“Pamela?” Sam questioned.

“Yes, I’m sorry. I tried to stop Ian but he wouldn’t listen. They were beyond my reach.” Anna murmured.

“So, he’s loose. It’s not over. There are still nine other mantles out there to locate. We’ll do better the next time out.” Sam encouraged.

Anna sighed. He was right their task was far from done. They’d lost this battle but the war was just beginning.

The End.

The

Mantle of the Gods

adventure continues

with...

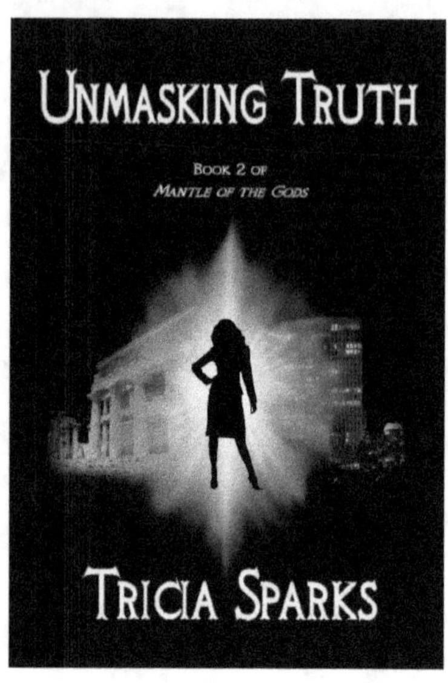

Mantle of the Gods

Book 2

Unmasking Truth

By Tricia Sparks

The search continues...

The lost city behind them, Annalynn Gallagher and Sam Abrams face the daunting task of identifying the other seven mantles, the ancient artifacts that can grant power – for a price. Yet while their task continues, an old associate makes a decision that will lead their paths to intersect once more.

...and a hunt resumes.

An earthen cup has been stolen from the Smithsonian Museum. The item may be innocuous, the theft illogical, but a crime is still a crime and Detective Lance Roman has just worked the longest day in his life trying to pinpoint the culprit. In his frustration, he almost misses it – a clue that reminds him of something he'd buried in the files long ago.

The past always comes back around...

Things take a strange turn when the FBI asks for his help – on a case he'd walked away from after losing everything. No longer working homicide and unwilling to get involved in an investigation that had already crippled him once, he hands over all he has. Yet the FBI aren't the only ones who remember the case and who'd worked it.

...to bite back hard when you least expect it.

A killer who is more than he seems is making his bloody mark on the world again – with Lance being the only person who can follow his trail. Forced back into the investigation, the detective is now in a race against time.

To defeat great evil, you have to know it for what it is...

The butcher has his next victim in the crosshairs, and when Lance deciphers the clues pointing to a clever writer named CJ Nichols as the next target, he calls in a favor from an old friend.

...and be willing to make sacrifices to gain victory.

1

Denver, Colorado

Anna sat staring at her fifth book of Scandinavian folklore. Her head was pounding and the letters were beginning to blur together on the page.

"Sam, I've got to stop for a bit, my eyes feel like they're going to bleed," Anna grumbled as she brushed a strand of her unruly blonde hair out of her face. It had managed to work its way out of her neat bun as she worked.

"Yeah, I think a break is in order. Have you had any luck?" Sam asked as he looked up from his own book of German tales. His blue eyes met with her ever changing eyes and he noted they were their normal hazel color. It relieved him. When he'd found her hours earlier in that god forsaken throne room they'd nearly been black with her fear and pain. He watched as temper flared and the color changed darkening.

"Nothing, I wish I knew where to begin there is so much to go through. I never realized just how many fairytales and myths there were not to mention this mountain of folklore from around the world. We could be at this for years," she said exasperated.

Sam raked a hand through his dark hair and sighed. He hated to admit it but she was right and they didn't have that kind of time here not with Artemis out there hunting for them to say nothing of Kadar's employer, Mr. York. "Yeah, didn't realize how big an undertaking this was going to prove to be."

"When I stop to think that I held one of them in my hands before this whole thing got started and that now it's gone. Stolen right from under the museum's nose it makes me want to scream," Anna groused.

"No sense lamenting something you couldn't have known at the time. Why don't we give Lance a call and see how he's doing with the investigation? Besides I should let him know we're in the clear for now and have him pass on our thanks to Catharine." Sam suggested as he marked his page and closed the book.

"Sounds good to me, don't want them to worry needlessly any longer," Anna replied. She followed his lead marking her place and setting the work aside.

Sam noting the time pulled out some of their provisions handing her a snack before pulling out his cell phone and dialing the detective's number.

2

WASHINGTON DC, VIRGINIA
SUNDAY
5PM

Detective Lance Roman sat behind his beat up oak desk studying the reports on his latest case. He looked at the earthen cup that had until recently been on display at the small auction house for the Smithsonian and groaned. The Crime Scene Unit had found nothing to help him identify the thief. As he stared at the forgery he willed it to grow fingerprints, he could track, with no success.

His gaze moved from the cup to the stack of photos sitting on his desk. They were copies of a similar stack he'd received anonymously at his private residence. The gruesome images were ones he'd hoped to never see again; the fact that he'd spent half his morning discussing them with the chief didn't sit well with him. He didn't want any part of that case again. It had taken quite a bit of dancing on his part to convince the older man that he had no business getting involved in the matter again.

But even that hadn't weighed as heavily on his mind as the major concern hanging over him that day. He'd tried to bury himself in his work to avoid it but nothing had truly been able to distract him for long. His thoughts kept drifting back to his phone call from Sam Abrams late last night.

"We got hit, they got Anna." Sam's words echoed around in his head like a record caught in a loop. Lance had contacted Catharine in LA on Sam's behalf and arrangements had been made to get the former reporter turned MMA fighter out to an undisclosed isle in the Bermuda Triangle – the city of Atlantis.

Lance laughed; the whole thing was insanity, from the place his friend had been headed to the reason for going. Mantle of the gods – nonsense! Sam had finally lost his mind. One too many blows to the head Lance reasoned. Yet he knew for a fact that when Sam called Anna had been in danger of some kind. Sam Abrams wasn't the sort of guy who called in a favor on a whim.

"Where the devil are they I'd have thought I'd heard something by now," Lance muttered. He contemplated heading home sitting here wasn't doing him any good and he couldn't take much more of the place. Too many reminders of a life, long gone, lingered here today, stirred up by the damn photos.

Lance shoved the photos in the drawer of his desk and picked up the troublesome cup. He had Sam and Anna to thank for that one too, he reminded himself with disgust. He switched off his computer and cup in hand started on his way to the evidence lock up. As he walked his phone rang. Lance took out the offending object which had been unusually quiet and seeing the number on the caller idea felt a giant weight lift from his shoulders.

"Hello Sam," he said as he answered the call.

"Lance, sorry I haven't called sooner. I got Anna out she's safe. Didn't have a lot of time to talk earlier we were on the run…"

"Yeah, I can imagine. Glad to hear you're both safe. I take it you've landed somewhere away from Miami and nowhere near DC or Vegas," Lance said interrupting, the less he knew about their mission the better he'd feel.

"Right, be sure to thank Catharine for us when you talk to her next."

"Will do, don't forget Abrams you owe me for this one," Lance stated.

"Yeah, more than you know, just let me know where and when and I'm there," Sam assured him.

"I'm going to hold you to that, Sam."

"Lance, I hate to ask for anything else but have you had any luck with the cup?" Sam questioned.

"No, wish I could say otherwise, but no. I'm getting nowhere on the damn thing and fast."

"Sorry to hear it."

"How are things on your end going?"

"About the same, we are buried under a mountain of research," Sam stated with a sigh.

Lance chuckled, "Well, I got to admit I think this whole thing is nuts, but good luck to you."

"Can't say I blame you for that or that I don't understand how you feel about it. Even to me this whole mess seems crazy even after seeing what I have. Thanks for your help and the luck; we'll need it. Good luck to you as well," Sam answered before he hung up.

Lance laughed if he'd been talking to anyone other than Sam about gods and powerful relics he'd have had them tested for sobriety and quite possibly locked up for insanity. Sam was not your average guy off the street. He knew things – Lance wondered how much Anna really knew about her protector and shrugged. Not his business, he reasoned.

Lance held up the evidence bag holding the cup in question and studied it again. This was a replica of the cup of a god? It seemed rather plain and unimpressive to him, a simple clay chalice. It had no engravings in it, no finery to it at all. It was completely blank – no he was wrong. Lance blinked, clearing his vision, verifying that the faint mark hidden inside the lip of the rim was real. Seeing that it was indeed still there he turned and headed back to his desk.

Pulling out a pair of gloves he opened the bag and with a magnifying glass examined the mark closer. The image depicted was that of a hammer leaning against an anvil with flames rising above it. In front of the image were two small rectangles with a smaller image within them that he couldn't quite make out. Lance smiled; it seemed that the forger couldn't resist signing his work. That had to be a maker's seal. Grabbing his digital camera Lance snapped a couple close-ups of the mark. He'd seen it before somewhere he was sure of it but where escaped him. Brushing the matter aside for later Lance picked up the phone and dialed the number of a local jeweler in the area. He'd used the guy in the past as a contact; he hoped that Frank would be able to identify the brand.

3 Atlantis, somewhere in the Bermuda Triangle

Zaharrah Lynch made her way past security headed in the direction of the city temple. Her brown eyes studied the dig site with disgust. Since Anna left things there had gotten worse. Any hope of trying to get into restricted areas was gone. Dr. Broody had tightened things up for reasons she didn't know. Whatever it was; it had to do with that chamber Anna had discovered beneath the temple.

Something had happened in that throne room early this morning. Zaharrah had felt the earth shift; watched the sky above darken without warning, seen the seas rage and boil as the weather went wild; waging war with an unseen foe. She wondered just what had taken place, in the hours before dawn, as she made her way up the steps of the temple and through its corridors in the direction of the library; where she'd spent more days than she could count reading through old texts.

Zaharrah was by no means a religious zealot she'd walked away from that life long ago but every fiber in her being urged her to abandon her task there and get as far away from the isle as she could. Something dwelled here in the shadows – it seeped out of every nook and cranny of the land and threatened to consume those who it caught off guard – whatever it was; it was evil.

Zaharrah recalled Anna's cryptic words before she left the isle "There are some secrets in this world that are never meant to be discovered." Zaharrah had heard similar words her whole life from her family; she'd never believed them – until now. She'd do as Anna asked of her not because she'd paid her well, though she had, no she'd do it to protect the people she cared about from this cursed places reach.

As she stepped into the library, Zaharrah was puzzled to find the torches already lit. She cursed as she realized she wasn't alone. A handsome young man with dark hair and blue eyes stood in her corner with a woman she didn't recognize. She had bottle blonde hair and whisky colored eyes. Zaharrah studied the pair with interest wondering who they were and how they'd gotten in here past security.

"Dr. Lynch, I see you don't take the weekends off either," the man said amused. His voice was familiar and yet strange to her.

"With all the added security it's difficult to get any serious work done when the rest of the staff is here," Zaharrah said, her voice cool and crisp, hinting at her anger.

"Yes, I'm sorry of that; but it can't be helped. We don't want another Ithaca on our hands," the man explained with a laugh. Zaharrah blinked with shock; the man before her was Dr. Broody.

"No, we wouldn't, how can I help you Dr. Broody?"

"Zaharrah please, call me Ian; we're old friends after all. I'd like you to meet my wife Pamela Walsh. She's fascinated by our work and I was hoping to show her the wonderful candle you found. "

"Hello, Pamela. I'd love to help you Ian, but I'm afraid I shipped the candle back to the Smithsonian. Dr. King requested to see some of the cataloged finds. It should be arriving there later this week."

"Oh, well, don't worry about it. I know how these things are. Zaharrah, I'm going to pull you out of the library on Monday."

"Why?"

"Well, quite frankly, with Anna gone, I need my best archeologist looking for additional artifacts, like the candle, things that will tell us more about the sort of place this is. I can put a grad student or low level researcher in here."

"Okay."

"Why don't you take a look through Anna's notes and see if you can find anything she found out about the candle or other items like it?" Ian stated as he handed her a copy of Anna's research.

Zaharrah nodded. She said a distracted goodbye to the new Mrs. Broody and set off in the direction of her office.

"What is he really up to?" She murmured as she closed herself in her workspace. She checked the room to ensure she was indeed alone; finding no electronic bugs or cameras Zaharrah breathed a sigh of relief before picking up the phone and punching in Anna's number. If anyone could tell her what was going on she was certain Anna could.

4 Denver, Colorado

Anna sat enjoying the warmth of a fire as she finished her simple snack of nuts and fruit. She sighed, relaxed, a break had been just what she'd needed. The headache that had been threatening to come on full force earlier had faded. She contemplated taking a soak in a nice hot tub but before she could consider the idea any further her phone rang.

"So much for that idea," Anna muttered as she pulled the offending object from her coat pocket. Sam looked up from the TV where he sat with question. Seeing the number she shrugged before connecting the call.

"Dr. Gallagher," a familiar voice said by way of greeting.

"Zaharrah is that you?" Anna questioned surprised by both the call and the unusual greeting.

"Yes, I'm not sure how much time I've got so let me make this quick. Broody pulled me out of the library, asked to see the candle. I told him it was in route to the museum. It should arrive there later this week."

"Thanks for the tip. Why the rush though?"

"Security here has gotten tighter since you left. I've given some serious thought to walking but I can't. He's looking for something in your research pertaining to the candle and any other artifacts they might mention; really closed mouthed about what though."

"I was hoping I'd have a bit more time before that happened."

"You know what he's looking for?"

"Yes, it's connected to the disk I had indirectly."

"Anna what is this all about?"

"Powerful relics known as the Mantles of the gods, the candle was only one of several. The clues he wants are in my notes; it's not blatantly obvious; but close scrutiny will reveal them. Do me a favor and stall him as long as possible he can't be allowed to find them."

"Okay, what are they, these mantles, so if I come across them here I can keep them from falling into his hands?"

"The ones still unaccounted for are, the sword of Ares, the bow of Eros, the whip of Helios, the Trident of Poseidon, the gauntlets of Hephaestus, the scroll of Chaos, and the crown of Zeus. I have the horn of Hermes, the candle you had and the cup is here somewhere in the USA, it was stolen recently. I've got a friend tracking it down for me. Zaharrah if you find one of them don't touch it directly – they're dangerous."

"I'll be careful doctor I suggest you do so as well," Zaharrah said before she disconnected the call.

"I take it our breaks over," Sam said.

"Yes, afraid so, Zaharrah said Broody came to her asked about the candle. It's apparently in route to the museum. I'll need to contact Dr. King have him keep it hidden upon arrival."

"So that's one that will be safe," Sam stated.

"Right, but Ian's started looking for the other mantles too."

www.ingramcontent.com/pod-product-compliance
Lightning Source LLC
Chambersburg PA
CBHW071052250626
47159CB00002B/448